Adeline

The Gayworthys

SALZWASSER
VERLAG

Adeline D. T. Whitney

The Gayworthys

Reprint of the original, first published in 1865.

1st Edition 2022 | ISBN: 978-3-75259-010-4

Verlag (Publisher): Salzwasser Verlag GmbH, Zeilweg 44, 60439 Frankfurt, Deutschland
Vertretungsberechtigt (Authorized to represent): E. Roepke, Zeilweg 44, 60439 Frankfurt, Deutschland
Druck (Print): Books on Demand GmbH, In de Tarpen 42, 22848 Norderstedt, Deutschland

THE GAYWORTHYS:

A STORY OF THREADS AND THRUMS.

BY THE AUTHOR OF

"Faith Gartney's Girlhood."

FIRST EDITION.

BOSTON.

1865.

PREFATORY.

Of threads and thrums: because a simple story of this mixed divine and human weaving we call Life; wherein are threads,—lines lying evenly along the loom, and made secure and perfect with a filling; wherein are also many thrums,—ends broken, or dropped midway, or reaching out unfinished lengths beyond the web. Wherein the fabric seems, so often, faulty; where much seems lost, left out, or wrongly joined; where correspondence is delayed, and full-matched beauty missed; where colors are confused; where the pattern, being vast, may never quite unroll to earthly vision; where Patience keeps her foot upon the treadle, and Faith must stand, with fervent eyes, beside the springing shuttle, knowing of breadths that shall be woven by and by!

CONTENTS.

THE GAYWORTHYS.

CHAPTER I.

DOCTOR GAYWORTHY'S WOMEN FOLKS.

Did you ever eat strawberry short-cake? If not, I am afraid I cannot put you in the way of that delight, further than to tell you that it is a delicious mystery of cuisine, known among certain dwellers in certain hill counties of New England, where the glorious scarlet berry blushes indigenous and profuse all over pasture slopes and mountain-sides at the early outburst of the short and fervid summer. A mystery, the manner of whose compounding is a grand, masonic secret among the skilful and initiated few; for it is not every farmer's wife or daughter, you must know, who has passed that high degree which entitles her to call her neighbors together for such annual regale and marvel.

I can tell you this only; that on the June day wherefrom I date this story, in the great, snowy-clean, pewter-shining kitchen of the Gayworthys, solemn preparations were toward; that on the broad dresser stood a huge pan, heaped high with the glowing fruit, wherefrom the whole house was redolent of rich, wild fragrance; that beside it, on either hand, waited, in plentiful supply, flour of the whitest, and cream of the yellowest; and that, somehow, by a deft putting of this and that together, the mighty result was to come.

Huldah Brown stood, bare-armed and waiting, before the whole; and looked calculatingly upon the gathered material.

"It's an awful lot, to be sure; but then they'll every soul of 'em come, from all pints of the compass; and when they're scalt and mashed, they do s'rink down!"

Huldah's utterance must stand, in all its horrible ambiguity, as to who or what was to be "scalt and mashed." I may not venture to throw light on one point, lest I trespass, with unwarranted illumination, upon another.

"And there's a manifest providence, comin' across the chip-yard!"

The "manifest providence" was a sharp-nosed, little, elderly woman, in a striped sun-bonnet, with a three-quart tin pail full of strawberries, which she changed from one hand to the other, wearily, as she came up to the open door.

"Miss Vorse!" cried Huldah, from the stair-foot: "I b'lieve my soul, we haint got berries enough, arter all!"

"You don't think it, Huldah!" came back, in a sharp explosive consternation.

"Wall, I do then!" returned Huldah, "and here's Widder Horke jest comin' along with a pailful. I call that clear luck!"

"See what she asks for 'em. I'll be down in a minute." Huldah Brown knew very well at which end to present a suggestion. The way to bring people to your own conclusion is to give them, not your last thought, but your first.

Huldah startled her mistress with the selfsame doubt that had startled herself, and then brought forward the "manifest providence."

Up stairs, in the white bedroom, were gathered the four ladies of the house; or, in country parlance, "all Dr. Gayworthy's women-folks." Mrs. Reuben Gair, Mrs. Prudence Vorse, and the two young, unmarried sisters, Joanna and Rebecca.

I mention first Mrs. Reuben Gair. Because, though she cannot claim the precedence of seniority, she holds the stronger right of paramount importance among the sisters; and is at this moment the centre and oracle of their group, as they stand, leaning eager faces in between the white festoons of dimity, about the great, old-fashioned, high-posted bedstead, whereon lie unfolded and displayed certain purchases, which the city lady has from time to time been commissioned by letter and pattern to make, and upon whose fashion and quality she enlarges with all the eloquence of a perfect *au-fait-ism.*

Mrs. Reuben Gair came up from Selport two days since, for her yearly summer visit in Hilbury. And so, the Hilbury season has begun, and the Gayworthys are giving their first summer party, and strawberry short-cake is the chief nominal attraction; while "from all pints of the compass they'll be sure to come," although there were no short-cake at all; since Mrs. Reuben will be to be seen, in her new bright green silk, of the freshest Selport style; and every soul (feminine) will be enabled to go home, having taken mental measurement and specification thereof, and knowing precisely the number of breadths in the skirt, and the width of the seven little "crossway" ruffles that garnish it.

The Gayworthy sisters have made an early toilet, and the house is in early festival trim, and there has been ample time for the production and discussion of the long-expected fineries.

Mrs. Vorse, or "sister Prue," is a woman of five and thirty, who looks to have taken life hard. She made "no great of a match" some fifteen years ago, and has come back within the four last past, to keep house for the old doctor, who is her step-father only, — her mother, his second wife, having been a widow with this one child, — while her young half-sisters have been away at school. Her son, Gershom Vorse, then a boy of eight, came with her, and here they still abide, greatly to the comfort of the worthy doctor, whose household Prudence guides in the true spirit of her name, and to the welcome enfranchisement of Joanna and Rebecca; not altogether, either, to the dissatisfaction of Mrs. Reuben, notwithstanding that the sisterhood between them is one of courtesy and association only; Mrs. Gair, although the younger, being the child of the first Mrs. Gayworthy; and thus, as she could not help remembering, at times, with a certain touch of jealous restlessness as connected with the present, and an as certain, but half-examined complacency as regarded the contingencies of the future, "really no relation at all."

"A double family of girls was quite enough in all conscience; and then, there was Prue's great boy!" Very clumsy and ill-judged, to be sure, this latter circumstance, on the part of Prue.

The world, as I have intimated, had been hard work for Prudence Vorse. Things had not fallen in comfortably or fortunately for her, as they do for some. She had had ten years of trying at life which was not life. If she wanted anything, every nerve was to be strained to get it. The people about her, instead of being helps to her wishes, were so many obstacles for her to overcome. She had always been heading straight against a stone wall; the more, because it had never been in her nature to take any circuitous way. Her face had got a hard directness and determination in it, so. Her voice had laid aside its softer modulations, and taken a short, strong, uncompromising tone. Her look, her movement, her whole bearing, had a searchingness, a promptness, a decision, almost aggressive, in them.

Many a woman hardens or sharpens, through the opposing or grinding of unkindly circumstances, who else might have been gentle, restful, round with grace in soul and lineament, through nestling lovingly among loving influences. Ah, well! God sees!

Mrs. Gair, on the contrary, has been one of those for whom all things smile; who have the world on their own terms; who have always pleasant weather for their pleasant plans, and timely tempest to make impossible that which they may not care to do. This, at least, was the look her life wore to others; she herself knew her own unsatisfactions, as we all do; whether hers were noble or ignoble discontents may be shown as we shall turn the coming pages.

There are only five years between her and her step-sister, as they stand there together; the one in her glistening, summer-bright robe, fresh and new as the new leaves of June; with round, fair face unlined by any perplexity, and hair untouched of autumn, dressed fearlessly in the simple style of the time; the other in her well-kept dress of not too costly black, having that air of *unusedness* which a black silk dress, produced only upon state occasions, may keep through whatever vicissitudes of passing fashion and fading gloss,—new always in its owner's idea however shabby it may come to be to eyes of others; cappy head-dress, that, although it is to the regularly instituted cap what spring eye-glasses are to spectacles, yet is, like them, the beginning of an acknowledgment; and the face that tells its ten years story as I have hinted;—who could have believed in but that five years' difference?

Joanna and Rebecca are young; wearing the look that only early girlhood wears,—unwritten of any past,—expectant of all future possibilities. What need to describe them? Round, laughing, and fair,—the one; slight, brown, delicate, serious-eyed, —the other; that is all. The years of their lives — perhaps the pages of this story —shall develop or contradict whatever prophecy you may read in two such faces.

Meanwhile, this sketch of the four is but a daguerreotype, flashed in an instant; the instant wherein Widow Horke still pauses upon the door-stone, and busy Huldah Brown, who, you may be certain, will not wait there long, yet lingers at the stair-foot.

And sister Prue smooths her new cap that has been brushed a little awry by the cotton fringes of the bed-hangings, and hastens down stairs with a great white apron tied on over the best black silk, and sleeves turned up, to superintend the strawberry short-cake; and Mrs. Reuben Gair, craving help of her two young sisters, lays shawls and muslins and ribbons and patterns carefully back into the great travelling trunk; which being locked, she plunges into the far recesses of the dark, narrow closet that runs back between the chambers their full length, lest half Hilbury may get accidental glimpse or confidentially crave full sight of these new summer things that have come from Selport.

"You're tired, I guess?" says Huldah Brown to the widow, as Mrs. Vorse comes down the stairs.

"Tired!" answers Widow Horke, emphatically. "I'm all gone! I don't know where."

"Walk in and sit down," says the quick, smart voice of Prudence Vorse, "while Huldah measures the berries. Three quarts? I don't want more 'n two. They 'd be clear wasted. I guess Mrs. Hartshorne 'll take the other. Ten cents! I have n't paid but six this week past."

So speaking, Mrs. Vorse led the way, pail in hand, across the kitchen toward the dresser, by the end of which, with a voluminous sigh, Widow Horke sunk into a seat.

"They 're wuth that, to me," pleaded the latter, with a low whine, the diminuendo of her sigh.

Mrs. Vorse turned short round, and pushed the pail toward her across the corner of the board.

"Very well, then," was the prompt decision, "the best thing you can do is just to take 'em right home and eat 'em. They won't be so valuable to anybody else, at that rate."

Mrs. Horke laughed faintly, as literally at her own expense.

"You 're allers jest so queer," she said. "Well, seein' its you, I 'spose I must let you have 'em."

"Just as you like. Six cents is a fair price." And Mrs. Vorse went over into the pantry, where she kept odd change in a blue mug, and brought back, presently, the twelve cents, and something beside, wrapped in a brown paper.

"That 'll help out your supper," said she, never minding that the plum cake was worth five times the difference in the disputed price of the strawberries. Mrs. Vorse was not stingy. But she had certain rules which she never let herself off from. She might give away, but she never would pay an exorbitant price. She had an uncompromising sense of justice which carried itself out into the least details.

"Sarah Gair!" she cried sharply, as a child of seven, sashed, pantaletted, and bronze-booted, running in before Mrs. Reuben, and across to the tempting dresser, straightway "thrust in a thumb and pulled out a plum," from Widow Horke's tin pail, — "if you want strawberries, take 'em out of the pudding dish! They 're paid for, and those aint!" and she deliberately put a berry from said pudding-dish back into the pail.

"Lord'a massy! ejaculated the widow, laughing genuinely this time, with a double tickle of Mrs. Prue's oddity and the aroma of plum cake, "if anybody ever heerd the like! You do hev the singl'rest notions, Miss Vorse."

"So it seems to me," remarked Mrs. Reuben Gair, as the strawberry picker took up her pail and departed across the chip-yard. "And they don't appear always to be quite consistent; did n't I hear you beating the poor woman down in her price a minute ago?"

"That 's just where the consistency is," retorted her step-sister. "Right's right, either way.—She may be poor," continued Mrs Prudence, "and she may be a widow woman; and she may be rheumatic, winters; and she may live all alone down there by Gibson's clearing; but that aint any reason why she shonld put it all on to the price of a mess of strawberries. When I give, I give; and when I buy, I buy. — Sarah Gair!" she cried again, suddenly, to the small, starched, ribboned, and beruffled creature who by this time was peeping in furtively at the pantry door, within which, on the ample shelves, stood the whole bountiful variety and array of country delicacies that were to sustain the ancient honor of the Gayworthy table, "don't you make up your mind to sponge-cake from the beginning, this time, and eat five pieces, as you did at the Fairbrother's!"

The child drooped down from head to foot, from her glad, eager attitude, in a moment; and a shame that only rebuked childhood knows, dreaming of nought more shameful than the present fault whereof it stands convicted, rushed over her, hot and scarlet.

"Mrs. Fairbrother asked me," she murmured faintly, "and ma won't let me eat plum cake."

"If Mrs. Fairbrother asked you five times, three times you should have said, 'No, I thank you.'"

"But," persisted the cnlprit, more confidently now, feeling suddenly to have the great Angel, Truth, upon her side, "she asked me if I *wanted* some more; and I did!"

Aunt Prue was silent.

"You should have said 'No, I thank you,' all the same," admonished the mother. "It was n't polite."

"Polite!" cried aunt Prue, aside. "Better tell her not to be greedy."

"And what *do* you suppose all those people think of you now?"

Mrs. Gair flung this last shaft,—a great battle-axe of world's-opinion against a mere gnat of transgression — and then the two grown women forgot the whole matter in five minutes, and the child crept out, and sat upon the door-stone, and felt her small pride crushed, and her character stained forever.

The strawberry party, at least it seemed so at this moment, was all spoiled now.

So, in our clumsy recklessness, we deal with souls!

Only, the dock always grows beside the nettle. It is God who takes care of that. Aunt Rebecca, in her white dress, with her pure, gentle young face, came out to the door-stone and stood behind Sarah.

The pleasant south wind was blowing through the great maples that stood in a row between the road and the chip-yard; the scent of early roses came up from the low flower-garden, to which a white gate, and a few rough stone steps led in and down straight opposite the door. Further on, beside the drive that wound with sudden slope around the garden to the right, toward the great barns, stood the long trough, hewn from a tree-trunk, and holding clear, cool water that flowed incessantly into it, through a wooden duct of halved and hollowed saplings, leading from a spring in the hillside away up behind the house. Here a yoke of tired cattle were drinking, — the ploughboy standing patiently beside; close by the great creatures' heads, upon the trough-rim, perched fearless chickens, dipping their yellow bills; and underneath and around, in the merry, unfailing puddles, splashed and quackled the ducks. The bright June sun, genial, not scorching, hung in the afternoon sky. There were birds in the maple trees, and the very grass about the door-stone was full of happy life. Out upon all, through troubled eyes, looked a little, tender human soul that had felt a pain.

"What is it, Say?"

Say turned round at the gentle voice, and nestled her face against the folds of the white dress.

"I ate all sponge-cake for my supper at Mrs. Fairbrother's," she murmured, like a penitent at confessional, whispering into priestly ears the avowal of a deadly sin.

"And that was —— ?" said Aunt Rebecca.

"Greedy. Horrid." So far she spoke from sentence of others, out of her shame; and then something in herself rebelled at her own words, and she added, with sudden defiance—"But I don't see why. There was plenty of it. And they asked me."

"Plenty for you, dear. But if everybody else had wanted all sponge-cake?"

Sarah saw the selfishness then, and there was no answer for her to make. She dropped, wretchedly, back into her self-contempt again.

"I wish," said the child, impulsively, "that I was a chicken. Only a little, yellow, peeping chicken. Like those down there."

"Like that one, running away to hide under the fence, with a barleycorn in his mouth?"

"Oh dear!" This soul that had been born into the world, and had had its tiny experience of the evil, might chafe in vain. She could see nowhere her escape, not even into chickenhood, had that been possible.

"Not that way," said Rebecca, more to her own thought than remembering the child. "Only toward God."

"We must *ask*, Say, to have the selfishness taken from us.

And we must try to give up. We can't turn into chickens, even if that would do. But we can grow — to be angels. This one little fault may make you better all your life. And," she added, with a delicate heart-instinct, "nobody will ever remember it!"

Say's face changed. She had passed through, in these few moments — sensitive children do, in a strange undreamed-of way, in these their little experiences — an epitome of the grand, spiritual experience of human life, and of the world. All things great are in all things little. Law comes with its rebuke, — its fruitless shame for what is past; Gospel with its word of mercy for what has been, its hope for better things to be. Aunt Prue was condemnation. Aunt Rebecca was redemption. The child loved the saintly young girl, at that moment, as men love their Redeemer.

She might overlive it, then; even this terrible misdemeanor of the sponge-cake. "Nobody would remember it." The words were a balm like that which comes to us grown sinners with God's words — "I have blotted out thy transgressions; I will not remember thy sins."

Say slid her little hand into Aunt Rebecca's. "Let me stay by you at tea-time," she whispered, "Why, Auntie!" she cried, suddenly, with altered tone, as for the first time she lifted her eyes fully to the kind face that looked down upon her. "You had your hair in those pretty puffs. Where are they?"

"I brushed them back again," said Aunt Rebecca, quietly.

This young girl of nineteen had renounced her vanity so. She had seen in her glass that her face was very pretty, set in its glossy frame of smoothly banded locks; and, lest she should remember it to her spiritual hurt, — lest she should so, thinking of self, forget her Lord, — she had put them back, and chosen to wear only her usual and unnoted look to-day.

Moreover, the Reverend Gordon King was to be of the strawberry party.

I do not say that puffs are sinful. I do not say that God forbids a simple joy in the beauty that He gives. I only tell you what this young creature, true to her own conception of duty, did.

Rebecca Gayworthy was growing into the character that primitive New England influences, and almost these alone, develop from certain natures. Out of these by-places where the Puritan air still lingers — out of these Bethlehems, slow of growth, perhaps, but the less tainted, come souls that rule. That walk sternly over self, — that choose the thorns, — that take up their cross daily, giving up their own work to do that of the Lord Christ. Taught from infancy that no Church or outside ark is to save them; that no cabalism of words said over them is to bring them necessarily into the kingdom of heaven; admonished of the spiritual birth, — warned of the spiritual death; set searching, each soul for itself, what this birth may mean, — how salvation from this death be won; the thoughtful, earnest spirit wrestles and reaches till it lays hold of sainthood.

A fugue of voices from within called Rebecca at this moment. Flour and cream and fruit had been carried away. The hour had come for laying the long table in the great front kitchen, the only room in the farm-house which might afford space for the expected guests at a real comfortable, sit-down, tea-drinking, whereat alone might strawberry short-cake be fittingly enjoyed. At other times, the Gayworthy ladies knew well how to order and preside over the stateliness of the formal "handing-round" in the best parlor. To-night was high festival, where mere gentility took second place.

The wide fireplace was garnished with greenery, and the flames that ordinarily poured upward through its capacious outlet were kindling unwontedly in the out-room, where Huldah Brown was already mixing and rolling, and would shortly be "scalding and mashing," — high priestess of the mighty mystery that she was. The dresser held now the wide tray laden with rare old china cups and saucers and plates; tea-pots of the same, tall, slender, quaint, long-spouted, high-handled; little pitchers with the "long ears," that shall forever be memorialized while little human receptacles with the like appendages continue to be; all these, and many of them; for in the days and regions of notable personal housewifery, and neat-handed Huldahs helping, grandmother's treasures of porcelain gathered and came down, with neither nick nor breakage, to second and third generations. Alas, for the days that have been, and shall be no more forever!

The monstrous linen-chest, that stood in the great "kitchen chamber" overhead, had delivered up its most voluminons naperies to shroud the extended board whose construction for the occasion, since no guests shall have need to spy, we, neither, need pry into nor explain. There was a sweet, nameless, delicate fragrance in the air, as the pure white folds were shaken out, such as is breathed only from old presses, and quaint bureaus, and great chests like this that had held these, wherein women of the olden time, who set store by their fair linens and delicate laces, and silken heirlooms of taffeta and brocade, kept daintily, with bits of musk, and sprigs of lavender, such wealth of house and wardrobe.

Rebecca was summoned to assist in the spreading and placing. An hour hence, and the early country party would have assembled.

Sarah Gair stayed outside, waiting to see what Gershom Vorse, coming up toward her from the orchard gate, with one of the farm men, might be going to do.

"Eben is going to feed the pigs now, Say! Come out into the shed-chamber, and we'll call 'em in!"

Say sprang down from the door-stone at that, eagerly; and skipped, in a dainty way, turning out the toes of her new bronze boots, over the bit of grass-plot that lay between her and the wide open doors of the great woodshed.

Gershom came up, with a certain contempt in the tread of his stout country shoes.

"I forgot you were all dressed up, and toes in position," said he.

Say had before this offered to teach him the small beginnings that she herself had made in the sublime art which includes "Deportment."

"That is n't a bit of matter," returned the straightforward little lady, not accepting the sarcasm, and picking her way among the scattered chips and litter along the shed, with a continued, conscious pleasure, — the pleasure of using pretty things, — in each separate planting of the trim, golden-gleaming little feet. "It's as nice out in my play-parlor, as it is in Aunt Prue's best room. Besides, my dollies want to see me, by this time."

The shed-chamber was a clean, floored room, rough-beamed and small-windowed, at the further end of the building. One window opened on the yard, toward the house, and the other overlooked the pig-pen, and pleasanter things beyond. Through the middle of the floor came up two square, box-like constructions—open conduits to the troughs beneath.

And this "play-parlor," as Say called it, was a really pleasant place. To a child, a bit of Paradise, roughly boarded in. Here, in any weather, Say could come, and amuse herself with her grand china-closet of broken bits,—luckily for the children, *common* ware *did* get fractured now and then,—ranged along the ledges in one corner; decorate the brown, unplaned walls with boughs of green and wild flowers or gay, coarse garden-blossoms that she had "leave to pick;" admonish and discipline, dress and array, her indefinite family of corn-cob children, and, above all, when everything else sated, stand at the "pig-pen" window, and look out over the green meadow stretching towards the bit of oak woods that skirted the opposite boundary of the wet land with its green mystery, which nobody but the pigs ever penetrated, and whither these happy animals daily betook themselves through a little wicket-gate left open from their board and lodging place.

The call from this window, in a high, peculiar monotone, "pig-pig-pig-pig-pig," would bring, first one, then another, and at last the whole drove, peeping out from the oak-grove, and scampering across the meadow to their roomy, and not unclean quarters within the wicket; where, at suitable intervals, buckets-full, not of common refuse, but of what to swinish appreciation, must have seemed the most sumptuous white soup,—a boiling of vegetables added to the surplus of the dairy,—rich buttermilk, or sweet whey, or plentiful skimmed milk, better than humans in the cities pay for,—was poured, a luscious flood, down the square conduits above mentioned. I think pigs were never so happy, so well lodged, so bountifully and delicately fed, as these of Grandpapa Gayworthy! What with the liberty abroad, and the dainties at home, it was the very poetry of pork.

At any rate, Sarah Gair was hardly ever more happy than in luring them out from their green, shady covert where the sweet acorns grew, and watching their eagerness as they scrambled along the meadow-path, and into their dining-parlor, and tumbled up confusedly about the troughs; lifting their small, keen eyes, like many a creature of higher organization, with a very assured expectancy of good gifts due, according to precedent, from above.

"Eben—ezer!" cried Say, from the window, as the man entered the chamber behind them, and set his pail beside the great wooden spouts. "The gate's blown to! The pigs can't get in! Make haste,—there's grandpa driving down the yard!"

"An' I guess he'll want his horse took out, afore I come back again. So you an' the pigs can wait. It 'll be sometime, too, I should n't wonder. You can't expect a man that carries a name as long as that, to stir round quite so spry as a Jack-be-nimble!"

Eben had so his sly revenge for Say's mischievous giving of the whole title, which, it was well known in the household, he very decidedly disliked. He left the pails as they were, beside the spouts, and went down to the yard below. As he set the wicket back, Dr. Gayworthy really did call to him. Meanwhile the children at the window called the pigs.

"How funny they look," said Say, "with their great ears flapping, and their queer, flat noses going, so!" and she turned her lips, very drolly, inside out and up and down against nose and chin, and tried to work them, pig-fashion.

"There they come, tumbling and grunting," as the creatures crossed their outer court and disappeared beneath the building. "And now, I wish Eb would come."

To pass away the time, Say skipped down from the block of timber upon which she stood at the window, and executing certain imperfectly learned "dancing steps," fell to admiring her new boots again,—chatting on, all the while, to Gershom.

"Did you know we 're going to have a little table, you and I, and take tea at the same time with the company?"

"I hate company," answered Gershom, gruffly. "People stuck round, mincing at little bits, and saying, 'No, I thank you,' with their mouths puckered up, when they want it, all the time! I hate company, and I hate company manners!—'Ma-l-vi-ny!'" he drawled, in a high, plaintive pitch of voice, "'take—your fingers—out—of the su-gar bowl! Do-n't—touch—the pie—until—it 's cut!' That's Mrs. Fairbrother. And then she gives her a lump of sugar, and a big piece of cake to eat in a corner, so as to make her behave. P—ff!"

"But then," put in little Say, quite seriously, "people *must* behave, you know. We should n't like to act like the pigs down there," as a fierce, impatient scramble and squealing was heard from about the empty troughs.

"I don't know," returned Gershom, a little less gruffly, but with a tone of cavil, still. "It 's wrong, somehow. It aint real. If they 'd *like* to be like the pigs, they'd better do it."

"I 'm sure *I* should n't like to be like the pigs," said Say, practising a waltz step pretty successfully. "I like to be nice!"

"O yes," returned Gershom, with a small sneer. "You like to wear new brown boots, and be fine, I daresay. But that aint it."

"Gershom! You 're cross!"

"No, I aint. But you 're proud. You 're thinking all the time of your boots. You 're thinking there is n't another pair in all Hilbury like 'em. What if there is n't? That don't make you any better than the rest. You 've got nothing but bare feet, like everybody's else, inside 'em, after all!"

"Gershom! You 're real ugly. I don't care for my boots!"

"Poh! That 's likely! Don't you pick round, like a cat, for fear you should wet 'em or scratch 'em?" And Gershom turned away, in utter disdain.

"I 'd just as lief spoil 'em as not! See here!"

Gershom turned his head, again, at the passionate tone and a sudden splash; and Eben re-entered the shed-chamber at the same moment. The two saw something astonishing. A small figure, dilated with an angry, desperate triumph, holding itself haughtily, erect, motionless, in a pig's-pail!

Gershom's scorn was the one thing Say could not bear. Woman-like, she vindicated herself impetuously and recklessly, from one suspicion, by rushing, absurdly, into an opposite excess. She had her reward, as women have.

"I don't see how that mends the matter," was the cool, slighting comment of the boy.

"You can't say any more about my boots, anyhow!" And standing there still in her ridiculous attitude, from which even the dignity of a righteous resentment now fell away, she burst into a passion of impotent tears.

Eben lifted her, quietly, by the shoulders, and set her, dripping, upon the floor. "Well, I vum!" said he, "that 's spunky. If ever I see the like o' that afore, my name aint Eben——ezer!"

Say stood sobbing, conscious of ignominious failure; remembering, with a rush, all that lay before her now,—the getting into the house again,—her mother's and aunt's displeasure,—all that was utterly impossible and horrible to do and to bear. She stood there in a shame, and fear, and agony; and in a great pause, that seemed like the end of all things. The next that life had for her might come; she could not move to meet it.

Then Gershom changed his mood. Conceit and vanity and self-satisfaction, — the shams of society patent to his early experience, — these he could battle with and put down. These, boy as he was, he had no mercy for. But humiliation and helplessness and tears,—these, the man-chivalry aroused in him to pity and to help.

He came and drew Say gently by the arm. Come," said he; "never mind! Sit down here on the block." Say let herself be put there, passively.

Gershom unfastened and drew off the soaked boots and stockings, and then brought a dipper full of water from the well, which he poured over the white little feet and ankles, and the unhappy pantalets. "Now," said he, "don't cry; but come up the back stairs with me. There 's nobody but Huldah in the out-room. And you and I'll have our supper in the kitchen-chamber."

There was nobody like Gershom for tormenting or consoling.

This childish scene betrayed something, on each side, of character, and foreshadowed much of what was yet to be.

CHAPTER II.

DOWN AMONG THE COMPANY.

"From all points of the compass" they began to arrive. Not that this implies necessarily any mighty concourse; there was no other way for a gathering to be made in Hilbury. It was one of those great, thinly populated townships that lie about among the hills in certain New England regions, which have a small settlement — sometimes that only of a single family, with its branches — in each corner, and a meeting-house in the middle. There were, in Hilbury, the separate villages of the Centre, the Bridge, Lawton's and Gibson's Corners, and Gair's Hill. So, from all these they came, — from up the road and down the road, — and, driving across the chip-yard, tied their horses to the garden fence.

Dr. Gayworthy's house stood, if mathematics admit of such an expression, in the edge of the Centre. It was a fair, prosperous-looking building, kept fresh with seasonable paintings, of a mellow, sunny, smiling straw-color; the color in the country, most indicative of well-to-do-ing. It had an air somehow, among the neighboring dwellings of dusky red, as of a dainty lady in primrose silk among rustics wearing common scarlet cotton print.

The children — Gershom and Say — watched the arrival of the company from the "clothes-room" window, — the clothes-room being a large, light closet, off the southwest end of the great kitchen-chamber.

Say's spirits were reacting merrily from her terror and disgrace. Mrs. Reuben, intent at the moment upon the placing of the iced plum-cakes, had but half comprehended the catastrophe which Gershom tried to convey to her knowledge, taking to himself as large a share of the blame as might be.

"I'll warrant it!" was her exclamation. "If there's a mischief to be got into, she'll be sure to find it!"

"She's very sorry about it, Aunt Jane. You won't scold her, will you?"

Something in this appeal, whatever it may have been, of word or manner, seemed to give "Aunt Jane" more annoyance than all the previous recital. She motioned — I might say, if it were elegant, elbowed — him off, with the arm against which, in his eagerness to follow her along the table, he pressed a little, to the damage of the new French embroidered cape, with its innumerable delicate lace finishings and frills, the like of which had never before been seen in Hilbury. The gesture was more pettish than it was like her usual self to be; for Mrs. Reuben Gair rarely allowed herself to be "put about," as the common saying is; she had a way of smoothly steering along toward her ends, whether great or small; without ever jostling against anything or anybody.

"There, go away," she returned, hastily. "I 've no time, now, for scolding, or anything else. If you 've got her into a mess, you 'll have to take care of her and keep her out of the way."

Gershom skipped up the out-room stairs, well pleased at gaining even this much.

"The worst 's over, Say," he said. "She knows. And she was n't so terrible angry, after all. She seemed more put out about my tumbling her new-fashioned vandyke, or whatever you call it, than anything else."

So Say was in spirits again; and sat, like a barefooted princess, upon the divan of blankets and "comfortables" that lay piled below the clothes-room window, and watched the gay arrivals; and Gershom, by and by, when the strawberry feasting began below, ran up and down the out-room staircase, receiving from friendly Huldah Brown nice bits of what he and Say liked best; and Say thought nothing in the world worth wishing for any longer, since Gershie was so good-natured.

"I told you I did n't care about my boots," she cried. "I'd rather be here than down among the company, a great deal!"

Down among the company, however it might be as to bodily wants, there was perhaps many a heart-hunger less abundantly ministered to than little Sarah Gair's.

Stacy Lawton felt no scruple about wearing her hair in the new puffs. She had thought of little else since Mrs. Reuben Gair appeared in them at Mrs. Fairbrother's sewing-circle.

She, as well as Rebecca Gayworthy, had heard the young minister, Gordon King, preach his two sermons last Sunday, the one upon "seeking first the kingdom of God and His righteousness;" after which, Stacy, with a party of other young girls, had adjourned to spend the "noon-time" with a friend close by the meeting-house, in eating cold pie, cake, and cheese, and in low-toned discussion among themselves as to how it—not this seeking of the kingdom, but the hair-dressing was done; the other, at afternoon service, upon the "mortifying of the flesh;" from which she went straightway home, and used her leisure hours of twilight in patient experiments before her glass, until the hairs of her head, which the Scripture-reading of the day had admonished her she "could neither make white nor black," took shape and place as she desired.

Rebecca Gayworthy shut herself in her chamber, also; but she sat there in a still, solemn presence that pervaded her soul; and in the fair garden thereof the Lord God walked in this cool of His day.

So Stacy Lawton came to the strawberry party with her dark hair banded stylishly from off her face; and the consciousness that she was looking very pretty, and that people were noticing it, gave a sparkle to her eyes, and a sprightly grace and ease to her movements that made her, as indeed she was very apt at all times to be, quite the belle of the occasion. Say what you will of violets, and unconscious charms, the perk little daisy gets the better of it in the eye of the world; and there is nothing that helps beauty so to its full success as just the spice of consciousness that gives confidence.

And Rebecca had put from her the like adornment, for conscience's sake. Foolishly, you say? I am not sure. There is somewhere this written—that "all things shall work together for good to them that love God." Even a mistaken or needless self-sacrifice, then. "There is none that hath forsaken anything for the kingdom of heaven's sake but shall receive manifold more." God's promise to pay holds good, I think.

Nevertheless, it is very true that Gordon King, as he stood talking for a few moments with Rebecca upon his first entrance, thought silently that "somehow, she was n't quite so pretty, after all as he had fancied;" and that Stacy Lawton's bright glance and musical laugh enticed him presently to that corner of the room where she held small, merry court; where she made room for him at her side with a beaming look that seemed warm welcome only, but was secretly, also, kindled of a coquettish triumph.

The Reverend Gordon King was very like other young men, it must be owned; and although he preached from the Bible on a Sunday the truth he found there, he went out from his pulpit of a week-day into the little world about him, and valued the things thereof greatly after the world's own fashion. "Take no thought for raiment, what ye shall put on," he had read and exhorted; yet here he was, quite appreciative of the results of Miss Stacy's "taking thought" which had brought about all this blooming prettiness in puffed-hair and pink muslin.

I do not mean that Gordon King was a hypocrite,—to be ranked with the Scribes and Pharisees in the condemnation. I mean simply, that he was no better than human; and as yet, perhaps, not wholly sanctified human. There may be snuffling, canting "shepherds,"—Stigginses, Chadbands, and the like in the world. I have not known them. I only speak of people of whom I know such to have been.

Preaching ran in the King family; as politics or doctoring, sailoring or soldiering, run in some others. The uncle of Gordon had been a divine, eminent in his neighborhood, degreed in due course, as Doctor Divinitatis, and now occupying a good college professorship. His elder brother was in Batavia, sent out by the A. B. C. F. M. His father was an influential deacon in the church; his sister had married the Rev. Felix Fairbrother; which brings him into the pulpit of Hilbury and into the scene of our story. He had gone through a college course; he had studied in the Divinity School; he had also, as needful preliminary to this,—not feignedly, but of good faith,—putting himself "in the way of grace,"—gone through what passed with himself and those about him for the genuine order of religious experience; he believed himself, and was believed, to have received the renewing gift—the intangible ordinance of the Spirit. How was he truly to know if what he had gotten were the same wherein another soul rejoiced?

Life was to test for him and teach him this. God, who worked, doubtless, in these very cues of circumstance, calling him outwardly, might have laid up for him in his future, a nobler, intenser experience than any whereto he had yet reached in these five and twenty years that were past.

Meanwhile, for this party at the Gayworthy's, he had dressed with thoughts not very different from those that any other bachelor of twenty-five might have had, in dressing for a ladies' party. There was an external difference. He folded about his neck the white cravat, at that time the still distinctive badge of his order. Two white cravats, successively, I should say; for the first that he essayed proving to be but limply starched, and the great house-clock below reminding him at the same moment of the lateness of the hour, he had flung it down with a very unclerical gesture of—to say the least—impatience; and an inarticulate ejaculation that, on ruder or unconsecrated lips *might* have gone nigh to syllable itself profanely. I don't say that it was n't a great deal better so than if he had actually said anything that would need to be spelt with a black ——; and I don't suppose he ever did use bad words. But I wonder if, after all, the angels up above listen so heedfully for the vibrations of these gases about our earth which feed and pulsate to our human breath as for the tremblings of the unseen spirit; and whether the state of mind of the Reverend Gordon King for the moment was really so widely unlike that of the poor man whose hay-cart I saw topple over in the field the other day, and who *did* say something with a dash in the middle. And I am afraid that, as a general statement men are but men, too often; and that, lest they might be worse, it behooves somebody to look after them pretty carefully, even in the matter of white cravats.

Howbeit, this was he whom Rebecca, in her innocent reverence, held as one sanctified of God above common men. For whom she would not use any harmless art of outer adornment; but rather hallow herself, and hold herself pure of earthly vanity, if so, at least, she might keep her soul upon the plane of such as his; if so, at least, she might be utterly worthy, whether it should please God that she might win his love, or no. Ah, there is a sainthood to whose companionship such life reaches, though that which it believes in seem to mock its faith!

If Gordon King had held the answering talisman in his own soul, he should not, this night, have been lured away to the false princess, while the true, veiled in her meek-heartedness, waited so near his side.

Rebecca, moving about among the guests with her Madonna hair and quiet look, grew even a shade more quiet, perhaps, but that was all. Joanna, bright and laughing, with a little positive emphatic way of her own of uttering droll or absurdly extravagant things, that made everybody else laugh with her, was somehow also a little more pronounced in her special characteristics, — a little more queer, and animated, and hyperbolical than usual. Nobody guessed, — as she kept a knot of the Hilbury girls in chimes of merriment with a carefully detailed receipt for the famous short-cake, in which she gravely asserted "soft soap, beaten to a cream" to be the chief ingredient, and described to their eager questionings the secret arrangement of "seventeen crash flounces" which she declared — ladies were not caged or coopered then — held Mrs. Reuben's skirts in such graceful rotundity, — the stealthy anxiety that glanced through all her fun, in the quick half-turn of her head at each movement near the door; or the disappointment that was gradually settling down cold upon her heart, as time wore on, and somebody, whom she looked for, did not come; and no one around her caught, as she did, a chance word of Mrs. Hartshorne's, who stood a dozen feet off, in answer to a question put by Mrs. Prue, that Joanna dared not, for her life, have put, herself.

"Gabriel's gone over to Deepwater, sailing with the Purcells. He promised a week ago, to go, when they settled on a day; and Aleck Purcell came over this morning to get him."

"Are the Frank Purcells staying there still?"

"O yes — the young folks. Mr. and Mrs. went back last Tuesday."

After that, Joanna laughed more merrily yet, and became yet more absurd. And her end of the room grew quite noisy with the "gale" the girls got into; and plaintive Mrs Fairbrother, away over opposite, quite worn out with continual mild, ineffectual remonstrances with "Malviny," who, as the minister's child, was privileged to be taken everywhere, said to her husband, — "It's Joanna Gayworthy. She's always in such high spirits. She'll get sobered down, one of these days, when she comes to see care and trouble."

Joanna Gayworthy, at the same moment, was thinking, in her secret heart, how nice it would be, when all these people were gone, and the china set away, and the house shut up, and lights put out, and she in bed, having a good cry to herself, in the dark.

Well, — this was a strawberry party. It makes no difference. That, or anything else, as it might happen. It was *life*, which finds slight outside seeming and excuse, and veils so its great workings. You don't hold out to people, undisguisedly, the hundred different hopes and motives which you know will bring them together, when you invite them to your house. You ask them to eat strawberries, or to listen to music, or to dance the polka. The rest is incidental, — thrown in. So we come to live double. Nobody says anything about it, but every one is conscious of something, be it what it may, that underlies the dressing and the dancing, and the feasting, and the words of the hour, which is the reality; else there is none, in it all. Take this away, and the whole crumbles into nothing. The game is not worth the candle. The candle, henceforth, goes out.

Doctor Gayworthy knew all this; but he had got past the time for thinking much about it. He could have remembered hours wherein all life had seemed to him centred; hours that seemed an existence, questioning nothing of a beginning or an end; a husking, or a quilting, or a winter dance, the simple scene of which had widened out with a breadth of experience that made it as a theatre whereon the pivotal act of a human life was played, while all the eager stars looked down; he could have remembered when, as his real life withdrew itself, and centred otherwise and elsewhere, such gatherings began to lose their charm, and he came to wonder how it was that there were no longer any such drives, or dances, or bees, or frolics, as had been when he was young. Now, even this was past; he neither participated nor wondered; but accepted or offered a hospitality that was part of a routine, and only looked to it, that, so far as depended upon him, everybody got their tea and cake, which was what they had ostensibly come for.

So, to-night, the Doctor, worthy gentleman, looked up and down among his daughters' guests, and saw that all was plentiful and comfortable; and he walked about the rooms after tea was over, and noticed everybody, and chatted with a few; and observed, indeed, that Rebecca was a little pale and still to-night, — tired, perhaps, with her preparations; and that Joanna was, as always, a gay little gipsey, and the life of the company; and it never occurred to him to imagine that these two or three hours wherein he wore his best coat, and submitted to this little temporary stir in the house, were any more to them, by chance, than they might be to himself.

As the company thinned off, toward nine o'clock, this little scene took place between him and Mrs. Reuben in the tea-room, whence Huldah was removing the "things," and whither the doctor had come for a surreptitious "third cup" which he had not got at the regular time.

"Where are the children? I have n't seen them to-night."

"Why, Gershom got Say into some sort of a scrape in the shed-chamber, while the pigs were being fed; and splashed her with the pails, I believe; I had n't time to dress her over, or to inquire much about it. I wish the boy was n't so rude and teasing."

"Got into a scrape, did they? I'm sorry for that. He's a very good sort of boy, though, Jane. A remarkably good boy; and steady, too, for his age. I don't know what I should do without Gershom."

Mrs. Gair was apparently intent upon a stain of something which had fallen upon the front breadth of her new silk, and which she was trying to wipe off with a wet napkin.

"He ought to be a good boy," she remarked. "He owes more to you than he'll ever be able to pay."

"Well, I don't know about that, — yet," said the doctor, "If things were squared up between Prue and the boy and me, I don't know exactly how the balance would stand, I'm sure."

"Everybody else knows. Why, father, you could not have done more for them if they'd been your own. To be sure," she added, as glancing up from her labor, she caught a darkening look upon the doctor's face, "I know, of course, they seem just like your own. And I don't suppose there was ever a mixed-up family like ours, that thought so little of the difference. But when you talk of squaring up accounts! By the way, father," — and Mrs. Gair laid down the napkin and reached the sugar for the doctor, standing by, with a thoughtful expression, while he bountifully sweetened his tea, — "now you speak of him, have you ever thought what it will be best for him to do, one of these days? He 's getting to be a great boy. I must have a talk with you about him when you 're at leisure, sometime, before I go. I dare say Mr. Gair might find something for him in Selport."

Mrs. Reuben was scrupulous in always speaking of her husband as "Mr. Gair," in this neighborhood, where he had some thirty years before, run barefooted.

"Time enough to talk about that," replied the doctor, a little impatiently. Then, setting down his cup, resting the knuckles of his hands upon the table-edge, and bending forward so, for a moment, he seemed to take thought, and come to a resolve.

"Jane," he said, seriously, after this instant 's pause, changing his posture and moving a pace closer to her side, — "don't speak to Reuben of anything of the sort; and don't talk to the boy about Selport. There 's time enough, as I said; and I have n't made up my mind. At least I should n't have spoken if you had n't begun. But Hilbury has always done well enough for me, and I 've been in hopes it might do well enough for Gershom. He 's all the boy I 've got, you know."

Yes, Mrs. Gair knew now just what she had wanted to find out. The good doctor had no thought of Gershom Vorse but as his boy. "All the boy he 'd got."

Jane Gair's work lay straight before her, and then and there she made an initial stroke.

She, too, held herself an instant in deliberation, the while she resumed again the napkin she had laid down, and with its dry corner wiped, leisurely and solicitously, the damp spot upon her dress. "O yes," she said, half absently, as people do when they are mainly intent on that which occupies their fingers, and speak mechanically. "There 's no hurry. And I don't know as it would have occurred to me to say anything about it, only that Gershom has been asking me some questions, now and then, since I came up, about the city. It seemed to me as though he had got a little restless. Boys will, you know. There," — once more dropping the napkin, and stroking down the folds of silk with her fingers, — "I don't see as I can do anything better for it, now."

"Better let it be," said Huldah Brown, coming in for a fresh relay of dishes, and catching the last sentence. "It 's grease, I guess. It 's easier to spot things than to clean 'em, a good deal."

"Oh, well, never mind," answered Mrs. Reuben, goodnaturedly, "I 'll manage it among the gathers, and it won't show." And she moved away into the front rooms.

"Jane Gayworthy, all over!" ejaculated Huldah, as she came into the out-room again, where Eben sat, eating strawberry short-cake. "She allus thinks it's no matter what's done, as long as it's tucked away in the gethers, out of sight. For my part, I like things good and clean, clear through. As soon as they're spotted they're sp'ilt, to my thinkin'."

Eben pushed his emptied plate into the middle of the table, and tilting his chair upon its hinder legs, made a quadruped of himself so, and walked himself back a few paces, as Yankees know how, till he rested comfortably against the wall. He had been seated within six feet, or thereabouts, of the steps that led up into the kitchen proper, through all the foregoing conversation. The busy handmaiden, in the clatter of her dishes, farther off, had caught nothing of it, save in her passages to and fro.

"Huldy Brown!" said Eben, emphatically, throwing up his arms over his head against the partition, and crossing his long legs in the air. "I tell you what it is! I don't want to jedge nobody; but I b'lieve, as I've got a created soul, she's thunderin' sly!"

CHAPTER III.

PEEKIN' AND HARKIN'.

When people decline peremptorily the discussion of affairs, you may be sure they go away and think them over all the more. An idea like this suggested itself to Mrs. Reuben Gair. Her hint of Selport, and something for the boy to do, had not apparently taken direct effect; but it might have set her father to considering, perhaps a little prematurely, as regarded her own secret wishes in the matter. Mrs. Reuben Gair was not mistaken in her surmise.

She *had* set her father to considering. Or rather, considerations which had long been passively revolving, as it were, within his mind, at this word of hers took shape, came out, and would be looked at. They grew to definite questions, and demanded, suddenly, decisions.

"You could n't have done more for them, if they 'd been your own!" There might be something more that he ought to do, because they were not his own. Somehow, after Jane's words, this thought pressed upon him obstinately, and refused to evaporate itself into mere vague purpose for the future. He finished his cup of tea, and, turning away rather abruptly, walked out upon the doorstone where Rebecca and Say had had their little talk together before the "company" came.

The company — those of it who still remained — were gathered at the front of the house, within and without. Laughter and merry speech of young voices came around from the pleasant dooryard, where the moon shone down upon June roses, and upon human life also in its June.

The good doctor stood musingly and listened; looking up to the still, night-heaven, unrolling the same slow-moving, gorgeous scroll as long ago, when it had been blossoming-time with him as well. And, standing there, he felt, rather than thought, how men change, and lives pass, and the great, unaltered skies look down on all. God laid His hand over him so, and sealed thought into action.

He scarcely knew why, but in those moments his "mind was made up."

"I won't leave things at loose ends another hour," said he at last, and turning back from the doorway, he walked straight through the long kitchen, passing on into his own little private room, which adjoined. Here he found his good friend, Parson Fairbrother, who, after having done his social duty among the company, had made his privileged way hither, to mouse, as he was apt to do, among the old books; and was at this moment quite lost in something he had lit upon among the pages of Burton's Anatomy.

"I want a little talk with you, Parson, if you please; and I've got a five-minutes bit of business to do. You shall take old Burton home if you like," said the doctor, closing the door by which he had entered — the parson had already shut that leading to the best parlor, to exclude disturbing sounds — and pushing two great leathern arm-chairs towards the table, in one of which he seated himself, while Mr. Fairbrother, turning down a leaf, carefully closed the volume, and came forward, in compliance, to the other.

When the parsonage party, — Mrs. Fairbrother, Malviny and Gordon King, with Miss Stacy Lawton, who had heedlessly let the Gibsons, her next-door neighbors, go home without her, fifteen minutes before, and who now availed herself of the Fairbrother escort, "only for as far as they went," — was gathering to take leave, the good minister, after considerable outcry, was found thus cosily closeted with the doctor; and when summoned a second time by Malviny, sent word that they "might step along. He'd come presently." It was nothing unusual. Nobody gave the circumstance a second thought, unless, indeed, the watchful, elder daughter of the house.

Presently — I should think, though, a good half hour after — Mrs. Gair, wondering very much, and waiting to put out the last candles, while her sisters were busied setting other things to rights, heard her father go with the minister to the front gate, and say good-night; returning directly to his own little room again, whence, in a few moments, stole out the deferred fragrance of his evening pipe.

There seemed to be a good deal revolving in various brains that night in the Gayworthy farmhouse. It might have been late tea-drinking, or strawberry short-cake, or the mental stimulus of social contact; whatever it was, people did not go straight to bed and to sleep, according to their wont.

Mrs. Vorse, having with her own hands set every precions bit of china back into the closet sacred to its keeping, departed up the staircase to the kitchen chamber with an armful of linen, enjoining on Huldah, as she went, to see everything safe in the out-room for the night.

Huldah had milkpans to wash, and bread to set; but she sang to herself cheerily, as left apparently alone in all the lower part of the house, she moved, not a whit loath or wearily, from kitchen to dairy, from dairy to the large, lonely out-room, where waited her last work for the night. She sang as she gathered her pans, whose contents had been rifled of their cream for the feasting; as she wiped down sweet-smelling shelves, whose purity neither drop nor dust might defile; as she poured away the skimmed milk into the large, tidy-tub that stood in the far corner to accumulate the dainty waste whose destination we know; sang on, with a sudden glee in her voice, as she carried the freshly-scalded tins out presently at the door, and set them gleaming there in the moonlight, catching, as she did so, glimpse of a tall, stalwart figure — *not* raw-boned and shambling, but sturdy, well-built, albeit Yankee to the vertebral main-shaft — that gathered itself up from leaning over the garden fence, and sauntered with great strides towards her. The song broke into a laugh as she turned back again, ignoring the presence, and said to herself, with a spasm of fun bubbling up among her words: —

"I knew it! I was certin he 'd jest go and be redickl'ous agin!"

Eben Hatch and Huldah Brown had grown up, boy and girl together, upon the Gayworthy farm.

When Huldah was eighteen, her mother, — who had been "brought up," as the country phrase is for expressing board-and-clothes-remunerated service, by the mother of Dr. Gayworthy, and who had married, had a child, been widowed, and returned to her old employ, as if she had been simply put out at interest,— Huldah, with the eight years start in the world, standing for the percentage of Mrs. Brown's ten years' absence, and accompanying her mother, to be profitably "brought up" in her turn, — had died, leaving the daughter to the comfortable hereditary position which was practically little less privileged or more precarious than that of a daughter of the house.

Since that time, Eben had had frequent turns of being what Huldah called "redickl'ous"; but as yet, owing, as he thought, to persistent ill-luck, — as Huldah secretly believed, to "special interpositions,"— he had never, however often he had shamefacedly essayed it, got the step beyond, which might have touched the sublime; in his own words he had "somehow never quite made out to fetch it."

They were always nervous occasions these, to Huldah; she

wouldn't care to have them go a hair's-breadth further than they did; she hailed devoutly the "interpositions," which Provi dence — usually, it must be owned, through the instrumentality of her own womanly artifice — threw in; she drew what would have been a long breath, if it had n't at the same time been a secret chuckle, when Eben, looking a blank surprise, found himself suddenly at the end of his opportunity, — like the sheep fenced in with such a crooked art, that when he had fairly, as he thought, jumped the enclosure, he found himself back upon the same side, — and the danger was for that time over. Nevertheless, at due intervals, she was best pleased after all that the peril should recur. If Eben had n't now and then been "redickl'ous" at home, there would have been no knowing that he was n't redickl'ous — nay, even achieving the sublime — elsewhere.

So Huldah drew herself back out of the moonlight, with an instinct of shunning any over-sentimental accessories, and disappeared down the trap stairway to the cellar, for the jug of yeast, as Eben stepped over the threshold.

"You there?" she exclaimed, when she emerged again from below, and found him just where she knew he would be, waiting in the night-shine at the open door.

"Yes. I 'm here, Huldy. Jest come an' look at the moon! of all the June nights I ever see, this is the crowner!"

Huldah understood him and his moon-rapture. The heavenly satellite had precious little, in reality, to do with it; the same old story veiled itself so, in his homely New England dialect, that Lorenzo breathed to Jessica out there in Venice, in the verse she never heard of. If there had never been a moon, there would have been lovers, doubtless, all the same, and they might easily have found something else to talk about. What they pretend to look at, or to speak of, is no matter; as well squashes as sunbeams; the subject is but as the indifferent third substance, in chemistry, — thrown in only that the others may unite; the thing is, to bring the two souls together.

Huldah however, eschewed the whole, as moonshine, all of it; and taking herself away out of its perilous gleams, walked straight over to her bread-pan; remarking, only, very unsympathetically, as she did so, that "she 'd seen the moon afore; she guessed there was n't anything special about it; at any rate she had n't time to look."

If Huldah once got her hands fairly into the dough, — there was where Eben's bread would be, sure enough; so while she measured the yeast, and scooped the orthodox hollow for it in the flour, and began to stir it in, gently, with her wooden spoon, he ventured with a fresh persistence.

"The folks out there in the front yard, was tellin', to-night, about the moon lookin' different to different people; come here, Huldy jest a minute! I want to know how big you think it is!"

"You great gander!" exploded Huldah, at this very barefaced and absurd artifice. But she glanced out of the open window, nevertheless, up at the moon's jolly disc, that laughed broadly down upon them both, through door and casement; and laughed, heaven knows, at the same moment, on how many others like them, of varied place and degree.

"They made it out," pursued Eben, not a whit abashed, "all the way from a cart-wheel to a tea-plate: for my part, it looks as much as anything like the biggest meller punkin 't ever I see!"

"I can find something that 's enough like that, without going to the moon to look for 't!"

As pumpkins are not ordinarily abundant during the strawberry season, there was no resisting the conclusion that Huldah meant to be metaphorical, with a dash of personality.

"Now, Huldy! I 'll give in that you 're a plaguy smart girl, 'athout your goin' on to hector me, that way, all night. — See here —do you b'lieve all them stars has got people in 'em, like us?"

"I should hope not, exactly. I guess the Lord's got his hands full if they have!"

Huldah would neither be drawn into sentiment nor speculation; she was bent, to-night, upon the purely practical; this was plain from the way in which she plumped her capable hands into the pan, and began the sort of calisthenics that had developed to their comely proportions the not ungraceful limbs whose drapery, tucked up to the shoulders, displayed smooth-curving outlines that many a city belle, with a two-pronged elbow, might have looked upon in a sickening of envy. Eben must choose a shorter road to his object, than all the way around among the constellations.

"Huldy!" began again the long-suffering wooer, approaching shyly the table at which, not devoid of a coquettish consciousness, Huldah tossed, and doubled, and patted and punched the wheaten mass that gave—and nothing, if you knew, gives better—opportunity for such varied charm of attitude, — "you *air* a master hand at makin' bread, that 's a fact! and as to strawberry shortcake! I 'll be — buttered — if ever I ate such a one as that was to-night!"

"Seems to me everything suits with you, just now,— from moonshine down."

(Ah, Huldah! that was a very badly played card. Eben had his trump all ready for that. He would have been obtuser, otherwise, than ever yet Yankee lover was.)

"Yes, Huldah, —" and he came as close as the now very vigorously busy elbows would let him, and his voice lowered a tone, and deponed with true feeling that struggled into homely expression, — "I 'm pretty well suited! I only wish — everybody else was! — Do n't you think — "

I hold that he was doing it very cleverly, now. He would have grown eloquent presently; truth and passion, let them once get utterance, can be nothing else. But there came an interposition, as usual. Huldah was saved the necessity of thinking. There came a tread across the kitchen within, and the tall figure of Dr. Gayworthy, in gown and slippers, appeared upon the upper step at the doorway. He held in his hand a candle that had been blown out.

"Things *air* overruled, certin," Huldah breathed to herself, as Eben precipitately made his way to the outer door again; thrown back now upon the apparent comparative measurement of spheres, cereal and celestial.

"Durn it all!" muttered the unfortunate suitor, nonsuited. I never come so nigh fetchin' it, afore! Now I 've got it all to dew over ag'in! Lord knows when,—I don't."

Dr. Gayworthy reached his candle to the lamp upon Huldah's table, and borrowed a flame therefrom; saying, as he did so —

"When you have finished, Huldah, will you and Eben come to my little room a moment? I should like you to write your names as witnesses, upon a business paper I have had to sign."

"Oh, certin," answered Huldah, giving her ball of dough a final roll and flop over, and smiting her palms up and down against each other, to shake off the flour. "Jest as soon as I 've washed my hands."

Very much flustered, inwardly, was Huldah at this summons; first, with curiosity as to the document to be signed; secondly, with the thrill of importance people who never had, nor expect to have, any personal concern with papers of consequence, are apt to feel at being called upon to make valid with their names the instruments that dispose of the affairs of others; thirdly, at the thought of the two names required in juxtaposition; "it seemed so redick'lous; jest as if they was bindin' themselves to something, together."

She had time to think all this, as she washed her hands and let down her sleeves, and Dr. Gayworthy, setting down the lighted candle, followed Eben out into the moonlight, to make sure of him, and to say something about the next day's mowing.

There had been time, also, for certain other things to be thought and done, elsewhere.

The excitement she had had, and the strawberry short-cake she had eaten, had made little Sarah Gair restless to-night. So she had tossings and dreams and starts, and wakings; and at ten o'clock she roused, agitatedly, from a fearful vision,—of a horse's head without any body, that came in at the windows and chased her about the house, till her feet struggled vainly to move, and she stood paralyzed, with his hot breath pouring close upon her, and enveloping her, — to find her mother standing by the open sash, where nothing worse came in than the sweet night gleam, and the warm southwest sighs of June.

Mrs. Gair was thinking. No, — not thinking, purely; for thinking is a good thing. Worrying, scheming, wishing, anticipating,—which half that we call thinking really is,—may be very different things; very far from good in themselves or likely to work good when they ripen into action. This is the sort of "taking thought," that we are warned against. Mrs. Gair would better have gone to bed, and said her prayer for forgiveness, and deliverance, and daily bread, and left the details she was anxious about to the Knowledge and the Power that were beyond her own, than have stood there in the beauty of that summer night, striving selfishly to conjecture and to plan.

What was there, you may wonder, for her to conjecture and to plan about? Here was no lordly inheritance, whose bestowal was a question for the forethought and competition of long years; that might rationally, according to the common acceptance of human nature, suggest motive for rivalry, and strategy, and craft. Here was only a plain New England homestead, and the property resulting from the thrift and industry that had held sway through a couple of generations, in which father and son, worthy and intelligent farmer-physicians, had done simple credit and worked steady benefit to name and estate. This was all. Therefore you need not expect, O devourer of high-flown and deep-laid romance, to find in these pages profound mysteries, diabolical contrivance, unheard-of wrongs, and a general crash of retribution and ecstacy at the end. Yet in ever so simple a New England family, there may be privacies and secrets; there may be conflicting interests; the Tempter may find a cranny wherethrough to whisper, beguiling souls by mean motives to questionable acts. "There is a great deal of human nature in the world;" and it is n't all over the water, where there are lords and ladies, and manorial estates; for upwards of two centuries it it has been growing in these New England hills, and bringing forth fruit after its kind. Besides, even among the granite, gold does gather; and the well-harvested results of two careful lives may present an aggregate at last, not at all to be despised, even in its distribution according to a law which recognizes no closer sonship in the first child than in the ninth.

Also I have never noticed that, as the children of a household go out and meet their own varied fortunes in the world, there is apt to be any greater indifference to original claims, when money comes to be in question, with them upon whom success has so broadly smiled that their share of patrimony might seem almost as coals to Newcastle, than with the rest. On the contrary, these Newcastles are curiously ready to take in all the coal they can get, if ever a little ship comes along and brings any.

So Mrs. Gair, with her husband owning four or five vessels upon the high seas, in thriving communication with West Indian and South American ports, — holding himself as a merchant of consequence on Change, — troubled her mind here at the old homestead, in Hilbury, during her little summer stay, as to what might befall, regarding it, some ten, twenty, who knows but even thirty or more, years hence.

And neither she nor little Say could sleep well this June night.

Say, after she had cried out and called her mother to the bedside, and gasped out the horror of her dream, and been soothed and hushed, and laughed at, and had the sheets and pillows smoothed, — got over her fright, and grew wide awake, and wanted a story.

"Tell me, mother," she said, "about the earthquake when you were a little girl."

Every child who has a mother, has also certain stereotyped "stories," for which, at all sorts of incongruous and inconvenient conjunctures, it teases her. This, of the earthquake, was chief favorite among Sarah Gair's.

So Mrs. Gair, with her mind running upon other things, told, mechanically, how, when she was quite a little girl, she and Aunt Prue were left by themselves one winter night, in the house; their father and mother having gone over to Deepwater to stay with a sick aunt; and how, after they had popped corn, and roasted apples, and eaten simballs, and told stories till ten o'clock, they had all gone to bed, and to sleep. How, long after, they were wakened by a strange trembling, and a noise as if a great wind shook the house, though it was a calm, still, clear night, — or as if somebody walked about heavily, down stairs. How they — the sisters — called out from their room to Serena, Huldah's mother, who lived here then.

"And the china rattled, mother! You left out that."

Whatever variety children demand otherwise, they will have none in the telling of a story. Leave out a phrase or a circumstance at your peril.

"Yes, the china rattled, — and they thought robbers were in the house. And Serena, half awake, laughed at them, and told them to turn over and go to sleep again. And then, in a minute, it came again —"

Something at this instant actually rolled, or rumbled, faintly, in the house below.

"Mother!" cried Say, bolt upright in bed, "there 's one now. Hark!"

And something surely rumbled back again.

"Nonsense, child! Lie down again. It's only Huldah, I suppose, rolling back the great table."

But, for all that, Mrs. Gair did n't quite think so; and after waiting a little while and listening, she said, suddenly, "I 'll go down and get you a drink of water, Say, and then you must go to sleep."

"But you have n't finished the story, mother!"

"Never mind. Let it be till to-morrow morning. I'll finish it then. I would n't think any more about earthquakes, to-night.

It was a simple thing, on the outside, Mrs. Gair's going down to fetch a glass of water for her wakeful child. If she had had nothing else in her mind, she might have gone and come back, and been led into no harm. As it was, it involved consequences that afterward she would gladly have gone back from. It is the double motive that makes the smallest doing perilous; that takes us out of the track of Providence, concerning us, and puts us where we have no business to be. Single-heartedness, alone, goes safely even among trivial things. If it had really been but care for the child which prompted her, Mrs. Gair would doubtless have finished her story, and gone quietly to bed. But she knew that people were still up and moving below; she had not heard her father go to his chamber; she was eager, restless, vaguely uneasy; so she would go down and get a drink of water for Say, and look about herself a little, as she went.

The stair-case upon which she stepped from her chamber door, and descended softly, came down to close within the front entrance of the house. On either side at the foot, opened doors; that on the right into the family sitting-room; on the left into the best parlor, between which and the kitchen was the Doctor's "little room," — office, library, or study, — so phrased.

Mrs. Gair set her light upon the lower stair, and passed noiselessly into the parlor. Here the shutters had been closed, and it was dark. The door communicating thence with the little room was ajar; the aperture showing by a faint gleam,—but only of the moon.

There was no other light there; and all was still.

But voices were distinguishable away out in the house beyond. Mrs. Gair glided back and took up her candle. She would just see how things looked. Without any definite idea, she wondered what her father could have been about, or occupied with in thought, to be kept so beyond his usual regular hour.

Very little, it seemed.

On the writing-table which stood in the centre of the floor, lay a half sheet of paper, folded back across the middle,—the doubled edge uppermost. Below the fold, a couple of lines, in the large, nervous, handwriting of her father, were visible to Mrs. Gair. Possibly only a prescription or a bill. She would see. Jane Gair! Are you in the line of Providential orderings, now? Has God or the devil brought you hither to search out this? In five minutes you will hold that in your knowledge which, hereafter, you would almost give five years of your life, if it might only, so, be stricken from your memory. So you should have had no sin. Henceforth, your sin remaineth.

"Signed, this night, June 27, 18——

"Benjamin Gayworthy.

"In presence of
Felix Fairbrother."

Jane Gair turned the paper. There were perhaps, fifteen lines upon the upper half of the page. Her eye glanced over them quickly, and a sudden flame flashed into her cheeks. Not shame. She had not begun to think of that, though it should surely come. For she laid the folded paper back, deliberately, as she had found it, walked out into the parlor again, blew out her candle, stood still, and listened.

Doctor Gayworthy's step was already heard, recrossing the kitchen. He re-entered his room and approached the table. Huldah's true-poised footfall followed, and then the clumsy tread of Eben, behind, making miserable work of trying to walk lightly, as befitted carpets.

Huldah moved straight on, close after the doctor, and only paused when he did; standing just behind him, leaning a little forward, one arm akimbo, the other hanging by her side, the fingers of its hand rolling, a little nervously, a fold of her gown. Flurried, but alert; all her keen, feminine senses, ready to comprehend quickly, and do creditably. Eben, less eager, more bashful, fell back. He took up his station, waiting, just beside the door-post, on the other side of which, in the dark parlor, stood that other figure, keen and alert also, listening at every pore.

It was only for an instant, but in that instant, Eben Hatch had the vague, strange consciousness that we have all known of an unseen human presence. The room behind him, beside whose open door he stood, did not *feel* empty. He made an involuntary step into the entrance. Jane Gair shrunk a little, as involuntarily; there was a slight, crisp sound,—it might have been the maple leaves in the night wind, — Eben had not time to conjecture, or to recognize the unfamiliar silken whisper.

The Doctor took up a pen, and glanced round. "This, you see,— both of you,"— Eben came forward,—"to be my signature;" and he rapidly traced over his own bold characters at the right of the sheet. "Now Huldah, your name here."

Huldah received the pen with a look of shy importance, thinly disguised by an air of matter-of-course acquiescence, and carefully straightening the paper before her, sat down, and occupied perhaps a minute in executing, in her handsomest style of hair lines and bulgy dots, acquired with infinite pains, the letters of her name, which had an appearance, when finished, as if constructed of some minute specimen of the seaweed which grows in an alternation of thin strings and leather bubbles.

Then Eben essayed; and with many slow vibrations of his head from side to side, accompanied with reverse, or balancing motions of his rigidly protruded tongue,—grasping the pen close down toward the nib, and inking himself profusely, accomplished, duly, "Ebenezer Hatch," the "ezer" a little detached and raised above the plane of the "Eben," as long unaccustomed to the conjunction, and the "Hatch" rushing headlong down hill, as if ashamed of, and eager to get away from both.

Doctor Gayworthy's "business paper" was signed. It had become a valid instrument. He dismissed his witnesses with thanks, and the remark that there would be no need for them to mention what they had done. No need, truly. They knew very little about it. The witness who did know all, but who had signed no name, stood passively, in the shade of the room beyond, and looked in, still, toward the light, to see what next.

She saw Doctor Gayworthy turn from the table, folding the paper as he did so, and stand with it in his hands, for two or three minutes, as if in deliberation, before the fireplace. Following his movement with her eyes, she noticed against the quaint, carved panel above the mantel, which formed, as she knew, the sliding door to a chimney cupboard but little used, and for many years but rarely opened, her father's keys; of which one, holding the others pendant, occupied the keyhole. Upon the shelf below, lay a large old, embroidered letter-case, the dim colors of whose cover she well remembered in the childish days when her most valued and eagerly sought privilege had been to see the panel cupboard opened, and be shown the queer old relics of the past which had been laid away there. For years, as I said, this cupboard had been rarely opened. For years, Jane Gair had scarcely thought of its existence. For all her life to come, she would scarcely forget it, now.

Doctor Gayworthy stood, and seemingly considered. Presently, he took up the letter-case, from which the faded string of ribbon hung unbound, and drew from it a packet of several sheets folded together, which he held and turned, hesitatingly, in his hand.

"'Such share and privilege as would *so* fall,'"— he said, slowly, to himself, in a half audible way. "By will, or law. Yes, that certainly secures it all. And if things *should* happen backward, and I should change my mind, its only this slip of paper, and the other would still remain. It's all safe, for the present.'"

The Doctor spoke these concluding words, more nearly aloud, and briskly, as one settling a perplexity; and changing his attitude from the limpness of a momentary indecision to the muscular up-gathering of satisfied and assured purpose, replaced the packet, slipping in behind it, the thinly-folded and just-written sheet, tied up the case, and putting his thumb against a carved projection of the panel-door, rolled it back, and laid all carefully away upon a shelf within.

Jane Gair took advantage of the sliding of the somewhat ponderous and unwilling door, to effect her escape unheard.

"All safe for the present," repeated the doctor, softly, as he turned the lock, and put the keys in his pocket.

For the present. Yes. But that paper, just written, is to lie there, unseen, for seventeen years.

And, meanwhile, many things will have happened.

Huldah had gone, upon being dismissed, straight out, as she had come straight in; crossed the great kitchen, and passed down into the out-room, to put away the few utensils she had had about in her bread-making.

Eben stopped in the great room. There was a door between the fireplace and that leading into the Doctor's study, which opened upon the passage — narrow here, behind the stairs — running the length of these two left-hand rooms, to the front door of the house. In through the fan-light, and side sashes, poured the full moonlight. Eben set the door softly ajar, by a space the width of his eye only, and applied thereto that useful organ. "If there's peekin' and harkin' goin' on, I might as well be in for a share of it," he said to himself.

There was a moment or two of utter silence, in which Eben began almost to think that there could be nobody "harkin," after all, except himself; but then came the heavy rolling of the cupboard door, and a figure passed across the light, and glided up the stairs. Eben heard also, quite distinctly, even above the other sound, the heavy rustle that was *not* among the maples.

"The doctor's a little deef, no doubt, Miss Gair," he said, to himself, again, with an emphatic nodding up and down of his head, as he carefully reclosed the door, and dropped the latch noiselessly, "but I kinder guess *I* aint, and I 've heerd considerble to-night, one way an' another."

When Huldah came back, he said not a word of this; but human-wise must have one upon the transaction of the night, so far as they had both participated in it. I say, human-wise; for, assert as you will, curiosity is neither male nor female, but belongs to the race. In a case like this, where the two are concerned, let the woman but hold her peace for awhile, and see, then, if the man don't speak!

"I wonder if that air could 'a ben anything about the property, now! 'T warnt a will, think,—was it Huldy?"

"Bless your benighted ignorance, Eben, no! Why, there warn 't half room for a will. 'T warn't but a half sheet o' paper writ on one side; and we put our names right in the middle o' that. I 've seen wills afore now, Eben. Twice. And I can tell you it takes an awful sight o' words to make one. Its jest like the House that Jack built. Whenever they say anything new, they have to begin and say the rest all over ag'in; so 't you'd think you 'd never get to the end on 't. Besides, the doctor's made his will, long ago. He altered it over jest after Ben died. My mother was knowin' to it. No, — 't warnt a will, nor nothing of the sort. You may make your mind easy about that. Most likely 'twas only some little church business, 'twixt him and the Parson."

"Well," said Eben, slowly, leaning his elbow against the kitchen mantel, and availing himself of leverage so obtained to scratch his head effectively,—"I—don't—know! maybe its a —— what's name! A —— thunder! I know well enough what the word is, only I can't fetch it! Something that 's second thoughts to a will. They string on a dozen of 'em, sometimes. You see, when they get the kite all framed and prepared, they begin, then, on the tail; and they can put on jest as many bobs as they like!"

"Blessed be nothing!" ejaculated Huldah, lighting a second candle for Eben, and turning away with her own. "I guess there won't have to be many bobs to *my* kite-tail; nor your 'n, neither, Ebenezer Hatch!"

"Mother!" cried Say, sitting up in bed again, when her mother returned to her at last. "I *know* there's been an earthquake since you 've been down stairs! I heard it!"

Perhaps there had, in a way. But Mrs. Gair only said "nonsense!" again, and bade the child go to sleep; and cautioned her not to talk about hearing earthquakes to anybody else, for they 'd be sure to make fun of her, — especially Gershom.

"But where 's my drink of water, mother?"

"I could n't get it. The light went out. You must go to sleep."

CHAPTER IV.

STACY LAWTON'S WALK HOME.

Stacy Lawton bade Mrs. Fairbrother a cordial good-by at the Parsonage door; and even bestowed a sudden kiss upon Malviny, who, glancing up in surprised inquiry as it descended, received it upon the snubby end of her little, freckled nose. Then, hastily, she held out a hand to Gordon King.

"Good-night. I'm *so* much obliged. No, indeed, you must n't come a step further. I shan't be a bit afraid, now." And, as if she were very honestly in earnest, she turned away, quickly, before the young minister could reply, and took the start of him, resolutely, up the road. How much of this haste and determination might have been accounted for by a glimpse she got of Newell Gibson coming around the corner of the cross-road at the bottom of the hill, and the perception that his approach might presently do away with the necessity for any persistence on the minister's part, I really do not know, and being simple-minded and charitable myself, will not attempt to conjecture; but of course, Gordon King did persist, and follow and join the self-willed damsel, whose trim little figure moved off so prettily and positively before him, in the moonlight, over the long, steep slope.

Newell Gibson knew better than to overtake them. Besides, he had his own thoughts to-night, that lingered pleasantly around the little brown house whence he had just come, down there in the cross-road under the hill. He, too, had been to see somebody home.

"You need n't have come," said Stacy to Gordon King, as he reached her side. "It's as bright as day. Does n't the moonlight make everything look beautiful?" And she swung by the strings, as she spoke, her muslin cape-bonnet, needless since the summer sun went down, and turned her bright face toward him, above which the night-gleam touched and crowned the full, graceful folds of her uncovered hair. Truly, he thought so, then.

"It 's a glorious night," he answered. "It seems a wonder that we can shut our doors, or our eyes, at all."

"I like moonlight," said Stacy. "But the stars seem awful when the sky is full of them. I remember the first time I ever saw them so. I was *so* frightened. It was when I was a very little girl, and grandma took me out one night to an evening meeting. I had never been kept up so late before; and, coming home, they blazed down, so bright and thick! I thought the Day of Judgment was come."

That word of Stacy's changed the tone between them. It pierced the surface, and went down, however heedlessly, into the deeps that lay beneath.

Gordon King believed in his solemn office, and in the things it handled. He gave no look at the pretty face, for a moment. He felt a soul beside him that had trembled at the Judgment.

"You are not afraid in the starlight, now?" This he said, inquiringly, meaningly. After the little pause wherein the thought-current of each had shifted.

They stood, at this moment, on the brow of the long hill. They stopped, involuntarily. Below, lay such a scene as lies, I suppose, hardly anywhere, out of New England. Among abrupt and picturesque heights, whose nearer wooded slopes were thinned and smoothed by cultivation, yet whose far horizon lines bristled everywhere with piney forests, untouched, unthrid; set in the centre of the great landscape, — held so in the scoop of the hills as almost in the hollow of an Almighty Hand, — the few white farm-houses that made up this little neighborhood in which was Stacy's home, clustered peacefully, and lay still in the moonlight around Gibson's Pond. So the country people had christened, in their homely, practical fashion, a great, glorious sheet of water that flashed up, now, its flood of silver, meeting and overbrooded by the more ethereal firmamental flood of light, that poured itself down, and rolled and gathered, as it were, in a huge chalice, against these steeps that held it in. A lake, which, — but that Hilbury pond was larger, and Deepwater larger yet, and that every village, almost, had one, greater or less, of its own, between this and the low lands of the sea-coast, where the great cities buzzed and grew, — might have had a name of music and grandeur, and held itself serenely here, in a royalty of beauty, to touch the border of whose robe men might make weary pilgrimage.

"Yes," said Stacy, falteringly, as they looked down on this together, "I am afraid. I am not good."

If there were art in this, it was the instinctive art whereby one soul draws itself toward the recognized and higher sphere of another. The child bethought herself of her soul at that moment. When the heart is stirred, if it lie at any depth at all, that which sleeps beneath must feel the thrill. She believed that he who stood beside her in this glory of the summer night, had a title to come closer to the spirit of it all, than she. In the one great overshadowing beauty she forgot, for a moment, the little coquetries of her own.

Now that it has come to this, you, Rebecca, — saying, "Thy Will be done" in your chamber, that is like a shrine for the purity of the thought and act it witnesses, and only half glancing, in your secret maidenly soul, at what might befall, to make that Will seem earthly-bitter, may school and strengthen yourself as you can, to bear and to do without. Since Adam followed his erring wife out of Paradise, — dearer to him, doubtless, than when he began to have pity for and patience with her, than when she came to him, faultless, from the hand of God, — there has been more hope, as to the love of man, for the sinning little Eves with the taste and perfume of the world's apple yet clinging to their lips, than for such as you. You are too far above him in your saintliness. You, who do not tremble at the stars, but who bend ever, in a sweet and holy awe, before their Maker, — who need no more the tears of a passionate penitence, because, in your noiseless life, you do daily the work that is given, and feel daily the patience that forgives your shortcomings, — you may not rival with the spiritual, any more than with the earthly witcheries of the pretty unregenerate, who needs yet something done for her; who leans toward a human help; who whispers with a new-born anxiety of her soul and of her sins.

Besides, any sort of professional dealing of man toward woman, where there is beforehand the faintest incipience of tender thought, is tolerably sure to do the business for them both. There is a sentiment in the one which loves to approach, shyly, the mystery of the other's strength and wisdom; there is a pride and chivalry in the other which is stirred pleasantly in the consciousness of extending help or protection. It is the very soul of the whole relation between the two.

"I think you will be," said Gordon King, presently, with a gentleness; and the thought of what she might be — of what he might see her, perhaps help her, to become — was more to him than all the beautiful attainment elsewhere. It was only human. One loves better the slip of green one cherishes in the rooting, than the fair, strong, perfect plant that flowers already without one's help.

So they walked on together, down the hill, in that light of sky and water. Two or three minutes more brought them to Squire Lawton's gateway.

"I think you will be," repeated Gordon King, as their hands met upon the latch, and he held his companion's, for an instant, with a friendly clasp.

And Stacy thought, very honestly, that she would.

CHAPTER V.

THE SECRET AT THE HARTSHORNES.

HUMAN histories and events go by periods and conjunctures, as well as the great planetary forces and systems. All are under one like law. This night of the 27th of June, which passed so seemingly unmarked, save by a simple social gathering, over the little town of Hilbury, and into the lives that revolved together, working out this story that I write, was a focus wherefrom radiated much. Hereafter, years may be missed in the narration; to-night, hardly a moment or a thought.

Mrs. Hartshorne went home early from the party; took "French leave," as she called it, making more bustle in doing so, however, through explaining to every member of the family the why, than could possibly have been accomplished in any other manner. But, underneath the bustle, her good heart was anxious, troubled. She *said*, that "Gabe would be tired after his day's sail, and she would n't wait to make him come for her;" that "father had a headache, which was why she came alone;" she knew, false-lipped woman that she was, that Gabriel had come back from Deepwater before she left her home, no more tired than a hearty young New-Englander should be, after a day's toil or frolic, and with no thought but to dress in his best and go to the strawberry party. But a shadow that was coming over their simple home, — a fearful something which they did not name, as yet, even to each other, — lifted its apparitional finger, and stayed them in this, as in many another hope and plan to come. There was a secret at the Hartshorne's; a secret surmised, as yet, by none but mother and son; but which should come to be more than surmise with all the little world about them, as such things do, long before they would acknowledge in words, between themselves, the terrible truth.

There was something queer about old Mr. Hartshorne. He took strange fancies now and then. He did things in odd ways, and at odd times.

"Gabriel," his mother had said, as the young man came down from his little corner bedroom that looked out toward the Gayworthy farm, and whence he could see the flutter of a white curtain at one particular window of the doctor's mansion, — he looked bright and handsome, to-night, in his new, dark-blue coat, and with the yellow-brown waves tossed back above the broad brow and beaming blue eyes, — "Gabriel, you don't care no great about the party to-night, I suppose?"

"Well, — no; nothing particular. Why?" returned Gabriel, forcing down heart and conscience with one great gulp, and holding them there with this lie that he laid upon them.

"Because, father's taken a notion that he won't go; he says he must walk clear over to the five-acre lot, to mow a piece round a turkey-hen that's settin' there, for fear the men should come foul of her in the mornin'; an' I donno how, exactly, to leave him to go alone. It's kinder pokerish over there, and he might cut himself, — or something."

"Well, — I'll go with him," said Gabriel, slowly, turning to go up-stairs again and take off the best suit. The cloud that came over his face, — the sudden quench in the beaming blue eye, — told nothing to his mother that her own heart did not answer to and explain.

And Gabriel inquired curiously after the turkey's nest, and "took a notion" in his turn, to walk over with his father to the five-acre lot, in the low sunlight, and fibbed again when he said he "didn't feel much like rigging up for a party;" which had been true but for the last five minutes, since he unrigged, and went his way, bearing the glittering scythe upon his shoulder, as any martyr might bear the weapon of his sacrifice; and Mrs. Hartshorne rendered herself at the tea-party as we have seen; and Joanna had hard, disappointed, bitter, mistaken thoughts, and carried them away to bed with her, and cried over them, as she had promised herself; and of all possible things never dreamed in her imaginings, of this, — that Gabriel might haply, be somehow as compulsorily, and painfully disappointed as she. The best reasons for human conduct are often, alas! precisely those which can never be given to them who demand of us the why. And so a story of misconception, which should not, for long, be made quite clear, began, between these two. So the threads of these lives, which seemed about to be caught together in a web of joy, were ravelled apart for awhile, and floated away from each other, reaching and feeling, — unfastened thrums, — into a hopeless void.

It was a good two hours before Gabriel Hartshorne was free of his father. The turkey's nest was islanded with a fragrant swath, — the "heft" of the crop noted and rejoiced over, — the tons of good timothy and clover calculated, — a circuit taken, — in a dreamy loiter by the old man, in a fever of impatience by the young one,—around by the brook, and up through the long meadow; and then there was a delay at the barn, — scythes looked to for the morrow; Gabriel sent down the lane, by a sudden thought, to see if the bars were up at the end; and, last of all, after they had fairly reached the house again, a fidget about the lantern they had lighted for a minute, in the tool-room, and Gabriel must go back to the barn and examine, lest by chance there might be any sparks about.

By the time all this was over and his father composed to the smoking of his evening pipe, the young man was tired. Tired in body and in spirit. Besides, the shoes he had blackened so nicely were all unpolished and dusty, now; his clean wristbands crumpled; the feeling of freshness and fitness gone beyond possibility of renewal by the changing of a coat; the hour was late, according to their primitive customs, and presently, deciding all question that he might else have had, he saw from the front gate where he stood and leaned, thinking gloomily, his mother's stout, comfortable figure moving homeward in the mingled light of sunset and moonrise, down the hill.

"Well, Gabriel. How's father?"

"Inside, smoking his pipe."

"You look tired. Where 've you been?"

"All round the lot. He 's been pretty res'less. How was the party?"

"Elegant. I wish you 'd a been there. Mis' Gair was as fine as a fiddle; and as to that Joann, she does beat all for carryin' on. I never see a girl in such spirits as she was to-night. It kinder frightens me, too, when young folks begin so. They 'll take such a lot o' soberin' down. I was pretty chipper myself when I was her age."

Good Mrs. Hartshorne ended with a sigh. In its fleeting breath exhaled a subtile distillation of many a sorrow that had come upon her since the "chipper" days. There were slabs in the churchyard to tell of some; there were care and labor-lines on face and hands, that might hint at others; there was something in the very breaking off of her report of the just past festivities, and the quickening of her footsteps toward the house, that had to do, as Gabriel knew, with an unspoken weight that lay upon her now.

He followed his mother into the house, asking no more questions.

Joanna had been gay, to-night, then. She had missed nothing from her pleasure. — Well!

From the corner bedroom he could see the white curtain still in the moonlight. There came a light that glimmered behind it, for a little while, and then went suddenly out, as somethiug that flared wildly for an instant, and quenched coldly, also, in his own heart. And night and stillness lay between the two homes.

O God! who holdest all lives in Thine own bosom, wherein all are quickened and commune together! what is this space, this circumstance, which Thou hast made, that can — ever so little of it — part them so; that can keep them so unwistful of each other, even in Thee?

Sunday came. The old meeting-house was full of its Sabbath fragrance. Do you know what I mean? Did you ever sit — a great while ago it must have been, to be sure — in one of those family inclosures in an old-fashioned country church, whose space is railed off in roomy squares, and smell the mingled incense that goes up, on a summer day, with the prayers and praises? The tender aroma of fresh flowers, held here and there in a hand that has gathered them just the last thing at home, or on the way; the odor of aromatics, — of peppermints, perhaps, or nibbled cloves; the lavender and musk that breathe faintly forth from the best laces, muslins, and ribbons; to say nothing of whiffs, now and then, that betray spice-cake and simballs and sage-cheese, stowed away carefully in sanctuary cupboards, under the hinge-seats, until the "nooning"? Whatever you may think, there was nothing disagreeable about it, — nothing even of coarseness or desecration; to long-accustomed nostrils, it was the very atmosphere of the Lord's Day; and the life-long, subtile association helped the people, doubtless, even in their prayers.

Little Sarah Gair found it all very delightful, contrasted with city church-going, where people shove themselves into narrow crannies, and sit with their knees against one board and their backs against another, — stuck in rows, like knives in a knife-box, — compressing the body, by way of expanding the soul. There was nothing Say liked better than to go to meeting in Hilbury; to sit in the corner, on the broad window-seat that came in so as to form a commodious place for two, and where Gershom was usually her companion; to listen to the full-voiced village choir, and look up with a sort of childish awe at the row of men and maidens who filled the "singing-seats," and bore part in the solemn service of praise; to glance from group to group of the crowded congregation, and, when tired of bonnets and faces within, to turn eyes and thoughts outward, where the stone slabs were planted thickly, marking the more solemn congregation of the dead; to walk round, quietly, from pew to pew in the nooning, or to go with Aunt Rebecca into the churchyard, and read the names, — it did n't seem a sad, but rather a pleasant and beautiful thing, to be lying there, where neighbors and friends came up and walked weekly, and talked gently, among the green graves, — or to go with Aunt Joanna to a neighbor's house, and eat simballs, and hear the great girls talk, which was pretty much all the little girls could do on Sunday; and as for the incense we were speaking of, Say always complained to her mother, when she got back to Selport, that it "did n't ever smell like Sunday there!"

These were her impressions. Quiet Aunt Rebecca, — merry Aunt Joanna, — pretty Stacy Lawton, who looked unwontedly demure to-day, — stout, good-natured Mrs. Hartshorne, and Gabriel, who, as first tenor, stood next, in the singing-seats, to Joanna, leading the treble, — with scores of others, whose hidden life it does not come within our especial province to trace, — had theirs.

Gabriel came late into the gallery. He was shy of meeting Joanna; fearful of the resentment she might show him for his apparent slight. He encountered something worse than resentment. An utter unconcern. Joanna was as blooming to-day in her "cottage-straw" with its blue ribbons, — her eye was as clear, her cheek was as fresh, as if that "cry" of the other night had never been. Her shoulder turned not a hair's breadth from the line of his, as they stood side by side in the opening hymn. Her hand shrunk with no disdain from the touch that met it for an instant, as they turned the pages of their books to find the tune. She settled a little, comfortably, into the corner of her seat which the narrow passage separated from his, when the sermon began, and the cottage-bonnet just shaded her face from his sight. After service, her "how-dye-do, Mr. Hartshorne," in answer to his greeting, was to the last degree *insouciante;* and then, just as he was about to say something more, she caught her name whispered from behind, and turning promptly, yet without any undue quickness, responded to some proposition or remark, and was drawn away among the girls, and down the left-hand staircase, which was the feminine exit.

She went, with half a dozen of them, down the hill from the meeting-house, between the rows of poplars, to Deacon Whittaker's; the deacon's daughter, Carrie, leading the way. Gabriel stood among a group of young men at the church-door, and saw them pass.

Presently, they disappeared round the corner of the large, old, unpainted house, whose great square open porch gave, not upon the road, but upon the smooth sloping grass-plat at the side. Here, buzzing and fluttering, as bees and maidens alone know how, they clustered and chatted, while baskets were opened and the simple nooning meal, that needed intervention of neither knife nor fork, was eaten.

"Where 's Stacy Lawton?" asked somebody.

"I can't tell you that, but I can tell you one thing, girls," said Joanna Gayworthy. "And before it happens, too. We 're in for a revival; and Stacy Lawton's going to lead off. She 's getting impressions, you may depend upon it. And some others, too, perhaps. You 'll see 'em in the anxious-seats, before long. The parson ought to have left *that* text for Gordon King, though."

"Oh, Joanna, how can you?" the others exclaimed, and laughed. The morning sermon had been from the words, "Give me thine heart."

"Well, I can't help it, when I see how things go on. Religion's *so* interesting when a handsome young man comes and talks about it. Why, poor Mr. Fairbrother might have preached his cheek bones through, and his eyes into hollows till they came out at the back of his head, and nobody would have been the least bit anxious. But those waving locks! and those heavenly eyes! and 'sech a figger!' as Sabiah Millet says! I'm sure I don't know what the sinners can be made of, if they *don't* come under conviction!"

While Joanna spoke, the three or four young men, of whom Gabriel Hartshorne was one, came into the door-yard, and passed the porch, going towards the well, which, with its long sweep and wide curb, occupied a central position in the space between house and garden, not so far from the porch as to be beyond conversational distance. There were almost always girls in the porch and young men about the well, in these summer Sunday noons. Joanna, standing upon the step, facing inward, neither paused nor turned, but talked on recklessly, as they went by.

"I never heard anybody run on as you do!" cried Eunice Gibson. "It don't make any difference what it 's about. It was just so at your party the other night. How you did train! You made fun of everything that came up."

"Yes; Satan entered into me. And I don't believe he's gone out yet. So don't set me going. I should like to be a little proper on Sunday. Here comes Mrs. Prouty. *Her* umbrella's always up. *She's* never caught in a shower."

"What *do* you mean?"

"Why, don't she always make you feel as if you were out in

the rain, and she standing under cover, chuckling? She does me. Her work's always so dreadfully sure to be done up, whether it's cheeses or salvation. She is not as other women are. There's never anything left over on a Saturday night, with her. Don't you see how her mouth's primmed up? That's as much as to say the washing and mending and churning and cleaning and baking are all through with, up to the minute, and her soul seen to, besides.—Mrs. Prouty! Where's Eliza? We 're going down the Brook Road, presently, for a little walk."

"Eliza stayed in. She's preparing herself for her Sunday School class," replied Mrs. Prouty, precisely, and with a tone of subdued self-gratulation. Her daughter, also, was not as other people's daughters were.

"Was n't that Christian of me, to give her such a chance? See how much good it 's done her," whispered Joanna to Eunice, as Mrs. Prouty passed them, and went in. "We 're such terrible creatures, you know, talking and laughing over our luncheon, and going to walk. And it 's such a satisfaction to her to see it! I don't know what some saints would do, if there *was n't* a world round them lying in wickedness!"

"Hush! there she is at the window!"

Mrs. Prouty had entered the deaconess' sitting-room, and taken a position where she could converse directly with that lady, and if occasion offered, send a few words also, over her shoulder, at the group upon the porch.

In a minute or two the side-fire began.

"Yes, it was a very feeling discourse; and I do hope we shall see some fruits of it. But it seems pretty hard to make any impression on our young folks, somehow. It 's in at one ear, and out at the other, with most of 'em."

"Might as well be so, perhaps, as in at the ear and out at the mouth," commented Joanna, in an under-tone.

"I 'm afraid there's some mischeevous influence, that undooes it all," continued Mrs. Prouty with a sigh.

"I know there is: but it is n't the sort you mean. Come girls, let's go and have our walk. I shall say something out loud, presently, if we stay here."

"I can't bear," continued Joanna, as the little party prepared to move, at her suggestion, "to be put into a dark closet, and have somebody continually coming to look in, and ask me if I'm sorry yet. I always feel like saying, as I did to my mother once, when I was a little girl. 'When I horry, I let oo know!'"

"But then," said one of the group, timidly, "I don't think we ought to make fun of such things."

"Nor I, neither, Abby," answered Joanna, quickly, and with a changed manner. "I don't make fun of the *things;* it's only the way people behave about them. It is n't real. It is n't natural. When folks really do give their hearts, whether it's to God or a fellow-creature, it is n't a thing, I think, that they run round telling about. There's only one concerned to know anything about it."

This sudden shifting to earnest, and of such outright sort, threw an astonished silence, for a moment, over the company. The girls did n't always know just how to take Joanna Gayworthy.

Whether the allusion to giving of hearts, or the approach of the young men, who now came up from behind, as if to join them, suggested the next remark or not, it came, with an unintentional "by the way," that made Joanna secretly wince.

"Why was n't Gabriel Hartshorne at your house the other night?"

"Sure enough! I don't know. I 'll ask him."

The quick, fine, feminine artifice of this, Gabriel, catching the words, could not discern. He took them at their surface meaning, and verily believed that she had never thought to miss him, or to wonder why he had not come. She, who had kept the whole company merry! Man-like, he turned off in a clumsy huff, and walked beside Eunice Gibson.

She put the question.

"I came home late from Deepwater," he answered; "and afterwards, I was wanted, — at home."

"A good plan, to stay where he was sure of that," whispered Joanna, as she moved forward with her companion. This was the word too much, which women are pretty sure to say when they try to cover up with words their true feelings. She bit her lip when she had spoken it. If Gabriel had not been already set off with such an impetus upon the wrong track, it might have gone far to guide him upon the right one. But men always do rush away headlong, at the first word; and another, sent after, drives them forward, rather than brings them back. There's where we have advantage of them.

The effervescence of Joanna's sauciness was over, however. She subsiding, the little party walked, in a new mood of quietness, tinged, perhaps, with a slight, half-recognized constraint, onward, down the Brook Road; paused a moment or two, upon the narrow bridge, listening to the Sunday song of the busy waters; and then, like the "King of France with twenty thousand men," turned, at her lead, and "marched up again." An evolution which, to them, as to the king in the old rhyme, had, doubtless, its own meaning.

With two of the number, it had at any rate, its own result.

A word, or the want of a word, is a little thing; but into the momentary wound or chasm, so made or left, throng circumstances; these thrust wider and wider asunder, till the whole round bulk of the world may lie between two lives.

CHAPTER VI.

THE DAIRY FARM.

"THE world is so full of other folks," said Joanna, wearily.

She was sitting by the pleasant garden-window in Rebecca's room. A great cherry-tree, full of fruit and birds, tossed its wide arms up against the house-front, and almost grew in at every opening. She looked out into its green intricacies and watched the robins, that feasted fearlessly, even when she reached a hand to the hither bough, and gathered, half absently, for herself, a dinner or two out of their crimson store.

Downstairs, the house was shaded, open, clean and cool, from end to end. The early country dinner was over, and cleared away. Huldah was turning cheeses in the cheese-room. Mrs. Vorse was taking her after-dinner nap. Say and Gershom were down in the garden, on a great rock, over which a plum-tree hung. Mrs. Gair had been gone to Selport a week or more. Say was left there with her aunts, until September. A box of clothing, with books and toys, had come up by the stage the night before. Among the rest, was that unfailing childish delight, "Swiss Family Robinson;" and for Gershom, a present from thoughtful Aunt Jane, a copy of Dana's "Two Years before the Mast." These books, and Say's life-size linen baby, kept the children abundant company down there on the great, green-canopied, granite divan.

There had been question, among the sisters, of plans for the remainder of the day. Mrs. Prue had said that somebody ought to go and see Mrs. Rockwood. Mrs. Prue rarely paid visits. "Somebody" meant the girls, of course, who were responsible for the social department in family affairs. Dutiful, compliant Rebecca repeated the suggestion, upstairs.

"We ought to go and see Mrs. Rockwood, Joanna."

"Dear me! and her third boy! I can't. I never know what to say to people in affliction. Besides, we should have to admire the baby. People are always astonished if you 're not fond of babies — and peaches. But they do come so done up in flannel!"

"Dear Joanna," said Rebecca, laughing, "don't be absurd. It will seem unkind if we don't go soon. As if we took no interest."

"Well, maybe we don't; just at this moment, at least. Perhaps, another day, we should. But people take for granted that we're interested all the time, and we pretend we are. And so we have to act up to it, whether or no, and hate it accordingly. The world's absurd. And, oh, dear! it's so full of other folks!"

Here is where we took Joanna up.

Rebecca said nothing for a moment. Dear and intimate as the sisters were, it was sometimes a puzzle for one to comprehend the other. Joanna's moods might mean nothing but absurdity and waywardness, or they might cover feeling that called for a deep sympathy. Rebecca could not tell. On points of feeling, Joanna never would be voluntarily communicative. To her, strong-thoughted, secret-hearted, masked with an impervious whimsicality that few would know how to approach with earnestness, the world would be likely, all her life, to seem filled only with "other folks."

Rebecca brought, presently, an open book, and laid it on the window-sill before her sister. These words were marked upon the page. "As Thou, Father, art in me, and I in Thee, that they, also, may be one in us."

"That is how it ought to be," she said.

"And just how it always is n't," said Joanna, leaning her head upon her right hand, with the searching look in her eyes of one striving to solve a problem, and gently pushing the Bible from her, with her left. "And these pretences only hinder it."

"They ought not to be pretences. Wherever there are Christians, there should be Christian love and sympathy, should n't there?"

"It's no use to talk in the potential mood. The present indicative contradicts it flatly. At least, among the Hilbury Christians. Take Mrs. Prouty. That woman aggravates me so, with her perfections! Why, the rest of the world, you'd think, was only made to be an offset to her righteousness. She's *so* faithful among the faithless, and always in such a small way! She darns her stockings — Wednesday nights — on the right side; and it is n't evangelical to darn them on the wrong. And not to get the clothes dried Monday, when *her* wash is over, is nothing less than Anti-Christ. It's mint, anise, and cummin, — gnats and needles' eyes. There is n't any room for Christian sympathy. And then look at Mrs. Fairbrother; with her whining ways and beautiful submission to her troubles and "chastenings." Other people are chastened too, I suppose. But she believes Providence keeps a special rod in pickle for her, and does n't do much else of importance but discipline and pity her. I 'm tired of going about among such people."

Rebecca stood, now, at the toilet, brushing out the soft, delicate cloud of her dark hair. She folded it back from her face, and wound it into the usual simple knot behind, keeping silence, waiting for the querulous mood to pass. Joanna sat, listlessly plucking leaves and cherries, through the window; biting either, as it happened, indifferently. Presently, she roused and turned.

"I 'm cross, Becsie, I know: and wicked. But it seems sometimes as if the world were all wrong. We must do something, I suppose. There are those books Jane left to be taken over to Wealthy. She always manages to leave that for us. Let 's take the children, and walk over. If anybody, but you, can set me straight when I 'm crooked, it 's Wealthy Hoogs. She 's real, and strong."

"Wealthy, healthy, and wise," assented Rebecca, playfully.

"I don't know about the wise. What did she marry Jaazaniah for?"

Down on the rock, under the pleasant shade of the plum-tree, two other little lives were getting, in their separate fashion, whatever the world had for them, to-day Say had set her doll upon a moss throne, in a high cleft, and crowned her with golden buttercups, and built a bower of asparagus plumes about her, and put in her hand a peeled willow twig, for a wand. This was her fairy queen of the grotto. And, mutely, lest Gershom should wake to consciousness of what she was about, and ridicule her, she was performing her favorite fairy tale of the Immortal Fountain. The asparagus, tossing its feathers of green, — the beans, winding their scarlet blossoms around the tall poles, — the growing corn, standing in stately rows, putting forth its young tassels, — these, filling with their ranks the long garden upon one side, were the fairy troops she essayed, according to the story, successively, to pass. The Immortal Fountain was supposed to be hidden in the vine-covered summer-house at the farther end.

Gershom, outstretched upon his back, lay utterly heedless of it all. He was rounding the Horn, in the forecastle of the Pilgrim.

Say came back to her fairy queen, after a breeze had swept the corn-patch, and refused her passage by the crossing of its blades. Gershom at the end of the chapter, flung down the book, and came back, also, from far Pacific seas.

"I've never seen anything but Hilbury rocks," he cried. "Say! how does the sea look? Come and tell me."

According to the spirit of the story, the corn-fairies should unhesitatingly have lowered their green blades, the next time, on Say's approach; so readily did she abandon her pantomime at the boy's call.

"The sea? Why, down at the wharf, where the Pearl comes in, it's black and dirty; and you're afraid all the time of falling in. But up on Harbor Hill, where papa takes me to walk sometimes, it looks wide and blue, and sparkles, way off, up against the edge of the sky. And you can see the vessels sailing. But I think it's prettier here."

"Poh! that's because you're a girl. I'm tired of hills and trees. I want to see the sea. And I mean to, sometime."

"Well, you're coming to Selport to see us, you know. And then, when the Pearl comes in, we'll go down to the wharf, and get oranges and pineapples."

"I don't care for the oranges. But I want to see the ship, and the captain, and the sailors."

"Well, they'll be there. And we can sit in the cabin."

"I shall go up the masts. To the very top."

"No, indeed! You'll fall."

"I shan't do any such thing. Can't I climb a tree? I brought home a crow's nest, last spring, off the top of a pine, higher than any mast. I wonder if grandpa'll let me go?"

"Of course he will. I'll ask him."

And Say skipped away, past the green fairies, and the scarlet fairies, and between the whispering corn-blades, triumphantly, and up to the golden sunflowers, that shook their radiant heads at her, and sent her back.

She took up Gershom's book. "That is n't pretty," she said, "'The Swiss Family Robinson' is nice. Mamma reads it to me. And I've got a story in my Girls Own Book, about a little boy and girl that went away to sea in a ship, and got lost among the savages."

There was ample present provision for Gershom's newly awakened craving. Aunt Jane had made her selections well. Yet, who could blame her, if the boy, like all boys, should grow restless, and feel a longing to see the world?

Aunt Rebecca, with her dainty white sunbonnet and large green parasol, came down the garden path and announced to the children the plan for the afternoon. A walk to cousin Wealthy's was the crown and acme of Hilbury delights to Say. Even Gershom, after a little balancing, let himself incline to the single thing that could have persuaded him away from his sea-story. Yet Say, after all, of the whole party, was the only one to whom came, unalloyed, the perfect joy of the golden summer, that day, among the hills.

Around by the high-road, it was a long, toilsome, unsheltered walk to Wealthy Hoogs's. The way they took, — down Hartshorne's lane, through the wild, ferny pasture, out by the pond side, and around its margin, to the opposite slopes, up which a wood-path led them to Jaazaniah's hillside farm, — this was purely fair and fragrant, green and still.

Joanna kept her face very straightforward, and her parasol lowered carefully against the side that was *not* sunny, as they passed down the lane; divining, somehow, without directly looking, that it was Gabriel who stood high up on the loaded hay-rigging out there at the left, pitching its perfumed freight, in mighty trusses, through the great barn-window. The footsteps of the sisters fell noiseless; but the children leaped, and laughed, and shouted. Gabriel never turned. After they had well gone by, he paused, though, and took breath, leaning upon his fork; his face toward the way that they had followed. Then he glanced round, westwardly, and raised his hand toward the sun; and then set himself, with more stalwart strain then ever, to his work again.

Down in the edge of the pasture, the Gayworthys met Mrs. Hartshorne, among the raspberry bushes.

"Well, now, I declare! You haint called in and missed me, have you? You've been as scarce, lately, as eggs in January. I was telling father, last night, that I had n't laid eyes on one of you, except at meeting, since Miss Gair went. And — speaking of meeting — I guess I've got some news for you. Parson Fairbrother was in, a minute, this morning; and what do you think he says?"

"Stacy Lawton's 'found a hope,' I suppose."

"How came you to guess, right off?"

"I thought she'd been looking for it."

"Well, yes, the Parson says she's been in a very interesting state of mind for some weeks; and he's very much encouraged. He thinks there's an increasing seriousness among the young people. But that is n't all; though, to be sure, that's what we ought to care the most about;" and Mrs. Hartshorne's round, cheery face lengthened a little, duly, for an instant, as she spoke, but sprang back to its jolly lines, by irresistible native elasticity, and lightened with a simple, womanly sympathy and delight as she went on.

"There's more coming of it. Only it is n't to be talked of quite yet, and so you must n't tell. But it looks as if there was work ready-laid out for her, and he as good as said so. I shan't mention any names."

"O no. It is n't worth while. It's been pretty plain that there was one thing depending on another."

"So, she's made sure of him! I knew she would, before she quite committed herself. And that's religion! with some people. I know yours, Becsie, is a better sort."

It was, and it needed to be.

Joanna said the last words as she left Mrs. Hartshorne and joined her sister, who had moved forward, and was disentangling Say's dress from the raspberry stems, among which the child had plunged, eagerly, after the fruit.

Rebecca had had an instant's time. It is all we need, at some crises, for hiding away our secrets between ourselves and Heaven. Her sweet face was, apparently, unchanged, as she turned, now, toward Joanna.

"We must not judge," said she. "And perhaps she has only had given her just what she needs to keep her fixed. God takes different ways."

And so they passed on; their feet following the same track; yet one of the twain, from that moment, entering, silently, without human sign, a path marked for her only. God's way. One taken, and the other left. How long?

They came down to the edge of the great pond. Away off, eastwardly and southwardly, it swept, shaping itself among the hills, its limit untraceable except just here about them. A light rippling line whispered up the mimic beach, — the hill they had just come down lay behind them against the southwest sky, and the birches and alders that fringed its base, shaded the calm water and its pebbly margin. They always sat down here to rest. It was a wonderful stillness. Nothing moved but the lazy-lapping water, and the tremulous birch leaves, and the little sandpiper that scampered along the wave-mark. Even the children could not begin at once to play. They sat down upon the pebbles, and dipped up water in their palms to drink.

Gershom, his mind stirred with new thoughts, looked out upon the shining expanse and upon the blue distant hills that shut it in, and wondered with himself where in the world was room left for the great sea.

The sisters talked no more. Each soul went its own way in the quietness. Only Say was supremely happy, with the water and the sky and the white clouds sailing about in both. Only Say had not come yet to look further than things visible, as, except from her fairy lore, she peopled the scene itself.

Well, that was all. They sat and rested there. And after fifteen minutes they got up and went on their way; and neither one knew what lines, in those few moments, life might have written for another.

They went half a mile around, to where a pasture-path led up again — more rocky and shaded this time — along the unfenced hillside of the Hoogs's dairy-farm.

Away up here, apart from all neighborhood, in the little red house built against a steep of granite, lived Cousin Wealthy. Between summer and winter — between churn and spinning-wheel — her life vibrated. Her husband Jaazaniah, lived here too, of course. Whatever may be to be said about him will say itself. If Wealthy Hoogs, "hungry for books," full of keen thought, energetic to a pre-eminence even among Yankee notables, had lived the high-pressure life of modern society,— if her Yankee "smartness" had taken a purely æsthetic turn,— which having never happened was no less a mercy to herself, perhaps, than to Jaazaniah, she might have discovered, as so many gifted beings seem destined to do, that there was something unresponsive in her sphere, that she had not found,— I am half ashamed to use the word,— her "affinity;" that she was a mismatched, misplaced woman. Apparently, she was; yet she comprehended nothing of this jargon; she had, seemingly, poor creature, never found it out; she lived here simply, where she had been put; made and packed her butter, wove her homespun, and loved faithfully,— and forbearingly, for the most part, — were it praise worth a woman's having to say more? the man whose name and home she shared.

If Wealthy Hoogs could have been spirited from her secluded mountain home, and set down bodily in a "cultivated circle,"— face to face even with such a one as soul to soul stood secretly her counterpart, — I think neither one nor the other of them, nor any among the congenial spirits near, who through fleshly eyes should behold her apparition, would at once have recognized the kin. Perhaps, for the strengthening and consolation of "misplaced" existence, in whatever sphere, the same conclusion might, in its behalf, be safely reached. It is quite possible that He who sets answering souls apart, shrouding them from each other's ken with unlike exteriors of form and phase, and joins by circumstance them of less correspondent mould, knows most clearly the fitness of His own work, and the fulness of His times.

Wealthy was a spare, "long-favored" woman. Her pale hair grew high upon her forehead, and could only be adjusted in the straightest of straight lines. Her rather small gray eyes were set in close neighborhood on either side the thin-bridged nose. This perhaps added, in effect, to the wonderful keenness of their glance. They pierced you with their intensity. They seemed always penetrating through things and people, to Artesian depths, searching after that she thirsted for. Sailors, they say, who daily strain their vision to the very earth-verge, come to attain a marvellous long-sightedness. Peering out, from her remote isolation, through such avenues of thought as opened themselves toward the world of things and thoughts that lay like a dream in the distance, reaching her spiritual treasures from afar,— she grew to place all whereon she looked instinctively, as it were, at long range and focus. So she got into her face the expression that people say, "looks through you."

"There's a great deal besides common smartness in Wealthy Hoogs," said her town's-folk. "And how on earth," it was not seldom added, with Yankee significance of incompleteness, "she ever came to take up with that Jaazaniah."

They found her to-day, on the little square, open platform, that, by way of stoop, was built against the angle of the house, under the shade of a great oak. She had a broad wooden tray upon her lap, in which she was cutting up a pure white mass of cheese-curd. Jaazaniah sat by; his chair — one useless fore-leg gone — tilted up against the red shingles. He whittled a stick, and whistled. It would be time, presently, to go after the "caows." That duty impending absolved the interval of time. Wealthy chopped on, following her own solitary thoughts, feeling a certain habitual comfort of having him at her elbow.

Voices first, and then heads, coming suddenly in view up the abrupt path, brought the visitors to their knowledge. Then there was voluble country welcome, and "laying off things." Say was made free of the curd-trough, and pecked away, eagerly, at the dainty white bits, like a bird lit in a seeded field.

"It's kind of an extra job, to-day, this cheese," explained Wealthy. "I don't mostly keep such work about into the afternoon. But I took a notion to set it after I'd got my butter out o' my hands. We had a famous churning, did n't we, Jez?"

"Eleven pounds, and jest as yaller as gold. Guess 't would do ye good to see the pats," said Jaazaniah, complacently. Lucky ye come to-day, for Wealthy 'n me's goin' down to Winthorpe to-morrow, with sixty weight."

"Come in," says Wealthy, proud of her dairy, and especially of this new churning, as a brain-worker might be of a last successful poem. "It's Lineback's cream; and you would n't think she'd ate anything but buttercups."

"If Wealthy's dairy was not poetry, it was very near it. Right up against the solid cool cliff, that formed one wall, — looking out, by its single-shaded window, upon a rare panorama of hill, pasture, and meadow, with the gleaming pond stretched far below, — redolent with a mingling of the cool mountain smell of rock and moss, and the fragrance of churned cowslips and clover, that had given up their essence into the golden rolls and pats that were ranged on shelf, or stored in boxes, — musical with the gurgle and plash of spring-water, that came in by a cleverly fixed spout, and flowed constantly through the large shallow, wooden receptacle wherein Wealthy worked and moulded, — there was such breath of purity, such suggestion of all delight of life and growth that culminated here, as no written word can give the feeling of.

Say drew long breaths as she entered. "I should like to live here," she said.

"I 'll keep you," answered Wealthy Hoogs, with one of her long, asking looks. Say thought it sharp, and shrank away, half changing her mind. In this little hillside home there had never been a child.

"We 've brought some books that Jane left for you," said Joanna. "She would have come up, but she had n't time. And it 's been so very hot."

"I know it has. This is the first comfortable breezy day for most a fortnight. And I 'm thoroughly obliged. It 's a great thing to get a book up here. Specially, when the winter nights come on."

"There 's something among them — a book of traveller's stories — that we thought Jaazaniah might like."

"Maybe he will. But he never took no great to readin'; more 'n a chapter in the Bible of a Sunday, or the newspaper once a week, or the Almanac. Sometimes I wish 't he would. It seems like goin' off and leavin' him all alone, when he sits here, and I get into a book. I 'm clear lost for awhile, that 's a fact. But then he 's always glad to see me back again, and that 's one good of goin' away, however you do it."

"Don't you ever read aloud to him?"

"Well, I used to try that, now and then. But it did n't do much good. I had to keep nudgin' him up all the time, or he 'd be sure to go to sleep. He aint one of the sort that can stand bein' read to. We aint much alike in some things, and I suppose it is n't best to be. He 's just as clever as the day is long; and you know that as well as I do."

Wealthy finished her sentence with a certain sudden, short defiance, as if she thrust down, with averted mental vision, some buried-alive thought that lifted itself now and then.

"If he got lost, as I do, there 'd be no knowing when we should ever come across one another again. But he 's a kind of anchor for me. He 's always right there, and I know just where to find him."

With this bit of wifely philosophy, Wealthy led the way out again, toward the house front, where Jaazaniah whittled and whistled still, with interjectional sentences of conversation with Gershom, and glances at the descending afternoon sun.

"You might think, to see him sittin' there, that he was lazy. His mother used to tell him he was. But I know better. He 's busy thinkin'. He is n't one that tells his thoughts much; but they come out, once in a while, in a way that would surprise you. And you ought to see him *at* a thing, when he once gets a going. He 's slow to begin, that's all. Come, Jez, make haste and get the cows home, and the milkin' done, while I get this cheese into the press. The folks 'll stay to supper, of course. And then, Jez, what if you take the boat and row the children across the pond?"

"Jest what I was a thinkin' of," responded Jaazaniah, slowly, shutting up his jack-knife, and coming down, skilfully, on the one forward leg of his chair.

"I told you so," said Wealthy, triumphantly, as he moved away. "He always gets ahead of me, after all 's said and done. I 've got into the way of always feelin' a kind of care of him, and remindin' him of things; but, half the time, there aint really any need of it. I suppose it 's partly because his mother's memory grew so short in her last days, and I had to look after *her* considerable; and when anybody's been used to doin', — no matter what it is, — they can't shake off the habit very easy. — Do you know what I think of every time I look at that old apple-tree, over there on the knoll? I do have curious thoughts about things sometimes. Well, it seems to me it 's just like the cares people have laid upon 'em, and by and by get so 's't they can't do without 'em. You see it grows right out from under a rock that happened to lay just there, and nobody ever moved it away. In the first of it, I suppose, it was a pretty hard chance. But it crept round, and climbed up, at last, into a tree. And now just look how the rock over its roots keeps it balanced! Why, if anybody should pry up that stone now, and heave it away, you can see, by the cant of the whole trunk, that it would n't hold itself up a minute!—And here I am, standing, moralizing, with the cheese-tray in my hands," she cried, interrupting herself. "It 's clear I want something to hold *me* down!"

It was pretty clearly suggested to the minds of her listeners how this want of hers had been permanently provided for, as slow-moving, literal Jaazaniah came out of the dairy, his arms strung with milk pails, and took his plodding way down the path toward the barnyard, wrinkling his brows in the level-glancing afternoon sunlight, with never an apparent out-glancing of any light within, kindled of all those heavenly shafts illumined.

"We all get that, one way or another, I suppose," said Rebecca, thoughtfully. "It's well when we can see the good."

"All the same," said Joanna, quickly, "I can't help wanting to give the rock a hoist. And I think in the beginning, somebody ought to have done it. At any rate, people need n't plant themselves in that fashion. — You 're just buried alive here, Wealthy Hoogs, and I can't help saying so. Nobody to speak to month in and month out, except Jaazaniah, and he won't talk back."

"Maybe I like that best, when I get a going," replied Wealthy, with a touch of quiet humor. "Besides, there 's more in folks than what gets said. There 's all sorts of hindrances; things don't always seem to correspond. It's just as it is with children. They want to say great grown-up words sometimes, but they don't dare. When I was four years old, I told my mother once, that I wished I was fifteen, so 's't I could say 'probable.' Clo'es is considerable. If Jaazaniah ever does come out more than ordinary, it 's on a Sunday, when he 's dressed and shaved, and gets the rough off a little. I don't doubt, if he wore a black suit every day, and kep' his hands clean, and his chin smooth, like a minister, he might talk like one. He 's got a soul, and thoughts. It comes out in his whistlin'. He could n't make such music as he does, out of nothin'. You never heard it, nor nobody else, as I have. Why, when we 're sittin' here, all alone, sometimes, as we were just now, before you come along, he 'll go on so, that I hold my breath for fear of stoppin' him. It 's like all the Psalms and Revelations to listen to it. There 's something between us then, that 's more than talk. — No, I don't care what folks think about it; nor I don't care whether it ever comes out any plainer as long as we both live; but I *know* I was no fool in takin' Jaazaniah. The rough 'll come off sometime, — over Jordan if it don't here, — and then, all I 'm afraid of is, whether or no I shall make out to keep up with him."

If you have n't cared for this little passing glimpse at Wealthy Hoogs's life, inner and outer, it has been very easy for you to skip it; but, however it may be with this, my poor presentment, if she had come to you as an episode in your own actual experience, I am very sure you would have done no such thing.

The tea-drinking was such as could only have been had in just that spot, and from just those simply hospitable hands. The sun was lowering slowly to the horizon, lessened everywhere, in those regions, by the multitudinous hills,— when Jaazaniah helped the children and Aunt Rebecca carefully into his little boat, and put off from the shore at the foot of the descent. Joanna refused to go. She would rather, she said, walk round the head of the pond, in the twilight; and there was n't room to take all safely. They would n't get across before she should come. They meant to have a row up the bend, first.

Joanna Gayworthy had a battle to fight,— after her own fashion. She must have it out with herself, and she must be left alone to do it. She wanted to stand up, face to face, with this great blank future that opened itself out before her, and see what its emptiness was like, and grapple with its phantoms, and put them down, once for all, if it might be.

There is a point we each come to, once,— and Joanna, whether she understood it or not, had reached it,— when a woman's life rounds itself out about her as the firmament, and in like manner resolves itself to her vision. One sun,— the rest a thronging huddle in a far ecliptic. Her sun had hidden itself below the horizon. Night was teaching her the secret of her day. Until Kate Purcell and her brother had come to Deepwater, there had never been a thought of doubt or loss to prompt her to look up and discover whence her daylight came. It lessened, all at once; she turned her back upon it, and could find nothing in the whole wide horizon, suddenly, but sharp-eyed, impertinent little far-off, self-sphered stars.

Gabriel Hartshorne had come no nearer than the garden fence, on some farm errand, since the Sunday I have told you of. Joanna was fractious and unreasonable; nobody knew why,— herself least of all, perhaps; nothing was worth while; the world was full of "other folks."

She had longed to get off, alone, somewhere; there had been no chance for it; Mrs. Gair's stay, her departure, the hundred little put-off things that had to be done to bring the family back into the ordinary grooves again,— all had teased and prevented her till it had become unbearable. Now, she *would* be left.

So she stood there by the water-side, as the little boat passed round the bend, Rebecca, with her calm face turned toward her as she sat in the bow, floating away into the placid shadows, and out of sight, leaving her to the wild solitude that hushed itself around her into waiting silence. How should *she* know?

Ah, me! the mute histories that run side by side! The hearts that seem to touch, whose electric currents never blend with the spark of inmost recognition!

"I should like to know how people come to bear their lives!"— It was in this wise she began the fight. "A whole winter, shut up there, with Jaazaniah Hoogs! Ten, twenty, sixty winters, perhaps!—" Joanna gave a little gasping scream, to herself, at the imagination. "And there's Prue! And Jane is n't much better, whatever she supposes. — And I wonder what I'm coming to! — I shall have Bessie for awhile, maybe, — she's all I've got, — and then — somehow — she'll slip away from me, as she did just now; she's too good for us, I'm afraid; or perhaps some prowling missionary will come along, as they do in the memoirs, and carry her off to the tigers and anacondas. And then I shall take care of father; but I can't keep *him* forever; and Gershie'll grow up, and go away, and Prue'll go after him; and I'm tough, and I shall live through it all, and grow fat, — that's what it turns to with people like me, — and nobody'll really know anything about it, or care for me; — and I shall just be 'old Miss Gayworthy' for forty years after I shall wish I was dead and gone! — Well! the world must always be full of other folks, I suppose; and I shall be one of 'em, — that's all!"

And with this she hardened her heart fiercely against herself, and walked on; punching great holes in the gravelly path with the stick of her parasol, and supposing that so, since she no longer worded them mentally, she put down thoughts. But they kept seething, confusedly, — the something in her short past, that she would not look at or acknowledge, except as she did it once, to her own sudden surprise, in the involuntary exclamation, "I wish I could just be angry enough not to care!" mingling and alternating with the dreary touches imagination laid upon that picture of the coming years.

By and by — she hardly knew it — the harsh, wild fancies began to soften; a furtive, unshaped suggestion crept in among them, that *other* lives too must go on; that there would always be something to know, and to think of, and to care for, if she pleased, however secretly; to be true to, however hopelessly. That lines not identical might yet run a great way parallel; that it would be hard if they should *never* cross or coincide; that people born into this world contemporaneously, could n't get off the planet, or into another generation; that, set at first in propinquity with like local ties and interests, they would scarcely drift away from each other into utter incognizance and separation; that they might, even, grow old before each others' eyes, and in a comfortable friendliness; and that she should n't very much mind being "old Miss Gayworthy" if only ——, and just then her thoughts took definite form, and flashed off to Deepwater; and she "did n't believe there was anything in that Purcell story; they were all off, now, and nothing seemed to have come of it. But why did n't Gabriel so much as turn his head to-day?" She knew he had n't, for she had heard the whish of every truss of hay that he had thrust in, without pause, at the barn-chamber window, until they had got round where he could n't see; and here she caught herself up indignantly, and leaped to her feet from the fallen log whereon, at the turn of the path, she had seated herself mechanically, wondering how ever she had come round to *that* again.

Just then a little boat—not Jaazaniah's—came up to view along the opposite shore, and veered this way.

I said she was at the turn of the path. Here, the bank became abrupt and broken, and the shore-path ended for a space. A little track bent off into the woods, and followed the curve around the head of the pond, which leaned itself coquettishly this side,—touching again, farther on, the strip of pebbly beach, and there offering choice of road,—by shore or on, within the fringe of wood, to the point where they had first struck the pond, this afternoon, at the foot of Farmer Hartshorne's pasture.

Joanna gave a flashing glance at boat and oarsman, sweeping, with vigorous stroke, toward her.

"Does he think, I wonder, I shall stand here for him to come and fetch me?" And the light muslin dress, that against the green had been an unwitting signal for his guidance, vanished from the rower's sight among the trees.

Quick as thought the boat's bow turned. It was a race.

If Joanna could only get past the turning first! But the little feet that hurried so along the mossy way, stood but small chance against the lusty sweep of oars that shot the light craft with such rapid impulse, along the inner line, toward the point of meeting. She could catch frequent glimpses out between the trees, and note its progress. She could measure odds, and she knew that she was worsted. That he must know it, too, and that to leave the path, and to dash away into the woods, as for an instant she felt temptation to do, would not only cause great uneasiness to her sister, but would be to those other eyes absurd and manifest flight. Since there was no help for it, then, she would keep her dignity, at least. So she walked slowly, again,—very slowly,—and gathered breath; and came out, leisurely enough at last, upon the narrow beach where Gabriel Hartshorne sat waiting in his boat, and confronted him, as one who knew no cause for shrinking.

The young man sprang ashore.

"I was determined to find you, Joanna. I had something to say. I should have been glad to have rowed you over."

"I wanted the walk, thank you. And now I must make haste, for I have been longer than I meant, and I daresay the others have crossed the pond below."

"No," answered Gabriel. "The children were getting lilies in the bend when I came up."

He had lain about upon the water, watching, a full hour past, for the poor reward of these five minutes. He would not have them shortened, now.

Joanna walked on, replying nothing.

"You 're offended, Joanna, and I suppose I can guess why. But there has n't been any reason. I can't explain everything. If I could ——"

"I am sure I would n't give you the trouble. I don't know why I should be supposed to be offended: and I certainly can't pretend to call you to account."

What strange, wayward words rush to the lips when the heart is fullest! These translated nothing of Joanna's self. Her sky was filling again with light. The whole east crimsoned with a coming joy. The impertinent stars faded out of her thought, and were forgotten. She could have sung, like a bird at dawn. And yet she answered frowardly. There was a curious delight in such very utterance. Like a child, she meant to be good in a minute; she meant to let herself be happy; but the last ebullitions of a relenting naughtiness, — the last throbs of an expiring pain, — there is a pleasure of perversity — a sweetness of torture — in the very prolonging of these.

Gabriel answered to her words.

"I wish I could show you my whole mind, this minute," said the young man, earnestly. "You would n't — that is, I hope not — find anything in it that would offend you. I told you I could n't explain. Things have n't gone, lately, quite as they used to, between us. I only want to ask you to believe it is n't my fault. We 've always been good friends, have n't we, Joanna?"

That nearly spoiled the whole. A little while ago, compounding meekly with fate, Joanna could have borne to be "old Miss Gayworthy," for a certain comfortable friendliness that might still be hers; now, was this all?

Had he pursued her so, to say only this? That he would like to say something better, if he could? Joanna felt inclined to be rather more indignant than ever. Spite of her capricious flight, the great solitude wherein she sat and dreamed had been so blithely broken by the coming of his boat! Such a thrill recalled her to the present, — such a nameless hope stirred suddenly, — and over the hard, lonely years she had looked out on, fell such a happy mist, once more, shutting her back into her youth again!

The first words, too, that had infringed, with a manly wilfulness, the silence that had lain between them, giving her a safe feeling in her own little petulance, that might be indulged, since, without humiliation to herself, it should presently be overborne, — meant they nothing more than this?

She felt very like the child, who discovers, after his naughtiness, that he may be as good as he pleases, yet it chiefly concerns himself: the world is to go on very much as it has always done before.

He only wanted to be friends, then.

"Of course," she answered, coldly. "There's no need to make a special talk about it. — When are you going to Winthorpe?"

"To study? I don't know. I'm afraid all that is put off for some time. Father seems to need me at home. Things don't look altogether clear, ahead. I may have to give up the law, after all, and stick to the farm."

"There they are, — coming round the point. They *did* cross below. We must make haste and meet them. It is getting late."

"Joanna!" exclaimed Gabriel, suddenly, placing himself before her in the narrow path, — "if it was fair and right to ask — as things are — I *would* ask you — ."

It was a blundering beginning; but he would have blundered on, blessedly, if she had let him; which of course she did n't.

"Better not!" she interposed, hurriedly; putting a full stop, so, after this, his third dash. Don't you remember what we used to say at school, when we opened our noon-baskets? 'Those that ask, shan't have; those that don't ask, don't want?' It always makes me contrary-minded, when folks come asking things!"

She put one foot on a great stone that lay in the water, and sprang past him, keeping on her way. He could but follow.

"It's clear she means to hold me off," was his thought.

"What in the world did he begin with a capital IF for?" was hers. "And why should n't it be 'fair and right,' — unless he's gone and made it wrong?"

Thrums again. This thread broke. Many things were to happen afterward to prevent its joining. But how should Joanna know that? She went home gayer hearted than for long past.

It would come right, somehow; she did not truly believe there was anything wrong, despite her captious coquetry. He would begin again, sometime; before long; without the capital IF; and say his lesson better.

There was a little quick restlessness in her manner, as she sat and chatted with Prue and the doctor, taking their tea together. She sang as she washed up the cups and plates, afterward; when that was done, she sang softly, still to herself, standing out by the doorstone in the great maple shade.

Rebecca complained that the sun had given her a headache, and betook herself quietly, with her pain, to bed.

CHAPTER VII.

WATCHING AND WAITING.

After that, for days and days, Joanna watched and waited. Not visibly. Hardly consciously. She never stood looking out of doors and windows, to see if anybody were coming. She omitted nothing of her ordinary share of household duties. She took care of Say; put on her long-sleeved tyers when she sent her out to play; changed her stockings when she came in with wet feet, from playing by the brook; told her stories; went down to the orchard with her, to pick up red, spicy summer apples; filled every moment of her time more busily even than her wont, with successive small objects and employments; never paused to think what it was that she expected, or that she expected anything; yet, each day, put some slight freshness of decoration to her simple summer-afternoon toilet, thinking, away down secretly in the heart that turned a deaf ignoring to its own whispers, — "To-night, to-night! surely, he will come!"

She could not think he would let it all end here. That he had taken her little flippancy for final answer to the question not yet fairly asked.

She avoided with marvellous ingenuity any little plan of walk or visit, that should appropriate those after-tea, twilight hours, when, nothing else occupying the time, they were accustomed to gather about the great open front-door, that faced down a grass-walk of some ten or twelve yards' length, to the white gate in the garden fence. Through this white gate, often, neighbors came, strolling in to spend a leisure half-hour. Down the green vista Joanna gazed as the shadows deepened, night after night, — sometimes left sitting there alone, — in an unconfessed expectation of a coming fate. And night after night the katydids sang in the maples, and the long summer twilight faded away, and the dews grew chill, and a dull soreness gathered and spread about her heart, and what she looked for came not. Everything else that could come, came, at one time or another, startling her with successive shocks of certainty and disappointment, as the little gate swung, clattering, after each entrance, and figures, that might at first glimpse be anybody's, moved up out of the shadow of the great trees. The minister dropped in for a minute with revival news; a farmer's wife had a word for Prue; village girls came, laughing and chatting, and stayed, and chattered on, till Joanna could have shrieked at them; little boys after the doctor; and then everybody, at last, in all Hilbury, was safe at home for the night; and Prue was locking up, and Rebecca's gentle voice called her remonstratingly in, out of the dampness; and the katy-dids were shriller and more insulting than ever; and the starch was all out of her pretty muslin dress; and that day's hope was over.

Forty rods or less away, down the road, at the Hartshorne farm-house, somebody else spent those same twilight hours, thinking and brooding, expecting nothing. Forty rods, at most, long measure; what had that to do with it? There was a space widening between these two not measurable by roods.

One night the doctor came in late to tea, — with something very evidently on his mind. He had been to the village at the Bridge.

"Prue," he asked, suddenly, "have you seen anything of Hartshorne's folks for a week or two back? Seems to me I have n't."

"Why, no," says Prue. "Not to speak of. And it's a little singular, too. I suppose Mrs. Hartshorne gets pretty well tired out with all the work she has, in haying-time, and we've been busy. But I can't think what's come of Gabe. He's rather left us off, lately, I must say."

"There's something wrong there, Prue!"

Joanna started up from the table, — all but the doctor had long finished the meal, — and hastened suddenly out after Say, who had run off, in her clean stockings and pantalets, to sail chips in the horse-trough.

"They say down at Barstow's that the old man grows queerer every day. He drives down and buys odd things in ridiculous quantities; things he can't possibly have any use for; and perhaps Gabriel comes along afterward and brings 'em back, with some excuse. Yesterday, there were half a dozen in there, standing round, and in comes the old man, — his otter-skin cap on, too, in the doggiest of dog-days, — and calls for 'axe-heads. Six of 'em.'"

'That's a good many,' says Barstow, not knowing exactly how to manage. 'Want any helves?' 'Did n't I say axe-*heads*?'

he snarls out, quite fierce. 'When I want anything else, I'll ask for't.' 'What yer goin' to set 'em to?' says old Hines, speaking up from the corner, in his shrill way, and winking to the others, that upside-down wink of his that takes all one side of his face to do it. 'Hallelujah metre!' roars Hartshorne again, and then laughs. 'No more *sense* to him than a patridge,' says Hines, chuckling. Just here, Gabriel came in, looking hot and hurried. He shook his head at Barstow over his father's shoulder, and he turned round and waited on another customer, and presently they began to talk of something else, and then the old man seemed to forget all about it, and Gabe got him away.—He looks strange, too. If they asked me, I should tell 'em not to trust him about alone. Gabriel does seem anxious and, keeps round after him as well as he can. But the old man fires up if he notices."

"O dear!" replies Prue, shocked. "I do hope he is n't going to lose his mind!"

The doctor moved his head slowly, twice, from side to side.

"I ve had my thoughts before now," said he. "I hope, whatever it is, it'll take a quiet turn with him. It's hard enough, anyway, on Gabriel and the old lady.—He ought n't to be irritated, though. It's queer what there is in human nature that turns out Hineses. People that never had any wits to spare themselves, always ready to egg on, and chuckle, when they see a better fellow going a bit astray. Every cur runs after and barks, when a noble-blooded mastiff gets a tin can tied to his tail. Barstow's is a bad place for Hartshorne."

"But, father," cried Rebecca, with an eager, horrified look, "can't something be done? Why don't you tell them?"

"Child," answered the doctor, almost impatiently, "what can *I* do? it's in the hands of God. And, next to Him, they know more than anybody else, already."

The doctor finished his tea, presently, and got up and went out.

Joanna came in. Prue turned round upon her with the news. She stood straight up between them, growing pale, and looking from one to the other, with such an expression as she had never shown them on her face before.

"I don't believe one word of it," she said, slowly, with a sort of trample in her tone. "And, you two! don't ever you mention it again to a living soul. It's a shame. It's Hilbury gossip. I wonder father listens to all they say, down there at Barstow's!" And with this, she left them and went out to the front doorstone, and sat down, alone. Could this be why "things did n't look quite clear ahead" to Gabriel? Was this the unspoken hindrance that lay between them? Had she from a heedless, unreasoning impulse, checked the avowal, that breaking through a harsh restraint, was ready in that moment only, to have rushed from his lips? Might she have given him love and comfort, that now he would never come to ask again? — She laid her hands upon her knees, and her face in them, and questioned herself of these things bitterly.

By and by, her head flung itself up again, with a sudden spring. "After all, he knew I could n't have understood. And they were all close by. There was no time. He would n't give it up so, if he meant anything. *I* would n't, if I were a man! At any rate, he can't keep out of the way forever."

With another sudden movement, she stood up. Then, she walked restlessly down the grass-path to the gate beneath the maples. She looked up the road, down the road, in the clear, early evening light. To the top of the long, sloping hill, on one side; to the red buildings of the Hartshorne farm, below, upon the other. A few steps would take her there; doubtless the old lady was wondering why some of them did not come. A month ago it would have been the most natural thing in the world to run down, and call in. Now, how impossible it had become! She and Gabriel might as well have been set apart on opposite ocean-shores. — Would this be so always? Would this mysterious gulf lie between them, unknown of others, holding them asunder, all their lives? — Might they "grow old before each other's eyes," yet miss the "comfortable friendliness?"

A man's figure came into view, moving up, in the softening and uncertain twilight.

Joanna's heart beat hard. He was coming at last. And she would not be shy and cold. She would even give him opportunity. Poor fellow! he had difficulty enough in his way, if all were true. She would be kind. She would stand still, there at the gate, — hold herself, forcibly, against her own wayward wish, — and meet him, alone. She would, — well it mattered not what she would have done. The figure drew nearer while these thoughts were flashing through her mind.

"What a fool I am!" she muttered, in a whisper, angrily, between her teeth; her hand clutching with a fierce pressure the upper bar of the white gate, as one clutches at any outward thing, to bear a horrible pain. She turned, and moved swiftly off under the screening boughs to the house-door, whence at the moment Rebecca came out.

"Here comes your revival man," said she sharply. "Stay

and attend to him. I can't." And she ran up stairs to her own chamber, shutting herself in.

The quiet enduring of some souls gets laid upon it, not only its own unstinted measure of pain, but half the burden of others' impatient suffering. Gordon King was coming to tell them of his betrothment. And Rebecca, of all the household, must stay alone and listen to his news. I think if he had known how this would chance, the young minister, clear as he might be of any falsity in word, would yet have shrunk, with a certain secret compunction, from the ordeal.

"I suppose," said he, after a few commonplaces, "you know something, already, of what I have to tell you. I hope you are glad for us?" So he asked her for congratulation. What could Rebecca say? Her face was pale and earnest in the dim light, as she answered him in words given her surely by that Spirit who teacheth His own in each moment of their need what they shall say and what they shall speak.

"I hope," she replied, slowly and solemnly, "that you may both be glad, all your lives, and forever, in each other, — and in the Lord!" And she stretched out her hand to him untremblingly, as an angel might.

Did no secret intimation whisper to him then, in the presence of that grander, purer womanhood, of something he might have missed in grasping after a mere witchery of prettiness?

He uncovered his head, involuntarily, with one hand, as he met hers with the other, and held it fervently. For a minute or two, he stood silent in the solemnity of such giving joy. In those instants perhaps, these two souls were nearer to each other, though they knew it not, than common souls, in common mood, can be even in the avowal and acceptance of what such call love; nearer than either might be again, to any other, while flesh should hold them darkling.

Afterward, he said, "I hope you will see Stacy soon. A friend like you will be a strength for her. She is younger than you, spiritually. Her feet, you know, are newly set in the upward way."

This almost went beyond. Something that Rebecca in her lowliness, struggled with as a motion of the old depravity, rose up within her at this demand from him. For she could not help — saint as she was — her own clear, native, common sense. Stacy was a good two years her elder, as the world reckons. A lifetime beyond her, in that which Rebecca Gayworthy had never lived at all. She might wish her well; she truly did; honestly, in her inmost soul, she prayed for her the prayer of self-forgetting faith.

But go to her! As she was now! In the fresh exultation of her double achievement, for this world and the next! To read, and to be read, as those two woman-souls would surely decipher each other, and to utter words of spiritual sympathy and earthly congratulation! What she did, she would do truly. Not this now.

"Stacy has better strength than mine to lean on. Even human. She will not need me yet. If ever she does, be sure I will not fail her. Give her my good wishes."

This was all; said with a calm, pure smile. Nothing to answer, nothing that he need translate beyond the letter. Yet Gordon King knew, dimly, as he listened, that he had wronged that gracious nature; knew, yet more dimly, — it was a thought away back in embryo shadows of his soul, that only years might give a form wherewith to haunt him, — that he also wronged himself.

This he shook off; thanked her for her friendly words; pressed once again the hand that let itself lie passively in his; bade her good-night; and passed on, up over the hill, in the golden, growing starlight, to Stacy's home, where there were sweet words, and bewitching looks, and winning smiles and willing kisses waiting him.

Rebecca, alone under the still heaven, as his last quick footfall came faintly back upon her ear, took up the cross that lay upon her path, and went away to God with it.

CHAPTER VIII.

EBEN'S COUP-D'ÉTAT.

Any one who had been by chance in the shadow of fence or bush by the lonely roadside, upon a certain August morning, as Eben Hatch came riding back from errands to the blacksmith's, and at the village store and post-office at the Bridge, would have seen something funny and rather unaccountable. If Eben had been ten years old, instead of six-and-twenty, and if it had been in the previous knowledge of the looker-on that one of those perambulating caravans of wonders, human and zoological, that make their appearance at certain intervals in our quiet New England villages, to set all the urchins' brains a madding, and their bodies more often than otherwise upside down, and to paper, gratis, with bright, monstrous pictured placards, bar-rooms, and offices, and variety shops, had recently sojourned at the Bridge,—he might have thought he understood the secret impulse of the mysterious and comical evolutions he would have so beheld.

Old Clumsy jogged on, in a mild, dignified imperturbability; perhaps it was a virtue born of necessity, like the middle-aged propriety of some humans, under otherwise exhilarating circumstances; they would have been queer antics, indeed, that her old muscles could have executed; while Eben, upon her back, the bridle dropped loosely upon her mane, an unfolded letter in his right hand, was giving vent to some unwonted internal excitement in a series of gymnastics that one would think could only have been learned in the Ring.

Now with a long, wide-mouthed cachinnation, he flung himself, backward, till his shoulders all but touched the horse's croup; then, flourishing his arms with a wild exultation, he bounded up and down in his saddle; and, presently, with a sudden "haw-haw," as if the overwhelming joke, whatever it might be, made itself abruptly palpable in a new and utterly irresistible aspect, performed a "right-about face" unheard-of in cavalry tactics, and set his sun-burnt nose in the direction of Clumsy's scraggy and wondering tail. Resting but an instant, however, in this position, he made a right-face again, bringing himself round with both legs dangling at the beast's near side; and here, pushing his straw hat up with both hands, in one of which the letter still rustled, scratched his sun-browned locks, and with the unsubsided grin of delight yet broadening his honest face, gave enigmatic utterance to the conclusion of this ecstasy of inspiration—

"Hooray! That'll do! That'll fetch it! I'll be — buttered — if it won't!"

And, resuming his masculine straddle, he stuffed the missive into his trowsers' pocket, and seizing the leathern bridle, strapped Clumsy's neck therewith, rather as a mild easing-off for his own effervescent spirits, than in any hope of altering a gait sublimely unaffected by all that had foregone.

When he arrived at home, having ridden in by the lane, and left his horse at the barn, Huldah was out among the "groves." You know what I mean, of course: among the lines of wet sheets and table-cloths in the clothes-yard; it being washing-day. Eben could see her stout-shod feet, and comely ankles cased in gray below the snowy drop-scenes; and, above, her brown hair ruffled by the breeze, and a bit of flushed forehead, as she struggled with the flapping linen; for the mountain wind was vigorous.

He wisely withheld the greeting he had ready. Without any theory about it, he had got hold of this bit of practical knowledge; a good nest-egg of everyday wisdom for a man to begin life with. Women are concentrative in their natures. They bend their force upon one point at a time, and that intensely, after the manner of a blow-pipe. Huldah, with a clothes-pin between her teeth, might give an answer from the right or wrong side, as should happen. Large-hearted and happy-natured, she would never sharpen or narrow to vixenishness; yet she had the little distinctive ways of her sex, for all. So Eben looked at her as he went by, reserving his fire; and passed on into the out-room, where he found his brown bread and apple-pie and cheese put up and waiting for him in a bright tin pail; and taking this in his hand, turned off again, marching away to his field-work, a secretly exultant man, with his *coup-d'état* in his pocket.

All day long it lay there, giving him boldness and strength. For the most part. A momentary reaction would come, now and then, of a doubt that struck him like a sudden blow with the thought, "What if it should n't work, after all?" It was his last shot. Well, if it missed, he would know at any rate where he was, and which way to beat retreat; the fight would be over.

"I 've got some news for you, Huldy," he said, as the maiden served him with his late dinner, on his return from the distant field. She looked rosy and pretty enough, after her cosmetics of vapor and breeze, in her tidy out-room, where the clothes dried from the wash lay heaped up, white and rustling, and odorous of sweet cleanliness, in broad willow baskets; her hair smoothed and a clean calico gown on, and a smiling grace of readiness upon her as she fetched the viands from the pantry; her energy concentred now on Eben's comfort, and secretly, upon making the most of this, their little hour of rest and companionship.

"I 've got some news for you. But I guess 't 'll keep."

"Not such a great while, I 'll be bound; if it depends on you. Good or bad?"

"Well, that 's as you take it. Kinder middlin'. I 'll tell yer to-night, when I come in from the chores. Hain't got time now. It 's consider'ble of a story."

Huldah looked at him over one shoulder, as she went into the cheese-room. There was a sparkle of determination in his eye, and a certain air of delayed triumph about him, as he spoke, that gave her a sudden thought of possible personal application in this story that should be coming.

"He 's goin' to be more redick'lous than ever. That 's what it is. And he thinks he 's so mighty cunnin' about it. We 'll see," and Huldah sparkled too, with feminine mischief, and made a pretty bit of picture, that nobody beheld, lit with gleams from under the dark eyelashes, and from between the ruddy lips, as she laughed to herself over the great sage-cheese from which she was cutting a generous wedge.

Eben ate and chuckled; and watched Huldah in and out and round the room, as if she were a little bird on which he could put a cat's paw at any moment. Huldah hopped tamely enough, but felt her wings stealthily and kept every feather trimmed and ready for a sudden unfurling.

"Concernin' whom?" she asked, abruptly, after a long pause, filled only by such pantomime.

"Oh, the news! You 're thinkin' of that yet, are ye? Well, concernin' me, mostly. Donno 's anybody else 'll care about it. May make some difference to the Doctor. I 'll tell yer to-night. Yer 'll want me to help stretch them sheets, I 'spose?"

Huldah was n't quite so merry and cómfortable after Eben went out, leaving her to clear up the dishes, and ruminate upon his words. "Difference to the Doctor?" Could it be that somebody was enticing him away from his old place with higher wages? Well, if Eben could be mean enough to give in to that, he might go. There 'd be no trusting him in anything. Huldah was quite angry at this imagination. And even when she had mentally repudiated it, as impossible, the mischief came no more back to eye and lip. The mystery might be perplexing, but it was no longer funny. She was off the scent again, and off her guard. So much the better for Eben.

After sundown, when the chores were through, and the milk strained and set away, they took up the little scene again, where they had broken it off.

Huldah had been sprinkling. All the small articles lay piled in neat, white rolls upon her fair deal table, and only sheets and table-linen lay waiting in the big basket, for Eben, as he always did, to help her "stretch." His rough hands were scrupulously clean for the operation; a weekly treat, which made Monday evening no less a blessed epoch to be looked forward to by the simple country lover, than the time-honored Sunday, when rural swains have traditional privilege to get themselves up in their best, and be, otherwise, as "redick'lous" as may please them. And he felt so strong to-night, with this foreclosure of the long mortgage he had held on Huldah 's heart, lying snugly in his pocket!

"Well, Huldy, I s'pose yer achin' to know?" This, as he gathered up in his hands, deftly enough for a man, the folded end of the sheet Huldah offered him, she walking off at the same time, with her own, to take her stand opposite.

"Folks that are in tribulation themselves, never see how anybody else can be feelin' easy," retorted Huldah, turning about and taking the cloth by the double corners. "Now, then, snap!"

Up went their arms, in admirable precision, each pair of hands uniting themselves, to be flung apart and downward, with a sudden jerk, and a mighty concussion of the bellying web against the air.

Huldah felt her power again, and her courage with it.

There was something illustrative in this little labor-pastime of theirs,—something suggestive in its likeness to their daily ways of going on, and what these were at last to come to. There must be just so many snaps, first of all; little hearty measurements of mutual strength and dexterity; then came the gathering up in earnest, for the "pull," when each drew away, apparently, with all force, from the other, yet taking care, the while, to hold stoutly by the good bond between, lest either failing, should so get the worst of it; then the final folding, bringing them nearer and nearer, hand to hand, till they stood close, at last, face to face, with their shared and lightened work between them. Eben felt the secret significance and symbolism, every Monday twilight of his life, though if the clumsy fellow had tried to put it into words, he would never assuredly, have "fetched it."

"If it 'll be any relief to your mind, speak out," says Huldah, again.

Snap!

"Oh, it 's not much," rejoins Eben, his arms going up for the third time.

Snap!

"Only, —" gathering up for the tug, — "I got a letter, again, this morning, from my cousin out in Illinois."

A long pull, — a pull together, — and a pause; a little twitch, maybe, of anxiety between the two hearts, as well.

"And he wants me to come out there, and settle down."

Another strain, as if each would tear away from the other, almost in anger; only for the something, woven too strong, that held them bound, and that neither would let go.

"And, — I 've pretty much made up my mind — when the crops are all in — to go."

It was time for the third pull; but one end gave way, suddenly. Huldah's arms fell, and Eben tumbled up, ingloriously, against the cheese-room door. Must a conqueror necessarily look grand and graceful, in the actual moment of victory?

Huldah laughed; but it was an odd little laugh, — her lips all a-quiver.

They gave the third pull in silence, somewhat feebly, as must needs be; a truer, mightier impulse counter-current to will and muscle, urging them, rather, to each other's arms. Then they began to fold. Meeting midway, the man, the victor, looked down, without a word, upon the eyes that shrouded themselves beneath proud, half-angry, trembling lids. They felt the magnetism, and flashed up.

"All the way out there?" says she, the vanquished, with a voice of tears. "Alone?"

"No, by thunder, Huldy! Not if you 'll go with me!" And the strong arms seized and held her. "Consider'ble of a story" had concentrated all its essence, by a heart-chemistry, into a few pungent words. The white folds fell to the floor. There was no interposition. Eben had "fetched it."

A day or two after, Joanna stood in her chamber, with a new bonnet in her hand; just sent from Selport. Pretty enough; but what use now? A woman has but one use for all her thousand little fripperies; to please the eyes she loves.

Joanna fingered, idly, the ribbons. All the family had seen

and admired it. Now it was going back into its box. She wondered if she should ever care to put it on.

Steps came up the stairs; Huldah showed herself, unwontedly, at the door; her face full of something she had to say. So full, evidently, that she could not quite easily begin; so she stood and rolled a corner of her apron.

Joanna looked up, in somewhat surprised inquiry.

"That 's a dreadful pretty bunnet," says Huldah; much as if that were not the thing, either.

Joanna wondered what strange fit of idleness and folly had come over the brisk and busy handmaid.

"I hate to be too curious, Joanna;" the girl resumed, a little desperately; "but would you mind tellin' me what they ask you for such a bunnet as that, down to Selport?"

"Nine dollars," replied Joanna, quietly, and marvelled again within herself, what next?

Everything else, however, seemed frightened out of Huldah's head at that amazing statement. She stood still, and looked at Joanna, with eyes that appeared as if they never would wink again. As if at least, were there any exaggeration in this, they meant to see through it first. Evidently, however, Joanna intended simply what she had said. She was busying herself with a little bending of the flowers, and a little perking of the ribbons, — I suppose a woman would do this, mechanically, though she were about to lay away the finery forever, for the sake of a life-long grief befallen her, — and gave not a glance after her words, to note their effect.

"Nine dullars! Well, they ain't bashful, down there, be they? Not the least mite!"

Now, Joanna did look up, and laugh. "Why, Huldah, she said, "What is it? Did you think of sending to Selport for a bonnet?"

"Well, no, — I donno 's I did; I was n't thinkin' decidedly of anything. Only I 'spose I might as well be pricin' things a little. I 've got to do some fixin' up before the fall. You see," — she continued, hesitatingly, "I never calculated to live out, all my life. I 've had a real pleasant home here, that's a fact; an' you and Rebecca, and Mis' Vorse, an' the Doctor, has been just like my own folks to me. But everybody likes a little change of some kind, now and then; and Ebenezer, he's got to be so redick'lous, — I don't see 's there 's any other way of pacifyin' him; and so — I 've pretty much made up my mind — to get married and try that awhile!"

These two brief little scenes, homely and absurd in the letter of their enactment, yet sweet and grand in spirit, with the blossoming of happy love and faithful purpose, forever the one, identical, divinely-beautiful thing in human hearts and lives, — decided and announced it all. After the crops were in, — a couple of months, or little more, hence, — Huldah and Eben were to take each other by the hand, and go. Changes were to begin at the Gayworthy farm. Who might guess what should come next?

Meantime, they had their own kite to fly, now; and there was nothing to remind them that they had ever helped to tie a bob to the tail of anybody's else.

CHAPTER IX.

"GABRIEL!"

MRS. HARTSHORNE's plum-colored silk and muslin pelerine were laid out on the bed in the best bedroom. The very cat, walking through, would have known by that, that it was Sunday morning. Old Flighty, — named in colthood, but long outgrown the correspondence to her title, — (don't Rose, and Lily, and Grace, — yes, even Patience, and Charity, and Comfort, and Frank, and Peter, and Felix, and Agnes, come often to outlive and belie theirs also?) stood harnessed in the wagon, and tied to the front fence; and Gabriel was in the garden, gathering as he always had done, since he was four years old, a Sunday nosegay for his mother, of late pinks and sweetwilliam, and southern-wood, and ladies' delights, and bits of coriander; when that good lady came reluctantly to the unusual conclusion that she "did n't feel hardly well enough to go to meetin', after all."

She told Gabriel so, when he came in with his accustomed little offering, and found her sitting pale, uncertain, and unready, a strange thing, indeed, for her, by the kitchen hearth. The farmer was shaving his chin by the looking-glass that tilted forward from the wall between the windows, and bore above it the common and morally appropriate country decoration, — a bunch of peacocks' feathers. Somebody always stayed in the room of late while he performed this Sunday morning operation; and Gabriel thought at first that his mother had only thus been detained from her own dressing.

"There, mother," he said cheerily, — he was always tender and cheery to her, the manly, gracious-hearted fellow, — as he and the sunshine came in together at the garden door, "here 's your posy. And you won't have much time to spare. The bell's just struck. I 'll wait here to see you off; or drive, if you and father like."

The old man turned about quickly, as Gabriel seated himself. There was an angry, suspicious gleam in his eye.

"What are ye allers waitin' round for, hey? Who yer watchin' of? Can't I drive ma'am to meetin' s well 's anybody?"

"You and father 'd best go along without me, I guess," said Mrs. Hartshorne. "I don't feel quite so smart as common to-day, somehow."

Then Gabriel looked anxiously in his mother's face, and noted the paleness of it. He began to say that he would stay, too; but she anticipated his words, and stopped him.

"Mary Makepeace 'll be at home. I shan't want anybody else. And you'd best both go."

Gabriel saw a queer look flit over his father's face; an expression as of a prisoner, who, through the inadvertence or mischance of a keeper, might perceive an opportunity before him. He had been very restless, lately, and impatient of their presence; he had had constantly an eager, watching air, as if what he wanted were to get away. From the beginning of the alteration in him, this had been its peculiar feature; a propensity to give them the slip; to make strange, sudden errands, and go off to distances, alone.

Gabriel wondered if his mother recollected that he could not sit with his father during service, — that he would be left to himself in the great, old-fashioned pew; and how he would be likely to comport himself. The presence of others, however he might chafe at it, seemed a force that held him to his old habits of outward demeanor. Gabriel had found him quite wild and bewildered, once or twice, of late, when he had tracked him out, in his ramblings away from home. So it was with a secret apprehension that he set off with him to-day, under the compulsion of circumstances, and in obedience to the wish of his mother.

The church-bell swung sweet and solemn on the air, as they drove along; it seemed to pulse forth a deep calm that should reach into souls. Old Mr. Hartshorne looked placidly forgetful, presently, of his momentary excitement, and seemed to fall, involuntarily, into the old Sabbath mood. Gabriel took courage. We know very little, I think, how outward sights and sounds and habitudes hold us safely by their myriad fine and subtle threads, in mental poise. How the whole creation travaileth with us, and all our minutest relations are adjusted, lest a single human soul should lose its wonderful balance and consciousness, and be lost. Let us take care how we discard and break away, despising, in our presumption, the value of that wherewith God, by His supremely-wise ordination hath hedged and environed us. A sharp pain, — an instant's giddiness, isolating us from ordinary perceptions, sets earth and heaven shattering and whirling to our thought. A calm touch, — the glance resting on some familiar, insignificant object, — a gentle sound, — brings back the delicate equilibrium, as by electric impulse, to the disturbed and endangered brain. We know not, hourly, how we are saved, or what we are saved from.

It is from an instinct of the spirit which touches upon this truth rather than from any definite apprehension, that children of fine, sensitive, nervous organization dread "the dark." I hold it an outrage and a cruelty to thrust them relentlessly into this void they shrink from. The soul craves things sensible and local, whereto to anchor itself. The first gift of God to the world was light; the dearest promise of Christ is that he prepares a *place* for us. The fearful threat to the unworthy is "outer darkness;" an apostle hath it — "the blackness of darkness forever." May there be, perhaps, an awful literalness in the phrasing — a "lost soul?"

Old Mr. Hartshorne rode up to the church-door, alighted and walked in, like any other of the comers. Gabriel fastened the old horse under the shed, and went up to his seat among the singers.

He noticed, as he glanced down toward the family pew, his father fidget a little with the hymn books, and then settle himself more quietly; looking round upon his neighbors with a certain expression of simple importance and self-appreciation, such as a child might have, sent to church, exceptionally, by himself; as if he said, "You see I am quite to be trusted." Alternating with wilfulness and petulance, and vagary, there often showed among the symptoms which Gabriel and his mother watched with the keen, silent eye of anxious love, this touching air of half conscious liability to go somehow wrong, and the pride of refraining. God only knows how mind, as well as soul, struggles and clings, before it goes down, borne under by some fearful influence of which He alone who permits it, can understand the might.

The prayers and hymns and reading of holy words began; continued. Gabriel forgot, by and by, to be uneasy, seeing, whenever he looked that way, his father quite composed, and outwardly himself. There was one beside him, though, who read his every glance; who felt intuitively, through her secret sympathy, his fears; who watched when he relaxed. Ah! how Joanna Gayworthy was repenting there, that day, that she had not seized, when he had half offered it, the right to share his trouble, and help him in his care! And now, it was too late. He would never ask again. He had only been betrayed, as it were, into that beginning of an avowal, which he had resolved within himself, — how truly she read him now! — must not be uttered, because he deemed it not "fair and right to ask, as things were." So men defraud women of their dearest rights; so women must wait silently, in pain, nor dare to claim them!

The sermon began. It was a "revival discourse," preached by a stranger; an exhortation unstinted in all the technical force and coloring of like discourses as such professedly; sermons that in times of religious excitement, it used to be common for men gifted in that specialty to go starring about with; starring, some of them, at least, it is to be feared, too much after the fashion of Samson's foxes; a fearful picture of God's wrath; tremendous warnings; all the awful imagery of Ancient Hebrew Writ, from Sinai to the final thunders of the latest prophet of that olden dispensation; reiteration of the text, — "escape unto the mountains;" a placing of God and man over against each other, — the One upon His Throne of Judgment, the other quaking, cowering beneath. God's Spirit was there, among the people, doubtless; there were hearts in that assembly, touched, softened, tender, who had come up asking humbly, secretly, for bread from heaven to feed their needs. But this man — did he not rather hurl stones among them? There were souls awestruck, scared; there were nerves thrilled, brains fevered, as they listened; was there a single spirit won back into the Father's bosom? Oh, be careful, ye who come with Law and Gospel in either hand, and on your lips cursing and blessing; be careful how ye apportion, and mete out, and construe. It is a fearful thing to deal recklessly with the feeble minds and hesitating hearts of men! How know ye what ye may be doing with those differently and delicately, perhaps perilously, attuned moods and vital crises of human experiences?

"Escape for your life! Escape unto the mountains!"

The voice rang out once again,—startlingly, sonorously. A hand reached over, almost in the same moment, and laid itself with a quick pressure, on Gabriel Hartshorne's arm. A hurried breath came with it, —

"Gabriel! Your father!"

The young man leaped to his feet; gave one look below; the pew was empty. There was a stir of heads; a pause in the preaching, and Squire Lawton and Deacon Gibson were moving quickly toward the door. Gabriel sprang to the gallery stairs and rushed down.

This was what had happened. The poor, misty brain that had been soothed by the Sunday bells, and by hymns and prayers, half followed, perhaps, but lifting in a dim way, his instincts to the One Strength and Safety, had felt a hot, sudden quiver at the first utterance of those detached words which the preacher had separated from their connection and chosen for his text. They had struck upon, and chimed dangerously with the morbid prehension of his mind. The old man moved himself along the seat, to where the window recessed itself into the wall, and stood open, letting in the summer air. He looked out, away, upon the everlasting hills that framed the glowing landscape. So gazing, — his mind and fancy wandering toward their mysterious distances,— his ears took in mechanically the burning, urgent words of the sermon. He felt no religious fear; but, as the sentences fell, they played upon that one diseased chord; they stirred wildly, like fierce music, that physical, unreasoning impulse. He moved his head, with quick, short, furtive turns, to right and left. He watched for a moment when no eye should be upon him, he changed his place, softly, again, and seated himself in the window, with his arm upon the sill. Then he held himself innocently quiet, for some moments, with the cunning of actual, developed insanity, looking round upon the near neighbors who had noticed his movement, with a peculiarly open, placid expression, till they turned their eyes away, and he felt himself again alone.

Close by, outside, pulling at her halter, and uttering, now and then, a quick, impatient whinny, stood Newell Gibson's fiery, half-broken young mare, harnessed to a light gig. She, too, wanted to get away. Every suggestion of word and scene, — even of animal sound and movement, at once an incentive, with its blind, brute sympathy, and a prompting to new, wild purpose, — conspired, strangely and fatally, to quicken the old man's fast maddening fancy.

He was spied upon — he was restrained. He knew he was going wrong, and he could not help himself. "Escape?" It was just what he wanted to do.

The impassioned, vehement sentences of the discourse swept on. There was a breathless hush in the old church. All eyes, save the straying eyes of children, — and, by this time, many of these were shut in sleep, — were fixed upon the speaker. He lifted his left arm, and stretched it out, right over toward those blue, shadowy peaks that filled the horizon, and the words pealed forth again.

"Escape! Escape, for your life! Look not behind you, nor stay in all the plain! Escape unto the mountain, lest ye be consumed!"

There was a sudden sound, — a leap outside; people started, and turned. It was at this instant that Joanna had touched Gabriel's arm.

When he reached the great outer door of the meeting-house, springing down the last six steps of the steep gallery-stairs and dashing across the vestibule, — he saw Newell Gibson's mare fling herself by, at a gallop, the light gig rocking and bounding after her, down the hill. His father sat in the frail vehicle, erect, his gray hair floating back in the wind from his uncovered head.

Gone! — To his death? It seemed so.

Another sound of wheels came round the building. Squire Lawton and Deacon Gibson, in the Squire's open wagon. They pulled up, for an instant, as they saw Gabriel standing pale, horrified, uncertain for the moment, on the stone step before the door.

"Will ye get in, Gabe?" The deacon spoke with the sudden, undefined distance in his familiar address, that people assume instinctively toward one fearfully stricken. "We'll do the best we can. 'Pon my soul, I'm sorry for ye!"

"Come with me," said another voice at his side. "It'll do no harm to be a minute or two behind. — We must n't make a chase of it." Dr. Gayworthy addressed the last words to the two men in the wagon. "You'd better take the turnpike, over to the crossing; and drive as fast as you please. We'll follow the old gentleman."

Gabriel turned mutely, and accompanied the Doctor to his chaise.

There was no word spoken between them, as they followed, along windings and descents, the headlong course of the runaway animal; noting the tracks of her fierce hoofs that had clutched the gravel in mad leaps, and the swerving traces of the wheels, as the vehicle had swayed from side to side of the narrow country road, most marvellously escaping immediate overturn. What should they find at last? For nearly a mile, the road, though in no part actually precipitous, tended downward all the way, — no great length visible before them at any given point. Beyond this, a long ascent traced itself to clear view up the slopes of an opposite hill; and there, presently, if it were possible that horse and vehicle should hold so long together, they would again catch glimpse of them. Over that hill, also, at right angles, stretched the turnpike, crossing just beneath the brow upon the hither side. There lay the bare chance of safety. If the two who had gone that shorter way, could head the creature, slackened in her speed with taking the long hill, it might yet be well. But the still, white line lay dustily distinct against the green mountain-side, and nothing moved upon it yet. Something must have already happened. There was an ugly turn by the brook, and the bridge was narrow. Gabriel grew paler as they came down into the shaded hollow, still following the wild trail that must end soon, and losing sight, now, of the way beyond.

Up in the meeting-house, — the momentary disturbance externally composed, — the minister was closing his discourse to restless ears that listened no longer; and men and women waited feverishly through the short prayer and benediction, unheeding either, in the eager human interest that had laid hold of them. All the little world of Hilbury knew that half-kept secret of the Hartshorne farmhouse, now.

Gabriel thought of it, even in those short instants of dread; thought of Joanna in her seat there in the gallery; felt, still, the touch of her hand upon his arm, and the friendly sympathy of it in his soul. He could never sit and sing there with her, again; If his father lived, he must never leave him, now.

So they kept their way down, — silent, breathless, — to where they came upon it all. The shattered gig, thrown on its side, crashed up against the handrail of the bridge, where it seemed to have been dragged and caught, — a broken shaft and splinters of the whiffle-tree, lying beyond, — some bits of torn harness, — the horse gone. This side the brook, across a decayed log overgrown to a bank with moss and weeds, a prostrate figure, — and a gray head flung back, with closed eyes. One arm lay bent, beneath the body.

Gabriel raised the poor, brain-sick, unconscious head, and held it against his breast. Kind, skilful hands moved and manipulated body and limbs; drawing, carefully, the limp arm from its unnatural position.

"Both bones of the fore-arm broken. And that seems all. That, and falling just here, is what has saved him." These were the first words spoken.

"Saved him, — for what?" groaned Gabriel, his long trouble speaking itself, at last, from pale, dry lips, and imploring eyes.

"We 'll hope," said the doctor, cheerily. "And now, I'd rather he would n't come to, till we can get him home. He won't remember how it came about; and that 's better. There 's the wagon."

"If my mother only might n't know it all!" cried Gabriel.

She never did.

CHAPTER X.

ANOTHER WEEK.

GABRIEL, leaning over his father's bed, heard the click of the bones as they came into place under the doctor's grasp. At the same moment, the old man opened his eyes. There was a quieter look in them, though with a vague amaze, than they had worn for long.

"Where am I? What ye doin' to me?" he asked, feebly.

"You've had an accident, and hurt your arm. Lie still," replied the doctor.

"An accident? I donno nothin' about it. Where's ma'am?"

"I'm here," said his wife, standing on the other side. But her white face grew whiter, as she spoke, and she would have dropped, if Mary Makepeace had not held her.

"She's clear beat out; and her head's been bad all day, and she must go to bed, herself, this minute," said Mary Makepeace, leading, or mostly, lifting her, along. Mrs. Hartshorne yielded, in a sick dizziness that made the faces round her all turn strange, and the look of the kitchen, as she moved across it to the little bedroom on the other side, like a place she had never been in before; and presently the doctor stood by her, in turn, feeling her pulse gravely, and ordered that nobody should talk to her, and that all the questioning neighbors in the front room should be told to go away; and promised that Prue should come over, directly, with something that she must take.

So that week began

A week of ceaseless watching, and nursing, and fear. Gabriel, except his coat, had never his Sunday clothes off, through it all. They could n't keep it from the old man that his wife was very ill. That, and the corporeal shock which he had suffered, seemed to suspend the workings of diseased fancy. He lay, in a childish sort of contented helplessness, asking, now and then, how "ma'am" was, and "when she was coming." "In all this time, he recollected nothing, apparently, of that which he himself had done.

How it would be with him, by and by, the doctor could not promise: though he still said, "We'll hope." For the present, he was simply, as it were, benumbed, subdued.

Joanna Gayworthy was angry in her secret heart with Prue, for the privilege she had of entering fearlessly the afflicted home, and ministering there, day and night. Because she was a widow, and almost forty, she could do it. She was "just the person to be there," as people said. What great difference did the years make? She felt herself grown old enough, of late, if that were all. And her hopeless life looked to her like a long widowhood just entered. But she must sit at home, — she and Rebecca, whom she almost hated, too, for her calmness, and keep down all her restless thoughts and questionings, and not dare even to ask what she most wanted to be told, when the others now and then came in; seeming indifferent almost, through fear of showing too much. She wanted to know how Gabriel looked, and what he said; she wanted to know if anybody said words of comfort to him, now and then, as there ought to be somebody to do; if anybody made him eat and rest; or whether he too were wearing himself ill, with nobody to notice. She wanted, — oh, this was not half! What her woman's heart wanted, was to go to him, in spite of all; to take her stand beside him; to tell him that his pain was her pain, and that she had come to bear it with him, for that she *would* not be divided from him now! — What a strange world and way we live in! This she did not do, she held herself back with a fierce might, because she must; because the words had never been spoken, — because she had stopped them, frivolously, when she knew they were on his lips, — that should have given her this right; because what another even like her might have done, in simple neighborly kindness, it was quite impossible for her, with her secret consciousness, to do.

Prue came and went; Rebecca asked, sometimes, if she could not do something to help or relieve her. Prue always answered, "no; it was not necessary. She and Mary Makepeace were getting along quite well." Joanna, if she had dared to say one word at all, — she thought so to herself, — would never have been put off in that tame way!

"About the same!" Who has not known the agonizing insignificance and delay of that sick-room bulletin, which denies not hope, yet, day by day, lets fear settle down more heavily? Gabriel heard it from the doctor, at each frequent visit; Prue repeated it, in the intervals, at each asking look from him, and to the old man's queries. "Will nobody tell me anything more?" his thought questioned, bitterly. Yet he dared not press them to say more.

Joanna heard it till she ceased to make inquiry. "What is the use?" she cried out, vehemently, to Rebecca. "They won't tell anything, till it tells itself."

That day came. On Saturday, Prue came back, needed no more.

"Here, mother, is your posy," Gabriel said again, through sobs, on Sunday, kneeling at her side. They were the last week's withered flowers. He found them in his mother's drawer with the folded muslin pelerine as she had put them away,— who knows with what foreboding? He laid them, reverently, on the dead hands that never would reach out for posy more, and went away into the garden, to gather her yet one, — the last.

On Monday, all the neighbors came, from all the country-side, and the church-bell tolled, and they buried her.

When everybody else was there, Joanna could come too. Yes, like any common curious acquaintance, — the motherless girl who had loved Gabriel's mother secretly, as if she were her own. To stand there in the hushed and crowded parlor, to hear the prayer, and to struggle against tears, till she looked, and wondered if she were grown cold, and stony, and unfeeling, — to see Gabriel go by, with bared head, unwitting of her presence, separated from her and all by the sacred isolation of his great grief, and then to go home, having never said a word to him through all, since she laid her hand upon his arm, and called him by his name, a week ago, in the church gallery.

The old man wept feebly, when Gabriel told him tenderly, that they had lost her. Then he grew quieter than before, scarcely speaking; and seemed to notice little of what went on about him. He slept a good deal, during the next two days. It was on Tuesday, just at evening, that he turned his head, with an earnest look, toward Gabriel, as he sat by the bedside; and spoke, slowly, most like one awaking from a dream.

"Well. — She 's gone. Aint she?"

Gabriel bent his head, and groaned, "Ay!"

"Yes, She 's gone. She can't take care of me, now. And I 'm,— Gabriel, — there 's something slipping away from me, like. I 've felt as if it was a goin', this long time. But I 've held on. Yes, I 've held on. I did n't want, — Gabriel, — oh, dear! to give quite up and let it go. And so I 've been contrary and fractious. I ain't now. But it's going; and there 's something I want to say to you, Gabriel, first, quick. You must n't let me plague you, when I get worse. Send me away somewhere; I wanted, sometimes, to get off; there 's places, you know, — where they take care of folks, — that — go out of their minds!"

He said these last words in a whisper, as if so, in the avowal of his strange, secret consciousness, he gathered up the last strength of his failing faculties, at the moment he also let go the sole cord holding him to safety; and looked up into his son's face with an expression at once bewildered, helpless, pleading, and defiant.

Then the young man stood up, in his strength.

"Father," he said, calmly, "I don't think that is going to happen to you. And — whether or no — here I am; and here I stay, and stand by you, as long as we both live; and no man — nor woman — shall hinder, or come between. So help me, God!"

The poor, harassed intellect that was just casting itself adrift, caught at the brave, loving words of promise, and struggled back. The old man laid his hand — the one hand he could move — in Gabriel's. His eye softened. There came a tenderness into it — a trust — a gleam of peace. "Will you?" he said in such a tone as a child might. "You was always a good boy, Gabriel."

"He has passed a mental crisis," Dr. Gayworthy said, afterward. "He will never be quite himself again. But the trouble has taken a different turn. He may live for years, — the longer for this feebleness of brain, in fact, — and be no worse than he is now."

This, then, was the likelihood that lay in the future. And Mr. Hartshorne, though I have spoken of him as his neighbors did, — and as it is the fashion of New England country-folks to speak, even of a man of forty, if he have a son arrived at manly estate, — was not, literally, an old man; He was yet under sixty. He might live twenty years.

Yet Gabriel Hartshorne, with never a thought of the how long, bound a vow upon his heart, and took up this, his cross.

The next Sunday, there were prayers in church, for "the young brother, sorely and doubly stricken."

Nobody prayed for Joanna. But she prayed — she who best knew how — out of her pain — for him.

Also, that same day, the banns of marriage were published between Anastasia Lawton and Gordon King.

I have not done with my two young sisters. But this — the story of their youth — is told. Many a life-story ends to human knowledge, as abruptly. Fate does not round and finish all, in the first, few years of mortal experience. Things don't go on, in eventful succession, day by day, in the real years, as they do, page by page, in a novel. God gives us intervals; and we can neither skip nor turn the leaves faster then they write themselves. Threads drop midway in the web, and only the Heavenly

Weaver can find or reunite them. We wait, and grow gray with waiting, for the word, the seeming accident, the trifle, that may or may never, He knows, — come into the monotony of our chilled existence, and alter it all for us; joining a living fibre once again, that may yet thrill with joy, to that we lost, far back in the old Past, wherein it throbbed so keenly.

But you will know, now, as you see them so, while younger lives press forward to the front and claim the fresher interest,— how it came to pass that, years after, there were these two maiden sisters, counting uneventful days in the old home at Hilbury.

All that most people knew was that " there *had* been once, folks thought, a sort of kindness between Gabriel Hartshorne and Joanna Gayworthy, but it never came to anything; and after his father's mind failed, and his mother died, he seemed to give up all thoughts of marrying, and just settled down to taking care of the old man and looking after the farm. As to Rebecca, she never *was* anyway like other young people. She was a born saint if the Lord ever made one."

CHAPTER XI.

MRS. GAIR WRITES HOME.

Three years after, Mrs. Vorse sat reading a letter, one day. This was it.

DEAR SISTER PRUE: —

The golden russets and the butter came safely to hand. Thank father for them, with my love. I write my letter to you, because I have owed you one this long time; and because I have some things to say, a little particularly, to yourself. I could not match your silk, near enough; the old gros and granites are all gone out of existence; but I have taken the liberty to manage for you according to my own judgment, and have used the money you sent towards a full dress pattern of new, plain silk. What was wanting, I made up; and wish you would accept it as a little present from me. Joanna is well, but I don't think she is altogether contented. I am afraid I shan't make out to keep her much longer. What under the sun, I wonder, can make a girl like her want to stay, year in and year out, in a place like Hilbury? She 'll go back, anyway, in February. That she 's determined on, and when she has once made up her mind to a thing, she 's as "set as a meeting-house." To tell the truth, the meeting-house seems to be at the bottom of it; she thinks she never can be spared out of that singing-gallery. You have lost a good many of your leading singers, one way and another, within a few years, to be sure; Eliza Prouty being married, and Stacy Lawton, and Gabriel Hartshorne giving up that, as he has everything else, to take care of his father. Well, he has been faithful to *his* duty, if a son ever was. Joanna tells me—I get things out of her, by degrees, with questions, though she don't somehow run the news right off the reel as she used to; she 's sobered down wonderfully — that they come to meeting regularly together, and sit there in the old pew, and that the old man keeps close to Gabe, and sits half the time holding his hand, as if he could n't be near enough, or have enough of him; and that, communion days, Gabriel takes the bread from the plate, and gives it to his father, and holds the cup to his lips; and that one day, the old man broke the bit of bread in two, and gave half of it back to Gabe, just as a baby might put the spoon up to its mother, feeding it; and Gabe took it, and looked at it a minute, with a face as if the tears were coming, and then ate it; though he is n't a church-member. I got this out of her, by asking first one thing and then another about how they managed, and saying things myself, until she warmed up all at once, as if she could n't help it, and told me the story; and then she stopped herself in a sudden, provoked kind of way, and would n't say another word about anybody. She does hate so what she calls Hilbury gossip. Well, here I am, running on about Hilbury folks,— I always do when I get agoing,— and forgetting my particular business, I think, and so does Mr. Gair, that father might let Gershom come down here this spring and make us that visit. He was to have come, you know, three years ago, only Eben and Huldah went away, and you all thought he could n't be spared. I suppose he could n't; but some mothers would have worked it, somehow. I think, if anything, Prue, you 're a little *too* conscientious about making Gershom do all and more than father seems to expect of him. Father is getting old, now; and old folks are apt to be a little one-sided and unreasonable if you humor them in everything. And it is n't quite fair to the boy, in more ways than one. He ought to see something of the world, to begin with; and besides, folks *will* think, maybe, (I say it because I know as well what you really are, and how you would despise anything that was not *more* than above-board,) that you are keeping him hanging round, with some hopes about the property. I think, most likely, father would be willing to let him come now, when he gets through at Winthorpe Academy; and he will have a little time to spare between that and college; if you and father have quite settled that he is to go; which I would n't, unless the boy's own mind was bent upon it; it does more harm than good, otherwise. To tell the truth, though I know father makes everything of him, I don't know that it might not be just as well to let *him* see that you and Gershom don't take it entirely for granted that he is to provide for him. I should n't say as much, so plainly, to everybody; but I know you are so independent that you would never bear to seem anything else, and I should feel just the same in your place. You need n't show this letter, of course; or mention what I have said; you would not be likely to; and I hope you always tear up all my letters; it is never worth while to keep them, and if they are at all confidential, it is best not to leave them lying about for people to get hold of who are no way concerned. I don't mean to interfere; only we stand ready, Mr. Gair and I, to give Gershom any opportunities we can, and I want you to know it. And if he could come and stay here awhile this spring, it would be a kindness to us; for Say, you know, is lonesome, and she thinks everything of him, and he is always so much company for her; and, having no boy of our own, we naturally think a great deal of Gershom. In fact, as father said once, "he 's all the boy we 've got," and I think it will be who shall have the most of him. You can consider of this, and if you think well of it, you can tell father we have asked you to let him come, and we shall be glad to see him at any time that may be convenient. Perhaps father will come down after Joanna, and bring him along then.

I had some other things to say, but I have filled and crossed my sheet, and must let them wait till another time. Hoping to hear from you soon, I am

Your affectionate sister, JANE GAIR.

Mrs. Gair's letter, you see, was by no means a masterpiece. Mrs. Gair herself was not a masterpiece. Yet she managed to carry out her little selfishnesses, and do her little mischiefs, and set going, in a small way, what grew to be quite sufficient evils in the end. It does n't take a *great* scoundrel, or whatever is the feminine of that, — dictionary men have been too chivalrous to tell us, — to accomplish every separate bit of Satan's work that gets done in the world. Catherine de Medicis may be wanted for one job, but Jane Gair will very well answer for another.

There was an inconsistency, somehow, in the woman who could write just such a letter as that. The old home feeling, — for Mrs. Gair said truth when she declared that she could n't help "running on about Hilbury folks when she once got agoing," — the capacity for appreciating a nobleness in another, — the little heart-touch in her words as she recounted what Joanna had told her of the Hartshornes, — all this was strangely enough mixed up with a very mean purpose of her own. People seem, often, in a marvellous way, to set themselves in contrast with themselves, and not to perceive it. Many a man to-day cheers lustily the old flag that heroes bear back from battle, having yet no idea of periling a button for it, himself, that he can help; nay, calculating its chances and mischances selfishly, studying the bulletin as a price-current. The same style of human nature comes out identical under great variety and degree of test. Jane Gair could discern the greatness of Gabriel Hartshorne's devotion; she could even speak of it with a little flash of enthusiasm; yet turn deliberately to her own intent of winniug away the chief dependence and comfort of her own old father's declining years. Only, she thought she knew better than himself what was really best in the matter. That is, she told herself she thought so. One must go down very deep to find the true throbbing of the mainspring, when once motives and reasonings begin to double and twist themselves within us. The real thing she was going to do — the real thing she meant to do — was, in plain words, to unsettle Gershom's mind if she could, and lead him to disappoint her father's intentions concerning him; to incite his love of adventure and boyish independence of spirit to some act or manifestation that should overturn the Doctor's plans, and decide a different future for him; perhaps, even, alienate the two utterly. This was the secret, unworded thought; overlaid and represented by argument that "the boy ought to know his own mind, or he 'd only be a greater disappointment in the end; that if he really wanted to go to college, looking forward, after that, to driving a doctor's chaise round the old Hilbury roads, for the remainder of his life; she certainly would n't do anything to prevent it; but it was n't likely he 'd be contented with that, after he 'd got ready for it; and what was more, her father would n't find himself quite in such a hurry to give up and make way, when it came to the point as he might fancy now; old men never did; and it *would* come to the point, and he 'd have to do it in half a dozen years or so, or else, there 'd be Gershom, standing round, waiting and spoiling, till he should step out of his shoes and leave them to him. There never was anything more miserable than that."

"Why, it would be enough to fairly shorten his days, to let him settle down into the feeling that his work was almost done, and somebody else was getting ready to take hold. It would be better for both that Gershom should go his own way, if father 'd only think so."

"*And then, very likely, it would make some difference about that bit of paper she had seen signed and laid away, three years ago.*"

This subtle little thought was neither boldly looked at, nor confessed; yet there it lay, palpitating and alive; imprinted in a very fine soul-type underneath everything else that had written itself above; and was the text and prompting of it all.

A little letter had fallen from within the larger, as Mrs. Vorse had opened it. This was from Say.

DEAR OLD GERSHIE: —

I am so glad you are coming to see us in the spring. Mother says she has been asking you. You must stay a great while, because there will be ever so much to do. The Dido has been in, and I have been down to the wharf four times and gone on board. And then I came up through the market and bought things. The peaches and pears are all gone now, but there are nuts and funny little shiny cakes and candies. Last week the Dido sailed, and I went down with father and saw her go. The sailors sing such funny songs. You have n't seen the sea yet. It looks just the same. And they bring back oranges and pine apples and sometimes cocoanuts. The Pearl is coming by and by. It 's always nice when the Pearl comes in. She goes a good way off and only comes back once in a great while. I guess you 'll be here when she comes. Mother 's going to do up her letter. Good by.

Respectfully, your obedient servant, SARAH GAIR.

Say had inquired out, you see, the abbreviated formality at the close of a business note. It contrasted funnily with the spontaneousness of her beginning. This is how the fashions of the world will always sit upon some natures. Her mother smiled as she read it, said it was a very good little letter, and put it in.

Prue was neither imposed upon, nor confounded, as she read what Jane had written. Brought to the test of her clear, just sense of right, the composition suffered instant analysis into its true elements. She saw plainly enough what it was that her step-sister wanted. Not all, perhaps; Jane herself, you know, shut her eyes to the full extent of her own purpose. But she discerned that whether other people might or might not think what Jane had suggested, — she did n't believe it likely, or trouble herself at all about it, — that lady's own mind was evidently disturbed upon the subject; had fully possessed itself with the idea that Gershom's "hanging round home" was, of design or otherwise, likely to affect her own rights and interests. And here was where, by indirect effect, Jane actually succeeded in touching that independence of spirit which she sought to provoke. Prudence Vorse read the letter through, twice, from beginning to end; then she laid it down, and discussed clearly with herself its main points.

These. Gershom must be dealt fairly by; that argument had force. He must decide with his eyes open; she would not shut him out from seeing or knowing what might reasonably affect his wishes and plans; it would be good for him to go away beyond the Hilbury horizon, and get a broader look at the world. Also, to accomplish this for him, she knew, at this moment, no other way than to accept for him the hospitality of her step-sister. It might lead to the disappointment of her own wishes, and those of his grandfather, as Gershom had been taught to call the Doctor; yet this thing would be only fair to the boy; she saw that; and, being fair and just, to Prue's mind it was, of necessity, the thing to be done. To be done, however, with a perfectly open understanding. The Doctor must know all her reasons, and thoughts upon the matter; must see the possible result, as she saw it, before he gave consent to what he might not otherwise think of as more than a brief change and recreation. Jane's letter? There was no need to communicate more of that than its message and invitation. It was with a certain generous, high-minded contempt that she settled, in a half-glance of thought, that consideration. A weapon had been put into her hands by her adversary, if she had chosen to use it. A hint to the free-hearted old doctor of its insinuations would have made him indignantly resolute to take and keep his own way in the disposal of his own; and might have put a purpose in his head, for the boy's benefit, if it had never been there before. But Jane knew well with whom she had to deal. This very possibility kept Prue silent; and the confidence of words written with the simple request of privacy, and trusted to her, beyond recall of the hand that penned them, held her with all the sacredness of her own pledged word. No, she had no thought of betraying Jane; the less that she perceived so easily how Jane betrayed herself.

That night, she read out to the Doctor, after tea, those portions of the letter conveying Jane's thanks to him, her mention of Joanna, and her proposal in the boy's behalf. Then she took her scissors and cut the sheet into narrow strips, and twisted them into lamplighters. This was Prue's prompt and economical fashion of disposing of such things.

While she twisted, she talked.

"I've been thinking it over, and the way it looks to me, is this. You've done a good deal, already, for Gershom; and before you do anything more, it would only be fair to both of you, that he should have a chance to make up his mind so that there won't be any danger of his changing it afterwards. He's never been away from home very far; and I daresay 't would do him good. And, at any rate, we can't keep it from him that they've asked him again; I don't hold to hiding things that folks have a good right to know; and there is n't any doubt but what he 'll be fierce to go. And that's the thing I want to come to. I think it's more than likely myself, that when he gets down there among the ships and things, it'll be hard work getting him back again. There! — Now, if you don't want him to go, say so."

The Doctor looked over at Prue's honest face, and laughed. "You're a funny special pleader," said he.

"I never talk all on one side," answered Prue. "Not when I can see two sides to a thing."

"Let's look at the letter. Oh, you've turned it into lamplighters already, have you? Well, it don't make much difference. If the boy wants to go, Prue, and you want to have him, that settles it. If he gets *un*settled, I shall be sorry; but if two or three weeks down there can do the mischief, it's as good as done already, and we can't help it. He's old enough now, to be put to the trial. And that's the way it looks to me."

Two straightforward minds come quickly to understanding and conclusion.

Prue answered Jane's letter thus: —

Dear Jane —

Your letter and parcel were duly received. Please accept my thanks for your trouble. I send you fifteen dollars, out of which you will please pay yourself whatever is due for the dress. I could not think of taking it as a present, for I had the money by me to send for a new one if it was necessary; only I always try first whether I can make the old things over.

As to Gershom, I don't know of anything to prevent his coming to Selport this spring. Your father seems to think it right that he should; and he'll be sure to like the plan, and be much obliged to you and Reuben for inviting him. I wrote to him yesterday, and sent him Say's letter.

I don't feel at all worried about anything that folks can think of me. It's plain enough, on the face of it, that Gershom and I owe our time and help to your father if he wants them; and he's given us just what he promised he would in return; a good home, and clothing for both, and Gershom's schooling. It was a fair bargain, because it *was* a bargain, though a generous one on the Doctor's part, as his bargains always are. If ever he does anything more, it won't be because we've waited round for it, or expected it.

There isn't much news in Hilbury. Gordon King preached here last Sunday. He's altered a good deal since he was married. Stacy didn't come. She couldn't leave the two babies. They say she isn't very well contented at Winthorpe. It's a large parish, and there's a good deal expected of her. A woman ought to be as strong as Goliath and as patient as Job, to make a good minister's wife. And Stacy never was quite that, I guess.

Gordon is improved in his sermons, though. Somehow, there seems to be more reality to them.

You must excuse short letters. I don't pretend to be much of a hand at writing, and I don't have a great deal of time for it. Give my love to Joanna, and Say, and remember me kindly to Reuben.

Yours truly,

PRUDENCE VORSE.

CHAPTER XII.

THE PEARL.

SPRING had breathed over the city. The light and joy that was in the country, among the hills and fields, somehow crept hither, also. There was the smell of tender grass in the narrow door-yards; the very sidewalks, as they steamed under the sun that climbed the great firmament, daily, higher and higher, had an odor as of the prisoned earth beneath, stirred with the sweet, universal impulse of growth, and giving out sighs of gentle, yearning pain, through every crevice. Little children were gay, they knew not why. Birds sang, in their cages, with a feeling of the far forests that they never saw. Houses stood with open windows, and the freshness of light and cleanliness were bestowed, where, all winter long, had been dimness and chill, and gathering dust and soil. Ladies walked out, apparelled in delicate fabrics and colors. There was a shining in shop windows of all manner of light and lovely draperies. Churches on Sunday, were beautiful with a sort of human blossom-time. Faces were bright; hearts, even the saddest, felt some instinctive spring of elasticity. Earth lay in her perihelion to heaven.

And the Pearl had come in.

From far islands, away over on the other side of the great ocean, that she left in the scorching heats of their torrid summer, she had come sailing, over and up, from clime to clime, meeting the seasons as the great globe wheeled itself, and bent its northern brow toward the summer solstice. And there she lay at the pier-end, dingy and weatherbeaten, breathing out the strange atmosphere that had hung around her, all the long way; a mingling of tropical spiciness, odors of dried skins, with which she was largely laden, and the tarry flavor that had distilled itself through everything, while shrouds and seams were seething there under that equatorial sun, with a glorious fragrance of rich, foreign fruits triumphing over all. For there were plenty of oranges and pine-apples; and, lying in the half-deck, with spare blocks, and rope, and rolled-up sails, great piles of rough-barked, sweet-hearted cocoanuts.

And Gershom Vorse had come to the city, too, at last. A well-grown fellow of sixteen he was now; tall, sturdy, like a young pine; with a mountaineer's uplifting of the brow, and a light upon it as if it caught the shining of some far-off sun. Full of quick thought, and manly hope, — ready for life, — glancing keenly, out of eagle eyes, into the world around him, to see what offered to him there. A boy in his imaginations and his faiths; growing speedily to a man in will and purpose.

Say was very happy in showing him about. Most of all, in "taking him down to see the Pearl," and doing the honors there.

Captain Burley was heartily hospitable on board his brig. There were gentlemen in and out of his cabin, sometimes, on business. Mr. Gair was often on board, for some quiet consultation, secure from the interruptions of the counting-house. There was always a plate of great, red-golden oranges, such as only came in the Pearl, or in vessels that went just where she did, — pine-apples and sugar, — or a glass of wine, — ready, either or all, according to the taste of his visitors. There was always somebody who would crack a cocoanut for Say, delivering up to her the fragments of the wonderful brown globe, with their lining of pure rich, delicious meat, and the thin luscious milk, saved for her in the glass she would get out of the captain's pantry.

The vessel lay, as I said, at the pier-end; there was a clear outlook from stem or stern. Say used to delight in lying curled up on the cushioned transom, in the little cabin, and looking through the open stern windows, down over the bright waters of the harbor, away off, into the broad, open bay. Overhead, the stevedore and his gang might tramp and shout; out on the wharf, might be all the bustle and noise and crowding of men, and teams, and merchandise, lading and unlading; but down here it was safe and quiet, and opened forth upon endless expanse and freedom and coolness. Gershom would leave her, established so with her oranges and cocoanuts, and go himself all over the vessel, searching out its hidden places, questioning, observing, studying; feeling a strange sort of reverence for the very ropes and timbers that had come, through sudden nights, and burning days, — in gales, and calms, and beautiful breezy weather, over half of the face of the round world. He would climb, as he had promised long ago to Say, up the rigging, and sit in the main-top, and look away where the blue water touched the sky-line; and think what it would be for him to go sailing down there, over the mysterious verge, to find the far-off countries and islands of the earth, — he, who had hitherto seen only Hilbury rocks, and traversed woods and pastures and mountain roads in a small circuit of a dozen miles.

Just over here roared the busy, growing, striving city; but that he hardly cared for in comparison; off yonder rolled and heaved the waters down the mighty planet-side, and his whole soul went out after his eyes, in his resistless longing to go and see the world.

They spent whole afternoons here; walking up at sunset through the quieting streets at last with Mr. Gair; whose mind, intent upon invoices and price-currents, caught no thrill of all that stirred so restlessly the heart and brain of the stripling by his side.

So things wrought on together, just as one at least among those interested in results had partially foreseen and tacitly intended.

Years ago, Jane Gair had laid a few little kindling sticks together, towards the building of a fire. Other and larger ones had laid themselves as it were since, or had been flung on by circumstance and opportunity. There was a pretty pile ready now, and a match was touched. When she saw little threads of smoke begin to creep up among them, she set herself judiciously to blow. There are two ways of using one's breath upon a flame. It depends on whether one wishes to blow it up or blow it out. Either may be done perhaps at first, and a heedless bystander might not discern at first which was intended. Mrs. Reuben Gair did not blow upon Gershom Vorse's kindling fancy as if she meant to blow it out. One real, cold, vigorous puff, at the right instant, might have been effectual. She blew; but gently. It was a mild show of remonstrance and caution, against which the flame curled only stronger into life. Presently, it would gain such headway that she might labor against it as heartily and directly as she pleased, yet the blaze would only grow and mount more mightily. Then nobody looking on could blame her, surely. Then she might say to her own conscience, even, — "It 's none of my doing. I have persuaded; I have opposed; the boy will have his own way."

"I don't know, Gershom," she said to him one evening, coming to him in the front window, after tea was over, — "about all this going to the wharf. I am afraid the Pearl has a little bewitched you."

"What if she had, Aunt Jane?"

"Oh, I don't know. It won't do to get *too* much taken up. It is n't what you 've got to do with, you know."

"I have n't found out what I have got to do with, yet. I 've just come down out of the hills. I 've only had books to tell me what 's in the world; I 've got out to an edge here, where I can look off. I think that 's it, — more than the Pearl."

"There 's a good deal to see here, without looking off."

"Yes; people walking up and down the streets, between their stores and houses, just as if there was n't anything beyond. I don't see how they can do it. I don't see how anybody can get as far as this, and not want to go farther."

"You'd better put those notions out of your head. They won't answer. Things are pretty much settled for you, already, I guess."

There came a cloud over the boy's face. This touched where human nature — young human nature, at least — inevitably rebels.

"Things get *un*settled sometimes," he said, half under his breath.

"I'm rather sorry," said Aunt Jane, "that you 've been kept quite so long at home. I always thought it would have been better to give you a chance to look about you sooner. It 's like coming suddenly out of the dark. You 're dazzled, at first. But it 's only the novelty. You 'll get over it."

"There 's more novelty out there, somewhere. And I never heard of anybody who wanted to go back into the dark."

Gershom's thoughts defined themselves, as they were drawn out in argument. His words declared as much to himself that he had hardly looked at before, as to his listener. More, perhaps.

"T—t—t!" Mrs. Gair's tongue made a little, untranslatable deprecating sound against the roof of her mouth. "That depends, some, upon what there is to go back for. People must think what is for their interest. What could you do, off in the world, alone?"

Pride and independence — yes, even honor, — got a prick in this little sentence. The boy was amazed, within himself, at the sudden start and growth, almost into determination, of his secret, settled wishes.

"I might find out what, perhaps. Others have. And I don't mean to be a good boy just for what I can get. I shan't be a baby, all my life, to sit in peoples' laps, and be fed."

"Why, Gershie, you 're spunky! as Eben used to say;" exclaimed Aunt Jane, and laughed.

But there were sudden tears in the boy's eyes, after the fire. The thought came to him, how he *had* been fed, and taught; and what he owed; and how he was held. A generous throb of gratitude and affection struggled with the strange, impetuous impulse just born into conscious life. Together, they burst forth in a short, quick, single sob. He put his elbow up, upon the window-ledge, and, turning his face half away, leaned his chin upon his hand, and looked, vacantly, through a great glistening, out into the street.

"Why, Gershie!" began Aunt Jane, again. "You quite worry me. I 'd no idea the mischief had gone so far. Or that there was any real mischief at all. I shall have to write home about you, if you feel like this."

"No," said Gershom, turning back suddenly, and rising to his feet. "Don't do that. When there 's anything to write about, I 'll write myself. Or go." And with that, he put his hands into his pockets, and walked off into the back parlor, where Say was spreading out her "Mansion of Happiness;" and offered to play with her. Presently, they were both busy with teetotum and counters, as if nothing else were in heart or head of either.

A little door, opened for an instant by an unexpected word, had swung to again upon the secret place in a human heart, whence motive power was fed, and a steam of purpose generated that should become the propelling force of a human life. But Aunt Jane had glanced in, and seen that the fire was burning, — well.

The next evening, Captain Burley came to tea. With an unusual blandness, Aunt Jane had herself proposed the invitation. "We ought to have him here," she said. "He 's been very kind to the children. It seems to me they have half lived on board the Pearl, since she came in." Mrs. Gair was ordinarily rather shy of proffering or even assenting to this sort of hospitality, to "business people." Captain Burley picked his teeth, put his feet on the fender, tilted back his chair, and spat in the grate. What if Mrs. Topliff and her husband should happen to come in, in a social way, as she had asked them to do? To be sure they never *had* happened in, since the Pearl went away before; but the possibility was always hanging over her head.

Mr. Gair very willingly conveyed the invitation which he had somewhat timidly delayed suggesting.

Captain Burley talked well. I do not mean elegantly, or eloquently; except so far as eloquence is understood as comprehending the power with which even an ordinary fashion of speech may convey from a mind fully possessed with its topic, its aspects and interests to the minds of others.

Captain Burley was a thorough sailor. He was a great, full-souled, generous man, too. It seemed as if he held the sea in his heart, and all his emotions became like the pulsing of mighty tides. This nature that was in him, flowing out into his common conversation, made it strong and salt; sparkling, too, when any little touch of sunshine played upon it. Gershom sat by, listening; something responsive waking up, within himself, to all he heard.

"I 'm sorry," said Mr. Gair, "that we could n't have kept Oakman for you, this trip."

"Can't be as sorry as I am," said the Captain. "The brig won't know how to behave herself, without him. He 's the smartest fellow that ever trod a deck and was n't master of it. Can't blame him though. If I'd an old mother out West, that I had n't clapped eyes on for three years' voyagin', I guess I 'd shake off salt water, and lay my course overland, too!"

"He 'll get that new barque of Kentley's when he comes back. They 've been after him."

"Likely he will. And he ought to. That, or something else as good. But that ain't what he 's workin' sail for. Pity you 've promised the new brig to Dixon. He 'd have been the man for her. It 's as good as a double insurance, to put him on a quarter deck. Saved the whole voyage, to say nothing of my life, that last time but one. We 'd have been hauled up there in Charles'on harbor, cargo all tumbled out, and crew off, in the middle of the yellow fever, if 't had n't been for him. And I don't know another man that could have helped it. I tell you, — he 's a kind of Tarpaulin Bonaparte!"

"You tell that story yet, don't you, Captain?" said Mr. Gair laughing. "Well, it 's a good one."

"Ask him to tell it now," whispered Gershom eagerly to Aunt Jane.

Mrs. Gair turned from the boy's kindling face to the sea-browned visage of the skipper, that was lighting all over also with the pleased recollection of difficulty met, man-fashion, and peril passed safely through. It would evidently be no less pleasure to tell than to listen.

"May n't we hear about it, Captain Burley?" she asked.

"Certainly, ma'am. 'Tis n't a long story. Now — to tell — I mean. We thought 't was a tolerable long story in the time of it. Or *he did*, at any rate. He did n't let me know it all, as it went on. You see," continued the Captain, bringing his chair down quietly to its four feet, as cognizant again of ladies' presence, and releasing his thumbs from the corners of his trowsers' pockets where they had hitched themselves, to place his hands upon his wide-spread knees, and lean a little forward toward his questioner, as he spoke, — "we was coming up from Rio. Cargo of coffee and sugar. Some hides. Been out thirty days; bothered about with calms and head winds on the line and all the way up, till we took the northeast trades; worked along up with them till we got just to the north'ard of St. Thomas.

"I was down below, sick, in my berth; got awfully knocked up, somehow; had n't been well all the way from Rio, nor before we sailed. Oakman had the handling of the brig. All at once — sprung a leak. Made two feet and a half of water before we knew what we were about. Could n't tell where it came in. Mistrusted some foul play on the part of the crew; had some troublesome fellows aboard. Well; we set the men at the pumps; had to keep 'em going night and day. Pretty soon they began to grumble; thought we ought to put in. Talked about making the Hole in the Wall, and getting in to Nassau. Nice place that would have been! Wreckers, and pirates, and general average, and hides all eaten up with worms! At last the third day in the afternoon, a gang of 'em came aft, to Oakman. 'What's the Captain going to do with us?' That was what they wanted to know. Wanted it pretty much in what you might call the imperative mood, too. 'Ain't he going to put in?' 'Can't say,' says Oakman, with a cigar in his mouth. 'Will if he must, I suppose; have n't asked him, though, and don't mean to, as long as I can help it.' 'Well, Mr. Oakman,' says the foremost fellow, 'if we don't see Providence Channel in a day or so, — we know we're somewhere off there, — we shall have more to say about it. We hain't had less 'n a foot 'n a half o' water since we've been at the pumps. Men have got some sort of a right to speak for their lives; be,' — well, so-and-so'd considerably, — 'if they hain't!' That was n't the only place where he put in the trimmins, neither. Well; Oakman just stood, and looked at 'em; straight, without winkin'.

"'See here, my men,' said he, 'd'ye think you're going to gain anything by this? The brig's in my hands, subject to the Captain's approval, as long as he's able to give me an order; and when he ain't, — whether or no. And as far as I'm concerned, I'm going to take good care of her, and all that's in her; lives, and cargo, and all. Best I can. My own life's aboard, too. Maybe you did n't think of that. You go for'ard again, and obey orders. If we find ourselves off 'Hole in the Wall,' ('t was n't likely, for we'd crossed the tropic, and the wind had come out from the sou'west, fair and strong; and we was in longitude seventy then, if we was an inch;) 'and the pumps don't tell a better story, I'll advise him to put in. And *if that leak is found*, — or *stopped*, — every man Jack of you gets extra grog as long as we're out, and a Spanish doubloon, atop of his wages, when we get into port!'

"There was always a kind of a look in that blue eye of his, that the men could n't stand against. 'Twas n't savage, neither. What with that, and the notion of the grog and the gold, they pulled forelocks, and took themselves for'ard, half pacified; and that lasted till we got up into latitude thirty degrees, just under the Bermudas. Then they began to look grumpy again. 'We 've run a good while before this sou'-west wind, Mr. Oakman,' says Kneeland, the second mate, coming aft. He was as bad as any of 'em. 'Why did n't you get in at Nassau?' 'You 've just said why,' says Oakman. 'Been running before a sou'-west wind. You did n't suppose I should try to make New Providence with a breeze like this in my teeth?' 'Guess we 'll have to see about something soon,' says Kneeland, 'or the men won't stand it. Them — so-and-so'd — 'pumps is working the hearts out of 'em.' 'Leak as bad as ever?' 'Don't s'pose' you need telling, sir; you know 't is.' 'Sorry for it,' says Oakman,' coolly, 'on account of the doubloons. Don't gain any, does it?' 'No, sir; nor the pumps don't gain on *it*; and if the men give out, there we go, to Davy's locker, sure as ——,' mentioning a place that some folks seem to be mighty sure of, and other folks ain't so certain about. 'They won't give out,' says Oakman, again. 'We 'll bear away for Charles'on; and if matters don't mend, we 'll put in there. Double their grog. — Eight bells. Call the watch!' Well, *there was so much west in the wind*, you see, that we could n't make Charles'on. Kept along up the coast, and came off Hatteras. Began to talk about Norfolk. Passed off there, — a good way off, — in the night. Good, stiffish weather; fair wind. If this holds,' says Oakman, 'we 'll be into New York by day after to-morrow. He 'd kept well out into the Gulf Stream, and we was then in longitude only a little west of seventy; and, by George, sir! while those fellows were keeping their eyes peeled for New York, we made Cape Cod!"

Captain Burley turned round, as he came to this climax of his story, warmed up by the recollection, to an apparent entire forgetfulness that he had ever told it before, or that Mr. Gair knew anything about it; slapping his right hand down upon his knee, with a jolly emphasis, and his ruddy brown face all aglow with delight. And Mr. Gair laughed back again, as heartily as if the Pearl had but yesterday finished her hazardous passage, and he were learning for the first time the clever daring that had opposed itself to threats of elements and mutinous men, and in the end made such a capital joke out of it all, for fireside rehearsal.

"Yes," resumed the Captain, presently; "it 's a good thing to tell; and it was a grand thing to do; and folks on shore can't take in the whole beauty of it, neither. I guess nobody but Oakman himself, and the Lord Almighty, ever knew what he went through, mind and body, to get that brig in, and save the property. I don't believe he had an hour's sleep, together, between the Bahamas and

Cape Cod Light. And he had n't a dollar's interest, neither, beyond his wages. It was just, as you might say, his own life against owners and underwriters, that he had to consider. And he stuck to his duty. I don't know how it appears to other folks, sir, but it don't seem to me that God looks down out of heaven on any braver or better thing, than a man standing on the deck of his vessel, out of sight and knowledge of every human being but the few he 's responsible over, in mortal peril between sea and sky, and doing the best he can, boldly, to the last, for what 's been trusted to him by men a thousand miles off, asleep, comfortably, maybe, in their beds. It 's easy to talk about; but doing as you 'd be done by is one kind of a thing ashore, and a *tre*mengious different kind of a thing, very often, I can tell you, out at sea!"

"Did the sailors get their doubloons?" asked little Say, after a pause. "I think they ought to, when they worked so hard. And I don't wonder they got frightened."

"That 's the strangest part of the whole thing. We 'd no sooner made Cape Cod Light, than all of a sudden, just as unaccountable as it had started, that leak stopped. Pumps sucked. Everything tight and dry. Might have turned round and gone back to Rio, if there 'd been anything to go back for. Of course, it looked more 'n ever as if the men themselves had had a hand in it; and when they found 't was no use, and they could n't put in much short of home, they gave it up, and saved their trouble and their doubloons. Well, they got 'em, — yes; your father's a man that keeps his promises, even when other folks has to make 'em for him; and now, see what turned up. When we got that vessel up on the ways, there it all was, plain as preaching; pretty good preaching, too, I think. There was the starboard garboard seam, close by the stern, had opened; long enough, you 'd say, to sink a seventy-four; and laid right into it, as neat as any caulking, was a fish. Long, narrow fellow, almost like an eel; sucking-fish, they call' em; made a-purpose, and a complete fit. Got hold with his big, round mouth, just for'ard of the leak, exactly where the water drawing in, took his body neatly along into the seam; and there it was. Thing done. Folks *talk* about Providence, but I *saw* it then, if I never did afore. That night, came on the first storm we 'd had from Cape St. Roque; and a regular peeler. Had to keep well off the coast, and beat about for a couple of days, before we could treat ourselves to a sight of land agaiu. If it had n't 'a been for that fish coming along just in the nick of time, like Jonah's whale, *we 'd* all have been swallowed up, fast enough: never could have weathered it an hour. I 've had queer things happen to me in my life; but, take it altogether, I don't think I ever experienced anything queerer than that passage from Rio."

"I'm so glad the poor sailors got their money, and it was all found out that they did n't make the leak," said Say, slipping her hand into her father's, and nestling closer to his side upon the sofa. "Would n't you like to see such a man as that Mr. Oakman, Gershie?"

"I'd like to *be* such a man," said Gershom, all afire, and speaking out, forgetting his boy's reserve.

"I could tell you more than that about him. People have chances for bravery, if it's in 'em, out at sea. It was only two or three years ago that he saved a whole ship-load of German emigrants. He was second mate of the Grampus, then, bound home to New York. Just this side of the Grand Banks, they fell in with a vessel in distress; dismasted, and sinking. Emigrant ship Adelheid, from Hamburg. Hundred and seventy poor souls on board, screaming and praying in Dutch. High sea running; could n't get a boat alongside. Bore up to windward as near the wreck as they could, and sent out boats and a hawser. Oakman was the first to be off, and carried the rope. Got as near alongside as he could and flung it aboard. There they made it fast, and rigged a running bowline. When the poor, scared devils found out that this was all that could be done for them, and they'd got to swing for their lives in that fashion, they all hung back and screamed and prayed in harder Dutch than ever. The Captain told the men to do as they liked; he should stay by the ship till the passengers were safe. His three officers stood by him; noble fellows, all of 'em. I tell you, 't was a ticklish time. Late in the afternoon, — the vessel settling slow and sure towards the water's edge, — the Grampus standing off to windward, and drifting away from her all the time, — and those poor creatures, mostly women and children, huddled together on the doomed deck, trembling and crying; feeling safer, poor fools, to keep the planks under them, than to trust themselves to a bowline-hitch over the raging water. The Captain and officers coaxed 'em, — stormed at 'em. No use. Nobody would go first. Then up came Oakman, over the ship's side, by the hawser, and sprung, dripping, on to the deck. Never said a word. Shook himself, and looked round. Nearest to him was a woman with two children, all on their knees. Youngest about six years old. Oakman grabbed him, screaming, made him fast with the bowline, and swung him down, safely, into the boat. Then the men began to cheer. 'Don't be frightened,' says Oakman, in a bright hearty way, that they understood, if they did n't his words, and picking up the other child; 'we 'll save you all.' Mother hollered Dutch at him, but he did n't stop to listen. Did n't know a word she said, and did n't want to. When the second child had been passed down, she stopped hollering, and made up her mind to go too. And that started all the rest. After that, it was which should go first. One after another, the boats were filled, and pulled away for the Grampus. Back they came, and filled again. A longer pull, each time, to and fro; the Grampus drifting, drifting, all the while, and the night darkening down. When the last boat was loaded, with every soul that she could safely carry, there stood the Hamburg Captain and his three officers, pale, and stern, and brave, refusing, every man of 'em, to set foot into a boat until the rest were safe. So they pulled away again, and left 'em. Wind and sea were higher than ever, and the Grampus farther off. Drifting, every moment, away; and the cloudy twilight coming on. 'Where 's the Captain of the ship?' shouted out the master of the Grampus, as that last boat came towards her with its load. 'Stayed by, sir!' was the answer. 'He and the three mates. We were all full.' 'My God!' cries the Captain, with a look at the scudding clouds, and the waves with their white caps on. 'I can't leave those fellows behind! Who 'll pull for the wreck again?' 'I'll go, sir,' says Oakman. And then, for half a minute, nobody else offered. It was a chance if they ever stood on that deck again, if they left it now. Oakman waited that half minute, and then, looking round at the men, — I can see how the blue fire would be lighting in his eyes, — 'which of you goes with me, boys? Don't all speak at once!' says he. So, out of bravery or shame, four of 'em stepped forward then, and went down with him over the ship's side. I suppose that Hamburg Captain and his mates had said their prayers, and taken their leave of this world, when that boat came climbing up, over a great, green wave, toward the wreck again. 'Here we are!' sung out Oakman. The four men on the wreck gave the beginning of a shout together, and stopped, as it were, in the midst. They said afterwards, it was to look round at each other, and grasp hands, with great, choking sobs. Two minutes more, and they were in the boat, pulling, for their lives, up and down those awful sea-ridges, towards where they hoped to find the Grampus. And from the peak of one, as it lifted them, they saw the Adelheid make a great swirl, and go down."

"Did they get back safe to the Grampus?" asked Say, breathless, when the Captain paused.

"To be sure!" he replied, lightly. "Has n't Oakman just come home with me, in the Pearl?"

"Oh, *wouldn't* you like to be such a man, Gershie?" cried Say.

Gershom sat still, and made no answer, now. In his heart, he said to himself, that, if he lived, he *meant* to be such a man.

After this story, Mr. Gair and the Captain got to talking about Hamburg, and Elsinore, and Copenhagen, and St. Petersburg, and the Russia trade, till Say curled herself up on the end of the sofa, and went to sleep; soothed by a confused, dreamy repetition of hemp, and duck, and bolt-rope, and pig-iron, and duties, and consignments, and bills of exchange, and Steiglitz and Co.; and Gershom sat, half listening, going over again, all the while, in imagination, the scenes on board the disabled Pearl, and the foundering Adelheid; till, by and by, at ten o'clock, the Captain departed, and the boy, as well as Say, went off to bed; not to sleep; to lie awake till after the slow, deep voices of the city bells had clanged out, one to another, from different points, the strokes of twelve; as a thought, wrought slowly toward the birth, in different souls, announces itself at last, from opposite sides the earth, when the hour is ripe; thinking, feverishly, of all that he had heard; of the free, brave life that enticed him forth to make it his own; of the ties that held him to his home among the hills; of how he would write to his grandfather, and tell him, truly, all he felt; and of what he should say.

CHAPTER XIII.

PROVERBS.

"But I thought you were all fitted for college?" said Mr. Gair, with a fresh recollection and surprise. He had been considerably surprised this afternoon.

"Yes, sir," returned Gershom. "But grandfather always said, that fitted for college was fitted for anything. He never made me feel as if I had *got* to go."

"I don't want to be the means of your disappointing him, though," rejoined the merchant. "I should n't feel warranted in encouraging such a notion, unless I knew what he would say to it, first."

"No, sir. That's what I mean to find out. But I did n't want to trouble him at all, till I knew whether I could have a chance or not."

"What do you say to all this, Captain Burley?"

The two gentlemen sat in Mr. Gair's inner counting-room. The boy stood there, before them, cap in hand, his eyes glowing, his whole face eager with the intensity of the wish he had come there to make known.

"I should say," replied the hearty Captain, looking upon the lad with a certain approving recognition, "that he 'd got it."

"What?"

"Ship-fever. The sort that nothing but a voyage 'll work off. And not that, if he 's the stuff he looks to be," he added, in an under-tone, to Mrs. Gair.

"Could you find a berth for him aboard the Pearl?"

The young fellow's eyes glistened, and flashed quick at Captain Burley from under their thick lashes. His fingers crushed nervously upon his cap-rim. Captain Burley saw it, although he seemed to be looking out of the window.

"There 's a berth for him *somewhere* I guess. Always a place in this world for everything that 's made, and he 's made for a sailor, if I know the signs. Write to your grandfather, young man; and when you get your answer, come down aboard the Pearl, and let me know.'

"Thank you, sir." With a great gulp back of his heart into its place, that had seemed to spring into his throat with the sudden throb of joy. "Uncle Reuben!"

"Well?"

"I think, if you please, we might as well not say any more about this till we hear from Hilbury. I don't think I could bear being disappointed of it, if it were much talked over."

"There 's where you 're right, boy. We 'll say no more till Saturday. Write to-day, and you 'll get your answer by then. The Pearl won't sail for a week, at least. An hour's notice will be long enough to get your outfit."

Mr. Gair turned round to his desk and his papers. Gershom went out, and down stairs. Up the wharf, to where the Pearl lay. He sprang over the gang-plank, and on board. Getting in cargo. All bustle, and apparent confusion. He went forward, and leaned against the bulwark, looking over the bow. He laid his hand lovingly on the solid timbers, as if the vessel were a living thing, to be caressed and delighted in with a tenderness. He looked down into the forecastle. That was to be his home. Here he should have bold, brave fellows for companions; here he should listen to stories of daring and danger, and the wild, strange happenings of sea-life, and the wonders of far-off lands. Here he should grow strong and hardy for great deeds of his own. It was all a poem and a romance. He never thought of brutal captains, or of coarse, degraded men; of mean tyrannies, or low contaminations; of all he might meet, all he must meet, in an apprenticeship of years to this profession that he would choose. He was to look up to men like Burley and Oakman; he was to stand, by and by, in places like theirs. The Captain's words were ringing in his ears; "God looks down out of heaven on no braver nor better thing!"

He stood there, with the firm, even deck under his feet, and longed to feel it bounding away upon the free ocean that he knew only in fancy. To be out there, "between sea and sky," even if it were "in mortal peril!

Captain Burley had said right. It was a fever that was upon him. The fever that a boy must have, — if the boy be but the possibility of a man, — when the fire within him kindles, whatever it may be that sets it alight. Books, or tools, or soldiering, or seafaring, — it is all the same; the force that is in him wakes, and grasps at something; and the soul that is in him lifts that something up, and idealizes it into a divineness of life, and wreathes it with a glory. Most of all, perhaps, when, from a quiet country life like Gershom's back among the hills, — where he has dreamed of the great waters, and the ships that go up and down thereon, — he comes first to behold the infinite glitter of the sea, and his eyes are smitten with its far-off gleam, and the tingle of its brine is in his nostrils, till he chafes to be off and away upon it, and any dry-land life grows tame compared with its boundless promise, its rousing demand upon all his flushing manhood.

There is no possession like the possession of the boy who craves to be a sailor.

Gershom could not have gone straight out from that counting room and gone up those stifled streets, properly, as if nothing had happened, and there were no need for him, any more than for all the rest of the lubberly people, to throw up his cap with a shout, when words were thrilling in his ears that offered a fulfilment of this hope of his that had slumbered within him, growing stronger in its sleep, for years. He must needs have stood first, for those few moments, on the deck of the Pearl once more.

Then he walked up through the town to Hill Street, quietly enough to outward show, but with a bound in his veins that made the bricked sidewalk seem to spring beneath his feet; his young brain busy with all manner of eager thoughts.

"Gershie's got his door locked!" cried Say, in an ill-used voice an hour or two after. "And when I called to him, he told me to run away. And I have n't got anything to do; and I wanted him to play Happiness with me; and it'll be tea-time presently."

Mrs. Gair's face took on a cloudy expression. "He's mighty independent, I think," said she, more to herself than to the child, "considering all things."

"He would n't take me down to the wharf, this afternoon. And he's been shut up in his room, ever since he got home."

Mrs. Gair's face grew suddenly placid. Her tone smoothed itself, also; and it was a very sweet and timely admonition to unselfishness that she was all at once inspired to give her little daughter.

"Well, never mind, Say. He'll come presently. I suppose he wants to be by himself, sometimes. You must n't be exacting. It is very wrong and disagreeable for little girls to expect older people to attend to them all the time."

Say seldom persisted in the wrong and disagreeable. She had been very patient, already; and appealed only when her small endurance had been tried nearly too far. She sat down to Happiness alone; such happiness as she could make out of it so. That was the child's nature. Ah, the prophecies that are in these dawning traits of temperament and capacity! Can the child bear quietly — console itself easily — wait long? There is never a power without a demand for it. It needs no reading of a horoscope, no palmister's divining, to tell something of the life-lines of such. Is there busy activity — skill — contrivance? An aptitude to make much out of a little? Be sure that when the germs of these were hidden in the baby-brain, there was no "silver spoon" laid ready for the lips.

Mrs. Gair got up presently, and left the room. When she reentered five minutes afterward, her face was even more beautifully serene than before. She told her parlor-maid, who came to lay the table in the inner room, that tea need not be hurried; Mr. Gair had not come in; in fact, she was busy herself, and should not object to its being half an hour later than usual. A little momentary pause, that she had made, upstairs, before a closed door, might or might not have had to do with this. I should not like to say she stooped, as well as paused, there, for an instant. People do stoop, sometimes, however, — when there is something they have special occasion to pick up.

Gershom Vorse was busy writing his letter to the Doctor. By and by, his step came down the stairs. A little softly, I must own; for Gershom had his own business to manage, now; and he had learned that in Mrs. Jane Gair's house business must often be managed softly. Mrs. Jane heard him, however; saying nothing; but making a sudden noise with pulling the heavy table a little nearer to herself, instead of moving her easily-rolling chair towards the table. Gershom got by the parlor door, and out into the street, without recall or hindrance. At the risk of being late to tea, and getting a glum look from Aunt Jane, he must post his letter, himself, to-night. Aunt Jane knew that, perhaps, as well as he did. But tea was a little late, as we have seen it was meant to be; and Mr. Gair was still chatting with Say upon his knee, when Gershom came in; his face flushed and his hair damp, with all the exercise he had taken, and the excitement he had had, that warm, summer-like, May afternoon.

"Well, Gershom," said Mr. Gair, as he cut off two or three of the curling spires from the form of fresh butter, that was done up, in a way they had in Hilbury, like a golden pine-apple, by some mysterious dinting and shaving, — "have you attended to your affairs as you proposed?"

Mr. Gair was always flying kites, and catching the electric current; learning no wisdom by getting so much more of it, often, than he at all wanted. Gershom wondered at Uncle Reuben's way of keeping a secret; and felt, with a flash of dismay, that it was all out, now, hopelessly; and must be discussed, over and over, through and through. Aunt Jane was quick on the scent, and a thorough mouser; no small rodent could show nose or tail out of his hole, with any hope of whisking it back again in safety from her nimble claw. But somebody caught something, once, and let it go again; to grow. Aunt Jane was busy with the teapot, which, she told the maid, had grown cold; and bade her, with some displeasure, fetch *boiling* water. "I have told you so often, Winny, that Mr. Gair *must* have his tea hot." And when she turned round again, it was to admonish Say to sit straight, and tuck her napkin under her chin, and to keep her elbows off the table. Gershom only said "yes, sir;" and found, to his very great surprise and relief, that question and answer both passed unnoticed.

It was astonishing how Aunt Jane entered into the children's amusements that evening! She played Happiness with them; and then they had out the bagatelle board, which she usually opposed; the balls, she said, made her so nervous. But she rolled, herself, to-night; and people don't mind a noise when they help to make it. She kept them ingeniously busy; so that Say was confounded when the nine o'clock bell rang; and after the child had gone to bed, Mr. Gair being quite absorbed in his *Journal of Commerce*, Mrs. Gair took up the *Lady's Book*, and when she was reading, nobody ever talked. Gershom was rapt and happy in Ross's *Voyages*. For the most part, therefore, there was a pin-drop silence, until they separated for the night. Mrs. Gair was reading, apparently; and looking at Fashions; really, she was playing proverbs; "None so deaf as those who won't hear." And, "let well enough alone."

I have no doubt that if Mrs. Jane had been only half as determined to hear, as she was *not* to hear, the whole matter would have come out, up stairs, after all, in matrimonial retirement. But she was very tired, and not conversationally disposed.

It is sometimes so well to have known nothing.

CHAPTER XIV.

THE EXPECTANT SYSTEM.

Now, Mrs. Gair exploded. Now, Mrs. Gair was righteously indignant at this that had been done. Now, it was quite safe to use the utmost of her breath against the flame, and she blew accordingly.

"Well! I wash my hands of the whole thing. Nobody consulted me. Gershom has been very sly. He knew I disapproved his going so much to the wharf, and hanging about the Pearl. I saw what it was likely to come to. I told him, a week ago, that I must write to his grandfather about it, and that 's what I ought to have done. It 's a great shame for him to disappoint father so, after all his kindness; and I doubt if he finds it answer to his interest, in the end. But it's no use to talk. There is n't any help for it, now. They can't blame *me* at any rate."

"But perhaps it can be helped," returned Mr. Gair, quite overwhelmed by his wife's view of the subject, and the sudden sense it gave him of his own guilt. "Gershom would n't persist, if he thought it was such a serious matter with the old gentleman. Had n't you better speak to him again?"

"No, — I ve done. The fancy ought to have been kept out of his head, in the first place. Now it 's there, and father knows it, there 's nothing more to be said. He would n't send him to college against his inclinations; but what he hoped was, that he might incline to go. It's all up with, now; the milk 's spilt; and it 's no use making anybody uneasy. Only, don't let them blame me. *I*'ve been kept in the dark."

Mr. Gair began to feel quite miserable. As if he had been doing something mean and secret; working against his father-in-law's wish and will. As if he had done Gershom, too, a vital disservice. This splash, and sense of uncleanness, he got by standing by while his wife "washed her hands."

Do you suppose Mrs. Gair saw her own double-dealing in its

true light? I don't. It is only to the single eye that self stands illumined. In the body that is full of darkness, there are secret lurking-places below where vision reaches; and here lie motives that are never looked at; thoughts that are never set in words; involuntary springs that send out their odyllic force without the intervention of even mental muscle. I think she told herself with a certain real outside indignation, strangely coexisting with a more interior satisfaction, that she had been set aside, — unfairly treated. And she made the most, to herself, as well as to others, of her injury and her position. None the less an injury because of the great good luck she felt it, and the little intention she had had, all along, of being treated precisely so. This she never took into the account. She meant to do nothing unjustifiable; she had done nothing. She had seen how things were tending; very well, let them tend; now, they had resulted, and she stood absolved. If, as it turned out, it were all the better for her, what then? She might not be sorry to have Prue's great boy well out of the way; she might not be sorry if even his altered course in life should alter her father's intentions towards him; yet, all the same, he had put himself out of the way, of his own free will. He himself, had forfeited whatever he might lose. It was no doing of hers. If he sailed away, some day, and never came back, even, — there were many chances of this in a sea life, — the responsibility lay not at her door.

Jane Gair! You will not find yourself able, to the very end, to forward your intents thus passively. Practice upon the "expectant" theory will not suffice for all crises. There will come test hours, when the hand must be put forth, or stayed; when the seal of *deed* must be set to the secret motive. Satan will have nothing less than the sign-manual of his own, at the last.

There had come an answer from Hilbury. Kindly, free-hearted; indicating little of the pain that must have lain behind. "I am sure," said Mr. Gair, reading it over for the second time, after that unpleasant sense of complicity had been put upon him, "I don't see that the Doctor takes it so much to heart, after all."

"There is scope for nobleness in every profession," wrote the good old physician, in reply to Gershom's enthusiastic reasoning in behalf of his desire. "It takes a *whole man* to be really anything. And even physical bravery may come in play, as you would find, not seldom, in the pursuit of a vocation that must now and then set a man's thought for his own life and limb, to say nothing of comfort, against his care for lives and limbs of others. I have spent many a dark night among the hills, here, whose peril was not less, perhaps, than that of the sailor in the same dark night, at sea.

Alone, too; I and my old nag; God with us, as everywhere, — that was all. And there have been men of my calling in camps and hospitals, in times of war and pestilence, and will need to be, now and then, as long as the world lasts, as brave in the face of death and destruction as God ever let a great soul be.

"——— Yet, if your whole heart is bent on this, — go, boy; and God bless you! Come first, and say good-by, though, if you can."

This letter, with one also from his mother, Gershom got on Saturday evening, sent down by way of Winthorpe. On Sunday, the subject was first broached openly in the household in Hill Street. We have seen how it was met by Mrs. Gair. She washed her hands of the whole thing, and went to church. She was a zealous churchwoman, here in Selport, where Episcopalianism was the height of fashion; and sat, every Sunday, in a pew behind the Topliffs, in the handsomest sacred edifice in town. She prayed God, to-day, with all the people, to "defend and provide for the fatherless children and widows;" to deliver her from "evil and mischief," and "privy conspiracy;" and all the while, away down in that dark place of her heart, among its unexamined things, the thought was lying, pulsing out by snatches — never acknowledged or entire — like a phosphoric writing: "He has made his own bed, now, and must lie upon it. The thing works well." Then, the glimmer of a doubt, — "father is foolishly indulgent and patient with him, after all. What if it should n't make any particular difference?" Still, in the fine soul-type I have spoken of before; not looked upon deliberately, or read. Heart-evil does not denude itself in shameless monologue. It never sets itself off, objectively, even to its most secret consciousness. Mrs. Gair was making her responses in the Litany; and she made them all, even to the last; feeling no shudder of dread at her desert, when to the utterance, "Lord, deal not with us according to our sins," she answered, with the rest, "Neither reward us according to our iniquities."

"Do you think grandfather is very sorry about it?" asked Gershom, suddenly, when he and Aunt Jane were walking home together from afternoon service.

"If you had asked my advice before, Gershom, — which you did n't, —" (Mrs. Gair meant that this should be well kept in mind, — "I should have said he *would* be, very sorry; perhaps angry; but he seems to take it more contentedly than I could have supposed. He *wanted* you to be a doctor, and come after him; there's no doubt of that; and perhaps if you'd known exactly on which side your bread was buttered, you'd have made up your mind to; but children always manage to drop the buttered side down, and seem to like it all the better; and if, as he says, your whole heart is bent on this thing, instead, he 's glad that you should tell him, honestly. I dare say he 'll get reconciled. Especially, if you show him you can stick to your choice, now you 've made it."

"No danger but I 'll do that," said the boy.

"He knows, at any rate, there's nothing mean spirited in your motives," said Aunt Jane, encouragingly; "and I will say, — for it 's as well to look on the bright side when a thing is settled, — that it may appear better to the rest of the world, perhaps, than if you hung round, all your life, dependent on what he could do for you; being, you know, Gershie, no blood relation, after all."

Wherever the current sprang from that ran in the boy's veins, it tingled a little, swiftly and sharply, as Aunt Jane said this; and a sudden quickened perception startled him with a glimpse at the depth of her meaning. Nobody had ever reminded Gershom, in plain words, before, that he did not belong, by claim of nature, to them whose love and care he had received, and to whom he had returned the love, and such service as he could render, for all those years of his young life; and the reminder thrust him off, for the first time, from his unquestioning reliance. Truly, life and death are in the power of the tongue! It would have irked him sorely, now, after those few words, to go back to the old place again, and make his home there, if he had not already chosen otherwise. Something brought back to his mind, also, associated with these, those other words Aunt Jane had used, that evening when they talked together in the parlor window at twilight. "That depends on what there is to go back *for*. People must think what is for their *interest*." She could talk both ways, then? Or *did* her words tend two ways? They touched him with a like feeling; a feeling that became now, all at once, quite definite. She was so ready to "look at the bright side, now all was settled!" She had been apparently so displeased when the plan was first made known to her, that very morning! What did Aunt Jane mean? Did she approve or disapprove? Was she, as he used to say of her fine notions and manners, in his rude honest childhood, all a sham? He drew away, a little from her side towards the curbstone, as these thoughts ran through his mind; he drew away yet further, in spirit; as he had never drawn himself from human soul before. The first chill of intimate distrust had touched him, with a shiver. In this world there must be offences; but woe to that one by whom the offence first cometh!

It was a hard day's journey, then, from the city to Hilbury;

and the stage that "connected" with the trains to and from Selport ran up and down on alternate days; meeting the afternoon "down train" on Monday, and waiting for mail and passengers by Tuesday morning's "up." So Gershom was to report himself aboard the Pearl on Monday; sign his shipping articles, and go with his uncle to get his "protection," and his sea rig; and on Tuesday, make his hasty journey to say good-by, returning on Wednesday; since to put it off till Friday would be too late. The Pearl would probably sail on Thursday or on Friday morning at farthest. So the plan stood until at noon on Monday; when Mr. Gair and Gershom, returning together to the counting-room, from the Custom House, found Captain Burley waiting there.

"I think, sir," said he to Mr. Gair, "that we could clear to-morrow as well as not, and be off next morning, if this weather holds. We must look for a change at the new moon; and a day's start, with such a wind as this, might make a week's difference in the voyage.

"That's true," rejoined the merchant. "Can Peterson manage it?"

"He says so, if those last fifty bales get down in time."

"I'll see to that. Come in to-morrow at ten, and I'll have your papers ready. I guess we'll get her off. — But, hallo! here's this youngster. What are we going to do about you?"

"Time and tide wait for no man," said Captain Burley, good-humoredly. "Nor a good vessel, when she's ready for sea, with a fair wind. I suppose it must be 'go or stay' with him. Are you sailor enough to say 'go,' and write your good-bys? That is, if you must have anything to do with them. *I* never do. Just take my hat, and walk off; and they never know when it's the last time."

The child and the man struggled together with Gershom at that moment. He was boy enough to yearn for his mother's kiss before he went; he was too much a man to shrink from what he had voluntarily chosen. He was sailor enough, or it seemed so, then, to feel that he could not let the beautiful Pearl go down that blue horizon, leaving him behind.

"I suppose there would n't be much chance of her not sailing?" he asked.

"Not much, I guess, if Captain Burley has made up his mind."

"Then I say 'go,'" said Gershom, with steady tone and eye, and a tender curve of lip that in no way weakened, but rather drew a dash of emphasis below his word.

"You 're the sort. Come aboard at nine, on Wednesday," said the Captain.

On Tuesday, two letters crossed each other between Selport and Hilbury. Gershom had written to his mother on Monday evening, saying how it was, and that he must bid good-by so, or relinquish the voyage for which all his preparations were now made; saying this in a sturdy, matter-of-fact way on paper, while his hand went up from the very writing to brush away a tear his mother might not know of. Manly words, with a child's homesick tenderness at heart. He thanked his grandfather for his consent and help; and, after that word of Aunt Jane's, could not forbear adding that "now he was put in the way of fulfilling this great wish that he had had so long, he felt sure he need never again be any trouble or anxiety to them at home; he could make a place and an independence for himself in the world; which was what he ought to be able for, after all that had been done for him in the past." These words, of a proud gratitude, touched the good Doctor a little sorely.

Mrs. Vorse wrote a letter to her step-sister, on Monday, which she sent down to Winthorpe by a private hand. It came into Selport by Tuesday's evening mail, and Mr. Gair received it at the office, on his way home at nine o'clock, from a meeting upon a reference case. Gershom had gone up to bed when he came in and handed it to his wife.

"Anything special?" he asked, as Mrs. Gair glanced down the pages.

"O no," Jane replied. "Pretty much, I suppose, what she has written to Gershom himself. Motherly directions; she wants me to see to this and that for him which she can't be here to see to herself. Nothing, I believe, but what has been done."

"I suppose they 've been looking for him, to-night; it 'll be considerable of a disappointment."

"Ye——s," said Mrs. Gair, absently. Her eye had fallen upon this little postscript to the letter.

"Of course we shall expect him up to-morrow. If it was n't for that, I don't think we could have consented at all. Tell him this. I *must* see him again; and his grandfather will take it almost harder than I, not to say good-by to him. Don't let him, on any account, be prevented from coming, if he has not left for home before this reaches you. To tell you the truth, Jane, though there is no need for any special worry, I don't think the Doctor seems quite so smart as common this spring. I can see he 's a good deal down-hearted about letting Gershom go, though he makes no opposition; and I can't help being afraid it may wear upon him."

Mrs. Gair put the letter in her pocket. She went round, presently, setting back the chairs, and looking to the window fastenings, for the night. Fastening something else, also, back in her own knowledge, for the over-night, at least.

Should she tell Gershom, in the morning, of this that his mother had written? She would not decide within herself that she should not; she would consider. Neither would she show the whole letter to her husband, and ask him what ought to be done. Ah, that might decide it too precipitately! So she went to bed, first laying the letter in a little side drawer of her bureau, among others that had come from home.

With the dark hours, came thoughts and misgiving. She hardly dared withhold this word from the boy. She wished Prue had not written so foolishly, throwing such responsibility upon her. She had been so resolved to *do* nothing in this matter, which had ripened itself so beautifully to her wishes. The "expectant" system had hitherto worked so well!

In the morning, she was braver. Her judgment was cool, and asserted itself. She knew best, being here upon the spot, what was best to be done. Prue had written in ignorance of the actual circumstances. There had been no idea that the vessel was to sail so soon. She had got Gershom's letter, by this time, bidding good-by, and explaining it all. The thing had been settled; how absurd it would be to unsettle it all, again! The boy would be good for nothing, if he were balked of this voyage, and sent home now. And, of course, it would be only cruel to give him a discomfort to go away with!

She knew very well, in her secret heart, that if Gershom Vorse had read those words, even at the last moment, he would *not* have gone away. Bitter as it might have been, he would have waited.

"It's very hard," said Aunt Jane to herself, as she went down stairs to the breakfast, that was to be somewhat earlier than usual. Gershom's sea-chest stood inside the front door. A carriage was to come at half past eight. "It's very hard," thought the lady, "to be placed in such a position. I daresay, whatever I do, they'll blame me. But I can only act as I think is for the best, under the circumstances. And then, my conscience will be clear."

She thought it for the best to tell Gershom, as he rose from the table, — the poor fellow's appetite would have been quite spoiled, had she mentioned home news before, — that she had heard again from his mother, chiefly in reference to the little matters of arrangement and provision for the voyage, "which," she said, "have all been made, I believe, very much as she suggests. You left out those four new linen shirts, didn't you? Your mother speaks of that."

"Yes," Gershom said. "The new shirts were in the valise that was to go back to Hilbury." He stood still, an instant, as if waiting to hear if there were any more particular message; I think he hardly dared trust his voice to ask; but nothing more was said. And that was all he heard about his mother's letter.

I have no doubt Mrs. Jane Gair's conscience, after this wise and prudent action, in the hard position she found herself placed in, was quite clear. People have their moral idiosyncrasies, which must always be taken into account.

The Pearl sailed that day at twelve o'clock.

At the same hour, the stage from up-country was reeling down the hill into Baxter's Mills village, the horses coming in upon their customary gallop. Inside was an old gentleman, who had not been so far from home before in ten years. Going down, by the train, to Selport. No other than our simple-hearted, splendid-souled Hilbury doctor.

He would try for it. Vessels did n't always sail on the day fixed. There was fog in the hills this morning; and there might be — who could tell? southeast wind and a coming storm down there on the coast. Mahomet could n't come to the mountain; the mountain would reverse the proverb, and come down to Mahomet.

He had reasoned so with "the girls," at home, last night, when the letter had come that set them at first looking in each others' faces with a blank, utter disappointment. There was only a chance; and Prue had best not encounter the fatigue, for the hope of it. But the doctor would go. If it were only to see her cast-off from the wharf, and shout a good-by, as the brig dropped down the harbor, it would be something; or to go out from the Point, maybe, in a boat, and speak her below. Vessels lay off, all night, and for days, at anchor, often, in the fogs that come up at this season. So he packed his portmanteau before he went to bed, and one of the farm boys drove him down to the Bridge in the morning, to take the early stage.

And the cars rattled and crashed along their level, shining grade, as if they could overtake anything. The swift motion exhilarated the old Doctor, and gave him a charming childlike confidence.

"You came up on the train this morning?" says he to the conductor.

"Ticket!" says the conductor to an oblivious passenger opposite, with a little backward touch of the left hand while nodding a reply to the Doctor on the right.

"Which way was the wind, down there?" asks the old man, anxiously.

Conductors get used to all kinds of queer questions, and answer them usually, if answerable, with a mechanical politeness, not interesting themselves greatly to follow out or piece together the indicia they offer to human histories.

"Getting a touch of east, I believe. This weather won't hold long. — Ticket, sir?" and passed on. Dr. Gayworthy was quite certain, now, that he should see his boy.

The train came into the station at dusk. The wind was sharp east, sure enough, and the smell of the salt water came up into the streets. The Doctor caught a cab, or the cabman caught the Doctor, and he and his portmanteau were whirled up to Hill Street. Jane Gair and her husband were sitting down to tea in the back parlor. The bell rang, and somebody came straight in, without a question.

"Jane! Where 's the boy?"

"Father! You here? Why, — the Pearl sailed to-day at noon."

A look, as of ten years suddenly added, fell over the good Doctor's face. Its lines dropped from their eager hopefulness into a strange, weary, dreary relinquishment. He set down his portmanteau, which he had brought straight into the room with him, and turned round to look for a chair.

"I did n't think she would be sure to get off. — I 'm very tired," said he, slowly, first finding out his fatigue now, and speaking as with the voice of another man.

They gave him his tea and answered his few questions, all about the Pearl, and the boy, and when and where from they might first hope to hear of him, and pretty soon afterward he went up to bed. Into the same room where Gershom had slept last night; swept, and aired, and made up with fresh linen, since then; as rooms are, out of which people have died and been borne away.

And there the good, great-hearted old man lay; in the sleeplessness of age in a strange place, — with all his strange, sad, disappointed thoughts; and heard the city bells clang out to each other, hour after hour, as Gershom had heard them, that night when he could not sleep for thinking of all the brave, beautiful things that men had done in the world; and for the boy-longing to go forth also, and be doing.

Leagues down, already upon the Atlantic, laughing at the fogs that lay gathering behind her along the coast, the good brig, her sails bravely set, making the most of what favor the wind had for her, was fairly away upon her voyage, speeding on towards the pleasant weather. And on her deck, standing his first watch, looking out under the stars for the first time, with an awed surprise, upon the restless and unmeasured sea, walked the boy of the hills;

his heart yearning back to them secretly, with a great longing and love; a wish that he might once more have gone there to say good-by; an apprehensive questioning whether all should be as it was, if he should come back safely and go home to them again by and by.

So these two were separated. Separated also by something more than the leagues of salt water that lay between them to-night.

A thought had been put into the mind of each that lessened perhaps no love, but that taught each to feel for the first time that he must learn to do without the other. The boy would be henceforth independent, even of ready kindness, from the friend who was no "blood-relation;" upon whom he could have no legitmate claim. The old man saw that he could no longer hold to himself the young life that sprang restlessly forth to its own place among the activities of the world, and would not fall obediently into a prepared round.

"He would go; there was nothing else for it," Jane had said. "I don't think anything whatever could have held him back."

It almost seemed as if he had gone without a pang, or a thought of those behind.

"Yes, yes; it's the way of the young;" said the gentle Doctor, and submitted.

Jane Gair slept very well to-night; after she had got over her little excitement of surprise at her father's coming. Why not? She had done nothing. These two hearts — these two lives — had drifted away from each other; she had only stood by, and looked on at what had happened.

I assisted once at a "table-tipping;" we were all novices, to be sure; there was no "developed medium" among us; we wanted the table to move, and move it did, at last, apparently by no physical agency; we rested the tips of our fingers upon it, and waited; and so, by degrees, it travelled across the room, we following; but somebody among, us by and by, when we came to talk the wonder over, was constrained candidly to confess, that "she might have pushed, — a little." I think human watching and waiting for the unfolding of circumstance to its wish, is often of this sort, precisely; and that a great deal of will works itself out at the finger-tips, — it may be with the best of us. It is, perhaps, hard to say at what point strong desire becomes responsible.

"Keep thy heart with all diligence; for out of it are the issues of life."

CHAPTER XV.

A SEARCH; AND ODYLLIC FORCE.

Dr. Gayworthy had nothing to stay for in Selport. He had no curiosity to "look about the city," as his daughter and her husband would have persuaded him to do. He had not seen it as I said for ten years past; and it had grown, as New England cities were growing, in those comparatively early days of railroads; and there was doubtless much to see; but in all its crowded area there was nothing left that the Doctor cared for, now, outside his daughter's dwelling. And his country patients would be waiting for him at home. So at nine o'clock the next morning, in a drizzling, soaking, sulky rain, he bestowed himself and his portmanteau again in the northward train, and was steamed away; touching and pausing, now and then, on outskirts of the towns that, twenty years ago, were quiet villages, through which the old road lay, along whose windings he had used to drive when he made his infrequent journeys southward.

He gave his ticket silently to-day when the conductor came his round. I doubt if the official knew him for the same man who had asked him yesterday about the way of the wind, with the eager look of a boy questioning his elders of the probabilities of weather, upon which some rare hope or pleasure hangs contingent. He felt dull to-day, — the good old Doctor, — languid in body and dispirited in soul. The miles were long to him. He was not hungry when he came to Baxter's Mills. He took a cup of tea, and a morsel of some food that lay nearest, and sat waiting in his place in the coach, when the other passengers, after their more prolonged refreshment, came clambering in.

All the rest of the day the slow, ponderous vehicle went tilting and lumbering and creaking on, up into the hill-country; and the persistent spring rain came down; and everything dripped outside and steamed within, and smelt of wet leather and damp overcoats: and at seven o'clock a chance wagon, hired at the Bridge, set down at the Gayworthy Farmhouse a pale, chilled, exhausted old gentleman, with nothing to tell his surprised 'women folks' but that they might get him some hot tea and put him to bed; for that he'd had the life pretty well jolted and drenched out of him; and the boy was gone after all."

Two days after they sent to Winthorpe for a brother physician; and a letter went down again to Selport, on Monday, from Joanna to Jane: "Father had taken a violent cold, and was threatened with a congestion of the lungs."

Dutiful Jane packed a trunk, took Say with her, and came up to Hilbury by the Tuesday's stage.

I have no desire to lead you through a whole chapter of suspense, for the mere sake of it. Dr. Gayworthy, though very ill, did not die. At the end of a week, Mrs. Gair and Say went back to Selport, leaving him, as the country saying is, "on the mending hand." Mrs. Gair felt no wish to prolong her stay: it was too early for her regular yearly visit, and there was all her own and Say's summer sewing to be done; besides, apart from the anxiety and dulness of a sick house, it had not been altogether an agreeable sojourn for her, this time, at home. Prue had asked her, plainly and straightforwardly, if Gershom had gone before her letter came, and whether she had told him of its contents. Jane Gair never told a lie. She had learned all about Ananias and Sapphira; and the fire and brimstone; and George Washington and his hatchet; and "Has my darling told a lie?" and all the rest that well-taught children knew in her day, long before she was as old as Say. She had read Mrs. Opie afterwards, in whose stories every variety of liars got surely caught and appropriately punished; and though she could live as false a life, in her small, protected way, as ever a woman did live, — though there was not a day of it all, perhaps, when she did not painstakingly put forth some other motive than the real one for her doing, — she shrank, with an in-drilled instinct of safety and decency, from deliberate, palpable falsification in word.

"Why, no," she said. "I thought if you yourself had known just how it was, you would not have written so. His shipping papers were signed; and the whole thing was settled: and the Pearl was to sail the next morning. I knew you did not mean for him to give up the voyage; and it was no use making him unhappy."

"I meant exactly what I said. I always do," said Prue shortly; and there she dropped the subject: and while Jane remained, she spoke no further word to her of Gershom. The mother knew she had been tricked of her boy. She knew that Jane knew she never intended to consent to such a departure; that it was with a sudden thought of its possibility, that she had finished her letter late that Monday afternoon, and walked over to Jaazaniah Hoogs's with it, that he might post it for her in Winthorpe the next morning before the mail went down. This knowledge lay between them, and it was enough. Mrs. Gair felt far from comfortable, even when that immediate danger to the Doctor was over, and she could say to herself, that "no great harm had come of it, after all." Come of what? What had her conscience been afraid of, after all?

The Doctor got well. That is, he did not die. But it was the first break in his fine old constitution. After this, "he must be careful;" a new text for the hearty, self-forgetful farmer-physician. A lung-attack, at any time of life — certainly when the threescore years and ten are passed — can hardly leave a man exactly where it found him. And as Prue had said, he had "been a little slim, before." He did not stouten much as summer came on. The haying was hard for him; he missed Gershom in that, and in everything; he came home from his round of visits, in the sultry weather, languid, and exhausted, and silent; and when Jane came up again in August — making her visit at a later season than usual, because of having been there in the spring, and also that Say might be in Hilbury in huckleberry time, — she saw that her father had changed; had aged; that he began to look a little broken. But it was now three months since the Pearl had sailed, and he made that unlucky journey, and fell ill after it. She did not choose to connect this with the other; or to see that circumstances had moved on to this result, through any remote "pushing" of her own. She "could n't help feeling anxious about father," she said to her sisters. But she had, at the same time, another little secret anxiety, which she said nothing about. It occurred to her now and then to wonder if certain matters remained just as they had been on that night in June, more than three years ago.

It happened strangely that she was put one day in the direct way of finding out.

Joanna and Rebecca had gone from home, to a sewing society, taking Say with them. Prue had withdrawn to her own room, where she was safe, according to precedent, for an hour to come. The Doctor had been summoned, just before dinner, to a patient four miles off, and had taken a hasty meal and departed. Mrs. Gair having no new dress to put on to-day that the Hilbury ladies had not seen, found herself unequal to the fatigue of a toilet and a half-mile walk. So she sat with a book, — very light summer reading, — just inside the open front door, enjoying the cool breeze that swept up under the maples.

A barefooted boy, on a bare-back horse, rode suddenly over the turf slope before the white gate, and with a touch of his dusty toes to the top rail, made a single spring from the beast's back to the grass within the fence, and walked quickly up toward the door-stone.

"The Doctor sent this, and this," said he to Mrs. Gair; "and wants what he 's written for."

"The leathern case at the right hand, in the middle drawer of my study table." This was one "this;" the other was a bunch of keys.

Mrs. Gair rose quietly, and entering her father's little room, procured the case, and came back with it to the messenger. The keys she put in her pocket. "That is all," she said. "You may go."

The boy departed; over the fence, and upon the uncaparisoned steed, as he had come; sticking his heels into the creature's rough sides, and larruping its neck with the bridle-end, till it broke into a wild canter.

Mrs. Gair sat still a few minutes after he had gone. She had first dropped the keys into her pocket, with only the thought of holding them safe; joined, perhaps, with an indefinite feeling that leads people of a certain temperament to cling instinctively to *possession*; even of what can be only temporarily and uselessly in their keeping. But, presently, something darted across her mind.

Among these, was the key to the panel-cupboard.

Prue was up-stairs, asleep. She was alone, in all this part of the house. She should never have a better — perhaps another — chance.

Mrs. Gair sat reading on down the page, comprehending never a word. Thinking, while the type lay in meaningless lines before her eyes, whether she should do this thing or not. When she came to the bottom of the leaf, she laid down the book. All still and solitary, through the house, and away out down the fields. Nothing to interrupt. Why should she not look into the old cupboard once more, and among its relics of time past? She bethought herself that the odd volume of Cecilia, which she could not find about the house, might have got laid away there. There were old books, or used to be, upon its upper shelf. Mrs. Gair's was a mind that could not be single-motived, even to itself. For such, the devil is always ready with his double reasons.

The panel door slid back with its old rumble; the earthquake that Say had heard before; softened by the care with which Jane handled it, but still sufficiently audible, or sensible, perhaps, in the silent, echoing house, and along the old timbers attuned to every long-accustomed thrill. Jane must be quick. Prue might notice, and come down. At this moment, the odd volume of Cecilia was not thought of. The faded letter-case lay there; back, upon the second shelf, with a worn leather wallet, and bundles of yellow, dusty papers, ancient, and mostly useless. Jane held it in her hand, and listened. No sound. She untied the green ribbon, and opened the case. There were two pockets. The upper and principal one, ample with inlet and once curiously-folded gores, stretched and bulged, now, with long use, still holding abundant contents. The other, a simple doubling, laid flat within the cover; protruding from which she saw the edges of a paper somewhat fresher than the rest. Not what she sought for. She remembered that well. It had been only a half sheet, twice folded. This presented multiplied thicknesses. She drew it out to look behind. This was what her father had held in his hand, that night, and replaced with the one newly written. She turned it over. It was superscribed and dated. Ten years back. "My last Will and Testament."

There was no time to unfold it. She heard a slight movement, somewhere, above. *Was* this the last? Ten years ago, was before Prue and her great boy had come home here. She put her fingers in the narrow pocket where it had been. Nothing there; where she had surely seen her father slip the second writing, behind the other. Something crackled a little, under her touch, though, as she felt along. As a new, stiff lining might have done; only this was an old thing, that had done crackling, long ago. In the back, just above this lesser pocket, was a slit, worn in the brocade that had faced it once so richly. Something had got in, or been hidden, here. She put the tips of her fingers under, carefully.

Suddenly she cared not to investigate further. She chose to tell herself that she knew nothing. And that it was best she should know nothing. And yet she did know, just as well as you and I do, what it must be that lay there, and how, with the dim candle-light, and her father's old eyes, it must have happened. But she would not look. Was it odyllic force, or a voluntary pressure of the finger tip that "pushed a little" upon what lay within, and crowded it down yet further, beyond discovery? Prue's step was distinct, up-stairs, now. The folded paper was put back,—the pocket heedfully smoothed down, pressed close,—the ribbon retied; and when Prue came in, a minute after, all in the lower portion of the cupboard looked undisturbed, and Jane was standing on the high round of the heavy old mahogany chair by which she had climbed, and was industriously rummaging among the shiny-covered leather-bound books and musty papers on the topmost shelf. She heard Prue coming, well enough; but she never turned. She was in no hurry. Why should she startle, or be afraid? She would just as soon Prue saw her there, as not. And here, good fortune that it was, quite justifying her procedure, — under her hand lay the very thing she had *come to look for!* The second volume of Cecilia, that had been gone from the up-stairs bookcase so long. Prue entered just in time to hear her exclaim with delight.

"How came you there, Jane? And where did you get father's keys?"

"He sent them home just now, for something that he needed from the table-drawer. And it came into my head to look here for this volume that I wanted so. I'm so pleased! I have n't read Cecilia since I was fifteen."

It was said with all the simplicity of fifteen. But when Jane was so very simple, good Prue, with all her own honesty, that had used to make her blind, had come of late to feel, vaguely, that there might be something unspoken. She reproached herself for this, and thought of the first verse of the seventh chapter of Matthew; yet the sensation would come.

"I don't think he likes those places meddled with. I never go there."

"Oh, I daresay you're scrupulous. But with me, it's rather different."

Jane never failed to imply her rights, when occasion offered, as born daughter of the house.

Prue did not reply. They heard Priscilla, Huldah's cousin and successor, moving about in the great kitchen to which the door stood open. Prue went out.

Jane rolled the panel to its place again; turned the key; dropped the bunch into the table-drawer; and went off with her old book; humming a tune.

A few minutes later, Priscilla came in, softly, with round eyes, and looked wonderingly about. She had heard, in her turn, the earthquake; and the little talk, also, between the step-sisters. These things impressed themselves upon her young mind, not over-occupied as yet with the urgencies of life, as those things do to which future impressions are to come and mate themselves.

CHAPTER XVI.

INTO PORT.

Gershom Vorse was standing his last night-watch at sea, upon the Pearl's homeward voyage. We left him upon his first. He has seen since then what a sailor's life is. He has found out a good deal of those eleven men who have been his shipmates; who disgusted him so at the outset, when they came reeling and rollicking on board, on the fair May morning when they sailed out of Selport. He has been half round the world with them, and back again. He has laid out with them on the yards, in stormy nights, reefing and furling sail. He has heard a prayer, or what was born a prayer, once, but has coarsened on rough lips and with irreverent usage to something little better, seemingly, — God knows, — than an ordinary oath, uttered in one breath, when they "tumbled up," at the midnight call, to face flood and fury; and downright cursing in the next, as they struggled at their task aloft, clinging for dear life to the swaying foot-rope, "fisting" the wet and bellying canvas. He has sat on the sunny forecastle deck in pleasant weather learning to make duck trowsers and listening to long yarns. He has looked, so, into strange lives. They had had "all sorts," as there are apt to be in a crew of a dozen men. There was the Italian, Joe, who always crossed himself before he went aloft in a gale, and swore hardest when he got there; who used to say in his broken English, wagging his head at his jolly companions, — jolly, so often, at his expense —

"Ah! you laugh now! Vera well! You laugh at me talk bad English, an' pray to Virgin Mary, an' San Peter. Vat you do when you go up dere, aloft one day, by 'm by? San Peter, he'll sit at de gate, wid de keys in he hand. He look over, an, see you comin', and he no let you in. He say, 'Vast, dere! Go below! Vat you do here, you 'a-retic?' Den by 'm by, you see Joe come along. An' San Peter, he look over de gate, an' he say: 'Ah, dat you, Joe? Glad to see you. How you do, Joe? Valk in, shipmate! Vat you take to drink?'"

There was Jerry, also, from the Vineyard. He had another

sort of religion, picked up at a camp-meeting; let drop, his comrades used to say, by some better fellow. Sneaking Jerry, they called him. He sneaked, and shirked, and snivelled; and the old salts despised him, and "damned his eyes," as they did "old horse."

This was all the religion they had — to speak of — in the forecastle of the Pearl. What had they, then? Well, there was sailor's fortitude; sailor's courage; sailor's patience; a rough sort of magnanimity; a spirit of share and share alike; one scorning to be better off than another, even in the matter of lobscouse and salt junk; there was coarse wit; shrewd invention; there was the strange bond of fellowship between men who, making a little world with each other now, might in a few months scatter to the ends of the earth, never beholding each others' faces again; or who might, with a moment's warning, go down together to a common death.

Here among these, for eight months, Gershom had lived. They had had a voyage of ordinary length and ordinary incident. There had been nothing high-heroic; only the heroism of every day endurance and exposure; and the glamour was a little gone. The second mate was a vulgar fellow; the chief officer a martinet; the Captain was Captain Burley still; a noble man upon the quarter-deck; but between the quarter-deck and the forecastle there was an infinite and impassable distance. Captain Burley and Gershom Vorse would be taking tea together soon perhaps at Uncle Reuben's table, talking over sea life, telling and listening again to sea stories; but for eight months one had been served his solitary meals in state by the steward in the cabin, and the other had fetched his kid from the galley; and words had been rare between them, beyond what the vessel's service required.

Gershom had seen the great sea, and the far, beautiful islands; he had been among the palms and orange groves; he had beheld unrolled a corner of the grand glowing panorama of the earth; he longed still for more; yet it had not all been a vision of grandeur and beauty, — a sublimity of scene and act; he was eager now for his home again; for a breath of the New England hills; eager, as if he had never fancied himself weary of them; never felt that they hemmed him round and held him in.

It was a bright, mild January night; the stars were out clear, and the wind fair; sails set, I shall not tell you what, nor how, for I have small knowledge of technical seamanship, — but all safe, and as it should be; the man at the wheel steering his steady course north-northwest, and the watch smoking and singing and skylarking on the forecastle, keeping themselves warm with antics and jokes. Gershom walked the deck, up and down apart, in the waist. He had little in common with the rest of the crew, to-night, save the common joy of nearing port. He knew nothing of their haunts, nothing of their shore life here in the city, though he could guess somewhat of it from their yarns and chaff. So soon as he should step from the deck of the Pearl, he would be the "boy of the hills" once more, as thoroughly as if he had never seen salt water. He was thinking of the Hilbury stage, and hoping the brig might get in before to-morrow night, that the next day might find him on his journey to the farm.

Ned Blackmere — English Ned — stood apart, also, leaning on the rail, looking gloomily over upon the water. English Ned was never jolly, coming into port. But then, when *was* he jolly? There was a fierce kind of spirit that waked up in him, when they sailed away out of sight of land, as if he had escaped something; and he flung himself into his seaman's duty, as if his life lay there; but he was never cheery and light-hearted. His gloom and reserve, strange always for a sailor, took on a heavier cloud, like the fog of the soundings, on approaching the homeward end of a voyage. He had sailed with the Pearl for six years past. They called him Old Barnacle, for sticking to her so. He loved the brig, I think, though he believed that he loved nothing. Gershom had never heard this man spin a yarn since they came on board together. Nobody knew much about him. He was a fearless, skilful seaman; a sure hand at the helm, or at an earing, in bad weather; but a moody messmate, caring for nothing but his pipe, from which he was nearly inseparable.

Gershom came close up to him, in his pacing to and fro, each time he turned forward. There was a spring in the boy's step, and a flinging up of the head, that had gone out of the man's bearing forever.

"Ye 're walking it off well to-night, youngster," said old Barnacle, turning suddenly, and clenching his pipe with his teeth. "Seems to help the brig along, don't it?"

"Well, I'm restless," replied Gershom, pausing at the end of his beat. "She 's going a good streak, ain't she? We 'll be in by to-morrow night, they say."

"You 've something to be glad of, then? What have you got to go to when ye 're in?"

He would not have asked this of those older men, who talked of sweethearts and wives, or laid their plans for a sailor's holiday time, with full pockets and a gay city to empty them in, — he knew, or thought he knew, what all that was worth; and he turned away bitterly from the merry forecastle group to the black water swashing by the sides, and to his solitary pipe: but he asked it of this boy, who had turned away also, — asked it with something between wonder and a sneer.

"I've got *home!*" cried the young sailor, with a warm outburst. He was so glad to have it to say out. He had been wanting to sing it, to shout it; but he could not say it to those men. "I 've got my mother and my grandfather, up in the country, among the hills. And, before that, I 've got friends in Selport; Uncle Reuben, — that is, Mr. Gair, you know, — and my little cousin Say. Where are you going to, Ned?"

He had been beguiled, suddenly, from the off-hand roughness learned at sea, that disguises everything with an indifference or turns it off with a joke, to the simple sentiment of a child. The child-side of his nature was uppermost just now; and, true to its impulse, he told all this to old Barnacle, as a six years' urchin tells all he has to tell upon the slightest questioning: and wound up by asking, — what nobody else on board would have dared to ask Ned Blackmere, — "Where are you going to, Ned?"

"To hell! If you must know." It was as true a speech out of the man's secret heart as the boy's confidence had been. They had called each other out alike.

"Stop! you need n't go. Since we 've begun, we may as well talk on a bit."

He took his pipe out of his mouth, saying this, and stood with his arms resting on the bulwark, and his head bent, the pipe held carelessly in his fingers, and his hand hanging idly down.

"You 've got a home, you say: I suppose you think so. You 'll find out sometime that there is n't any such thing. There 's places where people stay together awhile; but it 's for what they can get of each other, and because they can't help themselves. All at once something turns up, and sets 'em adrift, and what becomes of your home then? I 've seen it: I 've seen 'em go to pieces like a ship on a rock, — no two timbers held together. You 've got a mother? Well, that 's something; as long as it lasts; but the real ones mostly die. I can just remember somebody that used to cuddle me up, and tuck me in bed, and tell me prayers to say; but after that I don't remember anything but kicks and cuffs, and drink and misery. Then my father died; and my father's brother cheated us out of what living there was left; and my own brother cheated me out of what was more than living to me, or I was fool enough to think so; and my sister made a disgrace of herself, and broke the heart of an honest fellow as was my friend; and I went knocking about the world, and it 's all made up of just the same stuff. I 've been all over it; and God ain't anywhere in it. If he was, he would n't let things be as I have seen 'em. I set out once to plant a home of my own, and see if 't would grow; but I married a she-devil, and I tell you we made *hell!* *My* child never had a mother: it 's dead; and if God *was* anywhere round, I 'd thank him for it. She overlaid it in the night; she *said* she did. I knew she got tired of it; and it made her mad wi' crying, — that and the gin. She did n't get stupid wi' 't, only devilish; and the child lay smothered in the bed one morning. That 's where *my* home went to; but I go back there yet, and halve my wages with her, when the brig 's in: and I 'm precious jolly when we come in sight o' land, do n't you see?" And his white teeth glistened through the darkness as he set them tight, and his lips drew up from them in a horrible scorn. He barely relaxed their clench, and thrust his pipe between them again, and so held it fast.

"If I 'd gone my own way from the beginning, and never believed in nobody, I 'd ha' done." These words forced themselves, as it were, from locked jaws. "It 's all come o' trusting and expecting; and the women 's the worst. They 'll hold you up the most wi' trusting; and they'll let you down the hardest, — except the real mothers, and they don't last. If you 've got a mother, boy, hold on to her; but take care o' your bones, and keep clear o' the rest!"

Eight bells were struck as old Barnacle ended speaking; the larboard watch was called; and Gershom with his watchmates presently went below: but this epitomized story of a dark life, that he had heard, went with him, and haunted him. He could not forget Blackmere's look. He could not forget what he had said, — "I 've been all round the world; and God ain't anywhere in it." Should he, now that he had once come out from the safety of the hills, ever reach a desolation like this? Was this what must surely come of trusting and expecting? Was the great world, outside the shelter and the faith of his childhood, made up, even mostly, of stuff like this?

An unwholesome or unhappy life may touch our own, and pass us by harmless, as disease may do our bodies, except for a predisposition which it mysteriously finds, and seizes upon. We gather to ourselves nothing that we have not already some faint unnoticed symptom of. A sudden distrust, that had passed over him long ago, — that since, he had hardly remembered, or dwelt upon, — a doubt of one who should have been his friend, — recalled itself to Gershom in a vague way now; a feeling that he had also once known gave a holding point to this terrible history of a disappointed, utterly distrustful human soul, and grafted it, strange and fearful as it was, to the boy's own life. His own little experience of an ill in human nature added to itself this blacker knowledge; and the one verified the other. There was a glimmer whereby he could dimly comprehend this thing whereof he should have had no comprehension yet. It should have been a mere marvel to him; but it seized strong hold of him, and he could not shake it off.

It was a putting of two and two together; with Gershom Vorse, toward the acquiring of that bitter science men call knowledge of the world.

The lessons had begun longer ago than he reviewed them now; in the old childish days, with their perceptions of the shams of life; when Aunt Jane, with her fine city airs and fashions, had used to come to Hilbury; when she and her friends and neighbors met with such a seeming of simple, eager gladness, underneath which was yet the seething of vainglory on the one side, and jealousy on the other; when there were all sorts of quibbles and devices to get rid of lending Selport patterns, and painstaking contrivances to imitate them surreptitously; triumphant displays and wrathful recognitions, disguised with airs of innocent simplicity and bland acquiescence; when people who Gershom believed had it in them to behave like pigs, minced little bits, and said "No I thank you," to be thought polite; all this, as he saw or fancied he saw it, then had laid itself away within him, an early disgust, to color many an after estimate of life and the things thereof.

Gershom Vorse, with his uncompromising sense of honesty, drawn with mother's milk and incorporated with the strong, unyielding man-nature that was in him, was likely, unless something more divine and gracious should mingle and attune with it, to make a long quarrel of it with the world.

The world! Every soul of us knows a separate one. Over into each other's worlds, in a way we may look; and our own may borrow from what lies about the borders of those that touch upon it; but scarcely any two, however dear, inhabit literally one domain, — have one identical range and region.

What sort of world was little Sarah Gair feeling out into, with childish hands; glancing into, with eager, often puzzled eyes?

It opened differently to her than it did to Gershom; things that he was learning were as unknown to her as any concerns of another planet; things were forcing themselves upon her, as real facts of life, that to him would be nothings. Compared with better and stronger things, they were as nothings doubtless; yet they made up a certain sort of world for a certain sort of people, among whom Say was born and placed. They were the shape life took, just now at least, for her; she had a mother not too wise; and she was as yet only a little maiden of eleven years old.

Sarah Gair came home from dancing-school, in the January dusk, at the very hour when the Pearl came sailing up the harbor. She had had her hair tied up in a new way, with rose-colored ribbons; and this was the first day of wearing a bright brown silk frock with puffed sleeves and lace edgings, that Winny when she fastened it for her, had declared to be "the rale stylish thing, intirely." Yet somehow she had n't felt so fine, after all, as she expected. Pauline Topliff, wearing a blue dress, that just matched her eyes, and ribbons in her hair that matched the dress, had never once spoken to her; and had even declared, in a half aside, to Helen Semple, that she "could n't bear contrasts, or bran-new things; and pink and brown were dreadfully vulgar." This weighed upon Say's heart, and even upon her conscience.

She felt that she had, somehow, got with the wrong girls this afternoon, and that, if her mother knew, she would not like it. She supposed she ought to have stayed sitting by Pauline Topliff's elbow, even after that elbow was very unceremoniously thrust forward, and a hint given that the sofa was crowded. It had been very comfortable in the corner, afterward, with Lucy Briggs, who had a new book of fairy stories, and who let her "look over." But she knew that it had been all wrong. And yet the Topliff set would n't have her. What was she to do? She did n't understand why it was; Pauline Topliff was very pretty; and she danced the Gavotte beautifully; she and Helen Semple, together; and Say would have thought herself in heaven, almost, — so great was her spontaneous admiration, and so strong her instilled ambition, — if she could have once had Pauline's Topliff's arm thrown round her in the free girlish familiarity that Pauline showed to her especial friends, and that Lucy Briggs and other girls, of a more accessible order, were quite ready to show to herself. But ever since that afternoon of her first overture, made dutifully, in the spirit of her mother's injunctions, when she tried to "get acquainted" by offering half her book to Pauline, and the blue eyes had opened so very wide; and such a surprised voice had exclaimed to the friend with whom the young lady immediately got up and walked off, "Did you ever hear of such a thing? For a strange girl!"— "it had been all in vain. Beyond a certain point, — an uncertain one, I should rather say; since even a partial condescension depended on the caprice and convenience of the juvenile exclusives, — Say had never been able to reach. It was like the poor girl in the story, who could not find her way into the Enchanted Island. An invisible wall of adamant opposed her; she advanced impetuously; she was thrown back ignominiously. Say went straight at the wall of adamant; it was her nature to be impetu-

13

ous; she showed plainly what she wanted; it was the only way she knew how to try for it. So she seemed odd and awkward, and rude; so failure was made more positively certain.

So her little child-world puzzled and grieved her. She could not understand why things were so.

But behind the child-world was the great grown-up world. This she knew absolutely nothing of.

Selport — you observe — had its aristocracy. Of course. Every town and village on this continent that was a wilderness three hundred years ago, develops that, in its growth, by the inevitable, occult law of human crystallization. Selport, at this time of which I write, was a half-grown city. More punctilious and tenacious therefore, concerning its little dignities, as all half-grown creatures are, than it would be probably when it should get a little bigger. Why on earth Wilkins, who grew fat on nails and flatirons, twenty years ago, should contemn Simpkins who is doing the same thing to-day, as fast as he can, is among the unaccounted for, but palpable facts in social science. The thing is, and always has been. There were families in Selport who sold all their nails and flatirons, their soap and candles, — a generation or two ago. All these knew each other. This was the circle born, not made. Into this, one *must* be born. Fresh comers from the unknown up-country, making the beginnings of new fortunes, and the nuclei of new circles, could not for very long hope to wheel into an orbit concentric with these. Simpkins must roll forth, full-orbed, from his nebulous obscurity, before Wilkins can behold him with the naked eye.

The Gairs, pre-eminent in Hilbury, were in a nebula at Selport. The whole object of their lives — Mrs. Jane's more especially — was to find their way out, and begin to revolve as planets. It was slow work. With all her ambition, Mrs. Gair thought, at weary times, that she could almost give it all up, and relapse, contentedly, into chaos.

I don't pretend that my analogy is complete; a more perfect method obtains, doubtless, in the heavens, and the inchoate worlds are kept at safe distances from the established systems; but in the social firmament it does sometimes happen that a little concrete luminosity, trembling on the edge of one of its nebulæ, gets caught and drawn, once in a cycle or so, by some favoring attraction, to the outskirts of a sublime solar order. In such a case, it is for awhile, one of the most unhappy little objects in creation. It is not quite sure of belonging anywhere. Some great Jupiter, or benignant Venus, sweeps along, and almost catches it up, triumphantly, into the place where it would be. But its own tremendous forces bear the planet on, before the lesser orb can complete a perfect revolution, even as a satellite; and so it oscillates fearfully, in peril of plunging between opposing and disturbing impulses, down awful gulfs of wreck and annihilation. I suppose creation must go on; and it may be dastardly to say so; but I think, for my part, I would rather stay in the milkiest part of the Milky Way, forever.

"I don't know the person." These words from certain lips in Selport, were irrevocable oblivion. Human nature would find its way, sometimes, though, for all that. Good-hearted little Mrs. Semple — indisputably of the "best set" — was in continual peril of loss of caste, through mentioning people whom Mrs. Topliff "did n't know." She *would* have neighbors in the side street that turned down two doors from her own. Mrs. Topliff lived in a broader street than either, crossing the head of the first; and her house, standing opposite the opening, took in range of its outlook the whole length between its blocks. This typified properly her social position of overlook and scrutiny.

Mrs. Semple met the great lady one morning, walking down as she went up.

"Oh, Mrs. Topliff! Were you coming to me, I wonder? I'm so sorry. I've just come from Mrs. Norris, round the corner. She's in such trouble, poor little woman! Her eldest daughter, a sweet girl, just my Helen's age, has died, after an illness of only four days. Only think, what a blow! — I'm going down town for her, now, to order the dear child's burial-dress, and the mourning. I'm so grieved for her."

Thus far, Mrs. Topliff might have endured with only her chill look of well-bred, dignified patience, but when incautious Mrs. Semple, her whole mother's heart touched, went on to narrate some circumtances of the brief illness of this young creature, "just her own Helen's age," and the resistless tears stood in her eyes as she spoke, it became too much.

"My dear," she interposed, with a freezing emphasis, "*I don't know* Mrs. Norris!"

"But you're a mother!" cried the other, with a startle of honest, womanly indignation. She forgot to feel guilty, as she sometimes did, at her own lapse from the restrictions of her order.

I wonder if by any chance it ever occurred to this woman, who was a mother, and who supposed herself a Christian, to think of a possible moment in the mighty future when a Voice more awful might say, "I never knew you! Go your way!"

I wonder if the thought of that higher Recognition, or that

unutterably fearful Ignoring, might not sometimes set at nought, even to such as they, the petty human dictum, for whose favoring utterance setting heart and soul upon the aim, women like Jane Gair were laboring.

Laboring,—Mrs. Gair was,—and building up her own world about herself; nor for herself only. This was the world her child was to feel out into, wonderingly, with innocent hands. A world of petty, false ambitions; of mean subserviencies; of self-degrading shames.

A small consolation came to Sarah at the end of this dancing-school afternoon. If her mother had been at home to put her usual questions — "What did you do? Who did you sit by?" Say must have confessed, "I sat by Pauline Topliff a little while, and then I went and read a book with Lucy Briggs." But afterward she could have added the salvo — "And then Lucy and I walked home with Helen Semple." She was almost sorry now for what she had been glad of before: that her mother was away, and that she should not be required to give account. It might be long before she should have as much to boast again. Mrs. Topliff had called at the school early, in her carriage, and taken Pauline away with her; and then Helen had picked up the book which Lucy and Say had left behind them on the seat when they went to join their class. Two things bring children at once to a common level — sugar-plums and fairy tales. A paper of *bonbons* had often been a temporary propitiation; the story-book was irresistible. Helen condescended to linger on, even when the "bran-new" silk and ribbons came rustling and fluttering back, and, after a little timid hovering, settled themselves beside her. Lucy Briggs, in her dark merino, sat down, softly and simply, in the place she had left. She had been taught no mortifying ambitions, no false timidities. If Mrs. Gair could but have understood it, there was better chance in the world for Lucy Briggs, the wholesale grocer's daughter, than for the child of the merchant who brought home groceries in his own vessels from South America and the Indies. Lucy Briggs, in her plain, unpretending home, had a true woman for a mother. She was growing up in sweet, ladylike ways, unaware, with no especial thought about being a lady, at all. Here is where the two extremes meet; the highest breeding, the purest refinement, the most undoubted position, would account for its being, if its unconscious feeling were ever rendered in words, much as Topsy did; "Don't know; 'spect I growed." It is the half-way, restless, striving, self-sensitive state that is vulgar. Mrs. Gair had not mastered this secret yet.

Helen Semple borrowed the book of Lucy Briggs, and offered,

if she would walk home with her, to lend her the "Black Velvet Bracelet" in return.

So Say got into the front entry of Judge Semple's house, and waited there five minutes.

It had been a very praiseworthy thing, she thought, that had happened to her; and she wished her mother were at home to know.

A dear little dutiful, confiding girl was Sarah Gair; she trusted in her mother's supreme wisdom; the mother,— (thought of awe!) though she be but a fool, must needs, for a while, represent the Supreme Wisdom to her child; and Say's loyal little heart warmed at the hope of pleasing this worldly mother of hers, as few of our grown-up hearts, perhaps, warm at the thought of pleasing God.

"Now make haste, Miss Sarah, darlint. Yer late, and it 's moon-cakes there is for your tay to-night; and take aff your fine silk gown, an' pit an yer ould one, and come down to the basemint, like a good shild," said Winny, letting her in.

"No," answered Say, "I shan't take off my dress at all. And you may bring the tea up stairs. And I want the chandelier lighted."

"Arrah! is it crazed ye are, shild?" cried Winny, aghast. "Not take aff yer bran-new silk gown whin it 's yer mother wud always have ye pit back intil yer ould frock, an' it 's mussin it ahl ye 'll be, an' sorra ha'porth I can do till help it! An' the tay up stairs, and the shandler lighted. Well, well, well, what 'll I do at all?"

"Do what I said," returned Say, with a dignity. "I don't like bran-new things. I *want* my dress to get mussed, a little. My things all stick out and crackle so. Nobody's else do. And I 've been to Helen Semple's, and there was nobody in the parlor but her father and mother, and the chandelier was lighted, and they never said a word to her about taking off her dress. I don't believe she ever does. Till she goes to bed, I mean. It 's only making believe to have things when you pull 'em off the minute you get home. And when the chandelier is never lighted. I 'm going to have things real. Now bring up the tea and the moon-cakes." And Say settled herself down very comfortably in the great arm-chair by the fire.

"An' ye 'll never mind the shandler, like a good child?"

"Of course I will," said Say, impatiently. "Don't make me tell you over again so many times. There, take this, and get right up and light it now, — that 's a good Winny," she added, coaxingly, as she discovered the demur in the girl's face. "If you don't, I shall!"

"Arrah! but ye 're a quare one! I shuppose I must jist do it for yees, or ye 'll be afther smashin' ahl the glasses! Sorra know I know what's got intil yees the night."

The tea and the round short-cakes, christened "moon-cakes" years ago by Say, were brought up; and she sat there in the brilliant light, with her silk dress and her rose-colored ribbons, and made Winny wait upon her as scrupulously as if she had been a little princess. She felt, now, she was having things real. It was the truth of the child's nature rather than the foolish pride of it that indulged itself in this wise.

"I wish I was n't all alone!" she said to herself, after Winny had taken the tray down. "I wish some visitors would come. I wish I could have asked Lucy Briggs to come and stay all night."

Say had few companions. Even by grown-up acquaintances, the Gair's home was comparatively, little visited. There had been a snubbing of some people who would have been neighborly, and a waiting for others who seldom or never condescended to appear. Mrs. Topliff was President of one or two charitable societies, which Mrs. Gair had joined. Once or twice, partly on some business, she had called. Mrs. Gair was always expecting the great lady to "drop in, socially," as, with civil surprise, she had received invitation to do. Meanwhile, Jane put on "Topliff airs" with Mrs. Briggs and Mrs. Norris, who might have been her friends. Their daughters, also, and others like them, who might have been intimate with Say, were set aside, when the child suggested either of them, with, — "Oh, I would n't ask *her*. Why don't you invite this one, or that one, instead?" This or that one would not have come. Say was too proud to acknowledge this in words, which she and her mother both knew, secretly, very well. It ended, therefore, in a stiff, cold, unsocial living; a sad solitariness for little Say.

"Perhaps the Pearl has got in to-day, and Gershie 'll come!"

Say felt, secretly, that it would be very nice if Gershom should come, and Captain Burley too, perhaps, and find her in her best dress, with the parlor lighted.

"I 'm glad I kept it on. Only I can't go into the kitchen. I shall have to make Winny come up and sit here, and tell me a story." Which Winny was doing, an hour later, when the front door-bell rang, at last, and a voice, grown so deep and strong that Say, listening behind, hardly knew it for Gershom's, asked for Mr. Gair.

"He 's gone away to Hilberry; he and the mishtress; but Miss Sarah's at home, an' it 's she that 's been expiotin' yees," said Winny, at the door. Then Say sprang out.

"Oh, Gershom! I 'm so glad!"

But she paused when she saw the stout, manly-grown figure that stood there, in the rough pilot coat; and Gershom, after a quick movement to meet the little cousin who had been in his thoughts all through the long, dark watch on deck, last night, paused also, when he saw the fine little person that emerged with rustling silk and ribbons in the flood of light from the open parlor door. He could n't catch *that* in his arms! He had been used to tarred ropes and rough sailcloth. He had thought of Say, without her foibles or fineries, as we do always think of the lost or far away; and now, here she was, "dressed up, and toes in position," as he had said, of old, in Hilbury; and this to welcome him!

She put up her face to be kissed, and he kissed her; but she felt that "he was n't half so glad to see her as she had expected." She knew there was a disapproval in the look bent down upon her, as they went in, together, to the bright parlor. There seemed to be no great charm in the new silk dress, after all. Nobody thought much of it. She began to hate it herself. Somehow, things did n't feel so true to her, as they had a few minutes ago. She was a little ashamed of this great light she had got up in the room.

"When did Uncle Reuben and Aunt Jane go to Hilbury?" asked Gershom. He was afraid to add "what for?"

"Last Friday, I believe. Grandpa 's sick."

"Sick? How sick?" He turned toward her quickly, and the words came with a jerk.

"Oh, not very, I guess. He 's been sick a good deal lately."

There was a silence, then, for an instant.

"You don't seem to think much about it," said Gershom, presently, with something of the old, hard, bitter tone. "You 're keeping house in a grand way here all alone."

He felt indignant; but it was not that only. He spoke recklessly, anything, rather than ask on about what he was afraid to hear.

It was so, then, as he had dreaded. There had been changes while he had been away. He should not find all as it was in the old home that he had come back safely to. He had felt the premonition of this amidst his most joyful anticipations. When did he ever go away and come back again, after any of the few, short absences he had made before, and find all as he had left it? The first time he went a journey in all his life, — *to* Hilbury it was, with his mother, when Hilbury was not yet his home, — he had come back to find his dog dead; after his terms at school, there had always been something altered at the farm, though month in and out, while he stayed there, there had seemed to be no change at all. And he had known there would be something now. And this was it. This that he had not dared to let himself be afraid of, but that he knew now he had feared, ever since he sailed away without his mother's kiss, and the old man's hand laid in blessing on his head. That something should touch one of those two while he was gone.

He stood thinking this, and looking into the fire.

Say got into the corner of the sofa and watched him, with great tears coming in her eyes, and feeling mean and miserable in her silk gown, and wishing that it would turn to rags like Cinderella's, and that the lamps would somehow all go out.

"How long ago did he begin to be sick?" Gershom asked again, after a while, still looking into the fire.

"First of all?" said Say, tremulously.

"Yes."

"Why, ever so long. After he went home from here. Mother said he got tired out, because he would n't stay when you were gone; and then he got caught in a great rain; and so mother and I went to Hilbury, and he was sick a good while."

"Tell me exactly when that was," said Gershom, turning round suddenly and sternly upon her, as if she had been a culprit whom he was cross-questioning.

The sobs fairly came in the child's throat now.

"If you only would n't be so cross with me," she said, with a piteous falter. "It was — that night — after you went away in the Pearl — that grandpa came. And he was so tired and sorry. And — so was I, Gershie. And I thought — I should be so glad — when you came back!"

She crushed herself all down into a heap, as she finished, and hid her head against the sofa-pillow, crying.

Then Gershom came and sat down by her, and spoke more softly.

"I did n't mean to be cross with you, Say. Only it seemed as if you did n't care very much at first. And you were all dressed up so. I never liked you quite so well when you were fine, you know; and I 'm a rough sailor now. Besides, we can't be very glad if grandfather is sick."

"You think I don't care for anything but ribbons and new shoes. You always did. I wish you 'd put out all the lamps and let me cry."

"No, don't cry, Say. I won't be cross. But I want to know all about it. Sit up and tell me." He put his arm round her, gently, and drew her up out of her abandonment. "Did n't mother get my letter? I wrote and told her when the Pearl was going to sail."

"I don't know. I guess so," said Say, struggling with her tears. If Gershie meant to be kind, she would n't be sulky. "But grandpa thought perhaps she would n't go. So he came and went right back again, in the rain." Say paused here, but Gershom waited for more, and with an effort she went on "I don't remember exactly; but mother and I went up to Hilbury when they sent us word, and there was something about a letter, too; I heard Aunt Prue ask mother if it came before you went. I remember that, because mother said yes, and Aunt Prue seemed to be put out because mother had n't given you the message."

Here it was again. Something kept back and covered up, that he was to have known. He remembered well the mention of the letter, of which all that had been told him had been about the four new linen shirts. Aunt Jane, with her soft, sympathizing ways, had been double, both in speech and deed.

Say slid back again into her corner; she had exerted herself thus far rather than be sulky with Gershom; but it would not be quite right with her now till she should have had her cry out, let him be as kind as he might. He partly let her go; something in him at the moment shrunk away from Jane Gair's child.

Say drew little sobbing breaths, softly. Gershom seemed not to be aware. In a minute or two she looked around furtively.

"I could find the letter if you want it, Gershom. I know where mother puts them all. And there are only one or two of Aunt Prue's."

"I don't read other people's letters," answered Gershom, shortly.

"I only meant about the message," said Say, deprecatingly. She felt suddenly mean, again, as if she had tried to steal something and been caught. She loved Gershom dearly; and yet he always made her feel a self-contempt, somehow. She did not think he was fair to her, and yet he made her look at herself with his eyes. People she feared or cared for always did this. They over-magnetized her. She could not maintain her thought against theirs.

"Good-night, Say," said Gershom, suddenly. "I 'm going down aboard the Pearl again. To-morrow morning I shall go to Hilbury. I 've got some great pink and spotted shells for you in my chest, and a red basket. I 'll give them to the steward to keep till you go down."

Say kissed him when he leaned down to her, and said not a word to urge him from his purpose. It never entered her head to dispute Gershom's will. In a moment he was gone. Then she climbed up on the table and screwed down the lamps one after another, till there was only the firelight left in the room. And then she reached and tugged at the hooks of her dress, till she had unfastened them all, and pushed it down about her to the floor. She just set her foot upon it once, deliberately, as it lay there, and then flung herself back into the sofa-corner again, and pulled the pillow down over her head and her bare shoulders, and lay and cried, saying over and over to herself, "It was horrid, — horrid!" Half comprehending her own shame and pain, she cried herself to sleep at last; and Winny, when the game of cards was finished in the kitchen, came up and found her so.

Gershom went down through the dim streets to the wharf and to the brig again. The shipkeeper's watch — a couple of sturdy fellows — were pacing the quarter-deck; they took no notice as Gershom came up the side, and passed on forward. He had said, when he went ashore, that he might as likely as not come back to sleep. An hour after, Ned Blackmere also returned. The watch knew him, too; he passed his nights on board, more often than otherwise, when the brig was in port. Indeed, it had usually been counted on that he would; and Buxton, the shipkeeper, arranged his force accordingly. Blackmere passed quietly forward, also, and went down into the forecastle. He struck a match, and lit his pipe. His face showed sterner and gloomier than ever, by the instant's flash. He saw Gershom Vorse lying in his berth; and a kind of lurid smile came over his features, revealing rather than relaxing, their grim look, as the lightning shows the cloud.

"*He* wasn't wanted then, no more than I; he'll find 'em out, at last." Old Barnacle said this to himself, as his match went out, and, with his pipe alight, he passed quietly up the ladder and out upon the deck.

Gershom Vorse was not asleep. He heard Ned Blackmere pacing there, above him, — to and fro, to and fro, — for half the night after.

CHAPTER XVII.

COMING!

WEALTHY HOOGS went down through the long barn with her milk-pails on her arm.

She set them on the floor, and passed between the stanchions into the great standing-place. There she set open a side door that led into the yard; and one after another five great mild, milky-sweet mammals put their horned heads, with rimy, vaporous nostrils, in at the entrance, and presently offered their meek necks to captivity of peg and beam.

Wealthy tossed down great trusses of hay to them from the mow-side, and took a minute's rest, then, while they were feeding, sitting down on the shaft of a heavy hay-wagon, and leaning her elbows on her knees, and her chin in her hands.

"I wonder if there's never any end to *doin'!*" she said to herself. And I should like to know how it would seem, just once, to be *done for!* — I should like to be made much of, and tended, — yes, *babied*, awhile, for the sake of finding out. When I get to heaven, if I can have what I want, it'll be a good strong angel to follow round after me, and see to me all the time!"

"That's a pretty way of talking, too, Wealthy Hoogs!" she said, again, catching herself up after a pause. "As if you did n't suppose you'd got it now! — There's nothing given out, that is n't given in again from Somewhere. Tell yourself that."

The red winter sun, setting far to the south, sent its crimson shaft, ninety five million miles long, straight in at the low barn-side door, and told it her, too. "There's a way for it to come, though it's from ever so far!" This thought whispered itself to her, and she rose up again to her labor.

> "She took up her burden of life, again,"
> *Not* saying, even, "it might have been!"

The three deep pails were foaming full presently. But, before she carried them up to the house, Wealthy went round to where the "gray colt" — an equine youth of twenty — stood in his stall, and led him out, and put his harness on him. The sleigh, a small square box on runners, stood outside. Wealthy and her steed went forth together and the scrubby, precocious little beast helped all he could to put himself into the shafts.

Ten minutes after, the milk was strained; and Wealthy came into the kitchen where Jaazaniah, in a wadded gown of comfortable homespun, sat by the fire.

He had got a good deal of "the rough off," poor fellow, since we saw him last. Rheumatic fever had had him in its clutches, and had wrenched him in every joint. And now, feeble, and thin, and pale, with a "turrible poor appetite," and a "wearin' kind of a cough," he sat here, day after day, and waited; to get better, or worse. And Wealthy did the nursing, and the housework, and, as we have seen, pretty much of the out-door work, too.

"I 've put the colt into the sleigh, Jez," she said, cheerily as she came in. "And if you don't mind it, for an hour or so, I 'm going to drive down to the Bridge. There 's roots to be cut, and wood to split, and some little tinkerin' jobs to do about; and I must see to get 'Siah Ford up for a day or two. And, then, I don't durst to be any longer without that liniment; you might have your pain back, on a sudden; and, Jez, — I 've half a mind to get that new doctor to drop round here and take a look at you. He might think of something, you know, to start your appetite, and give you a little strength."

This last, you see, was what Wealthy had really made up her mind to go for.

There had come a new doctor to the Bridge, within three months past. Good Doctor Gayworthy's failing health had created an "opening." With nobody knows what instinct, from however far away, there is always an instant heading of eager capacity towards room so made. How do they find it out? How do the wild geese find out when the great icebergs are breaking up, northward, and the summer seas are widening, and they may go and build their nests?

The stage drove up to the Post Office, as Wealthy Hoogs came into the village at the Bridge. Post-office and village store were all one; and here Wealthy also drove up and alighted; and so met Gershom Vorse.

"Well, of all things! To think I should have lit right upon you!" she cried. "When did you get back from sea? Do your folks expect you? There don't seem to be any of 'em here. Jump right in with me. I can take you round, just as well as not. I've only got to speak to 'Siah Ford, and stop a minute at the new doctor's."

The new doctor's!

Those three words told Gershom how the last eight mouths had settled his life for him. His good old grandfather breaking down, disabled; his place already filled. Would it have been so if he had stayed at home; if he had taken up the life the old man meant for him; if everybody had known that he was coming, by and by, when he was needed, to follow the hereditary calling for which, for three generations back, there had not failed a son of the same house? He would have been nearly through a college year, by this time; and he had been ready to enter as Sophomore. Would his grandfather have been ill, but for the worry and exposure he had been the means of his incurring; but for the want of the help, also, that he should have given? They were painful, self-scourging thoughts the boy had, as he sat there, waiting while Wealthy Hoogs got her bottle filled with liniment.

"I suppose you 've heard all the Hilbury news?" said Wealthy, as she took her seat beside him.

"No," said Gershom. "There were only two other passengers in the coach; and they were strangers. The driver seemed to be a new man too."

"That 's part of the news. Abner 's gone out West. Where the smartest men and the laziest all go. He 's a lazy one. He 'll expect to stand out in the middle of a prairie an' p'int round; north, south, east, west; an' say 'Wheat, Barley, Oats, Rye,' an' see 'em grow! *Maybe* he will; but it 's a good way to go on a slim chance. Old Mr. Fairbrother's dead, you know?"

How should he know? Gershom started. The words smote him with a shock. Was everybody dead, or dying, or gone, that he had come back to see, after these eight months?

"Oh yes; he died, quite sudden, a month ago. I forgot; of course, you could n't have got a letter since then. I think that 's one thing that 's helped to upset your grandfather. They were always great friends."

"How *is* — the Doctor?"

Gershom was sensitive, all at once, coming back to his town's people, of using again the term of kinship, which might only set them thinking that he had no right to it; that there was "no blood-relation, after all."

"Well," — hesitatingly, — "you heard *he* was sick?"

"Yes; I heard that in Selport."

"He 's been pretty bad, that 's a fact. Most folks thought he would n't weather through it. Lung trouble again. But he 's got a wonderful constitution. And he 's had good nursin'. Those things come before doctors, both of 'em. And *I* guess, when Jane

Gair and her husband 's gone, and the house gets quieted down, he 'll pick up, and be smart again. It 's the worst thing in the world to send for sick folks' friends, without they can *do* something. They just gather round, and look on; and I believe half the people that die, do it because they see it 's expected of 'em. Nobody likes to make a muster for nothing."

"How is Jaazaniah, Cousin Wealthy?"

He asked it more for kindness' sake, and to change the topic, than from any doubt of the farmer's well-being; but he got Wealthy's last item of news for answer. Still of the same sort.

"Jaazaniah 's keeled up, too; he 's had a rheumatic fever, and been poorly enough all winter. That 's what I 'm coming here for."

And she motioned Gershom, who held the reins, toward the white paling of the little house on the corner of the village street. This was where the "new doctor" lived.

The world goes on, pausing for nobody to make experiments, or change his mind. Nobody can take up his old life-thread at any one point where he may have left it. Everything else has shaped itself to his first decision, with a facile, fatal mobility. Circumstances have flowed in around his act, and hardened to barriers against recantation.

In his first half hour at Hilbury, Gershom Vorse began to grow aware of this.

"Let me get out here," he said, at the foot of the hill. "And you drive right straight on. Unless you 'll come in, I 'd as lief not have them hear the bells stop at the house."

"Oh, I can't come in," said Wealthy. "Jez 'll be growing uneasy; and I guess you 're in the right to get in as quiet as you can. Nobody knows, that has n't *been* sick, or been a good deal with 'em, how sick folks mistrust all that goes on about a house. Oh, la," — to Gershom's thanks, — "it was no kind of trouble! come and see Jez, won't you? It 'll do him a sight of good," and Mrs. Hoogs made mild suggestions with bit and reins, to her well-broken nag, and drove straight on, as she was asked.

Gershom walked up the hill, and turned in by the garden fence, across the chipyard. He went up to the side door, and there he stopped; and stood still upon the great doorstone. If he could only see his mother, first, alone!

They were all expecting him, shortly. Only his mother, though, thought of him momently, and momently looked for him to come. The vessel would be in fair time, Mr. Gair had told them, at the end of the week, or by the first of next. This was only Thursday.

But Prudence Vorse was restless to-night. There was something in the air for her, though other nerves might easily not feel it. She could not pass a window, in her goings to and fro, without looking out into the winter starlight.

Jane was upstairs, sitting with her father; she always had the evening watch in the sick-room, as she could not sit up nights; Rebecca, who was to be called at ten, was sleeping in her own chamber; Joanna was washing up the tea-things in the sitting-room, and Mrs. Vorse was making a bowl of arrowroot at the kitchen fire, when Wealthy Hoogs drove by, her sleigh-bells leaving a cheery wake of sound behind her.

Nobody else noticed it; but it startled Prue. Why? It went straight on; yet the noise of the bells broke upon her like a summons, and seemed to ring a message to her, as it passed.

"Coming — coming — coming — coming!" If they did not syllable it, they put the feeling, somehow, with a fresh leap, into her heart.

She set down the bowl, into which she had just stirred salt and a teaspoonful of brandy; she stood, looking into the coals, thinking; sending her soul out to meet the child. Away out upon the deep she had gone in spirit, day after day, night after night; down upon the seacoast she had waited, thinking of the bright sails that should come up, some morning, in the winter sunlight, bringing her hope again; to-day, somehow, she had not yearned forth so far; she had thought of when he might be coming on the homeward road, up from the busy city, into the white stillness of the hills; and every now and then, let her be doing what she might, a joy that seemed hanging in the air would seize her suddenly, with a sweet electric pang. Now — this moment — it was close upon her. Farther than the echo of those bells, she could not send her thought out; but to the sound of them her pulse sprang restlessly; so she set her bowl down, and stood there, listening, those few moments while their resonance lasted; and then suddenly, she turned, as by some swift magnetic impulse, and went out toward the door. Not knowing why. She would look down the road. She would feel what the weather was.

She did neither. She looked no further than her boy's face, waiting for her there in the starlight. She felt no cold that came in with him. She folded him silently in her arms, and drew him in.

Joanna came presently from the sitting-room, and found the two standing together on the kitchen hearth. An exclamation sprang to her lips; but Prue put her finger up, and the habit of the still house checked her. She gave him a glad greeting, quietly; and would have gone away again, then, and left him to his mother.

But for the bowl of arrowroot, Prue might have been glad to have it so; as it was, she stopped her. "Never mind, Joanna; it is n't worth while; the Doctor must have this while it 's fresh, and he takes it best from me."

"Can I see grandfather to night?" asked Gershom.

"I wish you could," said Prue, slowly and emphatically, "or else — I wish nobody besides need know that you are in the house!"

"Why?" questioned Joanna quickly, in surprise.

"I don't know," answered Prue, still with the same slow earnestness. "I can't always tell why I *do* think things. I don't know why I went and opened the door just now; but I did; and I couldn't have helped it; and Gershom was there."

Prue was of too integral an honesty, perhaps, to understand the subtle shadows of doubt that warned her of a doubleness in another. But she had an uneasy feeling, although she did not care to define it, that if Jane knew of the boy's arrival, it would mix up things somehow; that some untowardness would result; either the old man would be sure to be unable for the meeting, or it would happen at some unfavorable moment. What Jane would have to do with this, she hardly thought; she could not certainly have told. There are unspoken instincts of knowledge between life and life, of which we can scarcely trace the growing up; we only know, surely, that they are there.

"Let me go up to your room, mother; you'll be able to come there presently, won't you? I'd rather not see them all to-night."

"There's no need of saying anything, if you don't choose," said Joanna to Prue. "The house is settled for the night, and it 's just as well to make no stir."

Joanna, who hated so all intermeddling of "other folks," could well see how mother and son might long to be together, and have each other quite to themselves. This was all she saw. The same straightforward independence which she would have used in her own behalf, she counselled in theirs. It was nobody's else business, if they chose to have it so, and nothing need be said.

It was all quite reasonable, and right, and easy; Joanna understood; to-morrow it would be enough to say that Gershom had been tired, and had not cared to see them all at once; and that the house was still, and so he had gone quietly up stairs; and before this need be said at all, when his grandfather should wake in the early morning, in Prue's watch, if all were well, she might bring him in, and have the meeting over.

But this was not quite after Prue's way for all; and she felt like a smuggler, going up the end staircase to her own room, Gershom following; and when she left him there, and turned away taking her bowl of arrowroot to the Doctor's chamber, where Jane sat, it was with a sensation foreign and intolerable to her nature.

Prudence Vorse would never have made a general. She would have never been equal to any magnificent strategy; she would have marched her men right up in face of the enemy, in broad daylight, and dared his guns; and beaten him so, in fair fight, or not at all.

She held her tongue as she came to the bedside, and Jane gave up her seat to her; but she put a force upon herself to do it, because, here, she must; and she was glad when Jane moved quietly off and went away, while she should give the old man his gruel. Afterward, when she met her on the stairs, coming up, as she went down, she passed her quickly, — almost roughly, — still without a word. Jane shrugged her shoulders, and smiled a little as she went on. "Prue's in one of her fierce fits," she said to herself. It must be horribly uncomfortable." And hugged herself placidly in spirit. Jane was never fierce; calm and good-natured, always; never forgetting to be polite. One got along so much better in the world, if one were only wise enough to know it.

At ten o'clock Prue went and called Rebecca. She stood there in the passage between Jane's room and the doctor's until Rebecca glided in and Jane came out. Then she stopped her, and spoke abruptly: —

"Gershom is come, Jane. I did n't choose that you should know it before; and he don't want to see anybody else till morning. First of all, if the doctor wakes comfortable, I mean he shall see *him*."

It was a fair fight, and aboveboard, now. By the very establishment of this, Jane's guns were silenced. She had not a word to say, — she, in her soft politeness. Brusque truth was not her weapon, as it was Prue's. She must have vantage-ground, and mask her batteries; Prue came upon them with a bayonet-charge of outright honesty, and carried the whole line at a sweep. There is nothing that so circumvents circumvention as a thorough, unlooked-for directness.

In the chill between midnight and morning, Prue took up her watch in the sick-room.

"Father has been rather restless: he wanders a little, I think. I can hardly tell whether it is that or dreaming. He talks about Benjamin, and even little Will that died so long ago." Will was Jane's brother, dead in babyhood, thirty years before.

Rebecca said this low, at the door, before she went.

"I think, Prue, he has never left off worrying about Gershom, he put him so in their place. If he would only come soon!"

"He *has* come, Becsie: he came last night." Her tenderness and joy welled up in these words, as she spoke them to Rebecca. Prudence was neither rough nor fierce now. The two women leaned to each other with a mutual impulse, and their lips met.

A low voice breathed from the bed, as Prue came up to it alone: —

"'Me have ye bereaved of my children. Joseph is not, and Simeon is not; and ye will take Benjamin away: all these things are against me.'

"Send for Ben, Prue;" and he lifted up his eyes to her face beseechingly. "Tell him to come to me. All the boy I 've got in the world; what did he go away for? Benjamin — it was right he should be named so, he was Rachel's son, — the son of my old age."

"Go to sleep now, father: he is coming; he will be here by and by."

"'One went out from me; and I saw him not since: and if ye take this also from me, ye shall bring down my gray hairs with sorrow to the grave.'"

The story of Israel wandered in his brain, — this old man, whose sons had died in babyhood and boyhood; from whom they had lured his last stay, — Rachel's child's child, whom he made in his heart as his own; who had grown up, reminding him, as his youth bloomed, of Benjamin; growing so into Benjamin's place that it had seemed like a coming back of the lost: so that now, in his wandering and weakness, he could not separate the thought of the two.

But he slept at last, quieted by that promise, — a real sleep, as if something of the peace Prue brought in with her had stolen over him also; and by and by, — hours after, — when the gray of the tardy January dawn began to crimson, he woke, quite calm and conscious: conscious of something that had come to him as in his sleep, — that was his first thought now; but that he was not sure of.

"Did you tell me he had come, Prue? or did I dream it?"

"I told you, father," said Prue, tenderly, coming to him with some warm, nourishing drink she had got ready; "and now when you have had this, and are quite rested and strong, I 'm going to bring him in to see you."

Prue knew just how to hold his head for him, and give him his drink comfortably; she knew also just how much to bring, — she never dismayed him with a cup too mighty; and, partly for this and partly from a childlike acceptance of it as a condition, the doctor swallowed it all, to the last drop; and then he lay back, with a sweet contentedness in his face, and looked up, his eyes asking for the better thing she was to give him next. She bathed his face, and smoothed his white hair, and laid the bedclothes even; and then she went and got the boy, as she had promised.

"An old man always looks far older for not being dressed, Gershie, or for ever so little of a sickness; you must remember that."

"I am afraid I shall cry, mother, like a girl."

"You won't do any such thing, Gershom," said his mother, quickly, turning short round. "It might kill him."

They went in together; and Gershom did not cry: but the tall, brown sailor stood by the old man's bedside, and laid his roughened hand in his; and every fibre of him trembled with deep feeling: for as Jacob had been to Benjamin, so had this old man been even to him.

And the legend of Genesis was still repeating itself in the sick man's thought; for he turned him toward the boy, and spoke the words familiar from many a heart-reading, "'Now let me die, since I have seen thy face, and thou art yet alive!'"

"*Grandfather!*"

It was all in that one word: The fulness of feeling that dared no further trust itself to utterance;—the pleading remonstrance against that word of death,—the sorrow, the self-accusing, the love; the very cry of Cain,—"It is more than I can bear!" There are single human tones that can say all this, and more.

The old man answered it.

"My son, it will all be well, and as God pleases. No other hath done or can undo. I have longed for you, and you have come. I thank Him!"

They understood each other, now: they felt each other; heart to heart. None could put a thought between them that could alter this.

"By and by you shall come and tell me all about your ship, and your sea-life. You 've seen a bigger piece of the world than I have, Gershie."

The voice was faint. The good doctor was tired with his effort and with his gladness; he could do no more now for awhile than to rest silently in his grateful thought. But he would not let the boy go away heavy with too great solemnity. He would say this cheerful word of common interest in common life first.

Gershom spoke no further till he stood alone with his mother in her chamber. Then he looked her full in the face and said—

"Tell me, mother, if you can, just what you wrote to Aunt Jane before I went."

His mother repeated to him that postscript of her letter, word for word. It had lain in her memory ever since. She had considered it well before she wrote it; she had reviewed it, mentally, over and over, in those forty-eight hours between the sending of it and the receiving of her son's letter. She had weighed the probable effect of every word upon him. She had not given him up, even on that Tuesday night when his own word came that he must go away without seeing her.

"That was it," she said, when she had finished. "And I felt sure that, let things be as they might, it would bring you back."

Gershom Vorse turned pale about the lips.

"Mother," said he, slowly, and without vehemence, "I will never forgive Aunt Jane for this."

And at that moment his mother could not find it in her heart to answer him a word.

CHAPTER XVIII.

BIDDY FLYNN AND HER NEIGHBORS.

There were tidy, white-curtained windows, with blossoming plants looking out at the panes, and rooms with clean-scoured floors, where bits of comfortable carpet were laid down, and all the snug, attractive living of the thrifty poor, in some other portions of that same tenement whereof the back room of the ground floor was rented and punctually paid for by Ned Blackmere. When he went off upon his voyages, he paid beforehand. His wife should not be without a roof to cover her and her shame.

So the landlord was forbearing, and the neighbors, for the poor man's sake, complained as little as they could. But they drew their little children inside their doors when her staggering step came over the threshold in the dusk; and Biddy Flynn, the washerwoman, would listen and look in on her at night, before she went to her own bed, for fear of fire. Biddy Flynn had a fine silk shawl that she wore on Sundays in the summer time, that Ned Blackmere had brought home to her from beyond the sea. They all pitied Blackmere, the sailor, — these simple neighbors, in their honest hearts; and when his sad, stern, weather-beaten face was seen about, and he passed in and out, at intervals, among them, they took a solemn look on their faces, too, as they might do for one who had death in his home. He scarcely knew whether they pitied him or not. He never sought companionship among them. He gave Biddy Flynn the shawl, for his wife was not fit for it, and it might help to keep her patient. He was afraid that, some day, losing patience, they might turn Susan into the street.

They were afraid, too, — the neighbors; afraid as well as sorry for him. He was such a terrible strong man, and there was such an anger in his eye, sometimes, when he came out.

"Lord grant he may n't be left to lift his hand upon her!" Luke Dolan, the carpenter, would say to his Betsy, in the room above, when the sound of fierce words, — gin made her devilish, not stupid, as poor Ned had said, — and of deep, stern answers, like the restrained rumble of an earthquake, would come up from below.

But the room below was sometimes empty for weeks, for months; then the neighbors had peace and respite. Sukey Blackmere was "off on her travels," nobody knew where. She had her haunts, her cronies; also, they knew that now and then, to get more money, she would go and "take a place." She had a decent suit of black that only saw the light upon these emergencies. She could look very respectable in this, with her black hair brushed, — it was silky black hair still, for Sukey had been handsome, — with threads of grey that only emphasized the respectability; and she wore a middle-aged dignity that one would hardly have suspected. She was a good cook, and an Englishwoman; that was a great thing. She had been brought up in the household of a county family, in the old country; hence her middle-aged dignity that could be so deferential, also; a manner sure to take here, where a rampant independence is ordinarily inspired with the first breath of republican air. So she got into good places, at high wages. The cloven foot showed presently, but she was seldom "overcome." Her fellow-servants got the worst of it. They called her what her husband did, — a she-devil. True to the traditions of her genus, she disappeared by-and-by in a grand explosion; then she came home with money in her pocket, — marvellously well lined, sometimes, after short absences, — and dropped to her lower parallel of life. On these two tracks she ran, leaving behind her a pretty little thread of history that only she, if any one, could trace.

I do not mean to enter into it; my story lies not here. What I have to say I will say quickly. Something came of it all, one January night; a tragedy, — a mystery; an added blackness over old Barnacle's gloomy life.

Sukey had been home three days; long enough to be at her worst. The third night she stayed out late.

The winter evening had closed in; the little families were gathered, each to its own fireside. Children were washed and put to bed, or crawled to their untidy couches, unwashed, according to the genius of the different homes; for there was not, of course, in every room of the old mansion that had come to be a human hive, that poetry of humble living I have hinted at in some; simple supper-tables were cleared away; bits of crockery were washed and put up on their shelves; the hour of domestic comfort or discomfort had arrived.

Biddy Flynn was home from a hard day's work. She had had

her "cup 'o tay," and wanted to go to bed. First however, she had a little routine of ceremony to go through. She had some money to count that was tied up in an old stocking-foot and kept behind the press. She had some more to put with it that she unfastened out of the corner of her neckerchief, — her wages for the day. This she reckoned over carefully, and added to the rest; and then to prove her sum, counted up all together, once more. Biddy was saving money — lone woman that she was — to bring over by and by a sister's child from the "ould counthry." Then she "racked" her hair, and tied it up tight, in anticipation of her early morning toilet, thereby reduced to the washing of her face, and the tying on of a clean cap; then she said her prayers; then one would have thought she must be ready for repose; but there was yet one thing more to do.

Against the wooden partition that had cut a large, old-fashioned kitchen in two, and made of it the separate tenements of Biddy Flynn and Sukey Blackmere, the sailor's wife, — hung a gaudy colored print of the Madonna. High up, so that it could only be reached by climbing on the deal table that stood beneath.

Every night, between her prayer and slumbers, Biddy so aspired; and every night the gracious Queen of Heaven came down, — from off her nail, — and Biddy had a vision. A surreptitious vision, — hardly beatific, — through a crack of the old boarding from which the paper had split away, and which, just here, the ingenious Biddy had enlarged, — to a comfortable breadth on her own side, and as far as she dared upon the other. Two thirds of the room, upon the further side, came within her range of observation; the bed against the wall below, took up most of the remaining third. Holding the Blessed Mary fast in her arms, Biddy made, first, her ocular examination of the premises; and then, applying the second feature of her face to the chink, would press into inquisitorial service a second sense. Usually, she smelt gin; and for its being only that, and not fire, she would thank the Holy Mother, and hang her reverently up again, and so betake herself content to bed.

A desolate room, — a worse than desolate man; these were what Biddy Flynn looked down upon, amazedly, to-night.

Ashes upon the floor, about the dead, dirty stove; a broken bottle on the hearth; a pail of filthy water, with a black mop-rag hanging over the side, conveying its contents by a slow dribble, to the floor; a sloppy table, with a crust and a tea-cup upon it; these visible by the blaze of an inch of candle standing flat upon the brick mantel, without a stick. By the miserable fireside, the man who had come home across the seas, to this; who had lighted as he could his forsaken hearth, and sat down by it, gloomy and despairing; his feet among the ashes; ashes of shame, also, upon his bent head, — ashes of hopelessness upon his heart.

"Beast!" he muttered, showing his white teeth, set with passion, and clenching tighter the closed fists between which he leaned his face, and sent forth his compressed speech. "And this stands between me and the chance of anything better on God's earth! — Dam-nation!"

Biddy Flynn shrunk back; she had no business with this, the horror of it was too sacred; she hung up the Blessed Mary with trembling hands, and prayed that glorified Womanhood, in her ignorant way, for mercy on what womanhood debased had crushed and maddened.

In a little while she heard his chair pushed back, and his step going out toward the door at the back that opened upon a narrow alley. He might have stayed there, waiting, or he might have gone away; she could not tell. She listened awhile, in fear, for what sounds might come back into that next room, but, hearing nothing, by-and-by she fell asleep.

It was going on to eleven o'clock when Susan Blackmere turned her unsteady steps into the alley. She put her hands out, reaching the wall on either side, supporting herself so, and feeling her dark way. A person looking in from the street would have distinguished nothing in the gloom. If Susan Blackmere, though, had but turned for a moment and looked outward, she might have seen, against the light of the entrance, the shadow of a something that came silently behind her. She was safe not to turn, however, groping her way so, at least until she came to the end. When she stopped there at the house door, the figure behind her stopped, and crouched down low, almost prostrate, like a dog, against the farther wall.

She passed in and shut the door. There was no lock upon it; the children had pulled out an old bolt and lost it, long ago; but the tenants locked their separate rooms at night, and it was no matter. It was Susan Blackmere's own affair, whether she remembered to fasten her door or not. As often as not, it was left as she left it now.

She stumbled in, over the pail, with a snarl and a curse. She felt towards the mantel, and searched for a match and the candle-end. This last was burned down and gone. She snarled and cursed again, and put her hand in her pocket and brought forth another. Then the match flickered through the darkness, and the flame fastened itself to the bit of wick, and the small, steady light showed, presently, the whole wretched, squalid place again. Showed it to two eyes that glared in at the window.

"Tree'd, — by G — ! Now we 'll see who 'll blab!"

And the figure crouched itself again and waited.

What it was that waked Biddy Flynn, when she had been asleep an hour or thereabout, she could never distinctly tell.

A dull blow, or a fall, and a strange sound of something crushed, — then two or three rapid steps, — whether she had dreamed or heard these, in her coming consciousness, she started upright in her bed, and tried to comprehend.

Dead silence, now. But something awful in the silence. A sudden horror in the air that seized her in every nerve.

Biddy crossed herself and listened, motionless.

Still no further sound.

"Was it a bad dhrame, I wonder, or the bit of herrin' wid me supper? Holy Mother! but I 've a strange feel, the night!"

It might not have been five minutes, or it might have been fifteen, that Biddy sat there still, with shortened breath and strained sense; but she calmed a little, at last, her muscles relaxed, she took a fuller respiration, and was about to lie back upon her pillow when there came a sound from just beyond the slight partition, — a faint, long, gasping, gurgling moan, like nothing but some creature dying in its blood.

"Ooh! — Ahl the saints! What is it?" she cried, and clapped her hands upon her ears, in a panic of ghastly apprehension.

For minutes more she cowered and quivered in an ignorant terror; fearful to move, fearful to stay where she was.

Then she slid down out of her bed, and, gathering up her shawl, which served her for an extra coverlet in the cold nights, she wrapped herself about with it, and crept toward her door.

This opened on the side of the room furthest from the Blackmeres, and directly at the foot of the broad old staircase, which ran up the back, and ended at Luke Dolan's door.

"Betsy Dolan! — Luke! Luke! — Are ye there at ahl?" came in a hoarse, gusty whisper through the keyhole; and the door was shaken, as if the wind had got in, and clattered it.

But the stout carpenter and his tired wife slept sound.

The call came louder, then.

"Arrah, darlint, waken, for the love of Heaven! — Luke Dolan! Betsy!"

And Betsy heard, at last.

"Whisht! don't rise the childher! — What is it, sure?" whispered Mistress Dolan, opening the door.

Biddy waited for no word or ceremony, but pressed in.

"The Blessed Lord knows what it is! It 's a fit or a murdher, down below, in Blackmere's! Mak' hashte, and come down wid yees, for it's feared I am of me life, there, me lane!"

A head came out at the opposite door, at this; and with the multiplied voices, and the opening and shutting, the alarm was spread till the whole floor was roused. There was a striking of lights, — a hustling into clothes, — a hurrying down the stairs; and, presently, into the dark, cheerless room where Ned Blackmere had sat brooding alone, three hours ago, huddled a crowd of housemates, eager with fear and curiosity.

"Stand back, all of ye!" said Luke Dolan, going first, and looking upon the bed. "There's wurruk here for the cur'ner, — an' the Lord be gracious to us all!"

It was the end of the dark thread that only one memory could have traced. And of the last hours through which it wound, there were no lips, now, to speak.

There was only a dead woman lying there across the bed, face down; beaten in among the clothes; blood welling from among the matted hair; beside her, the rough, stained, wedge-shaped billet of firewood that, in some human hand, had done the deed.

CHAPTER XIX.

THE SILENT SIN.

Mr. Gair went down to Selport, to look after his brig; and his child. People drop all to attend the summons, when message comes that a kinsman lies in danger of death; nothing, then, is of any weight, in comparison; but if death be long in coming, or hold off, uncertain, affairs become peremptory again. If any change occur, let them know. Mr. Gair was to be thus apprised. It suggested itself to Jane, in that underflow of thought that winds on, subtilely, among anxieties and emotions, strangely untouched of either — that this might be convenient, "if anything should happen." She never could have anything to do with that dreadful milliner at the Bridge.

Friday and Saturday were quiet, easy days; no alteration. The Doctor had Gershom in, and talked with him at intervals. He comforted and strengthened him, concerning what he had done. "All would turn out for the best. If he — the Doctor — could have had his health, and worked on a little longer, he might have preferred his own plan; but now he was quite content. People would not wait for a boy to go and get his learning. Sickness came every day; they looked for a ready-made wisdom to step in; ready-made gray hairs, if they could get them."

"Put your whole might into it, now, Gershom; and make a man of yourself; think of your mother; think of your God, boy!"

Between Saturday night and Sunday morning came the beginning of what they had feared. The Doctor himself had felt sure of it. A relapse. All day Sunday the good man struggled painfully with disease. On Monday, the word went down for Mr. Gair and Say.

God's word came down also into that still, sick-room, calling a soul back to Himself.

Before Tuesday night, when the stage came in at the Bridge and Gershom drove to meet it, all was over.

It had been a slow, painful giving way of nature. A laboring and failing breath, hour after hour, till the breath went forth at last, and was never drawn again. They sat by and watched, with grieved hearts and seldom speech.

There was no set leave-taking. There was no need. There had hardly ever been any word, that either could remember, of the good man going away from among them now, that, for its truth, or kindliness, or cheer, or simple, holy trust, might not fitly have been cherished by them as his last.

"Think of your mother. Think of your God, boy!"

These were what thrilled solemnly in the heart of Gershom Vorse, as nearly the last he spoke to him.

They sat all together at the family board for the first time since the Doctor's illness had gathered them at home, at that still breakfast on the Wednesday morning. The first coming together of the household in its old routine, after a blank has been left in it. How many a heart has felt that graveside solemnity!

"It"— the funeral — was to be on Thursday. Mr. Gair could not leave his business longer. He would come up again next week, and attend to anything that they might need him for. But just now his presence was imperatively required in Selport.

"With all the rest," Mr. Gair said, in that subdued tone that people use when they begin to speak of any outside matter in a house of death, "there has been a sad piece of work on board the brig since she came in. That English fellow, Gershom — Ned Blackmere — was arrested Friday morning for the murder of his wife. It's in the paper here," and he drew out a Selport Journal from his coat-pocket.

Gershom Vorse, startled out of thoughts that nothing less than a shock like this could have displaced, gazed for an instant in the speaker's face, as unable to take in the meaning of his words, then pushing his chair round suddenly, and almost springing from it, he exclaimed —

"He never did it in the world, sir!" After another moment's thought, — "he *could n't* have done it! Why, the brig only got in on Thursday evening, and he was on board all night with me."

"*All* night? You both went ashore, though? The murder took place, they say, between half past ten and eleven, and Blackmere was seen there, waiting in his wife's room, before she came in. The best we can get at for him is, that he was on board during the forepart of the night, and on deck for some time towards midnight. Buxton's men can testify to that much, but they can't swear to the exact time he came on board. And half an hour would make all the difference."

"It was n't fifteen minutes, sir, after the clock struck ten, when he came back on board!"

"Can you swear to that, Gershom?"

"Yes, sir."

"You may do something for him, then. At any rate you ought to be on hand week after next, when the case comes up."

No wonder, with this double weight of thought upon him, that Gershom was silent, and sought to be alone as far as possible all that day. In all this time, beyond the barest greeting at first seeing her, he had held no communication with Mrs. Gair. The circumstances under which they met made such avoidance easy. There had been little talk between any in that sad house, throughout those hours of watching and of grief.

Mrs. Vorse was busy with necessary cares. Miss Millett, from the Bridge, was up stairs with the other sisters, "making mourning." Gershom must get out of the way of all this. He could not have his mother to himself. He spent nearly all his time in the bay of the old barn, lying there alone in the hay, in the warm south window, where he had used to betake himself in the happy days that seemed already so long ago, when he was in heart and truth but a boy, dreaming boy-dreams of the world and of finding his way out into it; feeling now *thrust* out, with the door of his youth shut to suddenly behind him.

It all revolved itself over and over in his mind as he lay here. This terrible change; this loss that made him, for the first time, absolutely fatherless; the thought of what he should do with his mother; that she must not stay here now; that he would take her away, somewhere, and have her all for his own,— his own care, his one comfort. Of Aunt Jane, that he could never, would never, have aught to do with her again. The guilt of his grandfather's death, if it lay at any human door, lay at hers. Gershom had too much of his mother's clear, discerning justice not to see this, and cease reproaching himself weakly or unduly. He knew he would have come, laying aside all plan and preference of his own, at that summons which she had withheld from him. He was indignant, to the very depths of his nature, at this wrong that she had done them all; but he laid the wrong where it belonged. He would torture himself no more with self-upbraiding. He would take every loving, generous word that his grandfather had said, home into his heart and let it comfort him. Between them there had been truth and peace to the last. Between them there should only lie a peaceful memory.

He said all this to himself, not for self-solace only, but for honesty and justice. Yet he had to say it again and again. The cruel bitterness would come up. If he had only done his grandfather's bidding! If he had only never let that sea-fever get possession of him! If he had only been determined, even, not to go without a-coming home first! He might be strong enough and just enough not to torment himself morbidly, but this dreg of reproach would always lie in his conscience. Jane Gair had put this unsilenced, haunting "If" of fruitless regret into a young life that had never known it before; that henceforth should never be able wholly to cast it out.

And Ned Blackmere! This story, so sudden and awful, that he could hardly credit or conceive it clearly; this horrible doubt, this deadly suspicion, this mortal danger that hung over the man, who, in those very hours when it had been bearing down upon him, had been sleeping at his side, his sole companion! This terrible investigation with which Gershom, by the evidence that he could bring, would have to do! Truly, tremendous realities had swooped down, all at once, among his boy-dreams, and scattered them forever!

Say came and found him, at last. She had guessed where he might be, but she had not dared to come, till the red, level light of the setting sun streamed over the snow, and the tea-table stood ready, and she had heard Aunt Prue asking for him. Then she put on her India-rubber shoes and flung her little Scotch shawl over her head, and came to fetch him.

"Gershie!" she called, timidly, at the foot of the granary stairs.

"Well?" answered Gershom, from above, in the hay.

"Tea 's ready, and Aunt Prue wants you."

No answer.

"May I come up?"

"I 'm coming down in a minute."

Not permission, clearly. Neither dismissal, quite. Say gathered the little shawl tighter across her shoulders, and sat down on the lowest step. In a minute Gershom came.

It was a pale, sad little face — pale with the winter chill, sad with a look of some soul-summer gone out of it already — that turned itself up to his as he came down. There were tears, too, standing in the patient eyes.

"Oh, Gershie!" she said touchingly, putting out her hand for his, — "the old, good times are all gone. I don 't think there 's ever going to be any Hilbury any more!"

——"Something turns up and sets 'em adrift, and what becomes of your home then?"——

Those bitter words of Old Barnacle repeated themselves to Gershom's thought, and echoed the plaint of the child.

"For me — I suppose not," he said. "I've got to go out into the world and get my living. I can't be a boy any longer. I'm a man, Say. But you'll come here, summers, the same as ever. Aunt Joanna and Aunt Rebecca will be here. You'll come."

"No, I shan't," said Say, in a voice that trembled. "Mother won't want to come here, always, now. She said so this morning, when Aunt Rebecca spoke about the summer. I know she did n't want much to come, last time. She'll go to the Springs, now; or the sea-shore. That's what she wanted; only she said grandpa would be disappointed. And they said something else; about there being no knowing what would be done, now, with the farm. —And besides," the words quivered out painfully,— "it would n't be anything to come if you were n't here."

Gershom had been the centre of all Say's joys, in all the summer times that she could remember. Now, she was losing him. It is one of the gulfs that open at our feet in life, when one who has been dear and close — a sharer in the same thoughts, and wishes, and pleasures — springs suddenly as it seems away from our side, out of our sphere into another, that lies ready for him and not for us. When the brother goes out of his childhood and his home into manhood and the wide world, — leaving the sister behind in her home and her childhood still, whence the light of both has vanished. When, of the sisters who have slept and played and learned together, one goes forth to new loves and duties, and companionships, and the other stays behind in the same accustomed place, that yet can never be the same again. Ah! it is not the grave only which yawns between lives whereof the one is taken — on — up; — the other left, drearily waiting, in a world whose meaning is all changed; whose very vital springs seem deadened.

Say saw this fissure widening at her feet, between herself and Gershom Vorse; and her child-heart found it hard to bear.

"I've got to be a little girl ever so many years more!" she said, piteously.

Gershom would have been tender with her, but that he hardened so against her mother.

"You'll grow fast enough," he said. "And you'll forget all about Hilbury. You'll go to the Springs and the sea-shore; and by and by you'll like that best."

They were walking up, slowly, along the drive. Say stopped, and let fall Gershom's hand, and sat herself down on the rim of the great trough, determinedly, as if she would not take another step in that life that was leading her on, away from all that she loved best.

"I never shall, in all the world!" she cried, passionately. "I wish I could stop everything and everybody, right here, and not let 'em grow any older, or do anything else!"

"You can't," said Gershom, after a pause, in a quiet tone, and waiting, as expecting her to turn rational again directly. "We've got to keep going on. And you've got to get up now and go in to tea."

He set the palpable necessity of things square before her, as it is the way of man to do, when woman's nature is all in a white foam of tempestuous revolt against it.

Then she burst into tears. Gershom walked on, slowly. He knew not how to deal with this, and so he let it alone. Ah, if he had known it, that was hard dealing!

Say flung her shawl suddenly over head and face, and rushed blindly on, up and into the house. She vanished up the end staircase, and hid herself away in the old clothes-room.

Rebecca went to look for her presently, and found her there in an abandonment of tears. She sat down by her, on the pile of quilts and pillows, and put her arm around her gently, and waited till she should look up. Say, though she never moved, knew by the soft touch who it was. So she sobbed on: but there came a tenderer sound into the grief, at first so bitter and so sharp. By and by she rested; only a long-drawn quiver now and then. Rebecca drew her up against her shoulder, saying, in her old way, — as she had said years ago, when she found the child sitting grieving in disgrace upon the doorstone, — "What is it, Say?"

"It's all so hard!" was Say's strangely comprehensive answer.

"What, Say?" asked the same soft tone.

"Things that happen. People go off — and they don't care; and you've got to keep on; and you can't stop anything."

Only a broken thread in her own life, that Rebecca could lay her thought back upon, could have given her a clew to apprehend this first dreariness of feeling that uttered itself in Say's incoherent words.

"Yes. Things are hard, sometimes. And we must live on, and bear God's will. Because, He makes a plan for us; and there will be always something coming; we can't tell, day by day, what it may be; only He never forgets us, or leaves anything out; and by and by —— "

"By and by — what?" asked Say, after some second's pause.

"Shall I show you, Say?" There was a calm, holy light on Aunt Rebecca's face, as she stood up, and held her hand out to the child.

Say had a feeling of what it was that she would show her. She was not afraid. She got up, and gave her hand, and let herself be led away. Across the great kitchen chamber, — Rebecca taking up the candle she had left there, — and along the entry beyond, to where a door opened into the room Say had not entered since she came.

Rebecca set the light upon the mantel, and took her to the bedside. She drew back a closed curtain, and laid off a linen handkerchief from the pillow.

There was none of the grim rigidness about the bed or room that told of death, and death only. Rebecca would not have the form so tenderly cared for but a few hours before, left here, stark in the winter's cold, with only the grave-robing and the ghastly white sheet for covering. There was a fresh, soft coverlet spread over all, and the sheet turned back upon it, as a couch might have been made up for slumber. The drapery hung close about the foot.

Say saw the same dear face, — the white hair softly floating back from the temples; a beautiful quietness upon it, — and that was all.

"He has lived seventy-eight years, Say. Seven times as long as you. He was glad with all God gave him, and he bore every trouble that He sent. Now, this is what has come. A beautiful rest; and a waking that we cannot know of, into great joy.

"Do you remember the old dream you used to tell me of? When you used to think you had got lost, away from home, and it grew dark and cold; and you were all alone on the roadside, in a strange place? And how you would think to yourself, then, in your dream, — 'I will just lie down, right here, and go to sleep; and I shall wake in my own home again?' That is the way God takes us home to Him. He sends us such a sleep as this; and out of it we wake, presently, in heaven! It will all be right there, Say! It is all working for it, here."

Say held her aunt's hand tight; and spoke not a word; but her face changed from its troubled look to a still brightness, like the faces — the liviug and the dead — she looked upon. And so they drew the curtains again, and took the candle and went out together.

"Only," said Say, timidly, stopping presently, when they had got away into another room, and letting the words come with a long sigh, — "I should like to go to heaven from Hilbury, too."

Rebecca sighed softly, also, and did not speak. She knew how gladly many a heart would choose so its place on earth to go to heaven from. She thought how much might lie for the child in the years between these homes.

But Say was comforted.

Prue came to Mr. Gair, on Thursday, when the funeral was over.

"Will you keep these till you come back, or will you look, to-night, for any papers that he may have left?" She gave him, as she spoke, the Doctor's keys.

There was only the little room to look in. The merchant's time was valuable. He had better do, at once, perhaps, in these few hours when he could do nothing else, what might take him a half-day to do, on his return.

So he took the keys, and turned toward the study.

"Call the others, and come in here with me, all of you," he said.

Jane Gair had it all upon her conscience, now. Now, Satan came and stood straight before her, saying, Choose!

Of two direct ways? No. The devil never does that. There was only one direct way; to tell all she knew, if need be; to see, at any rate, that hidden paper brought to light. But there was a way, seemingly indirect; we never get a look from end to end, right down the evil path. She would *wait*, a few moments, at least; there might be something else to indicate; it might be, after all, that her father had changed his mind, and destroyed the writing. She *knew* nothing to the contrary. She would cling, still, to her "expectant" system. Ah! this was the very way the devil wanted her to choose.

Doctor Gayworthy had not died without a sign. He had implied, in his short talks with Prue and Gershom, that he had cared for them; how, or how far, they had no idea. Gershom, certainly, expected little.

"Think of your mother!" his grandfather had said; he had said, also, "Think of your God!" For aim and motive; for holy incitement and strength. But the boy had taken his mother, as his legacy, from the old man's hands; to care for her, — to labor for her. That was his one resolve now. He had little thought of possible money or land.

To one other the Doctor had spoken. As Jane sat by him in her evening watch, on Saturday, he had called her suddenly, — "Daughter!" and Jane had bent to catch his words.

"I have been easier to-day; but I am not deceived: to-morrow I may be worse again. If I die, Jane, — *when* I die, I think my affairs will all be found in order. There will be enough for all, — for *all*."

"Don't, father!" Jane had cried, partly from a genuine shrinking impulse, — for she had a daughter's natural love somewhere in that selfish heart of hers, — and partly from a dread of knowledge too solemnly imparted.

"I won't distress you, child. When the time comes, you will find it written. I put it in" — His cough interrupted him, — a long paroxysm; and he lay back exhausted after it.

Jane gave him his gum-arabic water, and wiped his lips, and the moisture from his pale forehead, and then busied herself across the room, restoring the glass to its place, examining what was left in the little pitcher from which she had filled it, and rearranging spoons and vials.

Then she turned toward the bed again. He raised his finger for her to come near; he pointed toward his dressing-glass, beside which hung his keys, which Prue had put upon a nail there. It was not possible to misunderstand. Jane brought them. Her father did not speak, he had hardly strength for that; and he feared to provoke the cough again: but he held the bunch in one hand, and with the other selected one, laying his finger on it, and looking up, while his lips and tongue just formed the syllable "There."

And Jane bent her head assentingly.

After that he seemed to trouble himself no further. He had left the clew to all in the hands of his eldest child.

And up to this moment, Jane had held her peace.

"Do any of you know — has the Doctor spoken to any of you — of any will or writing?" Mr. Gair asked this after they had all come into the little room together.

Jane waited a half minute or more. Nobody spoke. Then she moved to her husband's side, and answered him.

"He began to say something to me last Saturday evening; but a fit of coughing came on. He only said we should find it written. And he pointed to his keys, and I brought them; and he laid his finger on this." She took the keys from Reuben's hand as she spoke, and separated that belonging to the panel cupboard.

Had she not fulfilled her trust? I believe she thought so. She sat down, and waited with the rest for whatever should be found.

And in this very moment her punishment began. Her unlawful knowledge tormented her. She had told truly all she had been supposed to know. They might search, — they might find all.

But if not? Then it would have been better that she had never looked or listened. Why had she looked or listened? Only to lay this upon herself. She must publish herself a spy, or be a guiltier thing. She almost wished they might discover all. If she only had never meddled foolishly, all might have gone well. She could wish that this had been; she could have been satisfied to kill this memory of hers, if that were possible, and that they should all together, ignorantly, defraud the widow and her son. With a secret vehemence of regret, she deplored that this should not have happened. Her heart-desire was evil, her conscience-scruple was only weak.

Reuben Gair stood up on the very high-backed mahogany chair whereon his wife had climbed that summer afternoon last year, and rolled the panel back.

"Why, mother!" whispered Say, "that 's the earthquake!"

Jane Gair clutched her child's hand, with a grasp that pained her, enforcing silence. Say was ashamed. It had not been a proper time to speak so. This was what she thought. Years afterward, she remembered it with a different thought, — a hotter shame.

Prudence Vorse was reminded of the day when she had found her step-sister searching there. She looked straight over at Jane, suddenly, with her strong, discerning eye. The color mounted visibly in Jane's face. Prue had her own thought, instantly. "Whatever is there, she knows it."

Mr. Gair took down the leather wallet and the letter-case.

"It must be in one of these," said he. And he came down, and laid them on the table, and, drawing up a chair, sat down to open them, deliberately.

What could Jane do? She had placed herself quite upon the other side the room. She could not rush and seize it from his hand, and with her last impulse of truth, disclose its secret contents. If it could have been done naturally, and by apparent accident, she thought at that instant that she would have revealed it all. But Satan had her, and he held her fast; she waited still. It must be all chance, now, whether Reuben found it or not. Did she forget the little, little pressure of her finger, that day last year? It would not now be quite so easily found as then. It was thrust, smoothly and tightly down, along the very bottom of the pocket. It would scarcely even crackle, now.

But it might be nothing after all. How should she know what possibly in all those years wherein the old case had been used, had found its way there, and lain perhaps a lifetime?

It was not her business to imagine. Her father could well care for his affairs. There was the one paper, carefully preserved. The other had, most likely, been removed, destroyed. He might have written and revoked a dozen such.

She kept saying this, within herself, over and over. She looked anxious and *distraite*.

Prue saw the look. "There 's something on her mind," thought she. "Something she 's keeping back." Prue only thought of something more the Doctor might have said. She never dreamed of any other concealment.

Nobody thought of anything further to be looked for, when Mr. Gair drew from the under pocket of the letter-case the folded packet. The upper half was evidently filled with old, very old correspondence.

"This is it," said he, and read aloud the superscription.

"My last Will and Testament. Jan. 1, 183—."

"That was before Ben died, was n't it?"

"Just after," replied Jane, quickly. "Ben died in November, that same winter."

Mr. Gair unfolded it, and glanced over the pages. Then he began to read.

The will provided for them all. Jane soothed her conscience with this. There was no obvious discrepancy here with what her father had said.

"There is enough for all, — for *all*." That emphatic repetition had rung admonishingly in her ears; and if this instrument had done absolutely nothing for Prudence and her boy, there would have been an obstinate rough spot in her conscience that the smooth unction of false plausibility would have failed to cover. As it was, she sat back in her chair and breathed freer. There was no reason to force her to acknowledge to herself that this could not be all. She would not suppose it. She was very glad she had never looked any further!

By this time she had wellnigh persuaded herself that she was as utterly ignorant, and innocent therefore, as any of the rest.

There was property to the amount of upwards of one hundred thousand dollars.

The moneys and stocks — after certain legacies — were to be equally divided between his children. Certain real estate, in Winthorpe and Selport, was apportioned, — a share to each. The farm and homestead were to remain for the life use of any child or children who should continue unmarried and elect to live there. Then they were to go to the eldest direct male heir; failing males, to the eldest female.

Of the legacies, the chief was five thousand dollars in bank stock to "Prudence Vorse, the eldest child of my late dear wife, Rachel." There were five hundred dollars to Serena Brown; or, she not surviving, to her daughter, Huldah.

That was all. The paper was refolded, and laid back; not replaced in the pocket, only between the covers; and Mr. Gair wound the green ribbon around the whole, and tied it fast.

Nothing to be done, at this moment. Certainly nothing to be said.

They all rose, silently, as Mr. Gair put up the case into the cupboard, rolled the door back, and took out the key.

Prudence looked once more at Jane. The face she scrutinized was still hardly wholly composed. "She knows more yet. She has n't told it all. There's something lies between her and the dead. It must lie, then." She did not doubt it was some verbal request in behalf of Gershom; something for the heirs to do, that the old man knew his will, drawn up so many years ago, before the boy came home to him and grew into his love, had not contemplated. For herself, it never crossed her mind that there might be more intended. She had had, all this time, so much! His legacy to her was generous; more, by its whole amount, than she could have claim to look for.

The time for speaking was past. Jane stood committed to her sin. And yet she had "done nothing."

The next day she went down to Selport, with her husband and Say, to attend to her own household, and fit herself out with "decent black." The bonnet, constructed by Miss Millett, she would send back, she said, for the first poor soul in Hilbury who might have need of such a thing.

The will and the probable plans of the family were discussed in Hilbury, as such matters are. Of course there were many who "would have done differently in his place."

One piece of superhuman wisdom is always expected of a man; the absolutely just and judicious disposition of his property. One thing is, of necessity, closely investigated, as soon as he is dead, and the seal set so forever on his works, complete or incomplete, as he may leave them. And if this prove to have been in any way neglected or procrastinated, or left imperfect, it is so strange,— so unaccountable! Of all the hundreds of abortive beginnings and intents which the most methodical life may have numbered, this only comes out for posthumous criticism and wonder, that it was not done, or better done. The testator, one would suppose, ought to have shown forth in this word that should be spoken as from beyond the grave, an unearthly perspicacity and foresight.

"To him that hath" should never "be given"— overmuch. There should have been a prescience, we should almost think, of who should survive longest and require most; and apportionment have been made accordingly. The Hilbury people wondered that Jane Gair, "rolling in money,"— her husband making it "hand over hand,"— should have "come in for just as much as any of the others." They wondered that "Widder Vorse had n't got more; she 'd been perfectly *arduous* in her attention to the old man, allers." They wondered that "there 'd never been a codicil, nor nothing, to that air old will, to fix things a little mite straighter;" that Gershom Vorse, whom the Doctor always "sot by so," had n't been named at all. "He 'd cut himself out, though, most likely, by goin' off as he did."

So they talked it over, and settled the "whys" as well as they could; meantime, the young sisters were seen at church on Sundays in the dresses and bonnets Miss Millett had made for them, and grieved bitterly, in the quiet of their home, for the old man gone; and Mrs. Jane Gair busied herself among crapes and bombazines, in Selport, and took off, so, the first keen edge of her sorrow.

"If the girls want me," said Prudence, talking with her son, "I shall stay here till spring with them, and see 'em settled; and then if Jaazaniah keeps on failin', I shall offer to go and stop with Wealthy Hoogs. She has n't got a being in the world to help her."

"That 's just what I should like best for you, mother," answered Gershom.

CHAPTER XX.

GUILTY OR NOT GUILTY?

Ned Blackmere was in Selport jail, waiting for the court to meet, when his case should come up before the grand jury for indictment or discharge.

None but a sailor could conceive the misery of this confinement to him. Accustomed to a free ocean life, — to the hourly active use of all his limbs, — his cell cramped him, the jail air stifled him. "I hope, if they do anything with me, they 'll finish up the job and hang me!" The poor fellow feared most conviction of a secondary degree of crime, and condemnation to a prison life.

"They 'll have a Bedlamite in charge if they do that," he said.

Except for this, he had neither fear nor hope. He would as soon die as live. There was nothing in all the great world for him except his pipe. He smoked and brooded just as he always had done; only the people round him did not know anything about that. They said of him in the papers that he was utterly hardened and unconcerned.

A clergyman came to see him, and spoke to him solemnly of his situation.

"Do you think I need you to come and tell me I 'm in a fix?" said the sailor, curtly.

The good man, with the best intent, warned him against hardness of heart, and reminded him that he might shortly be sent to meet his God.

Ned Blackmere took the pipe out of his mouth. "I 'd like to see that Person. I 'd have a word or two to say to Him if I once found Him."

The words were blasphemous, perhaps; God's minister was shocked; it may be God saw deeper, and was more pitiful than angry.

The clergyman stood, and uttered a prayer; he would say no more to this desperate sinner; he would only plead with Heaven for him.

Blackmere remained motionless and silent, holding the pipe in his fingers that otherwise he would, doubtless, have replaced. When the petition was ended, he held out his hand.

"If you meant all that, I thank you, whether Anybody heard it or not."

The minister took the offered hand. "Lord! help this soul that Thou hast made, to find Thee!" And so he went away.

That same night Ned Blackmere had another visitor.

It was just at dusk when he heard the clank of the ponderous lock, and the door swung open, and Gershom Vorse came in with the turnkey.

Blackmere did not look up at first. The young man spoke.

"I 'm here, shipmate!"

Then a sudden quiver ran over the strong man's shoulders, before he got up, and came round.

"I did n't suppose I had a friend in the world that would do as much as this," he said. There was a quiver in the rough voice, too. The heart had not been trampled out of him quite, after all.

"You see, I *know* that you are here for nothing," said Gershom, in a strong, cheery way, straight out. And I 'm come to tell them so."

"You really did n't think it of me?" asked Ned Blackmere, with a kind of incredulous earnestness.

"I did n't think it, nor I should n't think it, anyhow; but besides that, I *know* better."

"How can you know anything about it? Did n't I tell you I 'd got a she-devil for a wife? Did n't I tell you it was hell I was coming back to? Ain't them the sort of circumstances that murder comes of? I went back there and waited for her, alone, at night. Biddy Flynn saw me there. She peeped in at me through a hole, as she would at a wild beast. She heard me curse the home that woman made for me. She heard me say it stood between me and anything better on God's earth. Ain't that enough to prove it on a man? Three hours afterwards, they found her there, with her head smashed in; hit from behind with a club. How do you know I did n't strike her down?" He asked this almost fiercely.

The stripling answered him with the strong, sure word of a man.

"Because, Ned, you 'd borne it all those years, not to do this at last. And if you 'd struck her down in anger, it would n't have been from behind, in the dark. That 's enough for *me*. But I 've got something more for them. Was n't I lying in my berth when

16*

you came aboard the brig and down into the forecastle, and lit your pipe? Did n't I hear you say,— thinking me asleep,— 'So he was n't wanted no more than I; he 'll find 'em out by and by?' Did n't I lie and think of that — being wide awake as I was — for hours after, and hear you walking all the time overhead, — back and forth, back and forth? Don't I know the clock had n't struck ten, fifteen minutes when you first came down? And did n't it go one just as you turned in at last? And they say the murder *must* have been done between half past ten and eleven. That 's what I know about it, Ned, and what I 've come down from Hilbury to tell 'em."

Ned Blackmere had seated himself on the side of his bed; his arms rested across his knees; his head was bent forward, listening; when Gershom had said all, instead of lifting it, he bent it lower, — lower yet. It was a minute, perhaps, before he raised it up, and looked the boy in the face; and there was a quick, upward motion of the hand at the same instant. Something came to his eyes, perhaps, that, for years of hard looking out upon a hard world, had not visited them before.

"You 've argied it out, shipmate; and it may be you 'll save my life, — whatever that 's worth. But it is n't that. *You did n't believe it of me;* and you 've taken the trouble to think it out; and come here 'o your own accord, to say it. That 's what pulls me down; I ain't been used to it."

He shook his head, and lowered it again, for a minute; then he got up, and made a step to Gershom, and held out his hand, a hard, seamed, callous hand, but with no murder-stain upon it.

"I would n't go to ask you to take it afore," said he. "But now, — there!" And Gershom's was seized with a grip that might well, of itself, have forced tears to his eyes. Be that as it may, the tears were there.

"If ever we two stand together on the deck of the same vessel again," said Old Barnacle, — "blow high or blow low, see if Ned Blackmere don't stand your friend. That 's all."

The few more prison days wore on; the sailor in his cell counted the hours that seemed almost years. Gershom lived on board the brig; slept there, that is, and got his meals at an eating-house.

Mr. Gair asked him to his house; wondered that he did not come; but the boy made excuse, at first, that he was better on board; all he had come for was to see Ned and give his evidence; he had left his shore clothes at home; his rough pilot-coat was n't fit for a parlor. He said this, at first; but the blunt, true spirit of Prudence Vorse worked in him, and came out, at last.

"I may as well tell you, sir," he said, one afternoon, in the counting-house, when Uncle Reuben urged him again to go home with him to tea. "You 've been kind to me; and you 've given me something to do; you 've been fair with me, and about me, always; and I 'd like to go on in your service if you think I 'm fit for it; but I can't keep such a feeling back, and put a smooth face before it. Aunt Jane *has n't* been fair and square with me, sir. If it offends you for me to say this, I 'm sorry; but you 've got the whole truth now, and it 's best."

Mr. Gair was surprised, perplexed; but there was no insult in the boy's manner; only a plain honesty. He could not be offended.

"I think there is some mistake," said he. "You must have misunderstood. Your aunt appears to me to be very fond of you."

Gershom was silent, out of respect; not from any hesitancy in his own opinion: Mr. Gair saw that. The fair-minded gentleman — for he was that — knew, from experiences of his own, that there were certain little crookednesses in his wife's methods, which he often wondered at; since the straight line seemed to him the shortest. He would not think of it as deliberate deceit. Still, the subject would bear no discussion even in thought: he laid it aside, as he had doubtless done before. He knew nothing, and he desired to know nothing, of any little manœuvre of hers against which Gershom's simple bluntness might have revolted. Let it pass: it would come right by and by.

A man can but resent for his wife, however, when it comes to speech of her. There was a little sudden stiffness, which he could not help, as he said, again, ending so the conversation —

"Let it be as you like, however. I don't care to ask any questions. Come if you feel like it; there can't be any very grave hindrance. Matters will work round after a while I suppose. It's never best to lay up any little misconception between friends."

Say came down with her father, and had one of her old happy hours on board the brig. Gershom was kind. He cracked a cocoanut for her; he opened his sea-chest, and showed her the little curious things a sailor contrives and picks up on a voyage; he had the red basket ready for her, and the pink and spotted shells; he even walked up with her when she went home and carried them; but he would not go in. He could not stop, he said. Say wondered; but she took what the day had given her, and laid it up among her pleasant memories. It had life in it, that served to help out many a dead day after.

The court assembled on Tuesday. Blackmere's case came up before the grand jury on Wednesday.

He did not know this, of course. He lay waiting in his cell, ignorant of the day or moment that might decide his fate; knowing only that the court met at this time, and that it was pending over him.

The Pearl had been in port almost three weeks; in less than another she would sail again. There were two things on earth now beside his pipe that Blackmere the prisoner cared for, — the hard man, who had thought he cared for nothing. He knew he loved the brig, now, that he had sailed in for seven years, — that had given him his sailor's sobriquet. He knew, at least, that it would almost kill him if a bill were found against him, and he were detained in prison to await a final trial, wearing out weeks or months there, while the ocean was blue in the coming spring-time, and the Pearl had her white robes on, and was dancing away over the waves. Perhaps he did not know yet that he had a human love in his heart; but he knew he had a thankfulness, and he thought of Gershom Vorse as he had hardly thought of a human creature since he was a boy. It was life or death he waited for at the decision of this grand jury; though the worst apparently that could happen to him would be that they should indict him for the crime and hold him for trial.

And the jury came together on this Wednesday, a score and more of sworn men, impanelled for this duty; strangers who never heard before of Edward Blackmere, who knew nothing of himself or of his life, who were simply to hear the scanty evidence of those two hours' time, and from their fallible human judgment decide, as best they could, the probabilities of guilt.

The district attorney entered his complaint on behalf of the Commonwealth, and brought forward his witnesses. They were summoned all together from the outer hall, and the foreman of the jury administered the oath.

Biddy Flynn cast an apprehensive look about her, as she came into the jury-room, expecting to see the prisoner there; bethinking herself painfully of what she was about to do; bethinking herself also remorsefully of the fine summer shawl that lay folded in the press at home. How could she ever put it on her shoulders again with an easy mind, — she who was going to swear away his life? She wished in her heart that she had trusted the Holy Mary to keep guard over the peep-hole, and to save her from her nightly dread. "Sure, was n't the Blessed Mother and ahl the saints enough, but she must go pittin' her nose intil this?" She wished to goodness it had been fire first.

Yet she held up her hand with the rest, and took her oath like a good Catholic; reassured in a degree by the discovery that Blackmere was not present; and then, the others being withdrawn again, and she retained to witness first, she drew her breath hard and prepared to tell her story steadfastly. "The truth, and the whole truth;" as to "nothing but the truth," she could not keep herself, except as she was repeatedly checked by the prosecuting officer, from throwing in, gratuitously, possible pleas and suppositions in favor of the accused, which occurred to her, Biddy Flynn, and might fail to occur to the minds of the twenty-three gentlemen who were to weigh and decide upon the evidence.

"What knowledge have you of the man, Edward Blackmere, now in jail accused of the murder of his wife?"

"Heth sirs! it's little enough, I or anybody. He was aff at the say, mostly. An' it's a poor home he had till come back to, an' that's thrue for him, whiddher or no."

"You knew his wife, Susan?"

"Troth, an' I did; an' a purty piece she was too, wid her tantrums."

"Tell the jury what you know of the occurrences of the night of the seventeenth of January last past."

"The night av the murdher, is it? — Will, thin, Sukey Blackmere had n't darkened the doures for three days. An' we knew well enough, whin she did come, it was she wud bring the sivin divils wid her. An' it's I was an the trimble for fear iv fire, thim nights; seeing, yer honors, as me bit iv a place, worse luck to it! was jist alangside iv hers."

"One moment. Explain, Mrs. Flynn, if you please, what you mean by the seven devils? Was Mrs. Blackmere in the habit of bringing home company with her?"

Sorra company, but jist that I tould ye av. The sivin divils that wud git intil her, wid the gin. I'm not saying, nayther, but there might likely be some iv her comerags in afther her, now an' agin; an' who's to know, yer honors, whin she 'd been aff an the straggle three days an' nights what sort iv riff-raffery might come trailin' afther her let alone a dacent man that was jist home from the wild says, and fetched back his wages reg'lar more shame till her for that same?"

Biddy rolled off this sentence of query from the tip of her tongue, in true impetuous Hibernian fashion, without breath or comma; and it was only the final interrogation point that gave the examining officer opportunity to draw curb upon her.

"We don't want any conjectures, or suggestions, my good woman. Your simple evidence is all that is required. The jury will take care of the rest, and draw its own conclusions."

"Humph! it's not Biddy Flynn wud be afther middling wid what was none iv her concerns; but two heads is bitter nor one, for all that, if one an 'em *is* a shape's head. An' yer honors may jist dhrah ahl the conclusions ye like!" Said, not insolently, but with a twinkle of pure Irish drollery, and a tossing up of broad, white cap-border that betokened anything but a sheepish consciousness on her part.

"You will be so good as not to interrupt the regular proceedings; but go on with your evidence in the case."

"An' did I inthurupt? Sure, I thought it was goin' an swately, I was. Will, thin, it was that night, the sivinteenth iv Jinuary, that I tuk me sup iv tay, an' redded up me room, an' was goin' to bed, tired enough wid a hard day's wash, whin I bethought mesel iv the Blissid Virgin."

"We do not need to know that, Mrs. Flynn. Do not dwell upon your thoughts, or any irrelevant outside circumstances; but give us the facts, according to your knowledge."

"Arrah, an' is it thoughts that's outside circumshtances, I'd like to know? An isn't the Blissid Virgin a fact? An wud I 'av known annything at ahl aboot it, but for hersel? Is n't it she that's hingin be the nail over the bit iv a crack in the boordin atwixt me room an' Sukey Blackmere's? An' how could I 'av seen a ha'porth iv ahl wint an, but for bethinkin mesel iv her, I wondher? — So, I tuk her down; an, bad luck till me, I jist luk 't in; for fear iv fire, yer honors. An, I see ——"

Biddy paused.

"Very well. What did you see?"

"I see a dishgraceful dhirty room, yer honor. Enough to make any dacent man shwear to come home till it; let alone bein eight months upon the say. An' I see the man there, sittin' his lane; Ned Blackmere; an' he had his ilbows an' his knees, an' his head betwane his two fishts. An' he lukt as if soometh 'n lay so heavy upon him as he 'd niver rise up from anundher it. An' are yees afther thinkin, gintlemen, I can fale it a purty thing to be shtandin' here the day, a hilpin to pile moor an? I 'll till yees the thruth, for I 've shwore me Bible oath an it; but for ahl he 's a dark an' a shtrong man, an' was an angered one that night, an' many times before, for rason why, I'll never believe, as God sees me, that he shtruck the blow! Don 't I know what he gave me the fine silk shahl for, coom Foorth iv July two years ago? Was n't it that I should n't complain iv the misherable jade, an' git her turned upon the shtraat? Don 't I know it, as well as if he 'd said the wurruds? An' don't judge hard, yer honors, as ye 'll be jidged yersels some day, what I 'll have to till yees nixt!"

"Go on," said the attorney, quietly, forbearing this time to rebuke her.

"He was a brukken an' an ill used man, I till yees; an' that was what was in his face, an' not murdher. An' he shqueezed his fishts tighter agin his jaws, an' the wurruds came out as if they could n't be hild in. He called her bashte, an' thrue for her, she was that, an' no more nor liss. An' thin he said it was this that stud between him an' any bitter home upon God's earth. An' whiddher a man says it or not, mush n't he think it, gintlemin, whin its druv doon upon him so? An' thin he shwore a big round wurrud as maybe anny one iv yees wud iv shwore it in his place, the night — An' thin, I hung up the Blissid Mary in her place agin, an' cript down, an' got intil me bed. For it was fitter for the pitiful Mother till hear more nor I!"

"Do you know at what hour of the evening this was?"

"Sorra know, beyant that the bells rung nine while I was washin up me bits of tay things; an' before I fell ashlaap, the clock struck tin."

"Was this the last you knew of Edward Blackmere?"

"Excipt that I heard him git up, prisintly, an' walk out. An' I could n't say whiddher it was beyant the door he wint or not; he might be waiten there, or he might iv wint away; but in me shoul, I believe he wint away intirely; an' whativer happunt afther, he knew no mooe nor I; but it was the Lard's own deliverance till him."

Upon further questioning, Biddy related, as clearly as she could, the circumstances of her waking shortly after, as the reader knows them; and of her giving the alarm.

She described the sounds which roused her. "Mixed up wid the shlape, they was," she said, "so I could n't iv shwore thin, whiddher I haard thim or dhramed thim; but I knew well, afhter, whin we found the wurruk that was done. It was a fahlin', an' a crushin', towanstlike; an' the shteps, thin, goin' aff. Sure, I know well it was sorra else than the murdherin' itsel; and the villain's faat that did it!" She testified confidently also to the long, moaning, bubbling breath that had terrified her at the last, just before she rushed up-stairs to Luke Dolan's door.

"How long had you been asleep, do you suppose?"

"I'm not afther shupozin', at ahl. What call iv I to go shupozin, whin it's an me Bible oath I am? It might iv been an oor, an' it might iv been — hoult! I can till yees this, thin. It was pitch darruk in the avenin, whin I pit oot me candle, an' whin I wakened there was a whisper iv light in the windy, for the moon was comin' ap, though she had n't got fair over the taps iv the houses. Maybe yer honors are knowledgeable to tell what time that might iv been?"

"Make note of that; it may be important," said the attorney to the juror who was recording evidence. And Biddy was dismissed.

Luke Dolan testified to the character of the deceased; and to the ill terms on which she lived with her husband; bearing witness at the same time, as Biddy had done, that Blackmere provided for her necessities "like an honest man;" and that though he had often heard high words between them, and "been in dread of worse," he had never known him to strike the woman a blow.

He testified also, as did other inmates of the house, that it was "full eleven by the clock"—some said a few minutes later—when the alarm arose. The finding of the body; the fact that life had manifestly but just departed, and the impossibility of the woman's having lived many minutes after such a blow was struck, were brought forward in testimony by the same witnesses who had given evidence previously, at the coroner's inquest and before the magistrate.

These points of time, therefore, were proved. That it was between nine and ten o'clock, when Biddy Flynn first made her investigation, and saw Blackmere in his wife's room. That it must have been nearly eleven when she awoke, and heard the sounds which alarmed her; since there was the "whisper iv light in the windy" and the moon, upon referring to an almanac, was ascertained to have risen, on the night of the 17th of January, at 10 o'clock and 24 minutes; this conclusion being strengthened also by the fact that the deceased was breathing just before Biddy ran up to Dolan's door. And that it was eleven, or more, when the inmates of the house gathered in the room, and found her dead. Therefore, that the deed must have been done as late as half past ten, certainly, more probably at near eleven.

Now Gershom Vorse, having been meanwhile, or at any time, in communication with none of these previous witnesses, was recalled.

"I will request your careful attention, gentlemen," said the attorney to the jury, "to the evidence of this witness. It has been volunteered since the accused was arrested and held to answer to the charge. You will please to bear in mind all that has foregone, tending to fix the points of time in relation to the case before you. You will proceed to tell the jury," he said, addressing Gershom, "all that you can recollect of the disposal of your own time, on the evening of the seventeenth of January last past; and all that you know, positively, of the movements of the accused, Edward Blackmere, upon that same night."

"I was on board the brig Pearl, which came into this port that evening, at about seven o'clock. We made fast to the wharf at about half-past seven. Edward Blackmere was one of the crew.

I left him on board at eight o'clock, when I went ashore, and walked up to the house of Mr. Reuben Gair in Hill Street. I remained at his house, perhaps, three quarters of an hour. The bell rung for nine, as I was on my way back to the brig. I stayed on deck half an hour, perhaps, before I went below. Then I partly undressed and turned in. I lay awake and heard the clock strike ten. Very soon after — it could not have been fifteen minutes, and, I think, hardly ten — Blackmere came on board. He came down into the forecastle and struck a match, and lit his pipe. He stopped beside my berth, and probably thought me asleep; for he said to himself, 'So — he was n't wanted; no more than I. He'll find 'em out, by and by.' I did not move nor speak; and he went up the ladder. I heard him walking up and down the forecastle deck, until after midnight. The clock struck one just as he came down and turned in. This is all, sir. I can simply say, upon my oath, that I know Ned Blackmere was aboard the Pearl, from fifteen minutes after ten, or earlier, till one o'clock; and I found him there when I awoke, at six, next morning."

"Are you sure that you may not have fallen partly asleep between ten o'clock and the time Blackmere came down?"

"I am certain, sir, that I never closed my eyes, nor lost myself, till after one. I had a good deal to think of. I had heard bad news."

"How was the forecastle? Open, or closed?"

"The doors were open, sir. And the scuttle pushed back just far enough for a man to pass in and out easily."

"Was it dark or light, above, when Blackmere came on board?"

"Dark, sir, when he came; but the moon began to come up a little after."

"How long after?"

"Fifteen or twenty minutes, I should think."

"How does the brig lie?"

"At the end of the pier; stern down the harbor."

"Toward the east, then?"

"Southeast; yes, sir."

"Thank you, young man; you have given your evidence very clearly, and to the point. You may go."

"The evidence is all in, gentlemen," said the presiding officer to the jury, after Gershom had withdrawn. "And my own opinion is, that you will hardly be able to find a bill in this case, especially under the aspect which it is made to assume by this additional testimony. The foregoing evidence goes to prove that the murdered woman had not ceased to breathe at a few minutes to eleven o'clock. The medical opinion given upon oath, declares that death would almost immediately follow such a blow. Mrs. Flynn, who heard that last struggling breath, and directly after gave the alarm, testifies to having heard also, at her first awaking, the sound of retreating steps from the adjoining room. The moon, she says, had at that time risen sufficiently high for its light to be perceptible in the street. It must, therefore, have been as much as half an hour high. You find from the almanac that the moon, on that night, rose at ten o'clock twenty-four minutes. The other inmates of the house declare that it was at or after eleven o'clock when they entered Mrs. Blackmere's room, and discovered her to be dead. It seems plainly indicated by these facts, that the murder, the escape of the murderer from the premises, the awaking of Mrs. Flynn, and the alarm in the house, and the finding of the body, must all have taken place in very rapid succession, and as late, or later, than a quarter to eleven by the clock. The last witness tells you, clearly, that the accused came back on board the brig at about ten or fifteen minutes after ten; and that the moon came up some fifteen minutes later. Setting all this aside, even, there seems a failure of direct evidence that could convict the man. But the positive proof in his favor must rest upon this question of half an hour of time. It will be your duty carefully to weigh the facts, and to decide according to the interpretation they bear to you."

The grand jury deliberated, and came to the conclusion that it could "find no bill."

Edward Blackmere was ordered to be discharged from custody.

Biddy Flynn's suggestions, however inappropriate as testimony, and unnecessary as addressed to intelligence fully prepared to devote itself to the investigation, found place also in the minds of the twenty-three gentlemen whose duty it was to consider them; and her "whisper iv light in the windy" was the first link in the chain of facts elicited which made it impossible to charge Blackmere with the crime. It would have done Biddy great good to have known this; as it was, she never put on the silk shawl of a pleasant Sunday without a "Thanks be to God I said as much for him as agin him, annyway!"

But it was Gershom Vorse's testimony, given with such simple clearness, that saved the man. The district attorney said this to him as they walked up the street with Mr. Gair, after the court adjourned.

"It was well for the fellow that you came forward," he said. "And also that the moon rose just at that particular hour on that particular night. It all hung on a very delicate hinge. The moon was the only witness who might n't be supposed to make a mistake of a half hour or so. Independently of the question of time, however, I felt that without further evidence against him, a jury could never have convicted him. He was seen there an hour previous, and that was all. Nobody could tell when the woman came in or how. As Mrs. Flynn observed, there's no knowing what sort of 'comerags' she may have had."

"Blackmore's a good fellow and a valuable sailor. He's odd and churlish, but I don't believe there's the germ of such a crime in his nature," said Mr. Gair. "He has sailed with Burley for six years. I've never heard the first ill thing of him."

"He's a noble-hearted fellow," said Gershom, warmly, "and everything has always worked against him. There's such a lot of cheating and meanness in the world!"

"You've found that out early," said the legal gentleman, glancing round upon the youth.

Gershom did not answer. He said to himself only, "He does not contradict me!"

The mistake of Gershom Vorse was, — now and for years through life, — that he overlooked the very good by contrast with which he judged the evil. He forgot what it was in himself that revolted against this evil. He saw a noble nature warped and soured by wrong, and failed to consider that but for this very nobleness the warping and the souring could not have been. He saw that there had been trusting and betrayal, faith and disappointment. He knew that he, too, had believed and been deceived; but the faith, and what it had first grown from and been fed upon, was suddenly lost sight of in the treachery that blasted it. He had "come out to an edge," as he had once said of himself, and looked forth for a little upon life; it was the night side of things that first revealed itself. He forgot the day that had been, or he believed that it was daylight only in the one home, and in the few hearts; darkness was the "stuff" the rest of the world was made of. The stars that shone out here and there showed but the black gulfs about them. There was his grandfather, there was his mother, there was Blackmere; but there was Aunt Jane, — there was the sailor's uncle, sister, wife. There were Aunt Joanna and Rebecca; but then there were all the little shams and malignities and hypocrisies of Hilbury; the Proutys, and the Hineses, and Stacy Lawton's silly set; and Aunt Joanna knew it as well as he did; Aunt Rebecca was a saint, and shut her eyes. There were Burley and Oakman, and the stories of their generous bravery and truth; but there were the yarns of the forecastle that had opened up a glimpse into the meannesses and cruelties and depravities of sailor life. He had got it all to live through, he supposed; he would set his little strength against the wrong as he best could, but he looked for wrong now rather than for right; he was taking up a position antagonistic rather than gladly co-operative with the world as he found it. He was *beginning* to do this, — he was setting his face that way; he was only seventeen, and it had not hardened in him yet; but the first joyous credulity of his youth was already gone. And whose fault was it first of all?

Gershom had got a new bitterness into his heart in these days of his waiting about the court. A new revelation had come to him of himself, and of all that Aunt Jane had thwarted in him. He had found out what it was that he ought to have been, — what this quick, keen, uncompromising sense of the just and right was given to him for. He could have stood up and pleaded for it as he heard it pleaded for by others. He followed the argument; he caught its points; they flashed upon him as he heard the evidence given in, and he anticipated them in the speech of the learned counsel. It was a civil case he listened to, hampered with technicalities, confused with intricacies of law; yet through all this his clear, honest apprehension grasped the inherent Right of the thing, and his heart beat high, almost to the forgetting of his anxiety for Blackmere, as he listened to the eloquent plea, and heard at last the verdict given for the plaintiff, and knew that one wrong at least had been rectified in the wicked world, that morning. This was what his instinct would have turned to when he had come to see more broadly what various work there was for men to do, and when his intellect had been trained to the point for choosing. "I could have done it, too!" he said to himself afterward, in a turmoil of excited thought. "Some time I could have done such things, too! If I had taken what my grandfather would have given me, if I had been in college, now, getting myself ready for it, instead of running off after my first fancy, and fixing myself in a forecastle for life, perhaps!"

"Grandfather said the truth; there is scope for nobleness in every profession; and I might have had a wider scope. If I had only gone back to Hilbury, and seen him! If I had only had my mother's message, that I *ought* to have had, — that Aunt Jane swindled me out of, — swindling me out of my life, too, at the same time! — There's nobody to send me to college now. I must never let my mother know I've had a thought of it; I can't take all her little property; and that is what it would come to. No; my life's fixed for me. I've chosen to be a sailor, there's no help for it now; I must make the best of it. And I was so glad to go in the Pearl less than a year ago! — But I've saved Blackmere 's life ; and there might n't have been anybody else to do that! — I 'll go ahead, now, and see what it leads to! I 'll put my whole might into it, as my grandfather told me ; I 'll make a man of myself! I 'll think of my mother. I 'll think of ——."

"Why had not God prevented this?" was the rebellious thought with which he ended. The first shadow of religious doubt fell on him at this instant.

Jane Gair! will you ever find out all that you have done?

Gershom Vorse went back to Hilbury; he stayed with his mother till the last possible moment; then he came down and joined Blackmere, and shipped for his second voyage in the Pearl. As ordinary seaman, this time; next it should be as able hand. His life was fixed for him; there was nothing to go back for, now. There were years of danger and hardship before him; of weariness and disgust, very likely; there was the hope of rising, of coming to be master of a ship, by and by; of doing great things for his mother yet before she should grow old: he had not done dreaming even yet.

In all his dreams the sailor Blackmere had a place; these two clung together; there was a fast friendship between them now. Shoulder to shoulder, against the world; not seeing the beauty of their own attitude; discerning only the necessity that set them so.

"You 're the only one that *knows*," said Blackmere to the boy. "There 'll always be doubt hangin' over me, for all. I wish a 'most they 'd found the bill, and I 'd had my trial. I 'd ha ' been one thing or the other then."

Blackmere had read the doubt in the looks of his old neighbors when he went back, and gave away his bits of furniture among them; he would sell nothing.

They thanked him; they were glad of his getting off; but they thanked him with a certain timid shrinking as if there were some strange spell and horror upon him still. They spoke of it as a "getting off." Only Biddy Flynn bade him "God bliss ye," and "knew that sorra thing he'd had til do wid it, at ahl!"

"They think its greatly luck, and having friends," said old Barnacle, moodily. "I'll never overlive it. It 'll come up agin me, yet. There 's a rope round my neck, though they didn 't hang me up by it."

So these two sailed away again together in the Pearl.

CHAPTER XXI.

THE ROUGH OFF.

SICKNESS and death come every day; as the good Doctor had said. Somewhere or another — yes; they are all around us; we hear of them; they make a staple of our daily news; yet there are periods, perhaps, in the history of almost every tolerably healthy country neighborhood, when there seems to be an invisible cordon of safety drawn about it; when for years, there happens no noteworthy death; none that leaves a felt vacancy. And then, suddenly, the Reaper comes, gathering in, in one short season, the harvest he has waited for.

It had been so in Hilbury. Except deaths of children, or of the very old, who must be dropping off in turn, the little circle in which the elements of this our simple story germinated, had been the same, untouched of vital change, for years; enough in number to take in the whole conscious lifetime of little Sarah Gair. Summer after summer she had gone up there to see the same familiar faces about the villages, and in the pews at church, and in the farm-houses where her aunts went visiting with her. Only Mrs. Hartshorne had died; this event, in its solemnity and suddenness, and from the emphasis of circumstance at the time, had stood alone, and been made memorable; minor affairs were dated from it — before and after; it was an era.

Now — within these six months past — death and change had been busy. Hilbury gave its quota of events into the chronicle of its district. Several of its leading townsmen had passed away. One after another, from their responsible positions, from the headship of their families, from use in the little community, they had gone silently; and from the places that knew them, and that scarcely seemed the same, they had dropped out, leaving only a memory, and a graven record in the old churchyard where their graves were not yet green.

Squire Lawton; Parson Fairbrother; Doctor Gayworthy.

And now, as the spring-time softened, and the farmers began to be busy in the fields, and the year's plans opened out to hopefulness and industry, it was growing evident that another — humbler than either of these, perhaps — yet so quietly useful in his place, and so wanted among them — so a part of their everyday associations, as many a simple soul, fixed and constant in its little round of life, grows to be in a neighborhood, — that when he should disappear wholly from their midst the townspeople would say, wonderingly to each other, "Who would have thought we should have missed him so?" — a man like this, it was growing evident, was about to follow meekly on in the great procession that moveth ever, soundless and grand, between the worlds — a bridge of souls across the eternal void.

Jaazaniah Hoogs "kept failing." Slowly, hesitating between life and death a long, long time. Temperament rules, perhaps, in all things, to the last. We are surprised foolishly when the vigorous and robust life, full of energy, quick and strong in all its deed, meets death as it has met all else before; and goes down, when the call comes, without a pause or parley among the shadows, and hides itself suddenly from our sight. The feeble organization resolves slowly; parts thread by thread, with its hold on earth; as old Hines said coarsely and unfeelingly, but with a certain basis of truth for his words, — it "can't seem to up an' die, even, *smart*, an' ha done with it!"

There is a beauty and a use in strength; there is a beauty and a use in feebleness, also. All are not made alike. God, who cuts no two leaves upon a tree after the same invariable model, shapes also His soul-work after His own will, variously.

Wealthy watched and tended, unweariedly. She knew her husband must die. She never thought that he was long in dying. She read a language in his pale, patient face, — in his large, soft, gentle eye, — that needed no spoken words for her. She made up his bed for him fresh and sweet, and lifted his shoulders — painless now, but with the stalwart strength gone out of them forever, — against the comfortable pillows; and pulled the curtain back from the low window near which he lay; unfolding so the sweet, growing greenness without; and put up the sash, in the mild sunny mornings, letting in the song of birds. Away down the mountain-side, among the rocks and whispering trees, and glittering trickle of water-threads, he could look; the calm, clear pond sleeping below, and the brightening blue of heaven bending over all.

She left him so, with his little Bible at his side, and went away; pursuing her daily morning work close within call; and when she came back, she questioned him nothing, after the fashion of her creed and people; but she knew that his simple soul had found its God, and got a comfort from Him. She felt, herself, a holiness about his quiet bedside and a deep love and knowledge between them that waited — that could wait — a heavenly utterance.

"He don't *talk* about the concerns of his soul," she said to the new minister, coming in with ghostly consolation. "He never did. 'T war n't his way. He ain't a man of words, about anything; and if you 'll excuse my saying so, I think it 's one of them experiences that ought n't to be handled."

So she shielded him, and ministered to him; demanding nothing; believing to the last in that which was unseen, unuttered; that "there was a good deal in him more than ever came out in words;" finding so a nearness and a mute communion of which more declarative lives may possibly fail. Speech builds up barriers, as often as it breaks them down.

She sat by him for hours; sometimes laying her hand softly down upon the coverlet, and letting his seek it, as it always would; and the spring breath and music in the air spoke gently for them both; and there was "something between them then, that was more than talk."

Prudence Vorse came up and stopped at the hillside farm. Wealthy was simply glad and thankful to have her. Not over thankful in words; it was no more than she would have done herself for another. She accepted frankly the help and companionship; and the days passed by, not without their pleasantness, — their cheer even, — in this lonely mountain home, wherein one was soon to be left, for aught that was spoken of yet, alone — utterly.

Was that last a true word? Was she really to be more alone than heretofore? I hardly think so. The unworded intercourse between this husband and wife was shortly to be lifted up, — made greater and surer; that was all. For this they must relinquish the outward community of work and daily visible living. The puny and the narrow for the full and grand. I think Wealthy felt it so, in her untranscendental way.

"He 's going where he 'll have it all; all we both want, and never got here; and he won't leave me in the lurch, if he can help me, I know. 'T would n't be Jaazaniah, if he did. He 'll have me in mind in the old still way; and there 'll be thoughts between us. He 'll get the start of me; and that 'll be right. It 'll be my work to keep on after him."

It was more like a new bridal to her than a parting at a grave.

People came up to see her sometimes, and wondered at "the calm way she took it." "But then," they said to each other,

"She could n't be expected to feel it as if 't was anybody else but Jaazaniah Hoogs." Neither her sorrow nor her joy could these strangers intermeddle with.

There came a day that brought a positive change.

Jaazaniah was too feeble this morning to be lifted up against his pillows, and look out and watch, as was his wont, the breaking day. They turned him toward the open window and let the breeze come in upon his face. He needed it. His breath was weak and painful. His eye had lost something of the gentle consciousness that had dwelt in its expression, and only lighted, momentarily, when it fell upon his wife. The "rough" was well off now. The thin hands that had lain helpless for so many months had grown white and tender, whiter and tenderer than Wealthy's, now. The lines of his face had softened; and the sun color had worn off. "He looked so like his mother," Wealthy said.

As night came on, the eyes were closed in seeming unconsciousness; not a sleep; and so he lay, without other change, through the hours till morning again; the breath easier but fainter still, Wealthy and Prudence watching by his side. Wealthy had had no sleep the previous night, either.

"You 'd better go and lie down awhile, in the next room," said Prue, when she came back from her bit of breakfast and brought Wealthy the cup of tea she would not go away for. I 'll call you if there 's any alteration. He is 'nt conscious now, and he won't miss you."

Wealthy looked up. The gray eyes were both keen and deep, as they fastened themselves on Prue's.

"You don't know that," she said in a low, strong tone. "Neither you nor I can tell what his mind may be about while his body 's sinking. I believe he *would* miss me. I believe it 's a comfort to him, having me here. And I shall stay." Still to the last interpreting his soul for him.

And so she stayed. Stayed, and had her reward.

The stupor passed off from him before he died. He lifted the eyelids they had thought would never lift again. The eyes found Wealthy's face, as having known where to look for it. There was the strange, deep imploringness in them that eyes have, sometimes, taking their last look of earth.

Wealthy leaned down close, answering them with that in her own which only the dying eyes might know of.

The pale lips tried to move. The rough was nearly off forever, now, and the spirit dared to speak.

"You ain't afraid, dear?" Wealthy whispered.

"No," came the faint reply. "It 's only going to bed in the

dark. God knows when it's time. He'll wake me up in the morning. Now I lay me down to sleep, I pray —"

"I pray the Lord thy soul to keep," said Wealthy, clearly and solemnly, falling softly to her knees beside the bed.

So their two souls stood hand in hand before the Father, in that moment of their seeming separation. So there was one beautiful uttered word between them at the last.

Now, she was newly wedded in the spirit. Now, it was "only her work to keep on after him."

She turned herself about to her life again, with this thought at its core.

"I like to have you with me. Stay awhile." She said this to Prudence Vorse the day after the funeral.

"I'll stay till you send me off again," said the straightforward Prue. "It's no place for one woman alone; but it's a good place for two. And I've got enough to keep up my end, if you like to let it be so."

This was all they said about it; and the two women henceforth made their home together.

"It's curious how pat things work in, after all," said the neighbors. "There's always a jog for every nick. I don't believe Prudence Vorse or Wealthy Hoogs was ever so snug in all their lives before."

They were snug, and content; they sat together in the summer twilights on the still mountain side, when their day's work was done, and sent their thoughts out, each her own way; the one upon the far restless deep, — the other into the infinitely near eternal Peace. They both believed and waited.

CHAPTER XXII.

MIXED NEWS; FROM HOME.

"There now, I'm happy! but 't won't last," said Huldah, letting every limb droop and every finger drop as she sank, utterly wearied, into her low wooden rocking-chair in the doorway, luxuriating for an instant in that beginning of rest that only excessive weariness can know.

The young baby was got to sleep at last, and laid in the cradle just within. The two old babies had been washed and put to bed in the little bedroom off the kitchen, built so after the New England fashion. It wasn't much of a house to keep: only these two rooms and a bit of a best room, at right angles; but it was hard housekeeping for all that, out here upon a prairie-edge in Illinois. Hard housekeeping! and the children had come fast. No wonder Huldah felt the faint blessedness now and then that only breathes over one with momentary relaxation, when every muscle has been strained as on a rack.

"Gin out? Well set and rest," said Eben, cheerily. He was sprinkling and folding for her from the big basket full of clothes, large and little, that the hard-worked wife and mother had got mostly through the wash that morning, before the nestlings had begun to peep. He did not look unmanly either, the stout farmer, so employed. He had gathered them all up from bush and grass and line, when he came home from the early cornfield to his dinner. By and by when Huldah had "set and rested" for a while, they would stretch the sheets together. This they did for old time's sake. There were only two full-sized ones, and the stretching might have been done without; but there was never a Monday night that they were not duly measured and pulled and folded as of old; and always when it was done, Eben would lean down to his wife's ear, with the same whispered question, "Ain't you 'horry' yet, Huldy? Had n't I better have come alone? And quoting still from the old homestead tradition of Joanna's childhood, Huldah would say, saucily, "Had n't you better hold your tongue? When I horry, I let 'oo know.'" Varied in their phrasing sometimes, question and answer; but this always the substance and the joke. There are some little foolish reiterations that grow sacred.

Huldah was tired: she was that every evening of her life; but she was not sorry. She sat looking out under the scattered oaks, toward the east, — they had built their rude dwelling with its face toward home, — and watched the reflected lights that lingered there, and remembered that it had been dark an hour and more already in Hilbury. Somehow, her thoughts went back there more strongly than usual, to-night. The early spring weather took them thither. It had been one of the harbinger-days of the kindling year. The air was mild at the open doorway, and the swelling buds of the oaks showed life in every sturdy limb. The woods would be green shortly; and the broad prairie jewelled with its flowers. She thought involuntarily of other spring-times: we always do, when this primal joy revisits us. She was in a maze of recollections and imaginations when Eben came to the bottom of the basket, where the sheets lay.

"Most ready, little woman? or shall I roll 'em up, athout the pullin?"

He knew she would never let him do that. If she had "gin out" to such degree, he would have dropped all in dismay, caught the horse, and galloped bareback two miles to the nearest neighbor, and four more for the doctor.

So they pulled and folded, and ended with the old query and reply, as I have said. Then Eben put his strong arm round the little woman's buxom waist, and drew her to the doorway, and they both stood there and looked out together.

There came the sound of a horse's tread along the turfy track, away up under the trees in the magnificent "oak-opening."

"It's Grueby coming home from Waterloo," said Eben. "He 'll have news, mebbe."

Neighbor Grueby trotted up, on his heavy, white farm-horse, and held out something in his hand. A letter.

"For me?" said Eben, coming to the horse's side.

"You, or your wife; it's all the same I reckon."

"Come in, farmer; wont ye?"

"Never stop when I bring letters; too much company's worse 'n none."

"What's the news? An' how's your folks?"

"My folks is all well, thank ye. There's your paper, I'd nigh forgot it. News? Nothin' but 'manifest destiny,' and takin' in Texas. Five new Slave States! Sounds big, don't it? But I reckon, Farmer Hatch, we may hurry in 't the large end 'o the horn, an' have to crawl out at the small one, by 'n by! Manifest destiny *may* turn out sumthin' mighty pretty — and then, again it may n't! Gee up!"

Neighbor Grueby rode on, and Eben and Huldah sat down together on the great oak log that served in place of a doorstone before their dwelling, to read their letter.

Mrs. Huldah Hatch,
Care of Ebenezer Hatch, Esq.
Graysonville,
—— Co. Illinois.

"Looks dreadful business-like an' important, don't it, Huldah?" said Eben, turning it over. "Esquire! Lucky it did n't make a misgo of it, superscribed like that! — Here — it's yourn!"

Huldah took it, and sat holding it, almost absently.

"Well, aint you goin' t' open it? 'Cause the daylight 's goin', an' the night-damps comin' on, an' I shall have you with the fever 'n ager, nex' thing, if I don't take care!"

"Eben," said Huldah, gravely, "somethin 's happened to home!"

"Things are allers happenin'! The world keeps turnin' round. You can't help that."

It was clear Eben was more curious than anxious. So Huldah opened the letter.

She held it so that Eben could look over, as she read. Eben made no demur at availing himself of the privilege mutely offered.

The clear, clerkly hand, large and strong, showed plain, even in the twilight. They read it through, and then Huldah laid it down upon her knees, and the two looked in each other's faces.

It was strangely mixed intelligence. Something to be sorry for, something to be glad over. Their simple hearts hardly knew which feeling to give way to first. Five hundred dollars was a great deal of money. More than Eben Hatch and Huldah had laid by together before they married. But then, the good old Doctor was dead.

"I suppose *we* might n't ever have seen him again in this world if he 'd lived to the age of Methuselum," said Eben, philosophically, after a few minutes. "It 's a long stretch atween here an' Hilbury hills, and I don't expect hardly we 'll ever fetch it, now, Huldy."

"It 'll pay off your mortgage and set you clear with cousin

Joshaway," said Huldah, thoughtfully. "And help to buy that pair of steers, besides."

"They'll miss him awfully round there, won't they? Fact, there 's nothin' now to hender their *all* goin' 's I see."

"I can't seem to feel it 's I oughter," said Huldah, with a pang of conscience. "I can't help bein' glad for you, Eben. It's an awful temptation havin' money left you. I spose it's lucky 't ain't no more, or my heart would have hardened up like old Pharaoh's. Lând sake, Eben! what *do* folks do that git their thousands?"

"He *meant* we should be glad, Huldah. It 's jest what he did it fur. But it 's your money; 't ain't mine."

"What kinder difference does that make, I should like to know!" Huldah spoke in capitals.

"It don't seem right, exac'ly, for me to put it inter land an' stock. I might git into diffikelty an' lose it all. It oughter be tied up somehow fer you 'n the children."

"Eben Hatch! You jest hold your tongue! You 're fairly ridick'lous. We got merried cause we expected to live together, did n't we? Well, that 's the expectation I 'm goin' on. I ain't agoin' to calc'late on any other condition yet awhile. I 'm a wife; I ain't a widder. If I was, I know Whose business 't would be to take care o' me an' the fatherless; now it 's yourn. An' all we 've got is to go to help. I guess 't would be a pretty fixin' o' things to lay away money against you 're used up and gone; and to leave you hampered up with worries enough to bring it to pass! I don't want to kill no two birds that fashion. More 'n that, it spiles a woman t' have property 'f her own. It 's queer, but a woman don't value anything else,—comfort, or health, or good looks, or what all; she lets 'em all go, an' never thinks twice of it; but she can't stand havin' money separate. Don't let me ever see it, Eben, or realize anything about it. I could n't stand it, I know. You 'd never hear the last of it. I don't see why the Doctor did n't leave it to you straight out."

"It was left to your mother, Huldy. Here 's the clause in the will, copied right off. 'To Serena Brown, or, she not surviving, to her daughter Huldah.' Huldy, that will was made more 'n a dozen year ago!"

"To be sure. It 's the will my mother was knowin' to. I never thought of that."

"Nor I, nuther," said Eben, emphatically. "But I think on 't now. An' it jest reminds me of somethin' else. Do you remember that air kite-bob, Huldy?"

"That what?"

"That bit of paper that we put our names to in the Doctor's study the night of the strawberry party, five year ago."

"Certain. But what 's that to do with it?"

"This is the kite, an' that air was the bob; the big bob at the tail end, Huldy, you may depend on 't. An' if 't warnt never tied on, the kite no business to be flew athout it!"

"Well, what then? What concern is it of ours?"

"I don't know, Huldy. I must think it over."

The baby cried, and Huldah went in. Eben stayed by the threshold, thinking. He came to a conclusion, apparently, at last; for he said to himself, "That 's what I 'll do. It 's workin' in the dark, and it may n't fetch it; for she 's thunderin' sly. But it 's the best I know of, and I 'll do it."

The result was this letter that Jane Gair got ten days after:—

MRS. REUBEN GAIR: —

This is to send our respects to you, Huldy's and mine, and our sincere condolements. We were sorry enough to hear of the Doctor's death, though he did remember Huldy so handsome. And that is what has set me out to write this letter. We was notified to draw on Mr. Reuben Gair at our convenience, for the amount of five hundred dollars willed to Huldy by the old gentleman. I say again it was a handsome thing of the Doctor, and we are as thankful as we ought to be. But there 's one thing lays in the way in my mind, and that is this: whether or no they 've found everything that has to do with the settling up. This money was left to Huldy's mother, showing it was a old will, for Widow Brown died more than a dozen year ago. Now, five year ago me and Huldy set our names to a bit of paper for the Doctor, witnessing to it. It might have had to do with the will, or a piecing of it out, or altering it, or then again it might n't. The Doctor did n't show us anything but his name. It was done the night of the strawberry frolic, five year ago, when you was up to the farm, after the folks was gone. *I see you up and round in the next room afterwards*, and I thought maybe the old gentleman might have been a showing it to you first. Anyway I suppose you might know as well as anybody the likeliest place to look for it. And so before we do anything towards the handling of this money that they say is ours, I think it right to put you in mind and tell you *what I know about it*, for fear as if there should turn out to be anything overlooked.

No more at present from yours truly,

EBENEZER HATCH.

The blood rushed quickly along her veins as Mrs. Gair first glanced this letter through. Then she calmed herself and pondered on it. Eben had written shrewdly. He meant that she should ponder. She wondered just how much or how little he knew of this thing. Possibly, all that she did. "The Doctor showed them nothing but his name." But Eben and Huldah had lived on in the house for six months after; and who could say there might not have been opportunities for them as well as for herself? "They might have done it as well as not a hundred times, I daresay. And that would account for their being so ready with their information. They 're sure enough it makes no difference to them for all their show of honesty."

There are persons to whom you must demonstrate the impracticability of a meanness, before you can convince them that it has not been committed. Could, would, and should, are to them indiscriminate signs of the potential.

Assuming for granted, then, as the safest conclusion, that Eben and Huldah knew it all, what course was she to take? She could not pass this over in silence. She must needs say or do something in reference to it, or the fact of her concealment would inevitably appear and implicate her.

She took up the letter again and read it carefully. She was alone in her own room. Her husband had gone to his counting house for the afternoon. He had given it to her just as he left home, having forgotten it before.

There was no help for it. He knew she had received it. He knew it must relate to the business of the legacy. She would have to read it — show it — to him. She dared not destroy it, and give her own version in words. That, of itself, would be strange and suspicious. Besides she had done — she had intended — no tangible wrong. This would be one.

"*I see you up and round in the next room, afterwards*, and —"

These words occupied the first line of the second page of the letter. They concerned only herself. She took her scissors from the basket at her side, and cut the sheet across, carefully. The date and address, upon the first page were safe below. She mutilated nothing that should be left. This was a happy thought — a fortunate practicability. The letter read connectedly, and *safely*, without it.

Then she took up the strip of paper, looking at those emphasized words once more. "*Afterwards*." Then he could not know — watch her as he might have done — that she knew anything more than he. Than he *professed* to know. He doubtless suspected, but he could prove nothing, not even to his own certainty.

Her course was plain.

Ebenezer Hatch was under the impression that some paper,

signed by himself and wife, five years ago, might be of a testamentary character. Had any such been found? This was the purport and inquiry of the letter. She had only, then, to submit it to her husband as executor under the will, and ask the question.

Such a paper might, on search, be found; very well; then it must be; then she would have been a very honest woman; and must comfort herself with that; honesty, as well as greatness, may be thrust upon one. If nothing should be found, they might all conclude that it had been either some minor transaction, some formal acknowledgment in an everyday business matter, whereof the record belonged in other keeping; or that, of whatever nature, it had been destroyed. She — Jane Gair — was bound to be no wiser than the rest. She looked at horself from the standpoint of others, and judged herself by what would be their knowledge.

And, all the while, those few lines — that half page of her father's own handwriting — stood clear in her memory. She knew — she only, of any living — what he had once meant, at least, to do. But hers was a secret knowledge; his had been a secret intention; if he cancelled it afterward, what right had she — even were it possible without shame and self-disgrace — to betray a private, transient purpose, never confided to her, learned only by an *accident*, and that no existing record could substantiate? She wished heartily — even with a resentfulness — that the accident had never happened. She felt ill-used of fate, that she had been led into this annoying cognizance. Somehow, she was forever being forced to feel responsible, when she would rather far leave all to its own working.

"If he cancelled it!" That hidden paper might alone reveal whether he did no no. And that she could not tell them of. She had no right to know of it, — she could not explain such knowledge. It might be nothing, and she might go all her life with a self-reproach that had no foundation. There it must lie, and she must doubt, — she had really made herself think she did doubt, — unless they found it. She almost hoped they would. Almost, but not wholly after all, else she could have bidden Reuben search well the old papers in the case where they had found the will; she might have managed to be with him; she might have rediscovered it herself. She let herself slide, half involuntary, into deeper wrong; she held her peace; she made herself passive. Her very soul lied unto itself in its false, bewildered reasoning; that is the inherent retribution of false souls.

Reuben read the letter and went to Hilbury. To his question "Did your father ever mention anything of the sort to you?" Jane had answered — "Nothing." Jane Gair had never told a lie.

She stayed at home; Say was not well, it was out of her power to go. The thing had been settled for her; she must wait.

Up at the old house they wondered at Eben's communication — Joanna and Rebecca and Reuben. Prudence Vorse had already gone over to the Hoogs's when this happened. Then they looked over again all the miscellaneous papers in the Doctor's tall secretary-desk, that held the papers of generations. They emptied its pigeon holes; ran over files of bills, packets of letters; examined even the bundles of yellow documents in the panel cupboard; opened again the ancient letter-case where the will had been; sorted the contents of its larger pocket that told the tales of old absences and intimacies and courtships; laid them back reverently, and found nothing.

Greater secrets than this have lain as shallowly concealed. Men have walked for generations over hidden treasures that a spade-plunge would unearth; murder screens its crimson stain with flimsy cover, and moves unchallenged among the living; science stumbles over truth that waits to be unveiled; invention lays her finger alongside the spring she seeks to touch, and misses it. All things lie near enough, if we knew but how to look.

Mr. Gair answered Eben's letter.

MR. HATCH, —

Dear Sir:— Yours of the —th ultimo was duly received. A re-examination of all the papers left by the late Dr. Gayworthy has been made, and nothing of the description you refer to has been brought to light. We can only conclude that it was either not of a nature to affect the disposal of his estate, or that he saw fit at some subsequent time to destroy it.

The legacy to Mrs. Hatch lies ready, subject to your draft.

I am, &c.,

Your Obt. Servt.,

REUBEN GAIR.

Mrs. Gair said to herself, when her husband told her of the thorough search and its result —

"Of course, whatever it was, they must have found it now. And it turned out to be nothing; just as I supposed."

So she told herself, asking no questions; and made believe to be quite innocent and easy in her mind. Laying something asleep there which would surely waken none the less at intervals her whole life long.

She made the most now of her mess of pottage. She flourished in her fashionable mourning, and in her self-conscious dignity as an heiress. She fancied all Selport knew that this was what her crape meant.

Now if Mrs. Topliff noticed whether it were black or blue, it was as much as she did. As to the death it stood for, it scarcely entered into her ideas that people of that sort had fathers to lose.

And forty thousand dollars! Why, if she had even heard of it, what would that have been in the ears of the woman who inherited a quarter of a million; whose husband was reputed worth a quarter of a million more?

Poor Jane Gair! She bit the ashes of her delusion, and knew not even that they were ashes. She put the price of sin in her bosom, and only the evil spirit that had tempted and betrayed her knew that it was turning already to dust and withered leaves.

Ebenezer Hatch was as fully persuaded as ever that there had been something to find out, if he could only "have fetched it."

And all went on their several ways, and these things bided their time.

CHAPTER XXIII.

MUSIC BETWEEN THE ACTS.

THERE is a music that only comes in the pauses of life. When the deafening pulsations of quick joy, and keen sorrow, and restless uncertainty and eager hope, are laid asleep for awhile, and nothing stirs them. When the every-day current of a common living bears us on, and the weeks and months and years glide by, each one with a look so like the last that we forget to count them, or to remember that we are growing old. When the whir of the loom that weaves our life-story grows monotonous; when the shuttle runs quietly, and makes no leaps that throw up vivid threads in bright, irregular spaces, flashing out, so, the design that makes it individual. When, in and out, the fibres intertwine, and mix a common, homespun web, like all the rest around us.

There is music between the acts; when the elements of whatever in our lives might combine into great utterances and sweeps of mighty melody, — into wonderful chorals and harmonies, if the divine touch were given, breathe low, one to another, whispering, only, We are here; we are waiting. It is an Eolian thrill, that tells of all possible ecstasies and passions; yet is sweet and calm; a present peace; a repose, it may be, after wails and discords that have gone over us.

The simplest life knows this; perhaps it is only to a simple life it comes. It came to the home in Hilbury, between the hope and pain of youth, and whatever ripened of these, later; it was the gentle ripening itself as it went on.

Let me show you if I can.

It is twelve years since our quiet chronicle began. The old Gayworthy mansion stands as it stood then, pre-eminent in its traditional mellow tint, among the dusky-red farmhouses about it. There is little altered here, in the Centre; where the old spire rises as it rose, not twelve, only, but a hundred years agone; where the churchyard, gray with stone and green with turf, holds its century of dead; where the farms lie out, field beside field, as they lay when the Gayworthy house was fresh and new; owned in the same names, mostly, even; or, if not, still spoken of by the same old family titles wherewith they had first been christened.

Changes had gone on all around, had crept within the very township; down at the Bridge, the quiet, primitive neighborhood was gone; and the gentle singing of the river to itself was gone, — lost; and the green forest that swept its robe down to the very borders of the stream was gone; at least, had had its skirts cut, like the old woman in the rhyme, till, whether it were itself or not, like the same bewildered ancient, it could scarcely tell; and in place of all this, was a great, whizzing, roaring, whirling, crashing, crowded, dusty factory village grown up; a conglomeration of steam and wheels, and fire, and shrieks; whence the railroad reached out, east and west, its iron length, grasping a great city, a hundred miles away, at either end.

But this was more than three miles distant, still; it would hardly creep this way yet awhile; it might go up and down the river along the rattling vertebræ of that backbone of iron, which joint after joint stretched itself those hundreds of miles up and down the country, a marvellous inception of growth that would throw out its limbs afterward, and develop bit by bit its huge skeleton, clasping in its prone embrace whole States.

As yet the old Gayworthy farm lay in its primeval quietude, save for the far-rending echo of the steam-whistle that divided the air sharply at certain intervals, and the rumble that came after through the hills, telling of that strange, swift intercourse, right and left, with the busy world that lay about its stillness.

And the two sisters lived here still. Changed little by the years, any more than the old home, but exactly because so little changed, grown, like the old home and its neighborhood, to seem, if brought suddenly to light and contrast, somewhat behind the times they lived in.

Rebecca was thirty-one; Joanna just beyond her in years; they had crossed the line of youth into old maidenhood; nobody looked any longer for change in them; they would count their years out as people did here among the hills; they would be the "old Miss Gayworthys" as Joanna had prophesied to herself.

Rebecca had the same sweet saintlike face, wanting something, perhaps, that a broader life might have kindled in it. Her ideas also had their gentle, limited range, wakening to the touch of all small, local sympathies; cramped and narrow, people of larger interests might say; yet this want, this cramp, were only earthward; she had a secret outlook toward the infinite; on the side of God her soul lay open, and her thought rayed wide.

She had never changed the fashion of her hair, even; put straightly back, — a little thinner, it was now, over the forehead, and turned up behind in the same simple knot. Prim? yes, perhaps so, but sweet also, as a late white summer pink, with no profusion or set-off about it, only profuse in the fragrant life that scatters from it, viewlessly, and makes a blessedness around.

Joanna was odd, quick, trenchant, and emphatic, as of old; full of little merry sarcasms and abruptnesses; you would think her life lay in looking on at life; she had her own secret, — a living secret still,— leavening all that was unseen and shaping her inmost experience and growth as God saw them. She looked bright and young, younger than Rebecca, even, who had the youth of seraphs, that is eternally old also; Rebecca had never been young with the mere bloom of earth.

Another of Joanna's self-prophecies also had come true; she "grew fat;" not obese, but round and jolly. It "turned to that," as she had said. She might as well be merry and quick; it was the only outside bearing for her. Pining melancholy had nothing to do with her constitution. Her heart might break, but it would be more likely to end with a dropsy, than an atrophy; on the whole, she preferred to keep herself healthy; this good sense also was constitutional.

The old house was a pleasant place to come to, under the rule of these two. It was quaintly and cheerily ordered. There were plenty and kindness there; there was speckless purity; you had a feeling that is only had in such old houses, that anything whatever might come forth for delectation from its fragrant cupboards, its teeming presses. All Hilbury was glad when the sisters gave a tea-party; the art of strawberry short-cake had not been forgotten; there was many another dainty art that had its season. There was no need or caprice of sickness that was not sure to be supplied from hence.

Old neighbor Hartshorne — living still, but very old and feeble — knew these dainties well. Wine of elderberry, blackberry, and currant; jellies of marvellous strength-giving; dishes of dexterous compounding, that Mary Makepeace could only lift her eyelids over; came like fairy gifts to the old man's board and store. Not officiously, or overburdeningly; there were kindnesses accepted — even asked for — in return. Gabriel came over in the twilights, and went down the fields and talked their farming over with them; he rented some lots that they did not care to use; he had man's counsel and a ready hand for them in all the emergencies of their feminine administration; It was a "comfortable friendliness." Was there ever a sigh in the heart of either that this was all?

Sarah Gair waked one spring morning — blissfully happy for the hour — in the old "red room" at Hilbury. She had come at night when it was too late to take in all the the familiar pleasantness. She opened her eyes now almost at the first dawn, listening with a joy of abundant content and satisfaction to the crowing of the cocks from farm to farm. She had come to stay for the summer with the aunts. Further than this summer — away from it — back or forward — Say did not care to look. It held in it a concentration of all delight and hope. Other hopes might wait; anxieties and disappointments — for even at nineteen she had these — were set by. It was "music between the acts of life" for her. This summer was an aeon.

She had left school the summer before; she had been a winter "in society;" the society uncertain and sporadic, that Mrs. Gair had scrambled into relation with.

Say had had a glimpse of fashionable life; not a full, long, every-day look, as some girls had, she knew; just enough to make her feel she only half lived; just enough to make her doubt whether she most longed for more, or hated it altogether. There were wearisome, companionless hours; her mother was capricious, irritable; Say felt she valued her more for the opinion she could win of others than for her intrinsic dearness to her as her child. This contradictoriness, — this wordless disappointment, — this lack of sympathy, — checked her exuberant youth; thwarted its life; made her begin, as the spring came on, to look pale and thin.

She was to go somewhere. She begged for Hilbury, and the kind aunts. Her mother said the seashore; she wanted to keep in the world's track; to go where its leaders went. Say struggled against this decision; she wanted the sweet country air; she did n't want to dress and worry; and her father took her part. For the hope of the bloom that should come back against the winter Mrs. Gair had yielded; for this, and also because she must, when once her husband said the thing. She, Jane, — would go to the beach; the Topliffs and Semples were to be there; she bore ever in remembrance the proverb that out of sight is out of mind. She would keep herself in sight, would keep a place warm for Say; the child would get tired of the woods and hay-fields by and by, and come down.

For herself she hardly ever went to Hilbury now. The keen air of the hills no longer agreed with her. It was too bracing, she said. Mrs. Gair had grown nervous and delicate. The twelve years past had changed her greatly in health and appearance. Her face was no longer round and unlined; it was graven with a deeper record than that of twelve ordinary years, lived as she had seemed to live them. She was full of whims; a great many old habitudes had become impossible to her. This of going to Hilbury, was one; she had "never been able to care for it since her father's death had changed all, so;" and now, the mountain winds must be eschewed. There was truly something in the air that had made the place unhealthful to her; there was a taint for her, in the old home; a dead thing lay there hidden away that she only knew; a reminder of corruption came with every breath; to none else — only to her. She thought she had forgotten this; she had laid it back years ago out of sight, and turned away from it, telling herself it was nothing. She knew, none the less, that she *should* remember, if she let herself glance back. She pushed all recollection from her; she would not exhume the old doubt and argue over again what she had once settled; her whole life was a resistance; a restless seeking for absorption in other things. And so, it fretted her away. And by her side, shadowed also by the cloud of the unknown evil, a chill upon her life, she knew not whence, — grew her young daughter; longing for a fulness of joy and warmth and love, and finding it not.

Mr. Gair was wholly occupied with business. "Your money or your life," is the daily challenge on the world's highway, to such as he. One or the other must be given up. Mr. Gair made money, and gave up his life — the best of it. He loved his child, — he labored for her; it was all for her; so it was all for her that Jane had sinned the old, secret, silent sin that ate her soul away, to-day; and the child, meanwhile, was alone in all the world. Orphaned, by her parents' very side.

There was pure, perfect delight for her, only here in Hilbury.

She woke there, this bright spring morning in the old, "red room." She lay, looking and listening. Listening to the sounds of arousal about the country-side; the far-off sounds that make it beautiful to listen, where such may be heard. In the city, there was only the rumble and clatter just under her windows; this smothered in upon her heavily, by the close brick walls; now and then the striking of a clock, or the chiming of a bell a few streets off. Here there was all the faint sweet music that comes floating over breadth of field and forest; the wind surging in the great trees; the whistle of the ploughman, and his cheery call to the oxen, beginning their day's work away over there where the brown furrows lay like a fine-lined carpet over the sunny side-hill; the distant singing of woodbirds, and wandering notes from high up overhead; the flutter and chirp in the boughs close by; the voice and stir of domestic creatures about house and farmyard; there were only these, in all the air; no din and bustle of more complicated life to drown them; they came in pleasant alternation, and succession, and blending, telling of space, and joy, and freedom. They ministered to Say's young, asking spirit.

What her eyes rested on was as simple, and pleasant, and quaint — as peculiar to the place — as its out-door tones. The faint crimson of the stained walls; the black stencilled diamonds of their border, following around, up and down and over, panels and frames; the antique-patterned red and white chintz that flounced the dressing-table, and draperied the windows, and covered the great easy-chair that Say could creep from side to side in, and hung about the high-framed bedstead; the old "mourning-piece" of flosswork, over the mantel, that some great-great-aunt had once achieved; the yet more ancient embroidery that companioned it, — the "Arms of Gayworthy of Yorkshire;" these Say never tired of; they rested her. Here was something that had grown with years; that had been as she saw it now, for lives'-lengths. There was no hint of restlessness nor striving; nothing "bran new," as there was in Selport. She did not make that analysis of what she felt, though; she only lay and drank it in at eyes and ears, and felt deliciously happy.

The door from the great kitchen chamber, into which half a dozen rooms opened, moved softly ajar. It was round behind the foot-curtains, and Say could not see.

"Auntie?" she said, with a bright little ripple of gladness in her voice. "Which auntie?"

She knew the soft step, an instant after, before Aunt Rebecca's gentle eyes looked in upon her, through the flung-back curtains at the side.

Aunt Rebecca had on a striped dimity "short-gown," old-fashioned for "dressing-sack," she carried a pile of fresh, sweet-smelling damask on her arm.

"Your towels, dear; I thought I could come in softly; did I wake you?" The truth was, Aunt Rebecca could not wait any longer for her morning look at the treasure that had been put away over night, in the "red room." She loved little Say, — who would be always little Say to her, — as only those gentle souls who never turn their love on self, and who have few immediate objects, can lavish their hearts upon such few.

"O, I was wide awake," said Say; "and have been for this great while. An hour or two. Oh, Aunt Beesie, it is so lovely here! And I 'm to stay all — summer!" The words came forth on a long breath of happiness.

Aunt Beesie stooped and kissed the bright, eager lips.

"Get up when you like, Say, and begin to enjoy it. There are wheat-cakes and maple syrup for your breakfast. Shall I hang these away? There was a pile of dresses over the sides and back of the great chair, that had lain above the linen, in one of the two deep trunks Say had brought up to Hilbury.

"I 'll keep that pink wrapper, auntie, to put on."

It was a dainty thing, with its rose-colored sprays dropped over a white ground, its narrow ruffles, italian-ironed, and its open skirt. Say always wore her prettiest — not her finest — at Hilbury. In the first place, nothing else seemed to suit the freshness and bloom about her; then she loved dearly to *be* one of the pretty things in the world; was that wrong? And then, the dear aunts always looked at her so fondly and admiringly; and the country people turned after her as they met her by the way, and stopped talking, and clustered nearer as she came up into the church porch of a Sunday. Perhaps it was weak, — even reprehensible; but I will tell the whole truth of Say; she had a liking for this, — the young, bright thing, in her teens. Nobody cared for her so in Selport; she felt no such warmth around her there. She might be fresh and dainty, — though oftener she was costly and elegant, — that was her mother's mistake, — but there was something else demanded that she did not reach; that she was at once too shy and too spontaneous to attain. Girls not half so sweet in their girlishness, were more certain of themselves, had more style, were more admired; she hovered about, of a circle, but not fairly in it; this was what her mother had got for her, bargaining away, in her behalf, all else; she felt little in her own eyes, often; her very mother undervalued her, she knew, when she stood alone, for ten minutes, at a crowded party; it was all a conscious, eager wrestling after what must come unlabored for, to be of any worth; here in Hilbury, there was a place ready for her, in all eyes and hearts. She was ten times as "stylish," even as the world pronounces upon style, up here among the hills, — she wore her graceful robes here, with a better air of grace, — than in the city. Because, the doubt, and the constraint, — the self-recollection, save as a pleasant, abiding sense of surely pleasing, were all gone. There was no *place* to achieve, no effect to aim at; both were certain. She had here the very thing that gave tone to the bearing of those "born to it" in the metropolitan aristocracy. If her mother could have seen her so, she would have wondered at her ease, her manner, — which was only no manner, — would have wondered that she could not bring it with her to the town. She forgot, or never understood how she had trained her in her town-life, to a diseased anxiety and self-distrust.

And Say liked it all; she forgot the old feeling of failure and of second-rate-ness; she found herself of consequence. Not that she cared to be first, after all; it was, as I said, to be *one* of the things in the world that make its brightness and its beauty, and to be sure of it; to be set among them, — not set aside. It is not natural to the young to sigh for pre-eminence; that, to them, would be a solitude. They gravitate to each other; they tend to troops and bevies; it is the more the merrier, always; only there must be one pulse among them all; a true community. They like uniforms and bandings; seats in rows; marches in file; dances in ring; songs in chorus. When Say, in her fanciful childhood, had used to endow all insensible life with the personality of fable, — when she had her myths of trees and flowers and stones, and dreamed what it would be like to have been created one of these, her thought was always of one among a many; she would not have been a palm or an aloe, or a cereus, or any grand and solitary, century-blooming thing, if she had known of such; she looked out on the early summer fields, and saw them golden with the buttercups, springing up, closely, on their slender, elastic stalks, and nodding gayly to each other in the morning sunshine, saying, cheerily, 'Here we are!' and she would have been one of them; one of the midmost on a hillside; she pitied the poor, scattered things away out under the walls. They were just as golden to be sure; but how could they feel it so? Any more than she could, on the outskirts of the "good society" of Selport? She did not care to be a *double* buttercup, even here in Hilbury; she did not wear her finest, as I said. But she made herself fresh, and pretty, and dainty; she had nothing else to do; and she found it worth her while; love and admiration gathered round her; and she liked it. She gave it back; the Hilbury girls were fresh, and bright, and heartsome; quick and intelligent too; and individual, as they were not in the city; nice and delicate, though simple, of array, also, in the hours when she saw them; nicer and more delicate for her being there, — though she never thought of that; it was the season in Hilbury when Sarah Gair came up; she brought fashions with her, and did not notice how they followed her appearing; she only thought there was not so great a difference, after all, beetwen these "countrified" folk, as her mother called them, and the people in the town. The clever adaptiveness which reproduced and reflected new ideas was so prompt, that it did not seem reflective but simultaneous. The decisive touches and amendments to half the summer apparel in Hilbury were made in the first fortnight after Say unpacked her pretty wardrobe there.

The large, pleasant breakfast-room, where the easterly rays struggled in, aslant, through the cherry-boughs, seemed full of spring bloom when Say came down, in her rose-colored wrapper; and she sat there, when she had done eating wheat-cakes and amber syrup, in the delicious after-breakfast feeling that one has, when the long fair day lies all before one to choose one's pleasure in.

Aunt Rebecca washed the china. Say offered to take a towel; but Rebecca did not care to have her; they had their own way, here, of doing things; and one of these was *not* the fashion of taking two to do what one could accomplish better alone.

"Plenty of towels and scalding water, and no standing to drain;" that was the rule. One thing taken out at a time, from the steaming tub, and rubbed to a polish as the quick vapor dried away from it. Say chatted, and looked on.

Presently a slow, shuffling step in at the end door and across the wide kitchen, towards them.

Joanna's bright good-morning had a tone of tenderness in it. An old man stood in the open entrance from the kitchen to the breakfast-room. An old, bent man, with a mild, asking face; always asking and dreamy; never lighted with any flash of certain apprehension. He came in, half feeling his way; the added vacancy in his eyes, of one not seeing clearly, passing from the outer sunshine to the shaded room. Say's dress was the brightest thing there; he made straight for that.

"Heaps of posies; whole heaps of posies; and a posy-face, too," as Say looked up at him and smiled in his old eyes.

"Jane's child; little Sarah, you know;" Joanna said, following in, and speaking with slow gentleness.

"Jane was allers a pretty little gal; yes; proper-behaved. No gals to our house; and marm 's been gone a great while. Gabriel's a good boy though; always a good boy, Gabriel."

"Going to the field, father?"

All the village people called old Mr. Hartshorne "father;" it is a natural, pitiful way that kindly hearts take towards such feeble folk. Joanna had a sweet accent on the word, that was a little different from her ordinary, aplomb fashion of speech.

When Gabriel was by, though, she never called him so. Many a heart has its little stolen luxury like this.

Gabriel was not far; they all knew that; he never lost the old man long, from sight. As for the old man himself, he was safe enough now, not to wander widely, from his "boy;" his boy of five and thirty, who, for the twelve last of those years had never been three days together away from him.

"Going to the field; to sow corn;" he said, with a childish glee. "I 've got it; a whole pocket full." And he shook the kernels, that rattled crisply one against another, as he plunged his fingers among them. "Farmer's gold, Gabriel says. Gabriel gave it to me. Good boy."

"It's a bright day, father." A little flush crept up to Joanna's cheek as she said this word the second time. She was nearly caught. Gabriel stood at this instant on the doorstone.

He came in, in a hearty way. He shook hands with Say, who laid her little white palm in his brown, generous, faithful one, with a reverence; for she knew all his story; all that any knew, that is, save Joanna Gayworthy in her secret memory, and —you and I, reader, of all others in the blind unconscious world.

Gabriel turned toward Joanna, last. These two rarely addressed each other by name. When they did, it was "Gabriel," and "Joanna," simply, as it had been of old from childhood up; anything else would have been absurd; but both, with a certain instinct, preferred to find themselves face to face before speaking at all; and they were quick to catch each other's glances; to feel, each the other, by an intuition, when there was a something to be said. There were times, though, when a name was given, for a meaning that was put so better than in other word; this was rare and beautiful; it stood for thanks; for perfect comprehension; for a thousand things. It was like a caress, that the receiver kept the happiness of for days, reward sufficient for whatever called it forth; the giver never dreaming how dear it had been held. Yet it had been as sweet to give as take. In one thing, only, these two mistook each other. It was a mistake of long ago with one; an error of conclusion grown from it, and established with the other.

"I looked in to say that we might change hands this morning if you liked. It 's drilling and sowing for us, to day, and if you 'd like to break up that south-side piece of the Peak-hill lot, you can have Rainer, as well as not, and send Landy to me."

Rainer was a stalwart ploughman, omnipotent with an ox-team; Orlando was a farm-boy of fourteen.

"We should like that, Gabriel,— thank you."

The frank acceptance, and the Christian name,— these were the thanks, the recompense; the rest was but a fashion of speech, common to common people.

Gabriel leaned down over the chair in which the old man had seated himself.

"We must make haste now, father," he said. "Farmer's gold won't grow in pockets."

There was no drawing-room lounging in Hilbury. The morning calls were of the shortest.

The old man got up and put his hand out, feeling for Gabriel's. Gabriel passed his own from the side furthest, and drew his father's up, upon his nearer arm. A kindly support, given with a grace, as it might have been to a woman, or to any old and feeble man. Gabriel Hartshorne never treated his childish father as a child.

"That's a good man," said Say, as the two went out of hearing.

"That's the best Christian in Hilbury," said Aunt Joanna, in a way that ended the matter, saying all that could be said.

Gabriel Hartshorne went forth to the field with his old father, and took up his day's work; the stronger for that moment in Joanna's presence; for that word of hers that he had caught. "It's a bright day, father." So the day wore a new brightness. For that, and because of the other word — "Gabriel!" On so little may hearts live. God keeps the breath in us, we know not how.

And she? She sang as she had sung at nineteen; going about the house in her quick, neat positive way, putting everything in Gayworthy trim; pure, delicate, smiling order. Old-maidish? I suppose so, since there were but these two maidens to be the soul of it all, and to dwell in its midst. Since there was such a quietness in the air; such a staying of things after they were put. But, whatever the life might look like, it was no stiff and solitary living; narrowed to the placing of a chair — the polishing of a fire-iron; there was a secret joy in it — an untold thought — content to rest so — asking for no more; yet sure of something that ought to be its own; that should be, sometime, let this world go as it might; that, meanwhile, none other might so much as touch.

It was the joy God gives us in His waiting-times. His music between our acts of life.

Say had her first flitting to do; out among the chickens — dozens of little live puff-balls of golden down, with just one note of faint, tender music breathed into each; into the shed-chamber, the "play-parlor" of old, where some of the selfsame bits of pink and blue china were set up on the ledges, against the boards, where she had put them, years ago; a glance out from the always-open window; a counting of little white and black and motley pigs, that were, at the very moment, scrambling after each other over the bit of meadow, toward the oak wood, — off thither, for their day's picnic; a stroll down through the great barn between the sweet-smelling mows, and so out, at the south doors, into the spring-meadow; through this, by the gravelled cart-path, running around two sides to a bar-place in the far corner, into the old "oak orchard," away beyond, where the great, precipitous gray boulder reared itself in the midst, on the brow of the hill-field, and beside it spread the huge branches of the ancient tree that gave its name to the plantation. A rest here, and a long look over the valley, to the blue, misty hills beyond; a ride on the old apple-bough, her steed in days of yore standing here, waiting, still, like the enchanted horse in the Alhambran legend. Back again, after awhile, more slowly; a peep into dairy and cheese room; a delicious pecking, in the old way, at white tender curd, cut up in cubes, ready for the press; and at last, half unwillingly, an acknowledgment of the one "must" of her first, bright day of multitudinous delights, —unpacking; she had all this to fill up the quick morning hours, and bring round the dinner-time, before she had really settled what to do with the day at all.

"Shall we go to Cousin Wealthy's this afternoon?" she asked of the aunts, sitting down with them to boiled chicken and dandelions; the "cruel dinner," that she had called it in her childhood, loving the doorside pets and the field flowers so; yet finding it very nice, for all, as she had them, with its garnishing of fresh eggs that lay like inlaid gold and ivory upon the dark greens; and its delicate sauce of new, sweet butter, melted into cream again, from the very churn. "Shall we go to Cousin Wealthy's and see Aunt Prue?"

"I promised to drive over to Winthorpe, one day this week," said Rebecca, "and this is Friday. We may not have so good a day to-morrow. And Stacy will have been looking for me."

"'The church and the steeple, and all the good people, and yet she complains that her hands are not full,'" said Aunt Joanna, merrily. "Did you ever find out, Say, that a leisure day gets crowded fuller of business, in the end, than any other? It 's just so with an old maid's life. Becsie was n't satisfied with being the chief spoke in the wheel in Hilbury parish; but she must take Winthorpe parsonage under her wing, besides. Stacy King has got a flock, you see. It 's very meritorious to have a flock, particularly because it provides something for your friends to do. So the minister came over here, one day, five or six years ago, whimpering: 'Stacy was greatly burdened, and very feeble; she was lonely, too; she wanted some friend to cheer her up, and would one of us go over?' Of course we would; people that have n't got husbands and flocks never have anything else to do but to go everywhere, and do everything, and all at a time. So Becsie went. And when she once begins on a thing, she takes it right into her life, and makes a place for it, and after that, it 's never off the docket. She 's like the man I saw in Selport, with the dinner-plates. One more never makes any difference. She keeps them all spinning. Turn by turn. And to-day's the day, it seems, for spinning Winthorpe. So you 'll have to go there, if, anywhere."

"That's beautiful. I like going to Winthorpe. It 's so lovely down that old street, so broad and green, with just a track in the middle, and the great elms reaching overhead. I 'm glad you did n't go before, Aunt Becsie."

"You need n't be under any alarm," said Joanna. "There 'll be opportunities enough. What with Stacy's ailments, and the vicissitudes of the flock, — seven of them, Say! there 's always an errand. Becsie goes one day, to find out what she 's to go for next. Last winter, they kept her busy with whooping-cough; the spring before, it was measles; and when the Parsoness gets pulled down herself, she goes and stays. That' s every six months, or so."

Rebecca only smiled. There was no open wound, now, to be touched with Joanna's raillery. Joanna had no suspicion there had ever been one. Their two lives ran on, side by side, each holding its own mystery. Such is sisterhood; and friendship; for the most part.

By two o'clock, the comfortable two-seated wagon was rolling along the downhill roads that led easterly to the Chinsittimie and Winthorpe. It was four when they came into the large, yet rural river-town. It was beautiful, as Say had said. Built on the wide, level meadow-reaches, it had, in place of the narrow, winding road that creeps from village to village among the hills, a broad, magnificent green street, running parallel to the river. Back from this, rods apart, stood the houses; odd and antique, many of them; for Winthorpe was an early settlement, and its fine academy was an old foundation. There were gambrel-roofs and overhanging upper stories; queer one-sided roofs, with slope from ridge-pole to door-post behind, and a mere flap in front, above the fair two-story elevation; deep porticoes and low stoops; all varieties of primitive New England architecture. Over all, trees older than the houses.

Up a turf yard, to the side porch, hung with trails and sweeps of woodbine, just growing tender with new green, they came to the parsonage entrance.

The pale, worn preacher saw them from his study window, and came out to take their horse. Stacy ran from some inner domestic sanctum, picking up a child by the way, and gave them greeting at the door.

"This is real good of you; and to bring Say, too!" she said. "I've been looking for you all the week."

Stacy King had no time now, for puffs and vanities; if not given up, they had been crowded aside. Her bright hair was put back over her ears, not quite unrumpled; the baby had been tugging at it; her face was thin, her eyes looked large, a side-tooth was gone that showed a gap in the pretty mouth, when she smiled, as she did now; yet her smile was sweeter, somehow, when it came, than it had been in the old, gay, careless days, when it had won Gordon King. The corners of her lips drooped into a quiet gravity, after the smile faded; there was a line between the eyebrows that told of perplexities, very like of petulance. Stacy had had a hard school to learn in.

You could have seen what Rebecca Gayworthy had been to her, by the look she turned and rested on her when she had got her indoors and taken away her bonnet. What she had been in the household, by the very baby springing to her arms as soon as it saw her face and caught her voice. What Gordon King thought when he came in and found her so, as he reached out his wan, white hand for a renewed grasp of welcome. But only God and the secret hearts of those two knew all that she had been.

The line had began to come in Stacy's forehead many years ago, when the first illusion of mere earthly love had faded, and the cares came in that thrust the husband and wife apart. This time arrives with the demands of earnest life, in some phase, to every pair. Every Adam and Eve must leave their early Paradise behind them, and while it lies there like a dream, turn from it to the wilderness that spreads wide and unrelenting all before. When Gordon King and Stacy stood so in their wilderness, an angel came to them.

Only she and Stacy knew the words that had been said between them, that day, long ago, in her first visit, as they sat in the two low chairs by the nursery fire; nursery and mother's room, as well; when Stacy flung down with a sudden, reckless impatience, the insufficient pattern of cloth from which she had been trying to contrive a little coat; and, with the stirring of a pebble, the whole pent-back stream poured forth.

"It's always so! I never tried to save by making a thing do that would n't do, but I ended in wasting the whole. It's miserable trying to get something out of nothing. And that's what my whole life has been. There was n't enough stuff in the beginning. And now it's all cut up, and there's nothing made of it, after all. I've worried, and tugged, and strained, and lost my good nature, and my strength, and my good looks, and all I had to make anybody care for me; and I'm cross, and old, and good for nothing, and spoilt!" And she put her two hands against her forehead, and leaned down, helplessly, and cried.

"You've done what God gave you to do, Stacy; don't say there's nothing made of it."

"I have n't. And He did n't give it to me. I took it. Rebecca Gayworthy, you know that."

Rebecca was silent at that for a half-minute. Then she came near, and laid her arm over Stacy's neck, — the thin shoulders, that had been so round and shapely once, — quivering, now, with the soul-pain that sent itself through the flesh, — and said tenderly —

"You took what you were made so as to long for, and what He let lie in your way. We can get nothing that He does not give. It is yours, — this life, — because you needed it."

"And I am not fit for it, Rebecca. I feel sometimes as if I had cheated my husband. And, — Lord help me! sometimes I think he feels so, too. I think he almost turns from me, and gives me up. And yet, I did mean to be so good! It was n't a pretence; but my religion was like all the rest. There never was stuff enough. I tried to make it do, but it fell short."

"We don't have it all at once, Stacy. It grows, as life grows. Out of all these things, perhaps, it is coming to you more and more."

"If I thought that! But no; it's punishment. I wanted to be religious, because he was; because I could n't be a minister's wife without it; because I loved him so. And I felt sure that with him I could be anything. I thought he would always help me. But he's had other people to help; and I've had my separate work to do. And when a person is once supposed to have got religion, it's taken for granted to be for good and all. Or else, they've been hypocrites and pretenders. I suppose that's what I've been; but I did n't mean it, Becsie. I believed in myself — then."

"And why not now, Stacy? What reason have you to doubt?"

"Oh, Becsie! it don't hold! It gives way with every strain that comes upon it. I have n't any strength nor any patience. I'm cross with my husband, and cross with my children. And I care just as much for vanities as ever; only I can't get them. It makes me angry to see my face in the glass, all pinched and pale; and to have to wear that old straw bonnet with the brown ribbon ironed out. And — it's gospel truth, Becsie, though he's a good man — he is n't half so patient himself with me as he was when I was pretty."

"Don't you tell him your troubles and temptations? Don't you pray God together for help?"

"Of course we have family prayers; when Dorcas comes in; there's hardly a chance now for anything else, with all his time so taken up, and the babies wanting me every hour. And prayers — it's dreadful — but they do! make me feel further away from him than ever, and from God too; when, perhaps, I've been fretful and tired all day long. Oh, Becsie! I want to be taken up and comforted!"

Rebecca drew the tired head, the pale face, down upon her shoulder.

"You're worn out dear. It's that. You must n't find fault with the soul for the ails of the body. You don't sleep well, poor child! do you?"

The tender words, — the "poor child," — the nestling down into a friendly bosom, — with these, Stacy sobbed in a gentle, passive, grieved way, as a baby might.

"I have n't had a whole night's rest in all these five years past. Sometimes not a whole hour. I've had my arms full night and day; when I wanted to be in arms myself and tended."

She breathed it out brokenly between her sobs.

"'The eternal God is thy refuge; and underneath are the everlasting arms.' We are only left to feel the other, that we might feel this. 'Flesh and heart faileth; but God is the strength of our hearts, and our portion forever.' Think that He is teaching you this, Stacy, and be willing to learn His lesson. But never think that He has left you, or given you over."

"Oh, that is what I have been afraid of," murmured Stacy.

"If the life had gone out of you, you could not have been afraid. It is the flesh that is weak; and for that, we must take care of you, somehow."

"God bless you, Rebecca Gayworthy! You *do* take me up and comfort me. And to think it should be *you!*"

"Hush, hush, dear!"

"She needs change and rest."

Rebecca had said so to the minister down stairs, after prayers that same night, when Stacy had gone up early with the baby.

"Next month," — the next month would be October, and Rebecca knew that then the baby would begin its little, independent life, and the mother might be spared from it, — "next month would not Mrs. Fairbrother come over and stay, and let me have Stacy a while at the farm? Annie and Gordie should come too. That would make it easier here, and they should not tease Stacy."

The minister turned with a quick, grateful look.

"You shall take your own way with us all. You are a true friend, Miss Rebecca."

"Being so, may I say one thing more, that only a true friend should say?"

"Whatever you please."

"Do you remember what you spoke of when you first came to tell us that this home was to be? Of the help she needed? 'Her feet,' you said, 'are newly set in the upward way.' "Has n't it been harder for her sometimes than you have thought, perhaps, with all these cares coming about her?"

"Have I been hard upon her? Does she think that?"

"No," said Rebecca. "But I am afraid she is hard upon herself. Because of little failures. I think she needs help and cherishing that way; more than she did then in her first hopefulness. I think she needs to feel nearer to her husband and his strength than ever."

Rebecca said this low, timidly, as going to the very verge of her friendly right.

Gordon King regarded her intently. His voice altered and he partly turned away again as he answered her.

"My strength is a poor thing," he said. "I have had my failures, too. I laid my hands on life presumptuously, before I knew what sort of matter it was. I took it upon me to lead others when, God knows, I wanted leading most of all myself. I was n't fit to care for Stácy, poor child."

"Yet her very love of God went up through you! and now she is afraid. Don't leave her alone!"

All the tenderness of the old days, — of the starlit evenings when Stacy had told him first "she was not good, she was afraid," — when it had seemed so sweet to help her, to lift his soul to Heaven for hers, — when he had thought he could be strong for both, — came back suddenly as he heard these words. A loftiness and strength came also to him, from the loftiness he recognized in her who spoke them. A new, generous love toward the wife for whom the old, first, passionate love even had borrowed a tender reverence, carried unconsciously from his thought of this woman, — this friend, — who was too high for him now, as she had been then; who strengthened him standing by; from whose presence he could bear strength to the other, — his own, — waiting for it. There are women who are born for ministry like this; not receiving unto themselves, ever, save from God; giving out always.

Gordon King thought of his wife as she had been in those old days; in her sweet girlishness, that any beautiful womanhood might grow from; with her fresh, bright smile, that grew brighter always for him; when her very little pettishnesses and vanities were like the spring breeze that tosses up a perfume. He thought of the weary mother above there, hushing her weary child. He felt life had been hard for her. It had been hard for him; but its hardness should not have thrust between them so. Tears and prayers should not have been so locked away in two separate souls. Please God, his yet young flower should grow bright again.

"I will not leave her alone. God forgive me if I have done so!"

He held out his hand to Rebecca as he rose. He grasped hers hard. "God has sent a help to us both," said he, tremulously.

"And that it should be you!" That was what his heart smote him with, also, secretly, though he spoke it not. The underlife that never had been spoken, — that lay between these three, — through the power of this Rebecca touched them both — the husband and the wife. It was possible for her alone; her purchased right. At her hand they must take help. Was it gift of grace or coals of fire? Gift of God's love, as comes with all scorch and pain, though we have earned the pain only.

The minister went up stairs; the baby was hushed away in the cradle. He and Stacy were alone.

Rebecca sat below, wistful of a beginning of new joy for them; a joy she had helped to make; that she also entered into.

I think it was the very "joy of her Lord." Of Him who came not to be ministered unto, but to minister.

More than six years ago that was. Six years, wherein, quietly and faithfully, Rebecca Gayworthy had taken Winthorpe Parsonage "right into her life, and made a place for it;" wherein there had grown to be no other consciousness any more between her and it than that of a gentle, happy friendliness; till to-day, because of her, there was here a life, toilsome but peaceful; there were hearts weary often, but undistrustful; love chastened, calm, patient; here where wreck of heart and faith and life had threatened: till to-day, a cheeriness lighted itself up about her as she came in, so that Sarah Gair, entering after her, felt on the very threshold the soul of the whole story.

Joanna had been set down in Shop Row. She had some errands to do and an old school-friend to see. Afterward she came to the Parsonage. And then it made itself evident that, for all her sauciness, she had taken up a cheery little mission of her own here, none the less.

There were sugar-plums in her bag, and the children instincted them afar off, like flies. She popped them into their mouths as they stood about her knees, holding up defiantly, now and then, before the parson's eyes, a glowing red or lucid amber bit, as she came to it. The parson usually approved only of white, unflavored candies for his children, when, poor souls, they happened to get any at all. But that was neither according to Joanna's hygiene nor philosophy.

"They're made to like pretty colors," she said. "We need n't poison them, to be sure; but the bright sugar tastes the sweetest, for all that, and it takes a little essence of something to help the double-refinements down."

So, after the sweetmeats came stories; truth essenced for them upon the like principle. White light broken up into rainbows. Aunt Joanna told magnificent stories. She went on, to-day, with a wonderful serial about a cat who exceeded in the brilliancy of her adventures all the cats of fable. In their fundamental morality, also, since she never lied, or stole, or slew, impunibly; but was trained gradually by the discipline of consequences, even as little humans, toward truth and honesty and mercy. And the story never came to a final end, any more than life does. She was never declared to have been "good and happy ever after;" there was always "more for next time." Aunt Joanna knew Mother Goose, too, from beginning to end, and she sang the old rhymes in her clear, beautiful voice, to improvised melodies of her own, sometimes gleeful as laughter, sometimes sweet and touching as old church-tunes. The others dropped their talk often and listened, to her inventions as well as to her songs. The grave minister laughed at her oddities, and Stacy declaring that there was never any chance of rationality after Joanna Gayworthy came in, was met by the avowal that it was precisely what she came for; to shake them up and unsettle them out of their primness, and give them all the trouble she could in getting back to it again. She was like a breeze that set everything fluttering, and left the whole house freshened after she had passed on.

Then as they drove slowly homeward over the hills, she took up her pranks of satire again.

"I've found it out; and it's something for an old maid to discover! Marriage goes by the Rule of Three. A two-legged stool won't stand alone. It wants a third prop somehow. Sometimes it's religion — when they're both of one mind about that, and when it really is the main thing; sometimes it's worldliness — when they've both one object; sometimes it's a friend — when there's somebody that's as much to both of them as they are to each other. That makes a three-strand rope. And for *that* couple it's Rebecca Gayworthy. She's married 'em both, as much as they ever married one another. And she's the *house-band* let me tell you, Say, of the whole establishment."

Say laughed. Rebecca smiled gently as she always did at Joanna's fun, but her eye had a far-away joy in it, not born of the smile. It was a look like one who hears a faint, sweet tone in the air. The echo of her own life-music, floating round her in this midmost calm, from all its pure accordant years.

"But what," said Say presently, "if they can't manage to get a third prop? There are n't many Aunt Rebeccas to be had, whatever they might do about the other things."

"Oh, then they lean up against a dead wall most of 'em, and just *look* strong and respectable. There's plenty of two-legged stools in the world."

"But, Aunt Joanna," said Say again, "I don't believe you take enough credit to yourself. It seems to me you're as much at home at the Parsonage as anybody."

"Oh, I go there, just as I do to dozens of other places. I like to see how different human beings manage. I borrow a little of everybody's life. That's what I go to church for, as much as the preaching. I know when old Mrs. Gibson has had the bows turned on her black Navarino, and it makes me feel just as comfortable for her as she does for herself; and it's nice to get a glimpse of Eunice when she is n't tailoressing; and to think how she's resting with her gloves on, and her hands folded. And I like to see when the Newcombe girls are home from Manchester on a visit, and to watch their mother's eyes; I don't know but her pride is as pious as most folks' prayers. And to see the different looks on different faces when a hymn's given out, or the Bible's read, or something special is said in a sermon. You can tell half that ever happened to people, if you did n't know it before; and pretty nearly what's come of it all. Yes, Say, I'm a gossip; weekdays and Sundays, a clear gossip. Old maids generally are, when they are n't saints like Becsie. And a gossip is n't a bad thing either, if you leave out the tattling part. I looked the word out in Johnson one day. It comes from "God-sibb, God-relation." It's what He puts between us in this world. And most of my religion I think, if I've got any, comes by relation; by feeling other people's experiences. I'd rather see a good face, and know of a good thing done, than to hear a twenty-headed sermon about it."

Not a word in all this, of Mrs. Prouty, as of old; there had been no sarcasm either upon Stacy; something in the years had touched Joanna's quickness with a broader kindliness.

Say remembered this talk, afterward, on Sunday, sitting by Aunt Joanna, in the old square pew; Joanna had left the singing gallery years ago, when there only remained Rebecca and herself, of all the Gayworthys, to sit together; Say thought of her words, and her Sunday "gossip," seeing Gabriel Hartshorne, — the "best

Christian in all Hilbury,"— in the pew before ; seeing him find the chapter and hymn for his old father, and hold the book for him to look on ; seeing him pick up his hat for him, when the service was over, and the people going out ; and lead him down the aisle, slowly, leaning on his strong, tender arm. She saw the light in Joanna's eyes, looking on all this, as they walked after; when Gabriel would have drawn back, to let them pass more quickly, and she refused to hasten by, but kept a reverent step behind ; when afterward, in the churchyard, they came near — the old man and the younger one — pausing at a white-tableted grave.

"Hepzibah Hartshorne," the stone said, — "aged 54."

Joanna Gayworthy pressed Say's arm, and drew her on. But she had seen Gabriel give to his father a little nosegay of spring-flowers. And the old man smiled, and laid it on the grave.

"She 's 'way off — an' it 's a long time ! But she knows we don't forget her Sunday posy, Gabe ?"

Gabriel bent his head ; and a strange, sweet smile came over his face ; a shining intentness into its lines ; as of one to whom a far, glad, solemn utterance comes, that is not for all. Some faint, beautiful likeness, I think it must have borne to the look that rested once on the One Divine Countenance when the Voice breathed "My beloved Son ! In whom I am well pleased."

Her Sunday posy — brought to her, even yet, by loving hands. In the tall-growing grass lay many such, already ; drying away there, week by week.

"Do they always do that ?" Say whispered.

And Joanna answered, in a hushed way, as speaking of something holy, — "always."

Even in a blank like this, a music. Sweet-dropping notes, summer by summer measuring the time, between far-parted acts of an old man's helpless life.

Aunt Joanna sat through the afternoon service, with her head upon her hand. Her face was paler than at morning, and there was, now and then, a look of wistful pain about the eyes. Say leaned toward her once, taking her little smelling-bottle from her pocket. A quick motion of Joanna's hand said plainly, Nonsense! and with a queer little quiver of the mouth, she pulled down her veil over the front of her bonnet and turned away.

"What was the matter, Auntie ?" asked Say, afterward, when they came out.

"Matter ? goosie ! replied Joanna. "Why, I sat looking at 'Senath Spring's new bonnet with the cape all on one side, till it gave me the toothache ! Nobody knows what I have to go through with the Hilbury millinery !"

CHAPTER XXIV.

THEN AND NOW.

JOANNA was out in the front yard, sowing her last annuals in the little beds under the parlor windows. Say stood behind her with the basket of seeds.

"Now, the nasturtiums."

While Say had her fingers among the paper bags, — rattle-te-clash! down came a country wagon to the gate. 'Siah Ford factotum, from the Hoogs place.

"Cap'n Vorse's got home!"

Joanna jumped up, and turned round, and Say thrust into her hand a big brown parcel of pumpkin seeds.

"Gershom! When?"

"Las' night. Much as ever, though. Ship all but went down in a harricane."

Then the two women turned pale, as if the news had come this end foremost, with the "all but" left out: and, in an instant, stood at the foot of the grass-path; basket, trowel, pumpkin seeds, and all.

"'Siah Ford!" cried Joanna, clutching the paper parcel in one hand, till the pumpkin-seeds began to ooze through its lower end, and slide down into the grass, while she threatened him with the trowel in the other,— "what-ever-in-the-world-do-you-mean?" Saying these words very deliberately and emphatically with the little catches between as designated, she sowed at least three pumpkins to the syllable.

'Siah Ford looked her in the face, solemnly.

"Sartin true, — black 'n blue, — give yer leave ter cut m' in two."

"Not the Ceres!"

"Ser 'is? Yes, I tell yer! Cant *nuthin* make yer b'lieve a feller?"

"The *ship* Ceres! You know what I mean. Say, make him tell!"

"*Ship* Ceres? "Oh, lor, no! I remember now. No, 'twant the Ceres; they left her, long shore, somewheres, out there in Indy; stoppin' fer, iv'ry, or sunthin; he'll tell yer. But the short on't is, he's Cap'n; an' I rather guess he's airnt his ship. One they put him aboard of to bring home. The Cap'n died out there. 'T all belonged t' the same concern. Spose likely I don't take in the hull o n't, but from what I c'n pick up 'bout it, he's done sunthin 'r other pesky smart, Cap'n Vorse has; or less he would n't be here."

Sarah Gair's eyes flashed a great, proud gladness, as she stood and listened.

"Something smart?" Oh, she knew! Some brave, grand thing, such as Gershom had always meant to do. Now, it had come. Now, he was a hero. And this noble thing, this glory, — it was hers, partly, also. Because she had been in the secret, in the old days, when it was only a dream. When he first wanted to go to sea; and talked out there on the big rock under the yellow plum-tree, of what he would do, if he ever got to be a man, and a sailor. Her hands trembled, holding the willow basket. The full, brilliant color swept up and deepened in her cheek, till it glowed — palpitated — like a flame.

Aunt Joanna had not quite got over her little paleness at the shock and the astonishment; at thirty-three the blood does not pulse back and forth with such suddenness, as at nineteen.

"Why, child," she cried, turning round to Say, "you're illuminated!"

With that, she sowed the last of the pumpkins, in a new spot, and was never the wiser. How they came there under the maples, she wondered, a month or two later.

'Siah Ford had driven round into the chip-yard. Rebecca was coming up from the barn, with a basket of eggs. Do the best they could, the women must go back through the house, to meet her. So he would be first with his news. This was his business, to-day, with every soul he could waylay in Hilbury. Nothing else under the sun had brought him down from the farm, with his horse and empty wagon. There was meal waiting at the mill, to be sure; and he was going for it: by and by, if he did n't forget it. This is the way they carry tidings in Yankee-land; much like the "bended bow and the voice" of Highland warfare; only without the avowed purpose. There is always meal at the mill.

He "could n't stop to talk over partick'lers; must come up to our 'us an' hear all about it. Cap'n was smart, an' so was the widders."

And the bended bow and the voice passed on; towards Hartshorne's, and so to the Bridge.

Dinner at twelve. Half an hour earlier than the Gayworthy wont. At one, a grand council of one, in the red-room, with bolted door, over four dresses.

The purple jaconet was fresh and new; but then the pink muslin was so bright and becoming; too dressy, perhaps, with its four little flouncings; Gershom hated finery so. Oh, dear! if one could only look one's prettiest, without keeping the reason why in sight! The dark-blue foulard was what she would naturally have put on for a common drive over to Cousin Wealthy's; and it would grow cool at dusk; but, oh, dear, no! that would never do for this occasion. An old thing, — mourning besides, somewhere, over there, on the other side the world, — and he just home, alive and well, by a hair-breadth 'scape, and who knows what marvel of courage! If she could have ventured on the white; — but that was too manifest a getting up. These first days of June had been summer in fact as well as name; but, up here among the mountains, people were slow in coming to trust the summer, — to the extent of white muslin.

Say turned back to the purple lawn; good sense and good taste compromised upon this. She huddled the other dresses into the press, and pulled her hair down with one hand, while she unfastened the door with the other. Aunt Rebecca was outside; come to see if she were ready. The hair must come down and go up again, though Aunt Rebecca would not have seen the necessity.

"In five minutes, auntie! If you come in I shall get chattering; just go off like a dear, and I won't be any time!"

But Rebecca and Joanna waited twenty minutes, talking with Mary Makepeace, who came in for a pitcher of yeast and to hear more, or over again, about it all. Then they began to call up the stairs, and called alternately, for five minutes longer; and then at last the little lady came down. Not gay, — not fine, but somehow things could not be fresh on her without proclaiming their freshness; there is such a difference in women about this: and from the straight white line between the dark waving bands of her hair to the tip of the little black gaiter boot, she was finished, — and *just* finished, marvellously.

"Is n't your dress too thin?"

"Oh, aunt Becsie! this jaconet! Why it's as thick as — pasteboard! It's only a nice kind of calico."

"I don't know, — it is n't out of the common to be sure, when you come to examine — and yet — it looks — well, if it was unbleached sheeting I suppose you'd bloom out in it!" Aunt Joanna's slight doubt worked itself off so, with an accent of pride, and a loving little tip of the chin, lifting up a bright face and graceful head that could but have bloomed truly from whatever sort of calyx.

It was only a simple white-grounded lawn, spotted thickly with tiny purple pansies; but there were dainty puffings about waist and sleeves, and delicate lace at the throat; and — altogether, she might have gone so to a ball, and looked lovely; or come down to breakfast in it equally lovely, and defiant of criticism.

Sarah Gair and Gershom Vorse had not met for five years past. Then it had been at Hilbury, as now; when she was fourteen, and he twenty. He was mate of a vessel then, sailing from New York; Blackmere was in the same ship, second officer. The old Pearl had been sold away; she went into smaller coastwise trade. Blackmere loved the brig, but he loved Gershom Vorse better. Gershom must rise; it was his duty in life, and he had chances. Education, which was the greatest chance of all. Blackmere cared for no advancement, whether he could have got it or not; he barnacled himself to Gershom now, and shipped with him always. Gershom looked out for that and carried his point, or gave up all the rest. They had been in the Ceres last; round the Northwest coast for sandal-wood and furs; home by China, to load with teas and silks. Gershom had seen the world — a sailor's sight of it — over and over.

And Say had lived on in her world: half a dozen streets; a couple of score of drawing rooms; four houses, perhaps, where she was intimate enough to go up stairs when there was no party. This world of hers opened out toward the great hills, though; this had saved her from utter narrowness and stagnation. And she had books; but they were to her life what Gershom's sailor-books had been to the great sea; *that* lay all beyond, in its might and mystery, transcending dreams.

Could these two join their sympathies at the point where their intercourse had broken off? Could they stand again at that instant of hope and resolve, and look in the light of it, at this moment of achievement? Hope and achievement never are so joined. The years and the labor lie between. It was a boy of thirteen that had lain on the gray rock under the plum-tree, asking Say, the child of seven, what the sea was like. It was a man of twenty-five, who had traversed the hemispheres, and measured his manhood against the elements, who came home to-day with a deed in his life where a resolve had been.

Say, who had had "all these years longer to be a little girl," had achieved it seems nothing but her growth, her bloom, and her woman-garb. Nothing else, that Gershom could apprehend. She could but put on her pansy-robe and come to him, so, with her best.

She could go back. Those moments under the plum-tree were fresh and vivid to her. It was to her as if Gershom had leaped from that to this. As if, an instant ago, he had said, I will do this, — as if, without conscious pause, she could cry to him exultingly, O Gershie, it is done!

She thought too, in her secret heart, that she *had* achieved something. To have grown into her womanliness and beauty, as he into his manliness and daring — was this nothing? Would he not be pleased to see her as she was to-day? This her little feminine—what-you-please, gave a warmer glow to her anticipation.

And what came of it?

A grasping of hands; a greeting of words; great asking of questions; brief, sailorly answers; a making light of whatever he had done; a holding back of the very thing Say secretly felt a share in.

He talked more to the aunts than to her. Once she caught a stray glance, — something of the old, measuring look, taking her in, from the little violet neck-ribbon to the hem of the wide-floating summer dress, — that made her feel suddenly flimsy before him, the stout, brave fellow, in rough dark blue, with hair tossed in an unconscious grace, and eyes that looked straight on, — that she could not fancy ever had stopped short at a self-image. Well, would he have her dowdy? A woman must do something to herself. It would be more painstaking to make herself a fright.

So she lifted up her head in a little assured, defiant way, as one who could not help it, and really did not care much that she *were* young and pretty, — the youngest and prettiest there. Also, there must be a first time of putting on anything; even a jaconet with purple pansies.

"She got away into the dairy, by and by, with Cousin Wealthy, going to skim the cream for tea.

"He does n't tell us half," said she.

"He is n't much for glorifying! He won't go round tellin' it over and over. He told his mother, last night. And I suppose he thinks that 's enough."

"But you know. Oh, do tell me, Cousin Wealthy, all about it!"

"I could n't. It takes a sailor. They were on their beam-ends, and the Lord knows what. And the sea made a clean breach, and they were knocked about amongst lee-scuppers, and cabooses and things; and two men were washed overboard. And the top mainmast went, and they cut away the rigging, and they drove before the wind till morning. And then the gale went down, but there was a great leak, and the men were for getting off in the boats. But the *Captain* — that 's Gershom you know —" Say nodded, — "and the mate — that 's Blackmere, his great friend, — said no; they should stick by the ship, and the women. There were two women passengers, one of 'em the Cap 'n's widow, and the other was a sick lady coming home from Calcutta. So, at that, the men were shamed, and made up their minds to stick by too. And they worked away at the pumps; and after awhile they found the leak; and they patched and rigged up again, somehow, and they had pleasant weather and they came on. And they say Gershie saved the ship, from first to last. It was all in the paper he brought home in his pocket; but when he 'd showed it to his mother, he just took it and poked it under the kitchen fire, as cool as you please. I think it kinder worked her, not to have it to put away; but she was prouder of him for his doin' it, after all. *She* don't *talk* about it; but she goes round *looking* — as if 'nobody was Corporal but your father and I!'"

"Oh, belay, Cousin Wealthy! Do you think a yarn 's the better for so much over-spinning?"

The Captain himself said this, coming in suddenly, at the door between kitchen and dairy.

Cousin Wealthy looked a little abashed, — an amateur caught meddling with his art by a professional, — and wondered how much he had heard, and how much she *had* mixed up the sea-phrases. Say dropped the spoon with which she had been stirring together a whole five-quart pan of milk with its twelve hours' rising of cream, while she listened to the story, — and made a spring toward him.

"Oh, Gershie!" she cried, "I knew it! I always knew you would!"

"Pshaw!" said the sailor. But he did not say it roughly, and he could but take, for a moment, the two little hands stretched out to him in eager enthusiasm. The next instant they were dropped, and Say burned all over at the thought of her forwardness.

All Captain Vorse did to help her, was to walk off, first, out of the dairy.

"If he is n't easier scared than pleased," said Cousin Wealthy to herself, in an amaze, "no wonder beam-ends could n't start him!"

Fine and affected! That was what he thought of her. That

was what she had done with her purple ribbons and puffs, and her gladness and her pride in him. People *do* feel things in their bones, or more interiorly. Sarah Gair was sure of this, though Gershom had given her neither word nor look that she could quite charge with proof of it. Though he had just treated her like anybody else. Ah, that was it! The old time was gone, and their relation in it. She had no claim, after all; no share beyond others, in this man-work of his, though she had listened to his boy-dreams and left her play for them; though she had first shown him the sea, and made him free of the wonderful Pearl. He was no longer "Gershie;" though she did forget and call him so, and put her hands out to him in that ridiculous way that he only "pshawed" at and did n't care for the feeling of; he was a great, brown, whiskered sea-captain; he never once called her Say; what a fool she was! how her breath quickened and her face tingled as she thought of it, riding home silently with the aunts, in the dusky evening!

She knew she had looked stiff and silly; she had not been herself; she could not do herself justice in his presence; she was so afraid — had always been — of his contempt.

It had ended miserably, — this glad day.

At the same moment, Captain Gershom Vorse was driving away the thought of how bright and pretty the girl had looked, with her glad, eager way, and her outstretched hands, and her proud congratulation spoken in eye and color more than in word, — with another "pshaw!", mental, and more emphatic.

He did not believe in her; he did not want to believe in her; she was Jane Gair's child; she had been brought up to that vain, pretentious city life; she was sham, like all of it. And she wore puffed muslin, and dainty boots, and looked like a thing in a shop-window.

At the best what business had such as Aunt Jane and she in a world like this, where there were poverty and nakedness, — crime and pain and danger? Where the weak were wronged, and the miserable trampled under foot, and the ignorant sat in darkness? Going up and down the earth had he not seen all this, — he, at twenty-five even? Living among rough, rude, brave, generous, coarse, vicious, ill-used men, how had he come to think of paltry life like theirs?

What would Ned Blackmere say to such a woman? The rough, stalwart, sterling fellow, whom the world had handled so fiercely, had battered and banged about, but had never banged the truth and courage out of? Who would stand by him, in his grand loyalty of friendship, to the last plank?

"You 've got a mother, boy, make much of her; but take care of your bones and keep clear of the rest!"

He remembered that Blackmere had said this; the man who had had sister and wife.

So he weighed by a harsh standard, and judged with a bitter judgment, borrowing from this man of sterner, harder experience, the girl-life of nineteen years.

Yet this very weighing and judging,—what did it prove? That he himself was but twenty-five, after all. That he could not put away, without much thought, this image of his little playmate Say. He might have been harder; he might have let her alone.

CHAPTER XXV.

BROWN BREAD.

Something was very pleasant; something was horribly uncomfortable.

These two flashes of sensation, or recollection in such quick succession as to seem mingled, roused Say next morning to complete wakefulness, after the first faint creeping back of consciousness, whereby the stray elements of existence concentred themselves, and made her aware, first, of her body lying on the bed, then of the life she lived in it, whose thread was to be taken up again.

This mystery of sleep! This greater mystery of waking! If we could fathom them, we should have fathomed ourselves, and Life, and Death!

From the child who goes to bed with his last new toy hugged to his bosom, or his new shoes by the bedside, to the man or woman with the last deep joy or mighty grief that is to lie still awhile and be lost only for an intenser grasp upon the whole soul when the soul regathers itself, — a world of human being vanishes nightly into the great unknown, and orbs itself again into myriad identities at the recall of Day, as the stars were born out of darkness when the Voice said — Let there be Light!

To begin where each left off. With the hope — the plan — the upfolding knowledge — to be taken up as it was dropped. Grand or trivial, base or beneficent, involving an hour's pastime, a revelation of science, a crime completed, a nation's fate, a soul's salvation, — human thought, interest, purpose, whatever it may be, recovers itself out of the pause and darkness, returning inevitably unto its own.

—— Gershom was come back. The old days could never come back. She was glad; she was disappointed; she was pained, puzzled, ashamed; a little resentful. She bit her lip and pressed her face down into her pillow, as a certain quick spasm of keen re-sufferance came over her.

She did not care! She had done nothing wrong, nothing to be ashamed of. Only — she would never do it again!

Life moved forward in its simple channel. To-day need not necessarily continue at once the chief interest of yesterday. That lives, but bides its time.

The day broadened. Breakfast was done. Say and Aunt Joanna sat in the south chamber window, with a little old-fashioned light-stand between them, holding their bits of work; and it happened that they held a talk together, touching by chance upon a certain other interest in Sarah's life, not wholly detached from or irrelative to the rest. Nothing is. In human history there is, really and strictly, no such thing as an episode.

It was Joanna's window; the very one wherein the flutter of white draperies and the shining of the night-candle had been watched years ago, and might be still, from that other window opening this way in the farm-house gable, down the road. Joanna loved this window. Had this and that to do with each other? She made her customary seat here. Every woman who loves womanly work, has her nook wherein to do it. Turn her out of it, and she is all astray; like a bird with her nest broken up. The brown light-stand, with the work-basket and the Bible, stood here always. And there was a holy time at night, when the answering gleam came from the red gable, when without ever a word of knowledge, two hearts told themselves of the one thought that held them both; two children of God felt themselves one in Him; their souls finding each other before Him. Non-professors these, both of them; hardly reckoned among the elect, according to old church rules, here in Hilbury; yet the one looking at the life of the other, divined its secret spring, and said of him, "That's the best Christian in Hilbury;" and the heart of the other hallowed the woman he had loved, and, thinking of her nightly prayer, he sent up his own to heaven beside it. So their feet walked separate paths; but their spirits went God-ward, hand in hand.

It is not the sunshine, or any other tangible why, that accounts for the pleasantness of old house-corners. It is the pureness and the pleasantness that have clustered there; the very walls have drank these in. Shall the leaven of pest lurk and infect, and these escape? The air of an old home is full of their beneficent contagion.

Say could not have told the reason, but she was always especially peaceful and cheery in this particular south window. It wrought with her now. The current of her thoughts was turned. Her spirits reacted.

"I wish I had been born in the country, and always lived here," she said. "I think it would have made more of me. People's lives are real, here; and everybody has one of their own."

Aunt Joanna lifted her eyebrows a little.

"And not in the city?" she said.

"Not half so much. For the most part, they seem to be trying to get into other people's lives. And then — everybody makes up their mind to all sponge-cake," Say said, laughing. She had never forgotten the misdemeanor of her childhood. It had grown into a proverb of expression with her.

"And the sponge-cake don't go round?"

"No," said Say. "And, oh dear! I've been so hungry sometimes, for plain brown bread!"

Under the parable, Joanna knew very well, what the child meant.

"It's my low taste, perhaps. Mother seems to think so; but I like nice people too. Only there's a kind of common, comfortable, really-in-earnest living, that I always wanted to know more about."

"Down Gay Street, for instance."

"O yes: how I did use to wish, sometimes, that we lived in Gay Street! I shall never forget the Carpenters in that second house round the corner. I could look from our windows right over into theirs. There were four of them, sisters: and I never had a sister! They went to some town school, and they wore dark calico dresses just alike, and white aprons bound with colors; and they used to come home laughing and singing, round by the alley, and in at the yard-gate. I've watched them, and listened to them by the hour, playing in that yard, under the horse-chestnut. They made fairy-slippers, pink and purple and white, pulled from off the balsam-blossoms; and set them, by pairs, along the brick-edge of the border. I used really to believe the fairies came at night and got them. In the winter, they stayed up stairs, and sat in the broad window-seats and dressed dolls. Oh, how I wished I was a Carpenter girl! They moved away, years ago. I've heard father say that Mr. Carpenter had grown a rich man in Boston. But I do hope those girls have as good a time together as they used to then!"

"And you never played with them?"

"Well, — not lawfully, or comfortably. I did get into the alley sometimes, and they 'pulled me in;' father used to laugh so at that excuse! But it was one of the strictly forbidden things."

"I suppose mothers know best, and city is different from country; but I don't think the brown bread would have hurt you."

Say, sat still a minute, her two hands on her lap holding her work, forgetfully; presently a smile crept up to her eyes, and she lifted them, smile and all, to Joanna, saying, with a quiet, quaint little mischief of her own, "There 's one little cupboard, though, where I do go and get a bit, now and then."

Joanna waited.

"And, rich or poor, Grace Lowder has more in her than any girl I ever knew."

"Who is Grace Lowder?"

"She 's a seamstress. I never go without my mother's knowledge; and most often it is about the work. But I carry her things sometimes, — fruit, and flowers, and books; and sit and read to her while she works. Mother does n't object to that; it is different; it is charity; Grace Lowder is *quite* beneath me; she never need be invited and meet other people, you know."

Joanna's lip curled a little, involuntarily. "How came you to know so much of her?" she said.

"She comes to St. James Sunday School. I never noticed her till one day Doctor Linslee brought her to our class. Her teacher was absent, and all her class, except herself. We all stared a little, I suppose, as she came in. But I stared because I could n't help it. Some of the girls looked at her in that hard, strange, astonished way they have, as if it were n't quite certain what order of natural history she belonged to. But I thought I had never seen anything more lovely. She had on a soft woollen dress, of that purple-gray, — just like those grass-blooms;" Say glanced across at an old china vase upon a corner shelf, filled with graceful spears and tassels, among which peculiar, soft, gray-purple, feathery heads, in the perfection of their natural tint, were heaped conspicuously; "and her shawl was gray, with a narrow stripe of purple in the border; her bonnet, too, with a plain purple ribbon crossed upon it. But her face was so sweet! She is almost always pale, I know now; her skin is fine and clear as a roseleaf; but she was a little frightened at us all, and she had such a bright, lovely color! And when she lifted her eyes, they were purple-gray, too, with long lashes. And her lips looked half sad and half happy, just dropped a little at the corners, and tucked away into dimples that showed with the least tremble. She was just like a picture. But she had a crutch, auntie; she was lame. And yet she was as graceful as she could be. She drooped down, somehow, into her seat, without any spread or rustle; and the gray dress fell round her like a cloud. Nothing she had on was new; but every thing was as nice as new, — without a speck. I think that is the thing; anybody can put on new clothes, and be spick-and-span; but everybody can't wear them, and wear them, and look as if they'd never been near any dirt."

"Well — that was the beginning of it. Her teacher was sick and had to give up her class; and the scholars were divided round. Grace Lowder stayed with us. Miss Westburn went to see her, and found out all about her; and she spoke to some of us about her wishing for more work to do; sewing or dress-making; her mother had been a dressmaker, and had taught her the trade; but she had died a year before. Miss Westburn was married the next summer, and she gave her her wedding-dress to make. After that she had plenty of work; and mother has let me go to her. She works at people's houses when they wish it, but I don't wish it; I could n't bear that, Aunt Joanna! Grace Lowder's little room is the pleasantest place I know in Selport!

"She boards and lodges just where she did for years, while her mother lived. A nice, comfortable widow woman keeps the house; she was very kind to her mother, Grace says; and Grace has nobody else in the world to go to. I asked her one day what she would do, if Mrs. Hopeley died, or went away. She may go, sometime, to live with one of her sons, who, she says, are 'likely men, both of 'em, and very forrard in their means;' but Grace only smiled, and said there would always be a place for her in the world, as long as God kept her here; she was not afraid."

Aunt Joanna broke in here.

"And this is Selport brown bread! I don't know what the fine wheat must be," said she.

"Tasteless enough, sometimes, — the heart all bolted out of it," said Say.

"But I must tell you about her room," she resumed, after a little pause of stitching that she made between her paragraphs. "It is a corner house, where two streets cross, two narrow streets; and the angles of the blocks are cut off, and the front doors set in at the corners. It is a queer little square; some person of odd taste must have been the owner of the property, and laid it out and built it up to please himself. There are the four sociable front doors, and four windows over them, facing each other diagonally, and looking each other right through, — like the four cats in the riddle. Grace Lowder's room is the second-story one. The two side windows she keeps for her plants. The corner one she sits in, at her sewing. Opposite this is a corner fireplace. On one side is her bed, and in the other a wide press-closet. She has a little round table in the middle of the room, with a few books; and the coarse old carpet — with bright, strong colors, though, that make it look cheery — is always swept up clean of every shred, and always has the sun shining on it, — that is, unless it don't shine anywhere, — for it is a southwest corner. And

Grace Lowder lives the happiest, sweetest, most contented life there!"

"Why Say, it's brown bread to make your mouth water!"

"Down the street, to the west, — that narrow street, auntie, between the high, close houses, — she has a *view*. She calls it so. The tops of a few green trees in some gardens in Front St, — a little sparkle of the bay, and a stripe of sky. And she watches every night for the sunsets! One little scrap of a crimson cloud perhaps, or the stripe of sky turned yellow and shading up into blue between the chimney-tops! What would she say to look out here over the sea of little hills? Or to get at Cousin Wealthy's dairy window and see down the mountain side, out over the great pond?"

"You say she goes to work at people's houses?" asked Joanna, rather irrelevantly, as it might seem, to the last sentences.

"When they want her, yes; but I think she likes her little room best."

"Would she come a hundred miles think, if she could be paid for it?"

"Aunt Joanna! You don't mean — "

"I don't know as I do. But I feel exactly just at this minute, as if I was going to have a monstrous deal of sewing to do, sometime or other. Next summer, perhaps."

As she said this, Gershom Vorse came riding into the side-yard.

CHAPTER XXVI.

UP BOAR-BACK.

Joanna went down stairs. Say did not stir. Further than to draw a little nearer to the window, and lean slightly toward the half-closed blind that had shaded them pleasantly from the southward-sweeping sun.

If Gershom wanted her, — or if he even got off his horse and came in, — but neither of these things did he signify or do; so presently Aunt Joanna came back again, and the horse's hoofs went crunching the dry, savory chips, and then struck off with sounding thud across the sward.

"Skylark has been out on a flitting," Joanna said, re-entering. She meant Miss Purcell, daughter of the Congressman at Deepwater, a youngest child left at home now, to be spoiled, since her elder sister and the boys were gone. She was a wilful, winsome thing; they called her Skylark, as much for her glad, bright, sun-loving nature, as for her merry, saucy, daring flights. Also her real name was an uncouth, grandmother's name, — Bathsheba. Nobody ever could call her so; it was folly to have demanded it. Skylark grew to be her ordinary appellative; shortened, indeed to Skylie; the nickname nicked.

"She lit upon Gershom at the Bridge," continued Joanna, without all this pause that we have made, "and chirped him an errand and sent him round. She's to chirp us all up Boar-back next Saturday. We're to meet at the Corners, and go up at two o'clock."

"Oh, glorious. Then you'll go?"

"I — don't know. It's eight years since I tried it. And I'm eight years older — and fatter, you see; and I don't know which dress I'd better tear to pieces."

"Pooh! make yourself just as lovely as you can, and never mind your dress till you get home again."

"Make yourself lovely! Well, you'll see! People come home from Boar-back in ribbons."

"That's gay, I'm sure."

"Strings and streamers, I tell you."

"How merry! 'Some in rags, and some in jags, and some in velvet gowns!' 'With a band of music — with a band of music, with a band of music sounding in the air!'"

Say quoted and sung, and danced her feet upon the floor to time. Her eyes danced too, with pleasure.

"Yes, I'll go," said Joanna, "Only I hope the two she-bears won't come out of the wood and tear the naughty children."

"Because they say, 'go up,' to their elders? that's the worst we've done; we've no chance at the 'bald head' part here in Hilbury where the old ladies all have such magnificent hair."

Joanna smiled. She knew her brown, wavy locks were as soft, and bright and abundant, as a dozen years ago. She cherished this and some other little vanities, quite quietly and secretly. She was glad her young looks waited. What for? She never answered herself; many a woman keeps young, she knows not how, because, without saying it, she feels her future is not dead.

Perhaps Say made the most of her impulse of delight; perhaps she over-acted just a little, feeling an under-pang of annoyance. Yet she was really joyous at the thought. She trembled on the verge of what might come to be a sorrow; but it was not sorrow yet; she knew nothing of her danger. It was vexatious that Gershom should be so chilling — so indifferent; that he should have "pshawed" last night, and refused to come in this morning; but then it was his way, and he was very likely in a hurry; and on Saturday they should all go up Boar-back together, and somehow, it would all come right. Say's was one of those elastic temperaments that until the last opportunity is over, — the last resource exhausted, — the last hope crushed, — will rebound from every check, spring up from under every disappointment. She was patient, like a sister, with Gershom. Had they not been little children together? Would they not always be something to each other?

For awhile this might last; but Sarah Gair was nineteen; she was no longer a child, but a woman; and her hour was coming.

Gabriel Hartshorne left his father with Mary Makepeace, and a neighbor gossip come in with her clean cap and her knitting-work, to spend a long country afternoon, and drove Joanna and Say in the wagon to the Corners. It was one of his brief holidays.

It was one of Joanna's young days back again.

Joanna had on stout country shoes, laced up high on the instep. Say wore cloth boots with patent foxings; nice, bright, trim little things, thick enough, but delicate looking, such as she walked in, in Selport.

Gershom helped them down from the wagon when they came up at the cross-roads below the mountain, where the party met. Say knew he glanced at the foot she put upon the thill; what woman with a pretty one does *not* know when it is seen? And, though he never said a word, she felt a secret shaft from his thought to hers.

"There, he 's disgusted again! At the very beginning! He thinks it's all show-off and vanity. And ti 's the very clumsiest pair I ever had iu all my life."

From the days of the bronze boots until now, the child's feet had inevitably walked her into trouble with the captious fellow. Don't hate him. He secretly saw the prettiness, just as we do. He was only provoked with himself when he caught himself admiring what he thought a flimsiness. And he was so sternly bent on not admiring Sarah Gair; because she was her mother's child, and he would not believe in her.

He is a sailor; he has learned to hold his position in the teeth of the wind; perhaps he may hold it now.

Say walked on without waiting for anybody. Some of the first arrived had gone forward already, up the hillocky slope, matted here and there with the close, flat junipers, that rose slowly toward the base of Boar-back. The mountain began away out here to gather up the earth into its mass, as the moon draws up the sea in breasted heaps.

They strayed along in little groups, winding in and out as they found pathway. They might scatter thus, for the approach was broad. By and by, they must file singly and toilsomely up the narrow, rocky footway where the real climb awaited them.

Skylie Purcell appropriated Gershom. Three or four village girls kept near enough these two to claim a share of attention. Say listened to the laughing and the jesting behind her, keeping her face straight on.

"How in the world did you persuade the Captain? We never can coax him into anything."

"I did n't stop to coax. I just told him he was to come. Have n't you country girls learned how to take hold of a thistle?"

"Was that it, Captain Vorse?"

"Something so, I suppose. She told me straight out what she wanted. I 'm used to short orders, you know."

"And I never get frightened," said Skylie. "I go upon the principle that the most terrible people are the most easily bullied. You see they never think of anybody's trying it, and it takes them right down. Captain Vorse, I want a moosewood stick, presently. You 'll cut me one."

"I suppose I shall."

"That 's very meek; but it is n't a sailor's answer, I happen to know."

"What is?"

"Ay, ay, — ma'am!" The first syllables round and full, in very pretty man-mimicry, and the last word with an indescribable comic tone of confessed absurdity, but a contradict-me-if-you-dare insistence.

They all laughed merrily. It takes little to make a young group do that.

Say felt herself getting cross. Did he like that? she wondered. *She* could n't have spoken to him with such pertness, though she had known him years for Skylie's days. It was the outrightness that pleased him, was it? People might well be outright where they had only little surface knowledge and interest. Say's thought went deep whenever she talked with Gershom, laying hold at the roots of their two lives. And he always seemed to measure her whole nature by her lightest word. A corollary to be drawn from this had never yet occurred to either of them.

Gabriel and Joanna and Ruth Gibson came round to Say's side from beyond the cedar clump that had divided them. Stephen Gibson and John Blighe, escorting the advance, lingered a little as they came to the edge of the woods above; looking round, as they said for "the rest;" their eyes turned with one accord toward Sarah Gair.

Into a little glade where a clear spring hid itself, they all came presently together. The young men filled canteens to carry up the mountain. The girls sat down on fallen trees and mossy rocks, chatting and resting. Gershom Vorse plunged into a thicket where the moosewood grew with its tough-grained stems and broad, thick leaves, and cut with his sailor's knife stout staves for climbing-poles. Gabriel trimmed and peeled one he had found already, rounding the end carefully, and gave it, smooth, finished, and delicate-white, to Joanna, first of all.

"Cut me one, please," said Say. And she sat watching him as he shaped it when Gershom appeared again with his three.

"This is mine," she said, scarce glancing round, as he held one toward her, after Skylie Purcell had chosen. "Thank you, Mr. Hartshorne," in a little ecstasy; "it is *such* a beauty!"

They moved on again, over braky ground, and among bosks of rampant sweet-fern. Say came next after Joanna, and gave her hand with an air of specially charmed readiness, to Gabriel, helping her in turn, along a huge, dry slippery log that lay over a springy spot. Gershom saw the little affectation, and set it down sheer, self-pleased vanity, not seeing it quite through. He had no business to condemn. There are hypocrisies of women, which, read aright, are truest truths. Should Say have gone straight up to Gershom, saying, "You are to come with me; it is you I want to help me?"

Skylie Purcell might do this, and it would be simple outrightness. It would not have told the truth for Say. That was better done by the little crookedness. Only, one can't read cipher without the key."

"They were to be all together, going up Boar-back." This was what Say had said to herself the other day; and the opportunity lay large and golden to her thought. Well — here they were; what then? Gershom was close behind her, climbing up the narrow path, as Gabriel Hartshorne was before. He might as well have been beyond the seas. Skylie Purcell chattered over his shoulder, and Say said never a word. Gabriel held aside the tangled branches for her, and Gershom caught them, in his turn again, smoothing the way for Skylie.

The ascent grew rougher. It was the old bed of a mountain-brook, long ago forced into some different channel from high above, that made their path. There were rocks where water had gone tumbling down, and logs lying athwart the narrow gully, making long steps and scrambles for them. Up these, sometimes, a strong arm lifted her; it happened so, from the necessity, — that was all, and so she scarcely thanked him, but kept on, not looking round.

A great barricade of fallen, tangled, mossgrown timber made an end of the brook-path, and stopped them, half-way up. This was the customary halt and resting-place. Here the single file was broken, and they scattered themselves in groups, again. Joanna, a little short of breath, and not slightly flushed in face, — yet bright, and even very, very pretty for all that and her old maidenhood, —leaned herself willingly back in a wild armchair of dead, curving, upturned roots, upon a huge gray log. Say sprang over this, and perched herself higher. John Blighe and the Gibsons found places near her. Skylie Purcell and Gershom coming last, were still left to each other, — Skylie contenting herself with a low, mossy cricket of stone, and the Captain half sitting, half leaning against the farther upturned end, above and against which all the lesser debris were piled.

It was a rough little amphitheatre of rocks and stems and branches; the fresh faces and graceful figures and dresses of summer colors filled up its irregular niches with wonderful effect of fitness and contrast.

They passed round shining little tin-cups, filled from the canteens, and drank and chatted; growing merry over their innocent tipple.

"Now, Captain Vorse, we want a yarn; a real sailor's yarn!"

Skylie looked up and said this with her most unrefusable expression.

"O yes, a yarn! a yarn!" echoed the galleries, away up to little Jimmy Gibson, roosting overhead upon an oak limb.

Gershom's brown face flushed red. He never cared to tell stories of his personal adventure, — and what else could a sailor's yarn be?

Sarah Gair listened with one ear, — waiting his first word of reply; the other she turned to Stephen Gibson, catching his sentences that she cared not a straw for, but which she answered with the mechanical dexterity women — tormented daily all their lives in this wise — have such special aptness for.

"Oh, I'm no yarn-spinner," said the young Captain, evasively. "Besides, I'm not old salt enough to have so very much to tell."

"We know better," said Skylie, decidedly. "Tell us something to make us catch our breaths, and think surely it's been all over with you half a dozen times, even while we're listening and looking you full in the face. That's what sailors come home from sea for!"

"Is it? But you won't understand half I say, if I tell you a real sea-story."

"Of course not. I don't know any sea-phrases except 'heave-yoy!' and 'ay, ay, ma'am!' That's the beauty of it. That makes the story grand, and frightens us so much more."

Gershom Vorse began then, taking them by surprise with his acquiescence, making no more preface. He was not a girl, to hang back, saying neither no nor yes.

"When we were out in the Pearl, seven years or so, ago, bound to Pernambuco, we had a young sailor in the starboard watch, — Jack ——"

"Oh! oh! we don't care about Jack anybody. We wanted a story about yourself!"

"I don't mean to talk about myself. Will you have the story, or not?"

The captain said this quietly, — pleasantly, — and waited. It was plain to Miss Purcell that he was captain, after all. She withdrew her point with a show of command still, insisting on the previous question.

"Yes, to be sure. We shan't let you off from that. I'm glad he was in the starboard watch, whatever that is. It sounds nice."

She settled her dress about her a little comfortably, and rested her chin in a plump, pretty hand, looking up with saucy expectation, into Gershom's face.

Quite unmoved, he proceeded.

"It is n't much of a story. Only a bit of danger, over in five minutes; and sooner, in the telling. We were nearly off Trinidad, — you know where that is?"

"Of course I do. That 's geography. And 'off' means, — anywhere between Guiana and away over, — to Guinea, say?"

"Anywhere less than half-way," said Gershom, smiling.

"We were in latitude about twelve degrees, just coming into the Doldrums."

Skylie clapped her hands.

"Have n't the least idea what *that* is," she said, *sotto voce.* "It 's growing very imposing."

"It 's the latitude of sudden changes, — calms and gales."

"Just my latitude," parenthesized the girl, in a whisper, like a child bent on mischief, but afraid of being chidden.

"We 'd been lying about for three days, — nearly a dead calm, — when one afternoon toward sunset, a fresh breeze sprang up from the eastward. Set all sail to catch it, and it came up fresher and fresher, till we were off before it, on the full jump. We made the most of it while we could, for we knew by the looks of a big black bank to the southeast that we should get more than we wanted before morning. At midnight the starboard watch went below and turned in."

"Turned in, — what?"

"Themselves, — into their berths. I thought you wanted it to be mysterious."

"O yes, so I do; go on."

"Things were creaking and straining, then; and we kept half an eye open, expecting a call. Sure enough, in less than an hour it came! All hands, — reef tops'ls! We tumbled up and found the mate's watch busy enough; all the light sails taken in, topsail yards braced to the wind, men hauling out upon the reef-tackles."

Skylie clapped her hands again, soundlessly, and gave a little ecstatic bounce upon her stone cricket. It was growing delightfully exciting and incomprehensible.

"The wind had shifted to the southeast and the storm was upon us. The night was black as Egypt. The darkness was like a weight. We groped out upon the yards, holding on for dear life, the wind blowing a hurricane. The best sailor on board had the weather-earing on our yard, and it took his best to pass it in time.

We had mastheaded our sail first, though, and were down on deck before the larbowlines, breathless and wet through; for the storm was a peeler and no mistake. The brig was pitching into a tremendous head sea. The waves came crashing over the forecastle, every now and then, with the *sound* of the shattering white foam we could not see. 'Lay out there forward and furl the jib!' Ned Blackmere was the one to go, as he always was when there was tough work to do. Close by him, as the mate gave his order, was a young fellow just down from the fore top; a mother's child, sent to sea by doctor's prescription for his health; never made for a sailor. It was his second voyage, and he ought to have been up to it, if he ever would; but he had no nerve, and precious little muscle. He was in the larboard watch, and it fairly belonged to him. But he hung back a little; in another second, he 'd have been ordered by name, — for our mate never stood any shirking, — only Jack, seeing how it was, and knowing if he was once out over the bows there 'd be a fair chance he 'd never come in again, sprung past him and took the poor devil's place. He thought of *his* mother before he got back between the knight-heads, again, I promise you.

"The boom was under water half the time. The big sail was jerking and filling, and the two had their hands full to hold themselves on, to say nothing of getting it down upon the boom."

Skylie broke in timidly.

"I *must* just know where the boom is, and how it could possibly get under water. I thought from the danger, it must be something very high up."

Nobody laughed. They were all too much absorbed by this time, with the peril.

"It's the spar that runs out beyond the bowsprit, — at the head of the vessel. As the sea broke over, and the vessel pitched, of course it went under. There was only the wet timber to hold on to, with the water dashing over you by the ton, and the canvas slatting out and in, in great bights, as soon as it was loosed; like the side of a house driving against you."

"Oh!" gasped Skylie; and her nonsense all went out of her in a shudder.

"Ned Blackmere shouted like the tempest itself, to the men hauling in on deck. And he tugged like a great brave tiger at the work; Jack holding on and helping as he best might; when, just as they had passed half a dozen turns with the gasket, there reared up a black, monstrous wall just ahead that they felt beforehand, as you feel a door when you 're running against it in the dark, and down it came with a hundred thunders over the bows and the whole forward deck. Ned held on by some miracle, and, coming up out of it gasping, found himself alone on the boom.

"I should n't have said 'miracle' so soon; for though it seemed one, that even he should have escaped being washed away, it was more than a miracle what happened to the other. He went down off the boom, struggling and grasping out. He felt the sprit-sail yard as the wave dashed him athwart it; and something caught him, or he it, hands and feet, he never knew how. But he clung, all blind and stunned, and smothered; and then — I take it — *he* thought of his mother. Ned Blackmere said afterwards, the time seemed like a month between his turning round and finding him gone, and catching his breath and shouting out, and the fellow's crawling up by the guys and dolphin-striker. But there he was, — a little bruised, and a good deal blown; and all Ned said was — 'Hallo, shipmate! Took the longest way round! Just make fast that gasket now, can you, inside the cap!' That 's all, Miss Purcell. Those are the sort of things that happen to sailors. Sometimes they come out of' em, and sometimes they don't."

They were all still an instant, as the story ended. Then Skylie drew a long breath, and exclaimed, half in real emotion, half in drollery, —

"Oh dear! don't tell any more, for pity's sake! I 'd rather not know it. I shall never hear the wind and rain, at night again, without thinking of poor fellows out in the 'Doldrums,' under water, holding on by their heels to dolphin-strikers. Let 's go on."

Say had meant to be very indifferent, and to go on with the Gibsons; but, somehow, on clambering down from her perch, she found herself very near Gershom, for a minute, alone.

Skylie Purcell had sprung forward, suiting her action to her own word; the Captain had waited, giving his hand to Joanna, who had passed him also and proceeded; and Say came next.

"Why did n't you tell them it was yourself?" she exclaimed, with sudden impulse, in an undertone, springing down to his side.

"Did you find that out?" said he, quite naively disconcerted. "I hope nobody else did."

"Nobody else among them knows you as well as I do, Ger — Captain Vorse."

Now he looked up, in simple surprise. "What do you call me that for?"

"Why, you are, are n't you? And — the other night — I forgot — and I felt quite ashamed."

Say colored intensely, as he looked at her, for a moment, with honest, uncomprehending eyes, and then turned away.

He made no answer. He wondered what she wanted, now.

Was it a mere affectation — a caprice,— to see what he would say? Or was it a way of setting him at a distance, of reminding him that she, herself, was now "Miss Gair?" Had it to do with the old rankling suggestion of "no blood-relation, after all?" He was sore and sensitive; he was ready to suspect her simplest word of profound purpose, because — she was her mother's child.

"I was sure you did not like it," she said, in a low voice, constrained to blunder into speech, the silence was so terrible.

"I don't know what you mean," said Gershom, bluntly. "I'm only half a captain at the best. I may never stand on the lee of a quarter-deck again. And here, I'm at home, and just what I always was. To those who take me as I am. I'm willing enough to *give* titles, but I don't care about claiming them,— Miss Gair."

"Why will you always take me wrong?" she cried out in a tone the more intense because it was kept under from other hearing. And she dashed on away from him, into the thickening wood, after the rest. There were tears in her eyes, and she caught herself blindly, in the tangle of branches, and tore away her veil impatiently, leaving a bit of blue barege behind, upon a stem, — the first of her "strings and streamers."

They began to go to ribbons, now, as Joanna had said. All the remainder of the way lay through the uncleared forest, matted with underbrush, intricate with interlacing branches, and rough with abrupt rocks and ridges, and wild obstructions of natural wreck and decay. John Blighe guided them. There was a way that a hunter could find, though there seemed no path. Out to the left, if they had wandered away from the right direction, they would have lost themselves among frightful chasms and precipices; and beyond, at the right, there was wet ground, and more impassable jungle. It was no trifling feat, this climbing of Boar-back. Ruth Gibson's sun-bonnet had lost half its pretty ruffling from the edge, and it hung back in a festoon over her neck behind. Say's veil was presently in tatters, and she put the fragments in her pocket; and then the ribbon of her hat got a sudden pull, unfastening the bow, and floating it off behind her like a pennant. Skirts were trodden on, and came out at the gathers; and there was more than one "barn-door" rent. But all this was nothing, so long as they got to the top; rather, it was one-half the frolic.

And in another half-hour they were at the top; upon the highest point of land for fifty miles around; the bare crest of the mountain rising above the forest they had passed, like the forehead of a giant above his bearded face. Only here and there, like a stray lock about his brow, a pine or a birch flung out its spicy tassels or its green silky rustle of new leaves.

Away back to the north lay untrodden wilds, — townships that had nothing but a name; — southward descended lower undulating ranges; — with bright valley views between, — and away off westwardly, they caught blue glimpses of real monarch-peaks.

It was a glory to have climbed for; to have lost gauds and trappings, and to have mutilated gay draperies for.

There were old stumps of huge pines scattered about, felled, or burned away, no one knows when; and a long, fallen log crashed in among a little group of younger growth. They found rude, comfortable resting-places here and there, choosing for themselves different outlooks; and for a while there was but little talk.

They were tired; they were also entranced with marvellous beauty, and beguiled with many thoughts that might not readily be spoken.

Fields and farms and houses, where their homes were, looked so little and so lost away down there. The rounds their lives ran in seemed so petty in their measure. The river came down — they could trace it all the way — from the far, northwesterly gap through the hills, and had so many like homes dotted upon its borders, and yet such wild, broad spaces between! The haunts of the fox and the squirrel looked so much grander than the small circuits men could reclaim and subdue unto their needs! The world was large; it was an edge here like the margin of the great sea; and one could discern more in the mighty off-sweep!

And the wonderful light that came pouring and surging down over all; on the evil and on the good; on the wilderness and on the town! How it gathered and rolled in golden mists through the gorges, and lay in purple radiance on the high, far crests, and left deep, dark-blue glooms of shadow in contrast on the eastward slopes and underneath!

They sat here and there, taking it in according to what each severally had; as the Scripture sayeth — and Life sayeth, evermore.

Joanna Gayworthy saw more, felt more, to-day, than she had done here eight years ago.

She drew herself apart a little from the others, just under the eastern brow of the great crown; sitting on the crisp, mossy sod, leaning back into a spicy cedar-bush, that held her comfortably, with thick, sidewise-spreading arms.

There came a hush over life and soul — a deep rest; a feeling of good and promise in all things — in all living.

She could discern afar down, the little apex of Peak Hill, and the dot of soft, light color beside its base, that was her home.

She knew just where beyond, out of sight, lay the red buildings of that other farm, close by. In that little space lay the whole scene and story of her life. Of hers and of another that had blessed and helped and taught her, and lifted her up to a higher, though unspoken faith, by its calm steadfastness and pure fidelity; that had done all this, though it had not fulfilled the dream of a far-past youth. There had been the "comfortable friendliness;" ay, there had been greatly more! And it had all been borne and lost, gained and gathered, enacted and beholden, there, — in that hand's-breadth of the great landscape, — that minutest point on God' vast earth, so full of life, of human experience, — of grief, and loss, and joy, and growth!

It was as if she were lifted up and separated from it, like a soul forever risen; measuring her little past against the wide sweep of that eternal Present that holds all. And the peace — the infinite hope of it — overspread her, and made her strong and glad. The mountain-joy swelled within her. She forgot how little distant was young, gay, heedless presence; she forgot her very self; and the spirit of the old hymn possessed her, and its grand, prophetic lines breathed themselves impulsively from her lips in the clear, stirring cadences of long-familiar "Emmons."

"O'er mountain tops, the mount of God
In latter days shall rise,
Above the summits of the hills,
And draw the wondering eyes."

With the third line, a broad, rich tenor joined.

From the rock above her came the voice; but she did not turn; only kept on, her tones swelling fuller, stronger; growing glorious as with an inspiration; and they sang the whole hymn through, before either singer moved. Then Gabriel Hartshorne came down and sat upon the moss beside Joanna.

"You struck it first, but it had been working in me," he said. "If you had not burst out, I should. This is a gallery to sing it in!"

Joanna did not answer, and for a minute Gabriel said nothing more. Old associations stirred in both. How could it but be so? You cannot do the merest thing, you cannot turn the corner of a street, you cannot hang your hat upon a peg where you have hung it once, you cannot, if you are a woman, turn a hem or fit a difficult corner as you sew, or pin a bow of ribbon, but you call up some mood, some circumstance of the past, however faintly, however unrecognized at the instant, that has been coincident, once, with the self-same triviality. Do you wish to reproduce another's by-gone mood? There is no surer art whereby to accomplish it, than to reproduce the little outward circumstance, if you can, which witnessed it before; which stamped itself twin with it, in the photograph of memory, that is always busy, that misses nothing, that works ever with a weird purpose, by a hidden, wondrous law.

"Do you know how changed you are in some things, Joanna?"

There was no need to say since when; the same old time was in the thoughts of both.

"Years change most people," she answered, with a difficulty. And then, with an attempt at the old lightness, she added, "I 've grown fat and old. I know that."

"'Tis n't that. You 're grown womanly, but not old. It 's no compliment, you know it. But I meant something else. Twelve years ago, you were like Skylie, there."

"Twelve years ago, I was —" a fool, was on her lips to say, but she suppressed it. It might mean too much, too definitely.

"I remember what my mother used to say of you."

"What was that?" Joanna asked the question quickly, almost sharply. Had his mother disapproved her, in her flippancy and recklessness? Had this had aught to do with the ending of that old story, twelve years ago?

"She said you would take such a lot of sobering down."

"I've had it."

"I suppose we 've all had just what was good for us."

He spoke it with a simple, reverent faith; a submission that had long ago grown into a large content. It brought back Joanna's mood of a few minutes since, that had been momentarily broken.

"I know you believe that. It is easy to see," she said, with a tone of feeling. "And so do I. Looking out here made me think.—" Here she paused. Joanna Gayworthy never had told her inmost thoughts; she could not now.

Gabriel waited for the space of a minute. No more came. Then he said gently, "We are old friends, now, Joanna."

"Yes, old friends," she answered, looking up with a bright, clear, sudden smile, and a content in her face that was like his own. The words expressed the utmost of her hope; the utmost that had been her hope, for years. It was very dear to her, this utterance of it, by Gabriel; very dear and pleasant, also, his calling her by the old infrequent name.

"Friends tell each other thoughts."

"Yes, some thoughts," said the woman.

"Why not these mountain thoughts?"

"I never can talk 'sanctified.' Mountain thoughts are high

thoughts. I don't wonder —." They stopped her again, these thoughts that could not be uttered.

"I don't wonder," said Gabriel, taking up the word, and going on quietly, as if it were not a strange, but a certain and natural thing, that their two thoughts should be the same, "that the Lord went up into the mountains to preach, or to pray, or to be transfigured."

"You 've said it. Now say the rest for me."

"It' s all said, plain enough, before us. Down there," — and he reached his hand out toward the little farm-buildings under the Peak, — "down there, are our lives; what they have been, so far; shut in there. Then, there is all the rest of it; room for so much!" The lifted hand swept round indicating the whole grand circuit of hill and vale under the wide horizon, whereon new glories played, in shifting lights and colors with each passing cloud, each hand's-breadth sinking of the westering sun.

A sudden instinct of dread came over Joanna. A terror, all at once, of the breadth of possibility.

"There is *too* much room!" she cried, putting her hands over her eyes. "I don't like to look at it. I have just learned to bear life as it is; in just that little spot. It must n't move nor change!"

"What may change, must. There are things that cannot change."

In the little pause between Joanna's words and Gabriel's answer, his thought had flashed to and fro, lighting up sharp points in the long history of years. His mother, — and the change that took her from their round of outward life, yet left the great love that made that life all full of her dear presence, even yet. — The young desire, — the hope that had been wrenched away, the work that had been given him in its stead, — the years of labor and of waiting, — and the unchanging force that held him steadfast through it all, true to his vow, — true, no less to the old, fervent passion, though it had calmed into pure, tender friendship that daily he thanked God for, — all these were touched by the gleam that kindled at those words of hers; and from the gathered feeling of it all, he spoke.

"There are things that cannot change."

If Joanna had looked up into his face, she would have read it in his eyes that rested on her, with nothing less than the old glow that had been in them years before, when he had tried to tell his love, and she had put him off with foolishness. Friendship, was it? A friendship, patient, holy; but a friendship born of fire; such as can be between two souls only; the souls of man and woman.

She did not look up. She rested, still, her head upon one hand; her face turned from the fair picture that had moved her so to hope and fear; the other hand she held out.

"Whatever happens, Gabriel, we are old friends, in all?" She questioned with an earnestness, an eagerness, — as if she dreaded something, she knew not what, and clung to him.

He took her hand and held it in a strong grasp that answered her.

"Old friends. Dear friends, Joanna."

A loud call interrupted them. A call for help.

CHAPTER XXVII.

OVER EAST SPUR.

Down to the northward the great mountain mass precipitated its descent, in steep banks and sheer escarpments, toward a wild ravine. They were like terraces; a bank, — a precipice, — a flat of sward, or a table-rock; another cliff, — another landing; each sucessive pitch a deeper fall; with shelving ridges that wound and sloped, eastward and westward, merging each ledge with the next, all down the giant shoulders of the hill.

From under the first cliff, the cry came. No cry of pain or even of fear. Only a call. Joanna's name, in Say's voice.

A few rods over on the westward slope, the greater number of the young party had settled themselves in closely neighboring groups. Say had been with them, and Joanna had supposed her with them still. They, perhaps, when she had risen and gone away, some fifteen minutes since, had thought her with Joanna.

There had been some merry, disputing claim of best places and outlooks.

"It would be just perfect, here," cried Skylie, out from a nook of pines, "only that impertinent birch-tree has grown up in the way. There 's nothing else between me and Red-Cap."

"It's the only thing that breaks the whole western view," said Ruth Gibson. "I 've been wishing it away ever since I got here."

"Has n't anybody got a hatchet in his pocket?" asked Skylie, impatiently.

"I 've got a jack-knife," said Gershom Vorse, quietly.

"Just whittle me down that tree, then, please."

The sailor, used to "short orders," went aloft, without ado. In an instant, he was in the top of the swaying birch; a tree of twenty-five feet height, perhaps, with a girth of more than two hands span.

He began to whittle down.

The feathery crown of upper twigs fell, rustling, to the ground. Then he lowered himself a little, and struck in a new place. A true branch was severed and crashed lightly among the others, underneath. Dropping a little, hands and feet, he worked away. Two, three, four limbs, each of successive larger bole, succumbed in turn.

It grew exciting. Would he really whittle down the tree? The party watched, and laughed, and cried out in applause.

Say got up, and walked away.

Why should Skylie Purcell order him up and down, so? Why should he obey?

Had *they* been brother and sister, with none nearer, in old childish years? Had he scolded and comforted, and laughed at and cheered *her*, away back in that time of the dear summer journeys and stays in Hilbury? Had *she* been afraid of his censure, and honored his honest bluntness, and brought all questions instinctively, to the secret test of what Gershom would say — how he would judge? Had *she* waited these five years for her brother to come back to her; longing for him with a great, lonely, childish longing, all the time? Having no other love to fill her want, like the love she had missed when her old playfellow suddenly went forth into manhood and the world, leaving her "to be a little girl ever so many years longer?"

What claim had Skylie Purcell, like this lifelong claim of hers?

Why should Gershom turn from her, his little Say, scorning her least word of sympathy and pride, and let this strange girl play her freaks with him?

She did not understand her own jealousy, that was growing sharper than a sister's. She only could not bear it, and she turned away.

She walked up the mountain crest; where it heaved itself into that slow, clumsy outline whence it had its name; beyond which, northward, plunged the steeps, one behind another into the wilderness. She went down a little, over the topmost height, where the first rapid slope tended downward, but had not yet become precipitous. She descended till the mountain summit hid her from sight; till she was all alone; till she paused at the very brink of the perpendicular declivity, where another step would be twenty feet straight down a face of granite.

She sat there on the verge; her feet over the cliff, resting on a projection of the stone below. She looked into the top of a tall, strong birch that grew upon the level underneath, and tossed its crown, quivering and whispering with every breath, close at her side. All alone, rooted in the rocks; a hard stern living; reaching up toward the far, soft blue, and trembling ever, with its sensitive pulsations, against the granite. There was human life like this; she had a dread that she must live it. She sat there thinking, listening, till the tears stood in her eyes; till the tree-whispers sounded like a syllabled sympathy; till, impelled with a tender pitifulness that was secretly for her own sadness, she reached out her hands caressingly to the green swaying boughs, that came lifting and dropping against her knees.

Suddenly, she heard her name, from above. She was missed.

The whittling down of the tree had been accomplished. There stood, now, only a bare, jagged pole, making a line against the western sky and the breast of Red-Cap purpling in shadow, to show where a tree had been, shutting out miles of hill and heaven.

There had been a shout of triumph; Say had not heeded; she had only folded more tenderly the young leaves between her palms, and looked through eyes suddenly dimmer with that self-pity, over upon the black surge of the wilderness.

Then they, above, turning one to another, had found that she was gone, — gone quite away, and out of sight; and somebody had called her by her name.

It startled her. She was in no mood to go back, just yet, or to be found; she had an impulse to spring up and hide herself away again. Still holding the birch in her right hand, she placed her left beside her on the rock to raise herself again upon it.

A strange thing happened. She threw her weight, for an instant, inadvertently, upon her right foot, resting as it did upon a shelf below. The shelf, — a thin shard of stone held edgewise in a crevice, — crumbled from its loose lodgment, and gave way. With the quick instinct of terror, she threw up, also, her other hand, clutching the birch-bole desperately with both. The lithe tree bent with her; she felt in a flash how it would be; she had "swung birches" before, many a time in sport; she was tossed down fifteen feet, and dropped. Dropped upon the thick moss and forest mould that bedded the broad platform below. She was safe; but the bough sprang back again, and she was left there. There was no way of reascending.

She lay where she had fallen a minute, trembling; she had not gotten over the convulsion of her momentary horror. Then she looked around, and the fact of her situation revealed itself.

Right and left were craggy shelving rocks; above, the sheer ascent from whose height she had come down, as by a miracle. The only foothold, either way, was downward still. One might, if one dared, pass out there, to the east, upon the narrow ledge to which this platform dwindled; where the upper cliff crowded out upon it; but whither? She was afraid, astonished. She was perplexed, and she was ashamed. Astonished and affrighted at this position in which, so strangely in a moment, she had placed herself. Ashamed to cry out and make known how she had come there

Meanwhile, the call for her had not been immediately repeated. She heard faintly a laugh. They were at some new jest.

She moved along to the eastward side of the hill, around a huge abutment of the granite, leaving the sounds behind and coming close under the point where she knew Joanna had been. Then she shouted in a clear, confident, yet appealing tone, her name. She had thought for that. If her cry reached them from this strange spot with an accent of distress or of alarm, they would be suddenly and terribly frightened for her. She wished to save them this. Above all, she wished if possible to avert a general commotion.

Gabriel and Joanna hastened up over the ridge. They came down cautiously to the verge of the cliff upon that side, and beheld below, sitting on a fragment of rock, half turned away from them, awaiting some answer to her call, the "child," Sarah Gair.

"Say! How on earth did you ever get there?" cried Joanna, in dismay

"Swung down on a birch, auntie!" she cried back, looking up half laughing; but her face was pale.

"What nonsense, child! On purpose? Don't tell me that!"

"No; my foot slipped, and I tumbled into it. How shall I get up again?"

"That's the thing!" said Joanna, turning to Gabriel with the question in her face.

"It's a mile around, by any safe path," said Gabriel. "Where 's the birch?"

"Around there, by the very top. Down behind the old log. But it might n't bear again," she cried with a sudden terror, as she saw them turn and walk away upward, rapidly, toward the crest.

Now they would all come. Now, they would all shout, and wonder, and ask questions. Now, Skylie would laugh, and Gershom, — well, she would stay here, where she was. So she sat down on her stone again.

Up there, above, they found the birch, and the whole party got together before anybody could make a mind up what to do.

The breeze had died away; there was no swaying of the bough, now, toward the cliff; and the strain that had bent the slender bole down nearly double, had not left it quite erect as it had been before. It swerved a little, outward from the rock.

Gabriel moved on a few paces, reconnoitring the crags upon the left; if haply any descent there might be possible.

John Blighe looked eager, nervous; measuring the height, — scanning the birch with doubtful, impatient eyes. Fifty pounds difference in weight might make a different jump of it.

"I know the way," he said. "Down under the Rump, over the East Spur by the old logging road. But that," — glancing into the crown of the light tree that trembled just beyond their reach, — "why, it's a thing for a bird to do!"

"Or a girl, or a very brave, quick-witted man," said Skylie Purcell, with a sharp little sarcasm in her tone.

For as they spoke the thing was done.

The sailor, Gershom Vorse, used to holding on with his eyelids, lowered himself suddenly down the face of the cliff, grasping its rough edge with his hands, and finding a seam to brace one foot in, threw out the other, catching so, and bringing toward him the yielding stem, whereon he flung himself with all his limbs, and clung as only a sailor could. Down it danced with him through the air, and dropped him safely. John Blighe looked vacant, as if somebody had plucked a purpose from him before he quite knew what it was, that took the breath out with it, and left him gasping.

Gershom looked up and spoke quietly, as if nothing out of the premeditated course had happened.

"We shall come out on East Spur in less than a half an hour. You can see us if you wait, and after that it's straight sailing. You need have no concern."

"You'll go down by the logging road, then?" said Gabriel.

"Yes, that is best; it's a bad way round to the south side again, and you'd ought to be gone long before we could meet you. Don't wait longer than just to see us safe out on the Spur."

"Where will they come out at last?" asked Joanna of John Blighe.

"Depends on whether he really knows the way," replied that gentleman, in a somewhat sulky tone. "If he has good luck, and they don't break their necks, they'll strike the Deepwater road somewhere over behind Hoogs's."

"Take Say home with you to Wealthy's," called Joanna to Gershom.

He nodded and moved on along the foot of the cliff, to find her. He had known just what would be to be done before a word had been said. He had scaled these ledges as a boy, years ago; and the old logging road down East Spur was no less familiar to him than to John Blighe. He knew that Say could never walk round the great mountain foot, by the winding Deepwater road to the point whence the party had commenced their climb that afternoon; it would be quite enough for her if she could accomplish the long, hard scrambling descent of East Spur; and if anybody were to drive round to meet them, there was no certain point within half a mile, at best, at which to expect them; for the logging road ended abruptly far away in rough pastures, where they must choose a track out as best they could to a travelled way. A short and smooth cut over a few cleared fields again, after crossing the Deepwater road would take them to the dairy farm.

"We'll go round there, and say they're coming," said Skylie Purcell to Joanna, "or, between you, they might be out all night, and nobody the wiser."

"I'm going there myself," said Joanna, quietly. "I'll go with you, if you'll make room, since it's on your way."

"I can take you round," said Gabriel.

"Thank you; but it will be late, and Rebecca will be getting anxious. I'd rather you'd go home and explain to her, if you'll be so kind."

Gabriel would be kind. There were no jealousies and misconstructions of young, hasty spirits between these two, now. They were old, sure friends. They would do each other best service, always, whether it were momentary pleasure, or no. Gabriel would go home and tell Rebecca, and Joanna and Say would be kept at the dairy farm till morning.

Gershom knew how it would be. Was there a little thrill of joy for him in it, spite of his stern will not to be pleased, — to let Say alone, and not to care for her — Jane Gair's child?" He did not ask himself what shade of other impulse mingled with his instinctive sailor gallantry and readiness when there was a thing to be done that called for cool nerve and trained muscle; what eagerness it was that he felt, as he sprang past John Blighe, and cast himself over the cliff, clinging by his finger-tips. Ah, the honestest of us have the little thoughts in the fine soul-type, that we put by and overlay with a sort we are more willing to look at.

"He should have Say all to himself, this little while, without being able to help it."

Gershom Vorse hardly knew that he thought this; yet some secret, detected content made him suddenly angry with himself, as he strode on, around the crag, and came upon her, sitting there, turned away, half ashamed, and waiting. It threw him back into his reserve again.

Say thought it was Gabriel coming. Round there, behind the beetling rock, the sounds of their voices had come to her with a confused perception of direction. She caught some of their words; she heard Gabriel speak, and Gershom; she heard them all talk together, scarcely distinguishing who might be above, and who below; and then came the man's step, striding and springing, and she knew somebody had come to take care of her. When he came close, she turned round. She started up.

"You!"

"Why not?"

"I thought it was Mr. Hartshorne." After a little pause,—"It was very silly and careless of me. I don't know how I did it. And you are very kind to come for me."

All her little resentment was gone. She was prompt to be grateful, poor child. A small kindness touched her, always. Even in what seemed her pleasant life, she had been used to snubs, and ready consideration took her by surprise. To be of consequence, —to be attended to,—this was what she had not learned to take for granted even in Hilbury. Her voice trembled, even, as she thanked him so.

It seemed to him beyond the occasion. There was nothing to make a fuss about.

"You must be got home somehow, of course." He was hard and matter-of-fact again. She crushed her gratitude back, and got up and wrapped her shawl about her, and was ready to move on.

The wind, that had been southerly all the early day, had come round to the eastward in the afternoon; and the air, cool always on these heights, was keen upon this shaded side of the mountain. Say had grown chilly as she had sat there on the cliff behind the crest, out of the sunshine; she felt the cold afresh now, coming out of the shelter of the rock and facing the breeze, as she followed Gershom on along the ledge, where it narrowed rapidly to a perilous pass.

He turned to take her hand, and help her round a point of rocks where the foothold was smallest. Beyond, it broadened again to safer space. Here he stopped and began to pull off the loose, rough jacket that he wore above his sailor shirt.

"You are cold," said he. "You'd better put this on."

The words and the act were kind; but the tone was matter-of-fact as ever.

"I can freeze as well as you," she said, shortly; and made as if she would pass him to go forward. He, on his part, replied nothing to that, but turned and resumed his leading of the way.

So they went on, in their moods, these two strange, young creatures, each holding such quick, magnetic power over the other, working as yet, it seemed, only for repulsion.

It was not in Say's nature to be haughty; to cast back scorn for scorn; she could flame out for an instant, with a woman's proud resentment, but a word would bring her back again to the sweetness of a child. And Gershom was not precisely scornful, either; he was only cold and rational; doing things for a reason; by no means for a sentiment. So she thought of him; so he too, thought, at present, of himself.

There was a wild delight of daring in the treading of this path they had to follow. To Gershom not so much, perhaps; he had been used to the hills and ledges from a child; to dizzy spars and slender ropes for years of hazardous life. But Say's cheek tingled and her eye glowed as, with her shawl tied tightly around her waist, and her dress knotted up behind, away from her feet, in a great, careless knob, she sprung like a bird, from perch to perch along the jagged and interrupted way. The little feet seemed made for dainty poising on the narrow shelves, and she held herself with sure and delicate balance, as if it were but a dance, on airy heights where an instant's uncertainty or giddiness might have been her death. She never thought of being afraid. Gershom could not help in his heart, a wondering admiration of the bright, brave young thing. He watched carefully for her safety. He reached a ready hand whenever it was needed for an instant. He was cool and heedful; it was his business to see her safe. But he did it as a business; he said never a word for a long while after that rejected offer of the jacket; he let no gleam come into his face of admiring surprise as she sped lightly on, never pausing or daunted, following with clean aplomb, wherever he himself could go.

Without him, she might hardly have been nerved to such intrepidity; it is hard to tell what goes to make a mood; she felt safe having him; she felt proud, he looking on; excited to do her best; to be as cool as he; goaded by his indifference to something that was no longer anger, but had a high touch,—was a little superb. Sarah Gair had never asserted herself so completely in his presence; she had never been so near seizing supremacy.

They came down at last, safely, to the second landing. They glanced back, upward to the way they had threaded. It looked almost like bare cliff again; seen from hence, one could hardly fancy there could be any path. The great mountain pile towered high above them, now; below a yet more enormous mass stretched itself out and clothed itself with forest. It was utter solitude. Dense shadow heaped itself, like a thing to be felt; cold, black glooms lay impenetrable about them. The whole great body of the mighty hill was between them and the presence of their friends; no voice could reach them; no ear could catch a cry. They were here together; they could only help each other.

There are moments in life when people stand so. When they look back on the path — broken and perilous — that they have traversed; coldly, perhaps, and in estrangement, yet together; when they can no longer return; when they can make no long pause; when they must help and cheer each other, or nothing human will. In such moments hearts come closer.

At first these seemed far enough.

"Are you tired?"

"No."

This was all they said, after the peril and the long silence. They stood a little apart, and the silence of the wilderness, broken only by this pebble of sound, closed up again around them. But the secret influence of the place was working. The solitude was bringing them nearer in spirit.

There came a crash in the woods, just down below them. Some forest animal, or a broken branch. Say started, and her movement brought her closer to Gershom's side.

"What is it?" she whispered, a little fearfully.

"Nothing," said Gershom, "but a fox perhaps, or a falling limb."

Say laughed. "I think it is the bears, coming to eat up the naughty children. Don't be cross, Gershom."

She said it with the very old accent of their childish days, when she had used to say it so often.

"I'm not cross, Say. Don't be silly." His old reply, — spoken very kindly now, for the old days came back, and the secret present charm had wrought.

"We had better go on."

Say felt the sound quiver as it came to her lips, saying but these simple, common-sensible words, with the thrill that only a returning kindness in Gershie had ever given her!

Both felt it would not do to linger. Say was warm with exercise, and she must not stay here to be chilled. They must wait for no reaction of body or of spirit.

So they went on, and the path narrowed again. Under the overhanging rock, they passed around, still working to the eastward and southward; making through the rock and tangle, for the great outlying shoulder of East Spur.

All at once Gershom paused, appalled. Had he missed his way, that he had felt so sure of? Had he taken some delusive turn, and followed a wrong shelving, that would end in middle air, against a hopeless face of rock? Or had there been a break, or fall, here, since he trod the path before?

They had come suddenly to a bend where they could see but a few feet in advance; those few feet a mere lintel against a precipice that reached itself up and forward, at a pitch that would not let them stand upright.

They might, though at great peril, crawl around; he had come to feel great faith in Say, by this time; but what lay beyond? If there should be no way to proceed, might they be able to turn and come back?

It was for him to go and see.

"Stay here, Say," he said; and there was suddenly something almost tender in his tone.

Was he frightened for her? Had anything gone wrong? She hardly cared at that moment, since he could be gentle once more.

It was only when she saw him stoop to hands and feet, and pass, carefully creeping, beyond her sight upon the dizzy shelf around the bend, that the thought smote her of why he did it; of what might happen to him, should the way prove a false leading. She saw it, suddenly, now; that he had left her here to test a dreadful danger alone.

She crouched down upon the lichened rock whereon she stood, covering her eyes with her hands; an agony of listening in her ears; waiting for a possible sound of horror. She refrained from the call of expostulation that had risen to her lips; she must not shake, by a breath, his concentration of faculty and purpose; she must wait, and let him alone.

Two — three — minutes: how many years did they seem like?

There came a small sound, — and then the stillness again. A sound of a stone, falling, rolling, losing itself, she could not tell whether in distance or against some resting-place.

The instant's silence after that was ghastly.

She had raised her head; she was gazing at the farthest angle behind which he had disappeared. She scarcely breathed; her vision was almost paralyzed by its own intentness; her whole being was gathered to a point, in fear and expectation; then she saw an arm reached into sight, — a hand planted — fingers outward — upon the rocky edge; a body lifted, so, sidewise, the feet hanging down over the abyss, and set, again, a little nearer. So he came back over a way where turning had been impossible.

"We must go down lower, Say; half-way to the bottom of the ravine; and cross over, so, to East Spur." He said it, coming to her side in safety.

Her tongue clave to the roof of her mouth. She looked up at him with wide distended eyes, speechless. The reaction could not come at once. Her senses held themselves at the climax of their strain

He stooped down and took her by both hands.

"Say! This won't do! What is the matter?" Then he put his arm about her and lifted her up.

It was well he had been cold and mechanical before. The difference now — the gentle words, the helpful touch — did what the sudden sight of his safety, not making itself believed in instantly, had failed to do. The tension of nerve and spirit gave way; she burst into uncontrollable tears.

"There will be nothing more like this, Say; and you must keep your courage up; you have been very brave."

"I 'm not frightened; it is n't that," she gasped out, checking her sobs, and looking up at him again, with a little nervous attempt at smiling, "What did you come to, out there?"

"Nothing."

"Nothing?"

"Just that. And when I found there *was* nothing, — why, of course, I came back again."

"It was horrible, — waiting! I did n't understand, till after you were gone."

There could be no sham in this. Gershom knew that she had borne a torture of terror for him.

"Can you come on now?" He kept her hand in his to lead her down. The way was steep, but it was a side-cliff, where they could scramble from rock to rock, together. There were no more narrow passes. From his perilous outlook, a moment since, he had seen this, which they could not see from hence, and that the descent was possible.

Say gathered her forces together, once more. She would not be a perplexity or a burden. She must go on with him, and she would go on bravely. The elastic joy was over; but she could be strong; she could persevere. She could do anything with his hand holding her, no longer perforce, but with a kind solicitude.

There were long spaces for them to drop down, descending this rough Titanic staircase; hands and feet were both needed, often; there were leaps, not insignificant, over rifts and chasms; they had got into the very heart of one of nature's wild and secret places. There was no path; the semblance of one that they might have followed, lay below; they should have descended to it from a point far back; but it was better to keep on this way, now. Half-way down into the ravine, as Gershom had said, they found it; it took them upon a new platform, or landing, of table-rock, that jutted from the overhanging cliff. A little trickle of water came down, through a cranny in the bare face of it, a shorter way, to meet them; it dropped upon the granite floor, and rolled away over its edge again, a thread of waterfall that went to help make up the brook winding itself in the glen below.

Gershom had his tin cup still in his jacket pocket. A little flat bit of a dipper, that would hold, maybe, two wineglass-fulls. He drew it out and held it to catch the drops. He gave them to Say to drink. They made her stronger. She looked up when she had swallowed them, and her eye searched the far-up, impending outline of the crag. Away up under its very top, was where Gershom had gone, clinging, till he came where there was — nothing! She could not trace from here, more than a faint line to show her where the narrow ledge had wound. If they had both ventured! She said nothing, but there came a shudder over her, and she turned away.

"We must go on," said Gershom. "They will be watching to see us safe out on the Spur; and the sun is lowering."

It was only to climb, now. Rough work; and the dress had new knots in it before long, where the strings and streamers had grown troublesome, and must be gathered up. The trim, dainty little figure was oddly metamorphosed. But Gershom liked her better so, somehow, perverse fellow, than he had done in the delicate array of purple-pansied muslin and lace frills and floating riband. She was no "thing for a shop-window," now, assuredly.

They stood out on the bare, high shoulder-top of East Spur, at last; and all this had been done in about five and thirty minutes. Down a little upon their way over the south slope, the rest of the party had paused and turned aside, and were waiting upon an opposite height that brought them marvellously near, by an air line, the point these two had reached by such a round of toil and danger. From this to that, there was no passing, though. They could hail each other, with shawls and scarfs tied upon bough and staff, and waved in signal. That was all. And then by their two roads, they went their ways down the two separate sides of stern, uncompromising old Boar-back.

There is no act or circumstance but bears its typical relations. We feel obscurely many times, a meaning and significance in what we do, — a method in our accidents, that startles us with a fear, a joy, an embarrassment; that carries us by a strange likeness or suggestion, into a past that we dimly, and perhaps mysteriously remember, or forereaches into a future moment that might come.

Not a word was said of it, in the merry party that turned off together down the south-side track, relieved and satisfied to have seen their companions safe, — far less between the two left so to their own separate pilgrimage. But it was like — and they all had a glimmer of the likeness — the setting forth of two together in such fashion, striking off and away into a strange and untried life-path opened for them only. Relinquished to each other; cheered away with friendly signals; but left then to their own shiftings; to make the best of it they might.

Say had a strange shyness come over her for a minute, that she did not try to define; Gershom had as strange a pulse, — a single one, — of something gladder than he cared to question, as they turned and met each other's faces, after watching the rest away among the shadows, and stood alone again with wilderness above, below, about them.

"Come!" he said, and stretched out his hand.

And Say came.

There was a joy of claim and confidence, unanalyzed, between them in that instant. A key-note struck, — responded; a phrase of music uttered, revealing the whole power and harmony life had for them. It should be played out, — somewhere. If only there were no discords that might lie between this and its full evolvement!

They kept the crest-line of the Spur, down to where thick woods began again; it led them straight to the opening of the logging-road, cut through a dense growth of trees, and winding down between tangled branches and underbrush. A mere gully it seemed, now; a path for a mountain torrent, or a wake left by some old tornado; it was the only way through impenetrable forest. Disused long ago, and fallen into more than its original roughness, by reason of rains, and gradual change of wearing earth and rolling stone, and forest fall and decay, it was no easy path, though a sure one, and devoid of all absolute danger.

It was down-hill, without break or rest. Say sprang, as she needs must, from rock to stump, — from log to knoll, — flying leaps, some of them, — on without pause; getting exhilarated again by the exercise and rapid progress, and not realizing the fatigue she was actually enduring. Breath failed a little after a time; and she caught herself up against the over-leaning trunk of an oak and looked back to Gershom, who was close behind, with a panting, comical appeal.

"I don't believe there's any 'down' to it; it's one everlasting tumble."

"Half-way down we shall find a rest; and then we shall be sure about our daylight. Are you warm?"

"Exhaling!"

"Thirsty?

"What's the use?"

He held out his tin cup, sparkling with its little treasure of water.

"Where did you find that? I 've seen none."

"I knew of a spring, just back here, off the road, and turned in luckily, at the right spot."

"I did n't miss you. How strange!"

"It only took a minute. I did n't want to say water, until I 'd got it."

"No, indeed. I should have choked, instantly."

"Drink now, then."

Simple little words these, that they exchanged; but they were very sweet with the old, familiar ease and sympathy; very sweet, also, was the draught Say took from the tiny dipper. It was beautiful to be cared for so, and by Gershom! It was like the old time of the clothes-room and the strawberry feasting. Oh, dear! why must they ever come out of the woods, and go back — she knew they would — to their distance, and their different ways, and their half understandings?

It was very lovely and pleasant, half-way down, where a huge rock upheaved and abutted itself, gathering against its sturdy back the soil and sod that made a soft, sylvan throne under wide oak branches, where Gershom lifted Say and placed her, and sat himself down at her side.

They had earned a rest; they had gained time to take it; there was no keen wind here; Say only drew up the folds of her shawl about her throat again, that she had pushed back upon her shoulders in the heat of her down-scramble. And the twilight was about them, soft and sweet; and little trickling music of unseen water, and faint evening chirp of early birds; and away off to the south-east lay other hills, purple in the level light; while, behind, the great might of Boar-back, with all its mysteries and grandeur of cliff and chasm, and piled-up solid heights, and unexplored ravines, and pathless woods, lifted and stretched itself too vast for them to see until they should get away from it, and it, too, should shape itself in purple distance.

Say could not help feeling very happy. Too quietly happy, too tired, perhaps, to talk much; so she sat and thought. Thoughts came abundantly. How different this day's life had been from ordinary living! How grand and awful the world was, with its high and hidden places, where people might come and look, but by no means abide! The great mountains, — waste land, — acres and acres of bare granite, and untamable wilds — that were nobody's land — but God's.

And then — as such do bring themselves to our remembrance — some words of Holy Scripture flashed bright across her thinkings. Over and over, she was saying them to herself, with a new perception.

"Say! What are you thinking about?"

Say hesitated a second, and then answered —

"'The strength of the hills.' I never knew what it was before."

"Well, what is it now?"

Gershom asked somewhat curiously. He had not caught the precise thread of her musing. She had not quoted all the words.

"The force that is holding all these rocks together, with such a might, and keeps them up in their terrible places. Particle by particle, you know."

"Cohesion, yes; and gravitation."

"That's what it says in the philosophies. But, Gershom, what *is* cohesion?"

"You said; one of the forces of nature."

"But those are only names. Gershom, is it something living? *Is it God?* working His work, right here, and everywhere?" Her voice lowered timidly, and awfully.

"I don't know." The young man's answer was a little constrained.

Say was out of herself for the moment. She forgot to be ruled; the press of a high thought was upon her; that she would not have uttered without urging; that, being urged, must be uttered in full.

"'The strength of the hills is His also,'" she repeated slowly. "It reminded me of that, and it seems to mean a living strength. Like ours that is in us."

Gershom looked round into Say's face. It was turned away from him, and up toward the towering mass that lay beside and behind them, filling the whole northwestern sky with its heights of gloom.

She was in earnest, then; and this was a real thought of hers. There was something curious about this child, with her bronze boots and her "behavior," with her grown-up elegance, that he called frippery and sham, her refinements, that seemed to him, often, grappler as he was with realities, the flimsiest of affectations, beneath which nothing real and true could be.

He was not startled or offended at this name of "God," as many a young man in society, going to church regularly of a Sunday, but holding church topics tabooed in polite talk of a weekday, might have been. He had had little church-going, these last eight years; he had seen little of the decorum of a trained Christianity; the Great Name had been often in his ears, when it was not a reverence but a blasphemy: but he had been among men who had their own thoughts, after all, of God, and the great beyond; who, when these came uppermost, spoke them, without whining or shamefacedness; rough, unscrupulous, even doubting thoughts, they might be; yet real, unmechanical; avowed as readily as any other thoughts; laid away for no set and proper occasions, and held an indecency at common times. It was not this that made his constraint; it was a something that lay only between him and Sarah Gair; the girl he would not have utter faith in; whom he would not willingly draw near to with any touch of a deep sympathy. "Trusting and expecting." He would have nothing of that; least of all with Jane Gair's child.

Yet he turned and looked at her; and he saw her face lit with a real, earnest thought. It was there, for the moment, at least; there was no discrediting it.

He had heard her speak Bible words — even utter her understanding of them — before; in the New England home where they had been so much together, under the sweet, saintly influence of Aunt Rebecca, it would have been strange if he had not. But it had seemed like hearsay; interpretation put upon her; Sunday school drill; matter of course; a part of the great system, deep or shallow, as you took it, whereof the text and platform was, as Say had expressed it of old, "People must behave, you know." Abstract theory, to which it was proper to subscribe, but which had little vital connection with any everyday doing or apprehension; except, perhaps, — as in the beauty of that home the exception had been forced upon him, — with grand, kindly-natured old men, and saintly, world-innocent women.

But here was a sudden, spontaneous recognition of "something living." Something living in the dead rock; something living in the old words that sung their mountain-psalm to the world three thousand years ago.

Against his will, there was something living touched in the sailor's soul.

And against this, came up the perplexity, the doubt, of a hard life, among hard, suffering lives.

"The strength of the hills is a very pitiless strength." This was what he said to her, after that silent look, in answer.

There came a shadow and a questioning over the face that turned now and met his look with its own. She waited for more. She hardly understood.

"If you or I had fallen from the cliff, among these rocks, what would their forces have done for us?"

"Crushed us." The words came with a low horror in their tone.

"Pitilessly. I said so."

"I don't know." Say spoke slowly, in her turn, using his own words, pausing between the syllables.

"No; we don't know. The world is full of awful strength, and men run against it everywhere, like helpless things, and are crushed. If the rocks are pitiless, the sea seems worse. The rocks wait; but the sea rushes after you, and beats upon you, and fights for your life. Then think of all the waste places, where beasts and savages howl, and tear, and torture each other. And safe people, in quiet little villages, sit together in comfortable meeting-houses, dressed up, to please each other, and talk about God! and think they understand something about Him! Handfuls of people, in little corners of the great world! And the wars, and the tempests, and the starvings and burnings, and drownings and cursings are going on, all over it, at the self-same time!"

Say had no reply for this, for an instant. It was too dreadful, in its doubt and its darkness; too overwhelming with its outside force of truth.

"But—" she said presently, "God must be there. He is everywhere. You *believe* it, don't you, Gershom?"

"I suppose I do. I suppose I believe pretty much what other people do. But I can't settle everything by rule and line as they do. I don't know much, and I see terrible mysteries in the world."

Say sat and thought silently. All at once she brightened.

"But these are mysteries of nature, and dangers of men's bodies. There 's the soul; and God's soul is behind his strength, as men's are behind theirs."

"You 'd better not talk to me, Say, about these things. I don't know, altogether, what I do think; and I 've some thoughts you might n't be the better of."

"Oh, Gershie!" was on Say's lips to cry. But she had an instinctive knowledge that with the first symptom of personal feeling the talk would be over, and she could not have it end just so. She was silent, but she did not stir. Gershom waited her movement, and she made none. She sat and looked, still, at the great mountain, with its hidden, living strength.

"It *must* be all right!" The words escaped her at length, half involuntarily.

"I wonder what you 'd say about men's souls if you 'd seen the things I have." This came, an utterance almost as involuntary, out of Gershom's silent thinking.

Say sat still, and answered never a word. Silence draws sometimes more than speech.

"Grinding, and persecution, and treachery, and meanness, and every sin and shame that has a name, or is too bad for one."

"You must have seen horrible things, Gershom," said Say, in a suppressed tone. "But have n't you seen *good* things, sometimes, too? I *know* you have!"

Here, again, there was more upon her lips that she dared not speak. His own brave, noble doings were quick in her mind, warm at her heart; but Gershom would "Pshaw!" if she breathed of these to him; and that would end everything at once, with a cold revulsion.

"They were like light in a great darkness," said Gershom, moodily.

"But you see you have not lived at *home*. You have seen the hardest part of life."

"I 've seen the largest part, and I 've found out something about homes, and your good, Christian people, too!" he added, with the old, bitter sneer. "I tell you, it 's a fine thing, and an easy thing, of a pleasant Sunday, in a comfortable church, between a good breakfast and dinner, with every nerve at rest, to believe pretty things about God and religion. But what if you were hungry, and had no home? What if your bones were crushed, and you were lying in some hospital, and nobody cared for you, and they only counted you as 'a bed'? I 've seen men so, — shipmates. What if your whole life was nothing but one great Pain?"

There was a hush again until Say said, tremulously and humbly, speaking beyond herself and her little experience, surely, that which was given her for herself and for that other soul also.

"I don't know; unless I found that God was in the pain, too!"

"But suppose" — Gershom went on, remorselessly now, swayed by his own bitter impulse of doubt born of the hard things he had seen and suffered, — "suppose you 'd been deceived, till you couldn 't trust them that ought to be your best friends; suppose that you had never known more than three people that you could believe in, and suppose you 'd known them cheated and ill-used till it was harder to think of for them than for yourself; supposing you had seen all the rest of the world outwitting and hustling and chuckling over each other like the devil's own children, till you were ready to hate the very sun for shining on such things? would you find God and goodness in all that?"

Say stood up suddenly before him. Instead of a direct answer, she gave, for all his questions, a single, searching one, that rang Where clear over the confusion that was in him.

"Gershom Vorse! do you think you are the only soul God has made capable of hating such things as these?"

Out of his very scorn he was answered.

He stood upon his feet, too, then. He looked again in the

glowing young face, that was almost angry in its bending upon him. It was better than if she had told him of his goodness, his bravery; she had charged him boldly with a haughty assumption in this noble hate of his; she had given him a weapon for his innate truth to grasp, against his own dark uncertainties. Something lighted and softened in his eyes as he looked upon her.

"That was a good word," he said honestly, with a changed tone. "A good word for a last one. We'll let that be the end of it."

The rest of the walk was nothing. The getting home to Cousin Wealthy's, the nice supper, the answering their eager questions, the being comfortably helped to bed by Aunt Joanna; all these were well enough at any other time, but she went through them all mechanically. At most, they were but interruptions.

"She is tired out," they said.

Say lay down to her rest with crowding thoughts; with some misgivings, but a great peace shining through them all. She had said "a good word" to Gershom. It had pleased him, for that it was true and bold. She had met him on his own ground. They had come near each other again, at last. She wondered at her own new strength; she, that had always been so timid, — so easily put down.

Would things be different after this? She wondered how it would be in the morning.

CHAPTER XXVIII.

SUNDAY.

In the morning Landy came over early with inquiries and a parcel. Say's dress for the Sunday, and other needfuls. When the sweet breath of the woods and the wild singing coming in upon her through the window Joanna had softly set open, roused Say to a full wakefulness, she saw, delicately laid out on one chair, the pansy-muslin carefully pressed over, and the puffings perked out in all the dainty freshness of its first day; on another, in the opposite window, the blue foulard, — looped and knotted and draggled and rent; looking like a banner brought home from battle. Beside it, on the floor, lay the little black boots, so trim and neat yesterday at starting, bursted and torn, trodden into such shape as no boot of hers had ever come to before; making her think of the twelve princesses in the fairy tale who mysteriously danced their shoes out every night. It was like a night-vision to her, almost, the recollection of that mountain dance of yesterday; like a dream, the strange, earnest talk with Gershom; but a blessed, present joy, — something that she grasped to her soul, — the tone that rang back to her recollection as she had it from his lips, at the last, his harshness and bitterness suddenly swept away —

"That 's a good word. For the last. We 'll let it be the end."

It was so honest and noble of him, too, taking the good out of it, when she had felt it hard and sharp in the saying, — launched with almost a passionate indignation.

She was half sorry to break the spell; to come down in her proper and nice array again; she would almost rather have put on the old, bedraggled, forlorn foulard, if so she could have kept the spirit of some of those moments of which it was like a sacred relic. She rolled it tenderly up with all its rags and stains, putting the demolished boots within it, resolving to herself, secretly, that it should never go the way of other rags and wrecks, but that she would put it carefully where she might keep it safely, always.

For Gershom had seemed like a brother again; and she had said one word to him that he had confessed was good.

Very sisterly, this was, all of it. Say thought so. She had never had a real brother; so how should she be supposed to know?

She could not help her habit of niceness; she could not turn away from that image in the little mirror until every wavy line lay smooth upon the bright head, and rolled itself away gracefully into the braids behind; any more than an artist could turn from his work, leaving a heedless or mistaken touch. It was habit, — instinct; sense of the pure and perfect; these more than vanity. She could not have done violence to her nature, — she could not deliberately make herself dowdy, — even though Gershom should have really liked her better, so. Which, knowing something of men and their contradictions, we may feel tolerably safe in doubting, after all.

She had slept late. When she entered the room below, she found only Joanna sitting there, and the table cleared, except of one pink-and-white china plate, and a quaint little coffee-mug and saucer to match.

Cousin Wealthy brought in two fresh wheaten rolls, baked since Say's footstep had first sounded above; two new-laid eggs, boiled since her door had opened; a little pitcher of golden-brown coffee, steaming oriental perfume; a tiny, shallow, silver sauceboat, filled with yellow cream; and a pat of June butter, with a daisy stamped on it.

There came a double tread of men's feet over the platform outside as Say sat down.

"We had company come last night," said Cousin Wealthy; and Gershom entered, followed by a tall, strong, grizzled, sea-browned man, with sailor gait, whose dark, searching eyes that had looked on strange lands and people everywhere all over the earth, glanced round him here, as if this port of home, of all others, were strangest.

"This is Mr. Blackmere," said Gershom, in an off-hand way, that sounded like "Now I 've mentioned it, you 've nothing more to do with it."

But Say had heard of Ned Blackmere; she rose from her chair, and walked to meet him, putting out her hand. Looking straight up, also, with a certain warm reverence in her eyes, into his hard, rough face.

I think Ned Blackmere had not touched a woman's hand before

for twenty years, perhaps. How do you think he felt, then, as the soft, pure little fingers lay for a moment in his, that had known nothing softer than tarred ropes and marlinspikes; and the eyes that had never learned to keep the soul back out of them, looked up, so, into his own?

Say saw something in his face that few had met there before; she thought he looked gentle and kind. She saw something that did not look quite strange to her; it was as if the look had somehow come into her life before. Then she remembered the old days of the Pearl, and the cracking of cocoanuts. There was where it had been; yet the familiar gleam came with its sudden grace of tenderness, that did not join itself to her memories of the rough sailors. Presently, it was gone; and when she looked again she could not remember that she had ever seen his face at all.

Gershom had been at home ten days. He had received a letter from the owners in New York whose ship he had saved and brought home, offering him the command again, when she should have been put in repair. He simply declined it, with thanks. To his mother he gave reasons; they were her due; for her sake, it was his business to rise, if he could.

"They expect work of their captains that I could n't do, mother. Work that is n't in the written orders, and could n't be, in lawfulness and honesty. When I 'm a merchant-captain, I mean to *be* one; and no smuggler, out or in."

"And now," he said, "I want you to do something for me. Write a letter to Blackmere, — a motherly letter, mother, — and get him up here into the hills. *I* can't do it; I 've tried. He says he 's no fit company for anything but his ship and his pipe. And yet, the man has got a soul like a king!"

Prudence wrote; such a letter as the "real mothers" only write. The kingly soul recognized its genuineness, through the wrong and prejudice of years. Ned Blackmere came; riding up into Hilbury hills that same Saturday twilight wherein Gershom and Say were having their talk under the shadow of Boar-back.

The sailor asked Wealthy for a match; and then he and Gershom went out again upon the platform and Blackmere smoked his pipe.

By and by, the sweet country chimes began. Through the still air they answered each other up and down the valley and sent their tender echoes from the hills. There were new churches in the factory village at the Bridge; but all the beautiful and holy memories clustered still around the ancient meeting-house at the Centre. No old Hilbury people thought of going to any other. Its mellow bell rang dearer, solemner tones than all the rest.

The "colt" — Wealthy never had any but a colt; the old one was dead and gone long ago, and she had driven his successor, now, for eight years — stood harnessed to the wagon; Say and Joanna came down in their Sunday bonnets; Joanna's ribbons and laces smelling of the quaint, faint breath of musk that our grandmothers loved.

"Will you go to meeting, Gershom?" Joanna asked him, as she stood in the doorway.

"I guess not," he answered, with a shadow of gruffness. "It's as good out here in the woods; and the dress-up takes down the devotion, rather, — for me."

"Folks will expect to see you; you did n't go last Sunday."

"*Folks?* I should suppose it was the Lord. And I don't want to be seen of men, — or women."

Joanna had n't her gentle human theory, — her "God-sibb," — ready at the moment, for answer; she let it pass; it was Gershom's way.

Say passed by him and spoke to Blackmere out beyond.

"Won't you go to church with us, Mr. Blackmere?" she said, with the same sweet up-look at him she had given him before. It was to the unused sailor very much as if a flower had lifted up its head and spoken.

"Yes. I'll go." He hardly knew whether he had answered of his own will; but the words came and he stood pledged. Gershom lifted his eyelids a little, and said nothing.

So they drove off; so Ned Blackmere, the rough old salt, used to the weather-earing in a gale, used to everything that was hard and perilous and coarse, with only a dream in the far back past, of a child's home and a mother; of a sister who had turned his love into bitterness; of a wife who had made him hate and forswear all women, for her vile and disloyal sake — found himself among women once more; found himself presently in the quiet house whence prayers go up to God.

He sat there in a sort of maze, as in a vision one might seem to see a world into which one had never been born.

He wondered if this were the real thing, and the great world outside that tossed and struggled and endured, were a huge mistake. For twenty years he had never stumbled into a scene like this; and here were people to whom it was the soul of their whole lives. Why had God given this, and that? If He were, and if this were His ordained way of finding Him, why was it only possible in safe nooks, while the wild world was roaring without, and the danger of it to be dared by souls made hard and reckless to meet it, and the labor of it to be done by hands that had no time to lift themselves in prayer?

The sermon did not help him. After a little, he tried not to listen to it. Once he caught himself in the beginning of a breath that would have been a whistle instantly. It was so hard for him with his vague, bewildered thoughts, and his habits of unconstraint, to remember the traditional sanctities of the place.

His dark features gathered themselves more than once into a heavy frown as sentences of the preacher broke in upon his musing, and forced a hearing. Only when his eyes fell upon Say, they sometimes softened. She watched him when he was not looking, and tried to imagine what the secret consciousness behind that stern face might be like.

In the nooning Say joined herself to Blackmere again, and asked him to come into the churchyard. She would show him old gravestones and curious inscriptions. She felt responsible for him since she had brought him here, that he should not feel strange or dull.

They stood by graves inviolate for upwards of a century.

"They rest quiet enough — all of 'em," said the sailor. "Don't they?"

"'In the hope of a blessed resurrection,'" read Say, from a gray stone, in answer.

"'Asleep in Jesus,'" repeated Blackmere, standing before another. "Well, they seem sure enough about that, some of 'em. Seems to me, when there 's so few to be privileged, it won't do to be too certain. How about them that never knew whether Jesus cared a hang for them or not?"

A shadow of contraction passed over Say's face at the reckless expression.

"I beg your pardon. I 'm a rough fellow. I 'd no business to come here at all."

"They have all been taught. We all know that He came to save us." Say answered his first words, now, as if they had been spoken in all reverence.

"Do we?" There was a curl of the lip, and a slight sarcasm in the tone.

The young girl looked pained.

"See here!" said Blackmere again; "you 're not the sort of person for me to speak out to so; and yet, somehow, I can't help it. I don't know why, but you 've got me here; and now you make me talk. So if it is n't just the sort of talk or the ways of thinking that you 've been used to, you must think what *I've* been used to, and overlook it. I 've never had much good of preachers; and till this blessed morning I have n't set foot in a church for over twenty years. And what do they tell me when I do come? You heard it. That man stood up and explained the Almighty's secret plans. He don't *mean* to save everybody. Now I'm only a poor, good-for-nothing devil of a sailor, and of course I don't know; but if *I* came with a life-boat to a wreck, I'd make no such half-job of it. I'd save every soul on board, or I'd go down trying!"

Say's heart swelled. She could find nothing to say. She felt the fearfulness of this Heaven-arraigning; but she felt, also, the nobleness that Heaven itself had given.

"He's laid it all out beforehand and forever. He's elected some to salvation, and some to damnation. I beg your pardon again; but that's the preacher's word; and the Bible word too, it seems. And it's the word my life corresponds to. It's easy to tell which watch I'm in."

"It's difficult to understand what they mean exactly, by these doctrines," said Say timidly. "I've never heard them much except in Hilbury. I think it was the hard, old way of taking Bible words. I could n't help thinking some thoughts of my own this morning, while Mr. Scarsley was preaching."

Blackmere went on again, when she paused, as following out his own reflections, almost unheeding her words.

"The damnation began when I was nothing better than a baby," he said, bitterly. The curse came among us then. And it's gone on ever since; been piled down upon me heavier and heavier. Did you ever hear about my life, young lady?"

"I have heard of a great deal that you have suffered. I have heard of very noble things that you have done."

"I've been in prison; for a crime. I've got a halter round my neck this minute, — or the brand of it. Did you know that?"

His tone grew sharp and fierce.

"I knew you were accused; and I knew you were proved innocent."

"No. Not proved. They only could n't make it out against me. Some of 'em believe it to this day."

"I don't think that. But it has been a hard thing. A hard thing given you to bear," she said, slowly, with a hidden meaning of consolation.

"A piece of the damnation. A thing to keep me down, and thrust me out. To make a vagabond of me, and clinch the sentence."

Say trembled, standing there, at the man's passion.

She had never had to teach. It was hard for her trying to guide even ever so slightly, the current of a human thought upon these themes of life and death. There was the shrinking every young soul feels at unveiling its secret faith. She was far from taking it deliberately upon herself to admonish; to set this doubting and discouraged spirit right with God. She knew, oh! very little. She had seldom asked herself, even, what she truly did know or believe. Life had not put its sternest questions to her, yet. But the thought of this man — hard, despairing, defiant with the reck lessness of one to whom the truth, whatever it might be to others, seemed only a relentless curse — this thought, this utterance, drew forth from her irresistibly, her own, thus, in her first close scrutinizing of it, — in its first waking to a conscious strength, — demanded of her instantly.

"I can't make it agree with what Jesus said, himself," she said, with modest reverence. "'Not a sparrow falleth to the ground, without your Father.' 'Ye are of more value than many sparrows.' 'The very hairs of your head are all numbered.'"

"It don't agree. But they 're both alike in the Bible," returned the sailor bluntly.

"'Knowing, brethren beloved, your election of God,'" Say repeated thoughtfully. It had been the morning's text. "It made me think, — just his reading it, and the few first sentences he said, before he came to the puzzling part, — how comforting it was. That everybody should be 'elected'— to their own particular life, and death, and all. Not forgotten; or let stumble into it by accident; but chosen. And I suppose the noblest souls — the dearest souls to God — might be chosen for the hardest. The best men in the ship are chosen for the hardest, are n't they, Mr. Blackmere?"

The sailor looked full at her, with a strange light sweeping suddenly over his face. The light of a new, gracious thought, gleaming up across confused clouds of doubt. There was doubt there, still, and hardness; but they were shone upon unawares.

"And the trust — the honor of it — makes it easy, don't it?" Blackmere looked at her for two or three seconds before replying.

"If I could think a thing like that!" he exclaimed, at last. "I can stand taking the toughest, when somebody must take it; I never shirk a weather-earing; that 's what I 'm cut out for; but a fellow's spirit's broke by hazing!"

"He does n't haze!" The young girl spoke it with an awe, a tenderness, an assurance. Blackmere stood gazing at her still; his own look melting.

"How the Bible-verses come up and explain each other, when one begins to think!" said Say. "'Whom the Lord loveth, He chasteneth; and scourgeth every son whom He receiveth.'"

The words fell slow and musical from her lips. The soul of the hard, life-buffeted man caught them to itself, like pearls.

They had wandered to the oldest, most secluded part of the cemetery. Down the sunshiny slope above them, came now Aunt Rebecca, looking for Say. The girl moved up to join her. Blackmere turned away abruptly, passing down where the far, shaded extremity of the burial-place joined itself to the natural forest.

"I have had such a strange talk with Mr. Blackmere," said Say; and she tried to tell it over as they walked up toward the vestry door at the back of the old meeting-house.

"'Elected!'" repeated Blackmere to himself, as he plunged along the rustling woodpath, unheeding whither. "That 's a new way to take it; and a different one from yonder howling doctrine. I wonder if the girl's notion is right. If I thought the tough job had been set me by Him above, there, and He cared how I came out, I 'd face it in a way that would n't shame the stuff He 's made me of. I could put a heart into it! But it never looked that way to me afore; and how should she know? And yet, when the child riz up to meet me so, this morning, holding out her hand for mine, it seemed somehow — I don't know why — as if she 'd come with a gift in it!"

CHAPTER XXIX.

LIFE'S WORD.

PRUE had not been to church. Wealthy went home when the morning service was ended. With her unwontedly large household, this was necessary. There was a plentiful tea-dinner to be got ready; and Joanna and Rebecca would come round with Say, after meeting, to "pick up her things," and take her home. So at least, the good woman had requested, and expected. But matters turned out differently.

The fatigue of the day before, — the exertion she had already made to-day, — the excitement of her talk with Blackmere, — began to assert themselves with Say. Coming up again in the face of the hot summer sun, the churchyard slope, her head began to throb, and remind her with fast-growing pain that she had done too much. When she reached the vestry just vacated by the Sunday School children, out now for their short "nooning," she seated herself languidly upon a bench, and her face suddenly lost its light, and her eyes contracted themselves.

"I believe I'm tired out," she said, with a little smile. "I've just discovered it; but I really am. I wish I could get home, — to Cousin Wealthy's I mean."

The child remembered her treasure of rag and wreck, and would rather secure it with her own hands, silently.

"I should be nicely rested by the time you came. Could Landy drive me, before meeting?"

To be sure, Landy could; the first stroke of the bell, recalling the worshippers, came after them on the air, as, round by the Deepwater road, Say and her escort reached the bar-place into the back pasture under Hoogs's hill.

"You need n't come any farther," said Say, laying her hand on the reins. "I'd rather get out here, and walk up."

She wanted to go quietly into the house and reach her room, if possible, unobserved, to get an hour's rest before they should know she had come back. So she checked the horse, peremptorily; and sprung out lightly over the thills. Landy, a slow fellow, had only time to get as far as "he 'd just as lieves" — when Say was through the bar-place, and he found himself alone in the road.

"She 's a whisker, I vum!" he ejaculated; and turned his horse's head Zionward again.

The path through the back pasture wound up along the side-hill, and came round under the dairy windows, at the rear of the house, and so, still further around its end to the square platform in the front angle. Against the building, at this projecting end, Jaazaniah had built, long ago, a rude bench, sitting upon which one could get the southerly breeze that came up among the pines, and, also the fair, wild, southerly view, through openings down the hillside to the gleam of the pond. Just over this rough seat, was the window by which he had lain in his long illness, taking in, for all joy and comfort, the sunshine and watershine, the shadow and fragrance and song whereto it gave blessed aspect and entrance.

Say got thus far and paused. Because she was tired, and the head beat with a new aching, and it was soothing here in the shade. Because also she heard voices in the angle, and waited; if by any chance she might yet pass in unseen.

They were the voices of Cousin Wealthy and Gershom Vorse; and these words came first distinctly to her ear.

"It 's all a queer mixing up of things, to me. That girl talked, yesterday, upon the mountain, about God; with a look in her face as if she felt Him; and to-day, she had on her little dainty airs and smiles again; and must go to meeting in starched muslin! It 's a curious world."

"The world's well enough, Gershom Vorse. And what 's more, if it was n't, you 're in it, and part and parcel of it, queerness and all! You can't stand off, and look down upon it, and judge it. There 's only One can do that. And He don't. He came down amongst us. You 're hard upon the world, Gershom; and you 're hard upon that child. She may n't be clear wisdom and perfection; but she 's a bright, loving little thing; and she sets by you as she does by her life. Only think; she never had an own brother; nor even a sister."

The woman instinct and *esprit du corps* it was that put in that, and the child, listening, blessed her for it; blessed her, while her cheeks flamed and her hot brow throbbed more wildly, and a strange shimmer of light seemed to show her, suddenly, a place in her own heart that she had never looked into before.

"You must take love as you can get it,— ore or nuggets,— and be thankful, or go without. The Lord never sends it for nothing, and however it comes, it 's a piece of His own. Sarah Gair has grown up with you in her very heart, and it 's a cruel way you take with her, slighting and faultfinding and watching and carping. I 've ached to tell you so, and now I 've done it."

"I like Say; I always did; but she 's had a poor bringing up."

"That ain't her fault, and I can't see as it 's done her so very much harm. I 'm an old woman, Gershom, and I know what things are worth. I 'll tell you something about myself. I did n't always take things right end foremost. I had a way once of twisting 'em about and looking 'em over, to find specks in 'em. I kept Jaazaniah off and on as long as his mother lived. It did n't seem to me always he was right up to the mark in everything, as I wished he was. Well, when she died of course I could n't go on staying here alone with him, so I packed up and went off, and lived along of Mrs. Gibson for more 'n a year; and all that time he was after me, and I was considering. I could n't give him quite up. There was n't as much more love left for me in the whole world as there was in that great clumsy honest heart of his. Sometimes I 'd as good as made up my mind, and then he 'd go and say or do something, or *not* do it, that would just upset the whole calabash, and I 'd have to begin all over again, persuading myself. But I never stopped spinning and weaving my piles of house linen, for all that; if I 'd only known, myself, what I meant by it. The thing that made me crossest was that he never took up spirit to answer me back in my own way, but just give in to all my tempers and impudence, when half the time the things I said were just to put the very words in his mouth that he ought to have said back, and if he had, would have made me feel a sight better. One day he 'd been a pleading and I 'd been a hectoring, and finally I just burst out at him. 'Jaazaniah Hoogs!' said I, 'you have n't got the character of a fly! I do wish there was more *to* you.' Of all the looks I ever see in a human face, his was the grievedest then, and the most humble; and yet in a kind of a way, it was the grandest. There was n't a particle of blame or anger in it, but a great, sorrowful, patient enduring. 'Wealthy,' says he, and his words did n't sound mean nor shuffling, but real manly and gentle, — 'I know there ain't much to me. I wish there was a great deal more for your sake; but you 've got all there is!' I took him then, for he belonged to me, and I 've known ever since that we belonged together. We belong together yet."

Wealthy's voice shook a little, but her words were clear as her faith was strong.

Gershom Vorse was silent. A minute after, Cousin Wealthy walked away into the house to lay by her Sunday things, and find Prue. Gershom lingered a little, and then his firm quarterdeck tread was heard across the platform and down the rocky path toward the great barn.

Sarah Gair was left alone.

She sat there in helpless pain; a pain of body, and an ache and shame and confusion of soul. She knew, by that shame and confusion, that the love she had called sisterly, when she had looked at it to call it anything, was more and different. She had "grown up with him in her very heart;" no love now, could ever come closer. Her pride, her joy, her glory, her claim in him — she had never felt these — she knew she never should feel them for any other. He had held the place in her thought — in her dreams, that but one can truly fill, and once, for any woman, whatever semblance may come after. His approval was gladness; his blame was suffering.

And he — "liked her; had always liked her;" that was all.

And Cousin Wealthy had stood and pleaded for her! Oh, it was bitter shame, — pain unendurable!

Notwithstanding those saving words,— that hint at brotherhood, — what, to his quick apprehension, his merciless insight, could it all mean, — that story of Wealthy's own love that had been the one love of her life — and its comparison with hers — what else but this, that every drop in her veins tingled to think of?

She was self-convicted. She could never shut her eyes to it again. She knew now what she had meant to do in cherishing those shreds up stairs, that she had rolled together and hidden away in the deep closet corner, lest any one should meddle. They might lie there now; she would never touch them.

"He liked her; but she had been ill brought up." He did not approve; he pitied, he was tolerant of her.

She had not suffered all that was set for her to bear, this day.

While these sensations, that were hardly thoughts, yet rent her, in her helplessness, a sound of spoken words reached her once again.

She was directly under Wealthy's bedroom window. Against it inside stood the bed. Wealthy approached, to lay her bonnet and shawl there; Say knew her habits, and understood the sound of every movement. At the same time she began talking; to Prue.

"I 've been saying something to that boy of yours, that 's done me good. He 's a noble-hearted fellow; but there 's other hearts in the world, as well as his; and he 's hard; and I 've told him so."

"He 's true," answered the mother. "Truth may be hard, sometimes; but he can't help that."

"Yes, he can;" persisted Wealthy. "Or, if he can't, I don't know but I'd as lieves he'd lie a little, now and then! He's cruel to that child. In his thoughts and in his ways."

Say's hands flew up, to stop her ears from further listening. She could not get up and go into the house. She could not stay there now. She must steal away presently, when they were out of hearing, and go home; and they must never know that she had been there. She lifted her hands to the two sides of her head. But she had no power to fasten them there. Words came that compelled her to hear on. One may refrain from deliberate hearkening to what is not meant for one's knowledge; but there is a momentary incapacity to resist what comes to one, unsought, seizing one's very life, and piercing it, as this did Say's.

"I suppose I might be half an hour pretending to try and find out what you mean, Wealthy Hoogs," said Prudence Vorse, in her strong tones. "But that is n't my way. I see it plain enough. As plain as you do. And to that, there's just one answer, in his mind and mine too. She's Jane Gair's child."

"She's a Gayworthy."

"The best blood may be spoilt by a bad cross. She's a Symonds: Hannah Symonds's grandchild; and the mother's clear Symonds, without the first redeeming particle!"

"I don't think much of Jane, myself; but you're very hard, Prue."

"I might be harder. If I called that woman to a strict account."

"Doubtful undertaking. She's a manager."

"Yes," returned Prue, with a peculiar deliberation and quietness. "She's a manager. She's managed my boy out of his home and away from me. By a lie, and a hiding. She's managed him into a rough, dangerous, distasteful life. She managed her good father into his grave. And — what with prying and poking, and concealing — it's my belief she's managed more. It would n't want much ferreting maybe, to find the rights of it. But I shan't take up the job. I'll leave her sin to find her out."

"You never speak without a reason, Prue. And yet you never spoke of this before."

"I hav n't been touched so near the quick before. It is n't a thing that'll be ever made plain in this world, most likely; but if that woman had a clear, honest mind when her father lay a dying, and that day afterward when we all sat together, while Reuben Gair looked over the papers that nobody ever touched — rightly — before, but the Doctor, and read that will — why, then an angel of heaven might wear Satan's own colors — that's all!"

"These are hard things, — hard things, Prue," Wealthy repeated. "And it was a hard time to judge her."

"She went round with a hard face, Wealthy, all those days. There was nothing soft or grieving; anxious enough — too anxious looking; in a strange, absent kind of a way, a sort of still flurry, as if she 'd something on her mind. Her father had a talk with her; and what it was, lies between her and the dead. *I know she kept back something.* And before Reuben laid his finger on the will, that night, she started, and her look changed. *She knew that he was coming to it. And she knew she had no business with her knowledge.* She 's false, and sly; but she is n't deep. I read her face; and it was the face of one who should never be a mother to my boy!"

Say put her hands to her ears, now, in an agony; she had been spellbound, to this point; but she could hear no more. The impulse that would have been a shriek if it had dared, brought her to her feet, with her hands held tightly, so, against her head; and she flew, with steps noiseless, though headlong, down the hill-side path that opened before her, between the pine trees, toward the Pond.

To get away, — from this house of her friends where she had been wounded, — to escape all sight of them, — to reach, somehow, in this bewildering pain that held her more and more fiercely, — a place where she could rest, and be alone; this impelled her desperately.

She followed the path around the margin of the pond. Through the perfumed summer woods; along by the still, plashing water, that throbbed up upon the pebbles; the nameless fragrance drifting over, or with it, that comes upon the freshened air wherever sweet water flows; with the blue, cloud-flecked sky bending down and repeating itself as of old; all this was as it had been in her childhood, when in these things lay sufficient joy; and the stricken woman passed them by.

"Elected! Elected!" The word kept ringing itself over to her inward ear. Now, she was beginning to know whereto. To this, and to no other thing. Her pain was upon her; her own separate allotment that was like no other soul's on earth.

Where was Gershom Vorse?

"I like Say; I have always liked her;" this was the most he had had to say to Wealthy's urgent, unsparing remonstrance. He said it quietly; almost coldly; then he listened without a word to all the rest she had to say; took in silently the simple pathos of her story of the one love God had sent into her life; and when she left him, turned and went his way.

To suffer too. In his strong, terrible, restrained, man's way. For he knew now, likewise, what that "liking" was; something grown up with him into his forceful nature, as Say's thought of him in her "very heart." What God hath joined together, man may not put asunder.

Man will try, though. Man will let his pride, and prejudice, and hate, stand between him and his love, making a fight of it all his life long. "I will never forgive Aunt Jane for this," had been his uttered resolve. "I will not believe in — I will not care for — Jane Gair's child," had been his secret unworded self-reiteration.

He stood in the great, open, west door-way of Cousin Wealthy's barn. He lifted his arms and leaned them upon the wooden bar across it; holding his head down. There was a working in his face. It would have been a shedding of bitter tears perhaps, with a woman; with this man, it was a swelling of every vein; a drawing of every cord; a red streak shooting athwart the eye-ball; a setting the firm teeth tight together.

"This, too, my enemy has done!" was the feeling in him. "All the rest was not enough, but I must feel her even here! I must love; and it must be her child! I was content to go through the world untrusting, expecting nothing; when she had killed my boy-trust, and sent me out among the hard, hateful things of life; but I must bear this after all! I must love that child and long for her; for her who has that lying blood in her veins; whom I *will not* take to my bosom; whom if I would, I have been set apart from forever, in my coarse, mean, struggling life. A poor sailor, — son of a widow; and she the rich merchant's only child! This, too, my enemy has done! — I have fought against it without looking at it; now I must grapple it face to face. 'She sets by you as she does by her life.' Why did Wealthy say that? Why did my head whirl when she said it? 'Slighting, and fault-finding; watching, and carping;' yes, I have done all that; I would never let myself see how I loved her; Thank God I never let *her* see! — Now, I've got this thing to do; to get through the world with this wind in my teeth; to set my face against it and take it! — Oh, Say! Say!"

The proud, stern, distrustful spirit groaned out its anguish in one deep, half-smothered moan.

Then he gathered himself up and strode away; as men stride, when they would hurry away from a passion.

Down over the rocks, into the deep woods; parallel to the very way Say was taking; a quarter of a mile of underbrush between them; God knows what impassableness between their two, suffering hearts!

An hour after, Say lay upon her bed in the red-room; the curtains drawn, and both doors bolted. She cried out all her tears; she spent herself in an ecstasy of shame and misery; then, at last, she sobbed slow and gently, with a self-pitiful heart-break.

"He will know me better, sometime; in heaven, maybe. And perhaps God will let me live to do something true and generous by him, yet, in this world. Something to make up, — oh, if I knew! Oh, mother! mother!"

When Rebecca came home, hastening directly, when she learned Say had not been at Wealthy's, she found the doors fast, and the room silent. The child had fallen asleep, Rebecca went away, and waited. By and by, she tried again. Still fast; no sound. She went round through what had been her father's room, and pushed away, there, a chest of drawers, that stood against a rarely used door. It opened into the narrow closet, running between this and the red-room. By this way, she entered, quietly, and went and drew the curtain softly aside from the bed. There was a crimson face, and tangled hair, upon the pillows; the chamber hot and close. Rebecca flung the curtains wide, unlocked the entry door and set it open; then lifted the opposite window and threw back the blinds.

The air, the movement, wakened Say; she turned and opened two swollen, glassy, feverish eyes. She lifted herself suddenly to her elbow, and glanced round, as if bewildered.

"Oh," she exclaimed, faintly, with a half-remembrance. "I came home. My — election — oh, auntie! my — head, I mean — was so bad. I could n't stop. I came round by the Pond."

She shivered a little, in the draught of the fresh air. Her eyes looked vague and troubled.

"Would you just — fold up — that tombstone? Oh, dear, what ails me? Shut it up — the door — I mean."

Say was in the first stage of violent fever.

All through the beautiful July days, when the haymakers were in the fields; through the calm, starry nights, when the dew was rich with perfume; while all over the hills and woods was the gladness of the country summer-time, — Say lay there, suffering in the grasp of disease. Her father and her mother came to Hilbury; Jane Gair was forced to it, now, and only her own heart and conscience could tell the scourge of punishment that mingled secretly with her natural pain. Ned Blackmere said, when they talked of Say's illness, — "She 'll die; she 's one of the real ones, and they go to heaven." Gershom Vorse kept his misery within himself, saying and asking little; but they knew, daily and nightly, at the hill-farm, how it was at the homestead; for Blackmere took it upon himself to go to and fro, bearing the tidings;

and a letter that came from Selport, offering Gershom command of a brig upon an African voyage, to sail at four days' notice, was quietly answered, destroyed, and never spoken of. He waited.

Three weeks of fevered pain and clouded consciousness; and then the tide turned, tremblingly, almost imperceptibly, toward life again.

Mr. Gair went back to his business; Jane was in a hurry, as soon as Say could bear it, to get her to the sea-shore; Gershom Vorse went down to Selport, and got a berth for himself and Blackmere; taking a voyage to Cronstadt; Say sat in the great easy-chair, or lay tired and feeble on her bed; and let her life come slowly back to her. A comfort came, also; came with the one word that had been given her, for a purpose, — that had rung in her memory through the first bewilderment of her brain, — "elected — elected!" She could bear what she had been *chosen* to bear. With this grain of mustard-seed, the whole kingdom came to bloom in her soul. It was her first childlike creeping close into the bosom of the Father. She had known that He was; she had believed His truth given to the world, and taught her through others. Now, she found Him, felt Him, as she never had before. She was "as one whom his mother comforteth." Her bodily state helped this; with exhaustion comes a peace; it is when we are strong, that we can suffer keenest.

Gershom came to say good-by.

"Shall I let him come up?" said Aunt Joanna. "Are you well enough to-day?"

A pink tinge came to the pale face. She caught her breath a little quickly; then she said quietly, "yes."

This, also, she must bear.

There was no disdain of her pretty daintiness, now. Gershom's face was very gentle as he approached her, sitting there in the warm, open window, with roses on the sill, and some especially sweet, late buds lying on the lap of her white-frilled wrapper, contrasting delicately in their pink and green, with the soft, pure muslin. The offending little foot was thrust out, too, unconsciously, upon its cushion, slippered with blue and golden brown, in embroidery of silk and satiny kid; but he saw only the kind, calm eyes that looked up, meeting his; and the white hand grown so slender, that reached itself out toward him.

There was a change in her beside the changes of her illness.

There was a quietude, a repose, that was not all of feebleness. She recognized it in herself. She would never be abashed at him again; she would never be in a flurry lest she should displease him; all that was laid at rest; she had faced the truth; she had borne its life-thrust; and the touch of truth had set her free. She knew now what lay between them; she thought she knew what he had given her; a "liking," merely; and a sort of pity; he should give her more — respect.

"You 've had a hard time, Say," he said, as he came and stood beside her.

"But it is very pleasant getting well."

It seemed to the stout sailor, looking at her as she sat there, that the getting well had not been very rapid.

"Blackmere sent you these." A basket of mountain raspberries, that Gershom held in his left hand.

"Mr. Blackmere is very kind. Tell him, please, how much I thank him."

"You 've won him over, however you managed it," said Gershom, lightly. It was hard for him this meeting and this good-by; he must get through it as he could.

A little touch upon the secret misery made Say wince.

"I don't *manage*," she said with emphasis. "I 'm glad if he likes me. I like him *very* much. He 's a good, brave, generous man. And —" she stopped. She had been very near saying, with the old impulse, "and he 's your friend, Gershie."

"And — what?" said Captain Vorse.

"I should know it from what you think of him, if I could n't see it myself. You 're hard to please, you know, Gershom."

"Am I? I 've had hard luck sometimes," the sailor answered.

This was coming closer though than either wished.

"I 'm glad you 're better, Say. And I 'm glad to know it before I go. I 've come to say good-by. I 'm going up the Baltic."

Say spoke not a word. She knew that parting now, they were to part for years, for all, perhaps. She knew it would be long before she should have another summer in Hilbury; their chances might never coincide again; and Gershom never came to Hill Street; she could no longer wonder why, or ask it of him.

All this was best so; still she could not speak.

"You look very sober, Say. Give me one of your good words, to go with." He spoke with that forced lightness, still; the strong man's pain clutching secretly at his heart, also.

Then Say looked up. She had a word for him. A word she had thought to send him, if she should be going to die, when she came out of that confusion and wandering into the consciousness that life hung trembling and uncertain; when she knew as well as those around her, that the last might soon come; when she read her mother's look, that bent over her in an agony; when her father's presence at her bedside told the why; when she saw in the tender, wistful, saddened eyes of the kind aunts, their fear for her; when her life, and all the love and hope, and pain of it, lay on one side, and Death stood waiting, close, upon the other; and in the twilight between the worlds, she saw things as they only see them who go down into the very shadow of the sunless gloom, and stand with feet in the very wave-break of the dark sea, and thence — look backward!

She had a word for him. She would give it, now. A brightness came into her face; an earnest self-forgetfulness. She put her hand out again and he took it.

"God *was* in the pain, also, Gershom!"

He knew in his soul that she was pure and true. He knew in his soul that he loved her. He knew that his very hold upon heaven lay with her. A strange look glowed in his eyes, for a moment, as he stood over her, her hand in his. That which was in him stirred mightily, and trembled on the breath of an avowal.

Then there came steps upon the stairs, and a voice. Aunt Jane's.

His secret went back into his soul again.

They said good-by, and he went away.

Threads cross, and break, and entangle; the pattern runs awry. Yet, God's Eye is over the loom; His Finger is upon the wheels!

CHAPTER XXX.

DRIFTING APART.

It began to come to her now. Now that she no longer cared for it, or distressed herself for the want of it. Now that the smile or stare of these fashionable girls, or their mothers differed little to her; now that even Jane Gair in her real solicitude, had forgotten for awhile her petty fussiness and obtrusive ambition, — it all began with the waywardness of things striven for and given up, to come, in a degree, of its own accord.

They were at the seashore until October. Mr. Gair brought his carriage down from the city. What he had refused to do for display, — taking his sensible business view of things, — he did for the comfort of his child. Say had her own way now; and Mrs. Gair's great object was her daughter's health. So they were simple and straightforward, minding their own business, for awhile. And people who would not have perceived them, arrayed elaborately, and presenting themselves, as had been Jane's fashion, without apparent immediate object other than expressed by that unmistakable air of "Here I am," in the piazzas and drawing-rooms; who gave short, surprised, civil answers to her overtures at conversation, and turned away; who had kept her in short, behind their elbows always; these people began to glance after the pale girl and her mother now, with a certain interest; had a word of inquiry when they met them in the doorway, just alighted from their drive; a word and a smile even, when they encountered upon the beach.

Mrs. Topliff discerned through her eyeglasses, "that there was something really quite distinguished about that Miss Gair; the mother was common enough, no doubt, but the girl's face and air were positively striking." It was simply that Say's face wore its own quiet look of thought and preoccupation, now; she had a life to live of her own; a life that took her strength to do it; she had no seeking, *distraite* expression of one trying, as she had said, "to get into other people's lives." And her natural elegance sat on her, so, unconsciously.

Mrs. Topliff had a comfortable sheltered seat beside herself, now and then, when the child came out, at sunset, to the piazza. Room for one only, and she would patronizingly beckon Say; Mrs. Gair found a place as she pleased, for herself. Mrs. Topliff drove an open English brett; one fine September day she offered Say a seat in it; took excellent care of her during the drive, and even remarked with a polite kindness, to the eager mother, meeting them on the steps at their return, proud to claim her daughter out of the stylish lady's carriage, in the eyes of all the standers-by, that "Miss Gair had got a little color in her cheeks." Whereon Jane went into an ecstasy of profuse thanks and familiar volubility; taking her ell in a great hurry, where but the brief inch had been accorded. Mrs. Topliff cut her very short, in a twinkling; had a sudden word for her coachman; and Jane was behind her elbow again, before she quite guessed at it; alone, presently, midway down the steps.

She was used to it; she was thankful for the little she got; to this abjectness had she come, — this absolute vulgarity of soul, through patient truckling to the vulgar airs of those whom she mistakenly believed to be great people.

There was a quiet room on the same floor with themselves, into which Say was sometimes invited, where she felt herself in an atmosphere of truer elegance and refinement than within the charmed circle of the "Topliff set" when they sanctified, for a brief half hour, a certain piazza corner,— mere boards and railing, when the spell was off, and open to any common comer, — or than even tucked cosily between the sumptuous cushions and blankets of the brett, driving *tête-a-tête* with its august owner.

It was the room of an elderly lady,— a widow,— and her maiden sister; persons necessarily, not of the gay set; but indisputably above the prevailing tone of it, and deferred to, in position, by people of that or of any set whatever. There are individuals like these, who make their own genus. Say was happier here, among their books and pictures, their gatherings of leaves and flowers and stones and shells, than she could be anywhere now, since Hilbury was done with.

It was literally the "*crême de la crême*" who had the privilege of this parlor; "Topsy" people; people who "growed;" who moved in and out among those below; whose place was where they chose it, but who showed their true metal only when rung against like coin. People who drew out Say's best; helped her to ideas and facts; enlarged the world to her, material and human. Among them she learned one thing that much of her former experience had tended to give her doubt of; that people may be true and yet genial; that the polite world is not all sham. She thought of Gershom Vorse in these days; she wished he might be here; she felt it hard for him that life should give him nothing better than it did; she remembered with a clutching pain and shame at her heart the terrible words of Aunt Prue, "she has managed him out of his home and away from me; she has managed him into a hard, dangerous, distasteful life;" she — Say's mother! Ah, she could only be half-happy, ever again!

The way was opened for her into a wider life after her return to the city. This winter was not just like the other winters she had known. She was intimate still at Mrs. Gorham's; people met her there who had passed her by in general society, where they had seen her tricked out, like scores of other girls, to be looked at, and wearing the telltale expression on her unfeigning face, of a vain anxiety, a mortified weariness. They saw her differently; she was different. She began to have friends. She was asked to new places. She ceased to be slighted, or half-noticed, anywhere. Mrs. Topliff could neither snub nor patronize where the Gorhams and the Grays quietly acknowledged. Say "had things real," now; these things, the outside appearance of which she cared not for. Mrs. Gair was beatified. They were wheeled slowly into the system. They had begun actually to revolve.

Say entered into this more positive life of society, into these very best things of it that met her need most pertinently, with a certain secret reluctance. It would separate her from the old life. That would lie back in the past; a thing left behind and done with. She should change; she felt herself changing. She should have new faiths, new interests. And her child-friend — her brother, — this was what she called him still, — with his nobleness, his hatred of shams and shows, his manly grappling with the life he had been set to live, — would be going such a different way! She got a glimpse in this, her larger intercourse, of things he might have done, as he himself had got it years ago, when it was too late. She heard grand words spoken for human right; she learned what true, loyal-hearted men, with power and education, and opportunity, were doing in the world. She saw a place he might have filled; where his stern justice, his heaven-clear honesty, his searching insight into motive and meaning, should have had their work. And he was away, and out of it all! Never seeing the good that she saw; weaning himself more and more from human fellowship, while she was drawing it more closely and kindly about her. It was not fair. She owed him something other than this. It was a debt; she was secretly bound to watch for opportunity to right him; to this end to hold herself still in the line of possibilities concerning him.

This one binding motive held her back from many things that might else have happened. Happened very naturally, whatever you may think I should make so of her constancy.

Gershom Vorse had been to her the ideal of man's nobleness. Of a truth that scorned disguise; of an earnestness that searched through all things even to unsatisfaction and scepticism; of a plain, sincere speech and bearing that were better than polite grace; of a bravery put to tests safe people never dreamed of; of a power and intelligence that gave lustre to the rough profession he had chosen, and made their opportunities, instead of yielding to and being obscured by circumstance. All this she honored, loved in him; longed that it should recognize its like in her; suffered that it misunderstood her; bore the bitter crisis of pain and shame at finding fully, for the first time, *how* she had loved and honored; how feebly she had been apprehended and requited.

But people do not go on and live in crisis; things subside again; life calms itself, and takes up what is left.

Sarah Gair might even have married. Then her life would have branched away, and separated itself utterly from this old life that she clung to, — that was sacred to her, — wherein she had a solemn, secret duty, grown from and joined to a strange remorse and shame that were for no doing of her own; for no positive doing that she knew or might ever come to know; but that she must wait to comprehend and remedy. This task of honor held her back, when other things might have lured and led her on.

She had learned by a sudden storm-flash what Gershom Vorse had truly been to her. She had learned by the same flash that he could be little to her ever again, even, perhaps, in brotherliness. This pang she bore; it crushed her down for the moment, but she lived through it; and life, like the waterbrooks, creeps under wreck and obstruction to find for itself new channels. You cannot help it, young dreamer of romance; it is your life also, and the very nature of it.

Say might even have married. She had men friends also in the sphere of her new companionships, — men of culture and of grace. She saw that there could be nobleness that was always gentle; that it was possible, even for her, with her mistakes and girlish weaknesses, to be borne with and counselled tenderly, and cherished; she who had been so little used to this!

My story will be long enough without it; since she did not marry him, I shall tell you little of a certain Doctor Robert Gorham, but his name, and his kindness to her this first winter of her actual, tried, woman-life; and that, before the winter ended, be made manifest that he would willingly give her help and cherishing through all the winters and the summers that they two might have to live.

It was not the old love only that withheld her. Old love sleeps, if it do not die. It has, too, its reactions, when it contrasts itself and its pains, and its unrequital, and the injustice it has borne, perhaps, with what might be, with what offers itself. There are moments when, with a breath refused it in this sleep, it might pass away and be no more ; when a slight added impulse given the reaction, it might fix itself beyond the point of possible return. It was not the old love only ; it was that she felt vaguely in the future a something waiting for her to do, for which she must reserve herself and hold herself free. That which she had prayed for in her trouble, and soothed herself with thinking God would give her ; something generous and true to do by Gershom Vorse. Something, she knew not what, that was owed him honestly. Something she trembled to imagine and shrunk from beforehand, but which time and the leading of Providence should make clear. Gershom Vorse should respect her, should think well of her, should know that she could neither lie nor hide. She would rather wait for this, than take even the gentle love that was ready for her. Something, truly, was strong upon her ; earnest as life ; drawing her surely to itself like death !

In the summer of the next year they went to Europe. Say, her father, and her mother. Dear old Hilbury was far behind. The world broadened out about her. She saw, and learned, and enjoyed, and was strengthened. Still she remembered. Still,— in the sea-storm or glory, — in the strange lands, — the farther she drifted out of the old years and places, — the deeper lay her thought and memory of him who was a wanderer also, not for pleasure, but for toil ; whose life, while hers was sweetening and ripening, might be shrivelling, and hardening, and growing bitter, still ; who, doubting earth, might also be doubting God and heaven ! He had been hard upon her ; he had thrust aside what she would have given ; for that she could have found it in her to be proud, resentful ; but he had been wronged ; she blamed, — she pitied, — she was tender of him in her heart ; above all, she kept her thought of him alive, longing for the hour to come, which should come.

CHAPTER XXXI.

A BIRTHDAY; AND WHAT IT BROUGHT.

JOANNA GAYWORTHY rose up one bright, early autumn morning — (it was a year from that time when Say had left them, after her illness, and at the end of the same summer wherein she had gone abroad —) with a wonderful blithe feeling at her heart. Something, — whether it were the crisp hill-breeze, bearing its ripened odors of orchard and forest, or the redundant golden sunshine, that itself seemed to have a crispness in it, or a happy physical harmony in herself, or an untraced association with some old happiness, — something, touching her subtly through every sense, carried her back to the feeling of her childhood; quickened suddenly within her its spirit of confident expectation, its perception of an infinite possibility in life; that every morning had used to renew itself in a rich, glad wonder of what *this* day should bring. This wonder stirred within her strangely, now; it was as if this day should not be quite like all others, for her; as if, somewhere in its breadth of brightness, in its atmosphere of joy, lay a special gift for her. A gift! She remembered. It was the gift of an added year. It was her birthday. She was five and thirty, to-day. Was that it? Was that a thing for a woman to feel blithe about? To-day, she turned her back upon her youth; it was all behind her now; she set her face, of compulsion, downward over the hill of life; she had passed the crest; the waters flowed the other way; they came no longer, springing from sweet fountains, to meet her; they ran from, and outran her; she might not choose; she might not even pause. Why should she have this nameless gladness at her heart?

She turned to her glass and tried to feel herself old.

"I've got a gray hair somewhere; saw it a week ago; I *am* old!" she said to herself, "And yet, I feel to-day, like a child."

Everybody told Joanna that she kept her youth; she knew it; she felt the spring of it within; she wondered, sometimes, as she wondered at this moment, how it was, and why. It seemed, she said to herself, as if a freshness in her had been kept hermetically sealed, waiting for something, for some festival time that was to come. Something in her that was unfulfilled, — that would not let life wholly ripen — that forbade it to decay.

"September — October — November, even. What matter is it which, if summer weather lasts? I *am* a child." She had turned, now, to her window again, looking out with pleasure sweet and new, and forever young, on the beautiful hills and the far-stooping sky, that had encircled her life these five and thirty years. "I *am* a child, still," she said with an exulting defiance. "God's child; with His Eternity before me, and the good in it that I have been waiting for, and coming to all these years, that, after all, are nothing!"

Leaning thus, and looking out with this recognized joy that had been but a nameless impulse, rooting itself blessedly in her heart, and growing into her face as real joys do, she saw Gabriel Hartshorne come quickly out at the front gate of the farm house, and turn his steps up hill.

Every sense was sharp in her, to-day; her intuitions keen, to grasp things drawing near.

"He is coming here," she said to herself. "He wants us. — Something has happened there. — And — yes — Mary Makepeace is away."

Mary Makepeace had been gone three days of ten, that Gabriel had given her, to visit her old home, a stage-journey of a day and a half eastward, among the hills. It would take three days to get her back again.

Joanna met Gabriel at the side door. His face was pale and his manner hurried.

"My father. Something is wrong with him; and I've nobody there but Abby and Hiram. Will you come down?"

"Yes, Gabriel, instantly." Joanna's face was earnest and pale as his, so bright as it had been a moment ago.

Gabriel turned without further word, and walked quickly down toward his home again. Joanna hastened into the house, and found Rebecca. The two women lifted their gingham bonnets from the entry pegs and followed.

How she blessed her five and thirty years! In that moment when her thought flashed back across fifteen of them, recalling the hour of her friend's first, bitter trouble; when she had been but a girl, and Prue, the woman, had been privileged to help him! How her heart sprang with half-acknowledged selfishness of joy, feeling that there was none nearer, now, than she, to give him aid and comfort! She claimed this, secretly, of life; claiming no more. That, stand at such distance as they might, each from the other, none should come between! So she was satisfied. Anything other would have been outrage. She knew God would not let it be!

"I'm old," she was inwardly saying, in the midst of her real pain and anxiety for Gabriel. "I've got a gray hair, somewhere. I'm thirty-five to-day. I can be his friend! I can help him always; and he will be sure to come to me. That was enough to be glad for!"

They went in at the open farm-house door. Gabriel met them in the great kitchen, coming out of his father's bedroom.

"I must go to the Bridge, myself. Hiram is slow, and blundering; and the doctor may be anywhere. I shall find him, and come back as soon as possible. Will you come and stay with him?"

They followed him into the old man's room. It was easy to see what was the matter. One fallen eyelid, — one corner of the mouth drawn down, — the soul gone out one half of him, — he lay there, speechless and helpless.

There were tears in the women's eyes, as they looked at him, and then at Gabriel. Gabriel's were sad, but clear and strong. He knew that the end was coming; the end of his long, faithful, loving work; the end, also, of all darkness and feebleness for him who had dwelt under the cloud so long.

They bathed, and chafed, and laid warm things about him; did what they knew; and then they sat and watched.

In three quarters of an hour, Gabriel came back with the doctor.

There was little to do. It might be a question of hours, or of days; it could not be a question of life or death, for long. There were few words said among them, after the doctor had given his directions and gone away; they quietly arranged things, or things fell naturally into arrangement, after the necessity. One must go home, for awhile; one would stay. Joanna took with silent decision her right of precedence; was she not the elder? Truly, there were almost three years between these two women, both so well past thirty.

Rebecca went home; she would come again by-and-by; Joanna stayed, watching by the stricken man, while Gabriel ate, as he could, his delayed breakfast; then she owned she had not eaten hers, and changed places with him; seating herself at his board.

It was strange; it was sad and solemn; but it was very sweet. The morning joy could not die wholly out of her heart; she was here with him; he relied upon her; she was more to him than any other woman in the world; this was the birthday gift God gave to her.

Hiram went away to the farm work; Abby betook herself to kitchen and dairy; these two, Gabriel and Joanna, were left to their watch.

Soft womanly touches laid all things tenderly straight and comfortable; prompt, quiet hands administered all that could be given; friendly woman-eyes met the man's, warmly, silently; heart and soul were very near; there had been no such presence in Gabriel's home, partaking the inner life of it, since the mother went away. Had there been, ever? Should there be, ever again?

Holiest joy — tenderest grief — touch often. If there be a joy left, sorrow magnetizes it to a counterpart depth of blessedness. There was a peace in Gabriel's Hartshorne's soul beyond where pain could reach.

The warm, September day climbed to its highest glory, and faded down. Down to a still gorgeousness, gathered among the western hills. Rebecca was with them, now. The two sisters would remain in the house all night. Gabriel would not let them watch. That was his office. He would call them if he needed them.

He could not keep her from his watch. She was there with him, and he knew it; though doors were closed between them, and the silence of sleep lay upon the house. He knew she did not sleep. He felt her wakeful thoughts with him, all through the midnight. There were but two hours wherein he had a sense of being alone. Those two, Joanna slept, sitting in the great, old-fashioned easy-chair by the best room window. She had risen noiselessly, from Rebecca's side, unable to close her eyes, leaving her sister quietly unconscious. And at last, relinquished sleep had come to her.

He knew she was coming. It was early dawn, and there had been no sound. But the felt presence was with him again; his watch was no longer solitary. As the morning paled out of the midnight, and the stars fainted, and the first blush came over the gray, he heard without surprise her step approaching; the soft sweep of her garments stirred the air of the hushed house. He stood up in the doorway as she came, and held his hand out.

"No change?"

"No change."

Could the heart help it, if, out of its complex meanings, a second wound itself to the words, and came thrilling after, like a blessed echo?

No change, between these two.

It might never be said plainer; the tangle of life might go on;

the flaw from that twisted thread of long ago might never be righted into perfectness; yet the inevitable truth — the pattern divined across the fault — flashed so, with now and then chance lights, and comforted them, they scarce knew how.

Joanna stayed in the kitchen; drew out the glowing embers from under the ashes in the wide, old-fashioned chimney; heaped them into a living mass, with tremulous, spirit-breath of fire; set something thereon; flitted between pantry and dairy; and brought Gabriel, presently, a great steaming, odorous breakfast-cup of such coffee as she could make.

"If you will take some, too," he said, as she put it into his hand. "I don't think you have slept much more than I."

So she fetched another cup and poured herself some; and they broke their fast together.

Hiram and Abby appeared presently. The world was going to be alive again.

"Now, you must go and rest," Joanna said. "Rebecca will be here. I will call you in an hour."

By that promise she prevailed; and Gabriel left her. To faithful watch and most sweet thoughts.

The morning wore along. The hour went by.

"I think he looks more as if he knew," said Joanna, coming from the bedside.

There had been a stupor like a sleep; now there was a clearer look, an opened eye, in that half the agéd face where soul yet lingered so strangely; the dead half lying so fearfully dead.

A glance met Gabriel's as he came close; there could be no sign; it was but a look. Asking — beseeching; recognizing sound; a quicker consciousness, than in the twilight of his faculties, the poor old man had shown for years.

Gabriel got the Bible that lay upon the bureau-top; he opened where there was a mark between the leaves; standing by his father's bed he read some verses; straight on from where he had read last, forty-eight hours ago. The asking eye calmed; the smitten face wore a look of listening; the one hand pressed Gabriel's as he took it, when he had ended reading. Bending above him, the strong, tender man spoke like a child, the simple words of the Lord's Prayer. It had been his morning service with his childlike father for many years. Joanna bowed her head and the tears fell. "The best Christian in Hilbury," her heart repeated.

The morning wore along. The church-bells rang. The people streamed by up the road, in country wagons. The Sabbath warmth and stillness brooded; and a rest lay upon the land. There was a hush and quiet in the house where Death was coming. All through the early day and the bright noontide, that seeming of sleep was upon the sick man; then again, at afternoon, the faint rousing: the glimmer of a life-light over the half-blank face; the eye that searched, and wandered, and besought; the hand moving restlessly till the strong one came and clasped it. And Gabriel said, gently, as the returning wagons began to roll down hill, — "I will go, father, for the minister. It is Sunday. It is Communion Day."

So he went; and Rebecca made ready. When he came back, bringing the preacher with him, — a man of grave, pure face, and somewhat sternly reverend bearing, — there was the little table by the bedside, with the white napkin covering it, holding fair bread, and red symbolic wine.

There was a voice of prayer and blessing. Christ's dear words were uttered, and the bread was broken, and the wine was poured; and the son held cup and morsel, as he had been wont to do, to the old helpless lips; and the women bowed and wept.

There was a fragment that the old man could not take; it was only a crumb, indeed, from the Lord's feast that might be given him. And Gabriel, without pause of doubt or question, shared the symbol as he shared the gift. Before, he had done this; in the church, when the old man proffered it childishly. or dropped a portion, unpartaken; Gabriel would not let it fall like common waste, but ate it with a quiet reverence. To-day, still calmly, questionlessly, he did more. For the first time in his life, he lifted the wine to his own lips, that had spoken no church-vow; and the Puritan pastor beheld it, saying no word. It was a pure assurance, a holy audacity; had not his whole life been a vow? Was not, in this hour, this cup of a last supper held out to him, above them all?

Rebecca joined in the gracious rite; the minister offered its emblems to her; it was her proper privilege. Joanna sat by and put forth no hand. But her soul was with the soul of him she loved; and inwardly she drank with him, the selfsame pain, — the selfsame joy.

After that the day went down. The light of a human life went also down. Slowly, flickeringly, flushing a little at the last with a parting ray, that told the coming night was as truly, over the verge, a coming morning; it changed and settled to the moveless Peace.

In the dropping shadow they went out at last, and left him. Alone, with his dead.

And a cry of the human went up from that closed room. A word gasped up from earth to heaven.

"I've been true to you, Mother! Mother!"

CHAPTER XXXII.

THE SCARLET OAK.

They came again and set the house in order for him, for the burying. They made all sweet, and pure, and orderly. They placed flowers about; common home-flowers, late-blooming; colorless asters and petunias. Joanna brought one white rose from her own window, twined with glistening myrtle, tied with a ribbon. She came to Gabriel and laid it on his hand. "It is for the mother," she said softly, and turned away. There was a thought in it the simple-spoken woman would not put in words. "For the new bridal. The golden wedding that was in heaven this day."

Gabriel came to her an hour or two before the service. He was freshly dressed in pure white linen, and his Sunday suit that was always black. He had in his hand a needle, that he had found somewhere and threaded. Mary Makepeace, just come, was in her own chamber.

"I must trouble you," he said; and held out a loosened wristband, from which a button had fallen. A simple, common need, coming in to assert itself among deeper need and loss, as such things do in this strange life of ours.

Joanna had been sitting by the window. She turned and came to him. She had filled tenderer office for him to-day, than this; she had ministered closer to his heart's asking; yet there was something in this homely, womanly service he came to beg of her, finding no other to perform, that moved and thrilled her curiously. Even to a girl's shyness. He held his hand out, and hers touched it, passing back and forth at her slight task. They stood close together. It was such a bit of help as a sister might give a brother; a wife, a husband. Suddenly she felt the color come; up, higher and higher into her face, that grew angry in shame at itself; at such unfitting hour, to be making foolishly much of a thing like this! Yet she was helpless; she, with her five and thirty years. She would not do her work at halves; she fastened her thread properly, and broke it cautiously; with the moisture springing to her very finger-tips, and a beating in her ears.

What could he think of her?

He only said, with his gentle, dwelling accent, invariable with the words, — "Thank you — Joanna!"

She could but hope he would forget; there was quite enough to make him. But he did not forget; he only put by.

For a fortnight after, they saw little of him; the time of helping and necessity was past; he had Mary Makepeace with him for all service; they were only neighbor-women again; he, a man, living alone; secluded, with a grief.

Of any definite difference these events might make to her, Joanna never let herself think; but she was perturbed, restless with a secret something that was not joy — how could it be? yet that had been never still in her — only overborne by tenderer, solemner feeling — since that birthday morning when it sprang like a mysterious premonition, unlooked for, in her heart. The friendly calm, the calm that she had thought for life, was leaving her; since that foolish, miserable moment, she had been afraid of herself; afraid of him; she held back suddenly from what she had eagerly claimed in virtue of her years; she let Rebecca go foremost now, in neighborly kindness. She said to herself she was a fool; getting into a girl-silliness, now when she had lived out half her life. Now, just when her friendship might be quietest and strongest; when it was bringing her toward Gabriel, as they should come nearer to each other, now that they both were growing old.

She was odd; impulsive; she made Rebecca think of the old Joanna, with her unreasonableness and whims; her petulance; her sudden despondencies; her gayeties, as sudden.

It went on so for weeks; and the autumn ripened. The early glories came and went; the maples flamed; the elms mellowed; oak and ash burnished themselves in bronze and crimson; and the winds came and fresheted all the waysides and woodpaths with a down-pour of color.

Over in the great orchard, beside the boulder-tower, the brave old scarlet oak burst out with tardy fires. Like a passion or a joy come late in life, it filled all the impoverished landscape with a deep strong warmth of radiance. Above it the blue hung tenderly; it was a picture of hope; a promise; a type of grand and sure fulfilment.

"It has waited to be more beautiful than all; it will last away into the winter. I'll go and bring home branches, and pile them on my hearth to warm me by," Joanna said, looking out through thinning boughs that opened toward the distant splendor.

She felt the life-meaning of it; the correspondence of its hope was in her soul. Nameless, restless, stirring fitfully, like branches flashing in an autumn wind; but large and real; planted there beside a rock.

She came down stairs with shawl and hood upon her arm.

"I 'm going off, out to the great oak orchard; to be glad and to bring home glory. Look there!" and she pointed out at the opened door, to the great dome of sunlight and color, rearing itself against a space of sky between the hills.

"But look here!" whispered Rebecca.

"Yah!" responded Joanna, in a snarl, below her breath.

Mrs. Prouty was within the yard, coming up over the chips with the security of a saint in her ordained place, it being her special afternoon for visits, and with most intimate aim at the side door-stone whereon Joanna was just about to set her foot. Country civility could not avail itself of "business" or "engagements" and walk off, straight before the comer's eyes, into the empty fields. Gladness and glory must give way; she must come in with her guest and pretend to be pleased.

Mrs. Prouty and the Deacon had been down to see Gabriel. A visit — *ex-officio* — of condolence and exhortation; a fag end of business appended, which leading the "men-folks" off towards the barns and cider mill, the good lady had bid Mary Makepeace good-by, and "guessed she would step on up hill and set with the Gayworthys till the Deacon came along."

People whose lives jog on in uneventful rounds, are greatly stirred at changes happening to their neighbors. Mrs. Prouty was exercised as to the "what next" with Gabriel Hartshorne.

"All alone in the world as he was now, and nothing to bind him anywhere, would he stay, and carry on the farm, or would he git res'less and start off?"

The great world suddenly spread itself out to Joanna's thought, as it had looked to her that summer day from the mountain-top. It was too wide. Too many things were possible. Her life, that been concentred in one point, might scatter itself. How should she bear it if it did? Oh, a friend was a troublesome thing! There was no outward ownership in him. He might take himself off, stretching out your heart-strings after him to the ends of the earth, and you should have no right to cry out. An impotent restlessness, an angry impatience, seized her again. She hated Mrs. Prouty. She almost snapped at her; and, catching herself at it, decided not to try to talk, but left the conversation to Rebecca, and sat by, her elbow pressed down hard upon the window-sill, and one foot treading savagely on the other's toes.

"It's my idee" — she caught the words up here, after a confused babble about the farm, and the expense of hired folks in the house, and the difficulties to a single man, during which her thought had hurled itself away on its own tangent of pain, "it's my idee — he's been tied down so close all his life — he'll go somewers now. I donno's I've any clear callin' to mention it, but I s'pose you'd know as quick as anybody if there was anything in it — Mary Makepeace *did* say something to-day about Californy. She's got a brother there; and Gabriel's been asking questions, it seems. She kinder mistrusts he's got a notion of it in his head; and the Deacon says the farm is ruther run out, some of it. He thinks very well of Gabriel, the Deacon doos; though he isn't an experimental Christian. But I hope, now father and mother has forsaken him, he'll look to the Lord to take him up."

Hot, indignant drops started to Joanna's eyes; her cheeks flamed; she whisked herself suddenly off her seat, and into the kitchen, where she put her head into the oven, to look after gingerbread that had been cooling for fifteen minutes in the pantry.

She was saved return; the Deacon's chaise seesawed and clattered itself, ricketily, to the doorstone; and Mrs. Prouty bustled out. She never kept the Deacon waiting. The ineffable complacency of the perfect woman spread itself over her face, and her features levelled themselves into a plane of benignity, as if they had been suddenly flatironed, as she took her privileged seat by his side, and departed sweetly to remaining duties.

Joanna shut the door in a silent rage, and darted upstairs. Rebecca had some housewifely business in the kitchen chamber, and followed.

"I wonder," she said, simply, with her head in a linen chest, close by Joanna's chamber-door, "whether Gabriel really does think of going away."

"*You*, too!"

It came with a sharpness so like a shriek, that Rebecca involuntarily sprang to her feet, and entered her sister's room. To see her fling herself passionately down along the bed; shawl, hood, and all, in a heap between her arms and under her face.

"Dear child! what is the matter?"

A sob; a little, quick, gasping laugh; a sob again; a hand stretched out and clutching Rebecca by the wrist; a tempest of tears, then; a real shriek, smothered with the head held down between the shawl and pillows.

Rebecca slipped from her grasp, and shut the doors, and brought sal volatile. This "old Miss Gayworthy," for the first time in her life, most unexpectedly to herself, yet with the utmost naturalness, was going into hysterics.

"That woman — she always — hears — with her elbows!— But to think — that you — should n't know — any better!"

She knew enough better, now. She wondered she had never known before.

She put her arms around her sister, tenderly; she drew her head down on her bosom.

It was all out; there was no help for it; and Joanna gave herself up, recklessly, to the comfort of a dear human sympathy.

"You never told me this," said Rebecca, by and by, almost reproachfully. She forgot she had never told her sister *that*. We live so close together, and yet so far apart!

"Did you think I would?" cried Joanna, lifting up her head, suddenly, with something of the old spirit of whimsicalness. "Did you ever know of a burnt hand I got once, when I was five years old, and nobody ever could find out how? There 's the scar; I wonder if you ever saw it before?" and she held up her fair palm, whereon was a whitened seam. "Well! now you 've seen it, and I 'm come to general confession, and I'll tell you. I took up a live coal in it. I was n't fool enough to tell that — though I did it; nor this; not even the smart of it. Only — the old hurt began to ache so, all of a sudden!"

And Joanna laughed and cried, again, together; and turned herself away, and hid her face in the pillow; all but one crimsoned ear, that looked as if it had been boxed.

After awhile, in a smothered voice, with her nose down among the feathers, —

"Are n't you gone? You 've got it all, now; why dont you go away?" As if she were a dog that had come for a bone.

Whereat Rebecca rose, silently, from the bedside, and went.

An hour after, down-stairs, by the sitting-room window, she lifted her eyes from her needlework to see Gabriel Hartshorne coming, with his grave air and steady step, up among the red and yellow maple leaves. At the same instant, something in a shawl and hood whisked out at the end door, and flitted down the barn-road, by the garden fence.

Years ago, she had been left, just so; to bear her own hurt; now she must receive the first pang for another.

Gabriel was come to tell them something. Of himself, perhaps; this very news. It did not seem impossible to Rebecca that it might be true. In the prime of life — alone — with untried capacity yet waiting within him — what wonder would it be if this man, always of a power beyond the scope he found for it, should go forth from his solitude into the great world, at last?

She stood up, and glanced after the flitting figure. Safe; skimming along the cart-path through the spring meadow, already; making straight for the oak-orchard and the great scarlet tree. Then she went out and welcomed Gabriel, and drew him in; lest, left to wait an instant on the doorstone, he should turn and see what she saw.

He came in, and sat down; sat silent, for some moments; he was apt to come and sit so, in those days; and the sisters never took it strange, or hastened him with speech.

"I 've been thinking," he began, after awhile, "a great deal, lately. And I 've come to talk some of my thoughts out."

"You can. You know that, Gabriel."

"I know; and I do; all that can be talked of.—It seems to me sometimes as if my work was done here, — for the present."

"I dare say it does, just now," she answered.

"The farm would be as well let out, no doubt. I don't seem to feel spirit for what it needs. The soul of the old place is gone. And yet it's *home* to me. You can't tell *how*, Rebecca! Out in the world somewhere, there may be something waiting for me to do — and to get. If I could go and bring back money——. Rebecca, I 'm not well off, and the farm won't make me richer. Things have run down a good deal in all these years. If I could ever stand in the right position, there might be ——." Gabriel paused. He had not come to think *all* his thoughts out, after all.

She wondered to herself if she guessed rightly. This was a proud man; with the grand, honest pride that keeps men upright of mind, though nobly humble, also, of soul. They — the Gayworthy sisters — were the heiresses of Hilbury, with money and culture more than their neighbors; more than this faithful son who had waited God's time; who seemed not ever to find his own time.

"Hilbury would miss you sorely," she said, with a tremble of regret and sympathy.

"Not as I should miss Hilbury," he answered, in a sudden, strong way, that was almost like a spoken sob, the feeling burst so with it. My whole heart is here, as my life has been. And my grave must be here, as theirs are."

They were silent for a few minutes, and then Rebecca asked —

"Where would you go, Gabriel?"

"To the place from which I could come quickest back again. To the gold country."

Upon this moment might hang all. It was laid upon her to speak. But how?

Out of her true, friendly heart.

"We might bear it. But it would be very hard. Gold does n't

buy friendship, Gabriel, or make it any richer. You might come back to find more graves. You might not come till we should all be old. Don't go, Gabriel!"

He flashed up a strange, earnest, appealing look to her face. Some women might have misunderstood it. She herself might have wondered at it, but for what she had learned this day. She read it truly now. If other lips had so besought! If this, or something like, yet more, might be in another heart for him!

She was sure. With her pure insight, she discerned it all. She spoke to his silence. She reached straight down and touched the secret of his soul. With a quick, sweet, electric surprise.

"If you must go," — she spoke slow and steadily, yet with a low thrill of womanly timidity, — "if you find you *must*, come and tell Joanna yourself. I don't dare!"

Two breaths were audible in the still room. A fluttering respiration of a woman frightened at her words the moment they had fallen. A deep, hard pant out of the bosom of a man.

Rebecca stood by the window. She had risen and turned her face away outward. A step came up to her; a hand lay on her shoulder. The strong, eager breathing was in her ear.

"Where is Joanna?"

"Away down there in the oak-orchard. Gone to the old tree."

Gabriel snatched his hat and strode away.

She heard him coming, sitting there under the spread of the great flaming boughs, and looking off from this lower edge of the orchard over the yellow stubble of cornstalks down the slope to the still, sweet river-glen, and across to the rising uplands beyond, — the fields that joined the Hartshorne farm, and had been rented and used by Gabriel.

She sat there trying to take it all in; how Hilbury would look without him; what her life would be; and whether she could bear it. She took up this live coal of pain and tried how long she could hold it; and a cry was rising to her lips as the anguish grew too sharp; and then she heard him coming.

She sat still, moving not a hair; not even to look up; as one cowers under the coming of a blow. She waited to be crushed.

"Joanna!" and two hands were held to her.

She put hers up and let him take them, but she lifted not her face.

"Dear friend, I have come to tell — to ask you — something."

"Ask, Gabriel."

He seated himself beside her on the fallen leaves; over their heads the red, shifting lights of that late forest-fervor; in their hearts what ripeness of strong love, waiting the frost-touch for its perfect revelation!

"I have had thoughts, — I don't know whether they are wise ones, but my life turns here. I must decide what the rest of it shall be, and I have come to-day to tell my thoughts to my best friends. I am not yet old; there may be something that I can do in the world. Ought I to go and find it? and come back, — that of a certainty, God willing, — when I have found and done it?"

"Why do you come and say this to me?" The face still turned away, and the eyes downward; a strange forced tone in the voice.

"Because — I must, Joanna. I have said all to you, always."

"No, you have not!" It was a cry of the heart in which the words came. "And this — you know I cannot bear it!"

Then she started to her feet, and flung herself away from him.

For a moment the great surge of joy that swelled up in him would not let him speak. The crimson flush was on his brow; the tardy glory of his life had crowned him. She stood, scarlet in her woman's shame, in the low, red sunlight under the scarlet tree.

"Why don't you shame me? Why don't you pay me back? Why don't you tell me what I told you years ago?"

She pelted the sentences at him over her turned shoulder; she scourged herself with the smiting questions, in their rapid tones like lashings.

But before she had finished, he held her in his arms. In his strong, tender arms, that had waited with their first, pure longing, all these years.

"God gives, at last!"

The golden afternoon light, — the autumn glow, — were over and about them. And a like light shone radiant on the hidden beauty that their life had woven; the pattern different from their own purpose, — traced after God's thought for them. Had any brightness been left out?

"We might have been together in it all. So many years we lost," said Gabriel.

"We have been, Gabriel; close together, always in our hearts; the years are not lost!" So she answered.

CHAPTER XXXIII.

VIEWS; ACROSS AND BACK.

In the narrow city streets, people who cannot see clouds and fields, and hills, see something else. There are other "views" for them than the brick-vistaed bit of far-off green, or the pinched gleam that comes to them of the broad sunsets. They have human life. They look in at opening doors and at uncurtained windows. They have views into homes, imaginative peeps into hearts. "Across the way" there is always something; an arrival, a departure; a funeral, a wedding; or the daily uneventful coming and going of the same steps, in the same rounds, — the apparition of the same faces at the same panes, — that make the quiet continuance of things that seem as if they had always been, and always must be.

There are lives that look out so, and borrow; feed continually upon the life they find about them; love, and pity, and surmise; weave histories and hopes, — find all the play of human interests and affections, in the little cognizance they get of human creatures, whose real hopes are but a guessed-out story; whose very names and voices they may never come to know.

Grace Lowder sat so, day by day, in her little corner window, and read, as best she could, the simple chronicles that evolved themselves in her sight; having a great joy and interest in the activities so unlike her own helplessness, — the vigorous living she could never share.

Diagonally, across the square, was old Crossman's; and his second story corner room, that corresponded to her own, had a never-failing fascination of mystery, an occasional very absorbing charm of attraction in its aspect.

Nobody could get anything out of old Crossman; he let his rooms or shut them up, or hid himself away in them, in his surly, solitary living, and "nobody," as Mrs. Hopeley said, "knew the who, or the how, or the why, or the wherefore." There was something odd, and quaint, and strangely pleasant to Grace, in the glimpses the sunlight, glancing in and reflecting itself through the windows, opening like hers, from street to street, gave her, now and then, of this opposite chamber. Sometimes, for months, — for a year and more, even,— it had been a blank, with its closed blinds; then the life came to it again, and the light was let in, and the curious feeling came over her that friends had got back.

She did not pry with intent of impertinence; but she could not help looking, and when the day poured in and out, or the lamplight shone there, and the curtains were not drawn, as they hardly ever were for hours of an evening, she could not help seeing.

Antique-looking pictures; queer things in cane and carved work; shells; a parrot in a cage, which, whether it went away in a trunk when the lodgers took themselves off, or was secreted in the rear with old Crossman, Mrs. Hopeley avowed herself "conundered" to tell; a narrow bed, — a fixture in the recess of the wall, in whose like space was her own closet, — overspread with covering of some strange, rich, oriental stuff; a painted lantern hung from the ceiling; over the mantel, some foreign-looking weapons fastened against the wall; books; instruments; spy-glasses; maps; every available space crowded with what seemed the heterogeneous drift of a roving and busy life, that had gathered itself, somehow, into this little cove of temporary rest.

In the midst of it all, two men, as curiously unlike each other, as any other two things there. Father and son? It was hardly possible. Brothers? It could not be. Master and servant? The one was a gentleman; but the other was too much of a man. Companions they seemed, and friends; friends that had found each other across some social chasm; there was a rough deference from the older to the younger, that, beside his different bearing, evidenced this. The older man came first, always; sometimes he would be there for days and weeks alone. Then the parrot hung in the front window, and he would sit there and smoke his pipe; the very puffs of it came, often, in pleasant weather, through the opened sashes, into Grace's room.

Grace used to sit and sew; and these two, with a dozen yards, between them, — with two utterly distinct and unknown lives holding them apart, — thought many thoughts about each other in a dreamy way, that was hardly an active, conscious interest, but that made, none the less, a real place for each in the other's living sympathies.

It was strange how much they thought. The gray, rough man wondered at himself, half impatiently, when he found himself missing, uneasily, sometimes, the little figure seated at her quiet tasks, on the infrequent days when she worked away from home.

He watched her coming back in the dusk, after her day's labor; and he saw with a strong man's half-comprehending pity, that the little thing was lame. She knew his tread upon the pavement, when he came up the street; and was glad when he went in at the door, and listened for him to fling up the window; for, winter or summer he did that; he was a hardy, out-door man, who could not endure stifling. It was somehow pleasant to her to know that there was such a grand, defiant strength in the world; to her, a feeble, little lonely creature, that had never known father or brother. She felt safer in the nights, when these neighbors had come back, and the corner room was occupied; she thought, if there was a fire, or robbers should get in, she could call out loud, and help would come; she said her prayers and slept trustfully; but this was good also.

Once, on a winter day, something happened that caused this feeling — of pity and reliance — to grow suddenly, from a secret sense, into a proved reality.

The narrow sidewalks were slippery with ice; more slippery, in these by streets, with long "slides" which the boys had made; ground glassy smooth, with fine-scored lines, tempting to all young feet. One of these stretched from below Mrs. Hopeley's, quite out, along the fronts of two houses, to the curbstone at the corner. The widow had n't the heart to put ashes on it; she and Grace both loved to watch the merry groups that gathered there; rosy little girls, in hoods and mittens, with a run and a hop, and a stoop, launching themselves, with small momentum, along the shining way; boys, dashing with fearless velocity, upright, from end to end; even a grown man, now and then, taking it in his way, as if he did n't mean it, an old-times feeling getting him, nevertheless, by the heel. They had only, in their comings and goings, to keep the inside; a narrow path to be sure, but room enough; so the slide remained, and widened.

And late one afternoon, — late, counting by the rapidly-falling twilight of a winter's day, — Grace Lowder and her crutch came round the corner, just as a great grocer's boy, with big boots, and clumsy elbows set akimbo, and a parcel under his arm, plunged himself along, turning about and ending his slide backward upon the glare.

The wind drew through the street, and carried Grace, with her insecure footing, a few steps further than she meant. Exactly where she met it full, — big boy, and bundle, elbows, boots, and all. The little figure was borne down; the slender crutch, dashed from her hand, flew out into the street, and a wheel went over it.

"Blast me!" came a strong voice from above. "If ever I see

a little craft like that capsized, and the sticks knocked out of her that fashion!"

All but the first ejaculation was uttered tortuously, in the narrow, intestinal windings of back entry and staircase, down which the speaker plunged, making his impetuous way out of the crooked little building opposite; and then a stout pair of arms were round the delicate shoulders, and there was a breath, pungent with pipe odors, but with nothing worse, close to the girl's cheek, and she was lifted tenderly, — not to her feet, poor child! that might not be, — but to an upright posture, and borne across the narrow, slippery sidewalk, to Mrs. Hopeley's door.

Some strange, dormant instinct stirred in Grace Lowder's heart, as she balanced herself between her one strong foot and the other hand, catching the door-post, and was forced to lean also partly against the stalwart support that would not relinquish her. The sweet, womanly sense of being protected by manly power, — the power that had never been about her for her aid. She had hardly so much as had the touch of a man's hand, the strength of a man's arm given her momentarily, in all her crippled, helpless, creeping up from childhood. Her mother was all; and she had been gone for years; and then there had been Mrs. Hopeley. Beyond these there had been nothing between her and the Almighty Strength.

She had seen, while she was a child, other children led along by fathers' hands; a maiden, she had looked on other maidens kept close in brotherly care. She knew there was all this in the world, — for others; this beautiful vigor, made to offset and defend delicate helplessness; and with her helplessness, that was beyond all ordinary need of woman, she stood alone; with her crutch, and her Father who was in heaven.

She never dreamed of the dearest earthly reliance of all; that of course, was not for her; it had never troubled her with a longing; but if she could have had a *father*, to care tenderly for her; the more, that she was his poor lame daughter!

This instinct it was that warmed and stirred with the strangeness of its first answering; she trembled in the great sturdy arms. If it had been a gentleman, she might have been only shy and thankful; there would have been, perhaps, no heart-consciousness in it; it would have been a chance help, that she would have known would be forgotten, the instant it was rendered; but this was not a gentleman; he was only a rough, odd, honest, kindly man, not above her own station; for age, he might have been her father; there might have been such an one, if God had willed, to cherish her; to feel life even, brighter to himself through her, feeble and helpless though she was. All this did not come to her in clear order as she leaned there, waiting, for that moment; it was a confused thrill, born of thoughts that had been hers before; of a nameless missing she had felt of an unknown thing desired.

And Blackmere — you know who it was, as well as I, — how did he feel? The man whom life had hardened; who had had no woman-love, of mother, sister, wife, to keep him gentle, for more than a quarter of a century that had gone over him in a stern, hopeless striving with the world?

Three years ago, a girl's hand had held his; a girl's voice had spoken gentle words to him; words of a sweet, natural faith, that had set his soul for the time, in a new attitude toward God. Since then, he had been less hard; that and his one friendship, fervent with all the restrained might of his proud, silent, fiery nature, had begun the salvation which begins by a little sometimes, and afar off. He had doubted; doubted fiercely, and upbraidingly, as one who felt there *ought* to be a God and a Guidance, — and a good in the world; but who had been hard-used and bewildered, till he was all adrift and could not make it seem to be; but he had not positively denied. In his darkest hour, when, with a seeming blasphemy, he had wished that he might "see that Person," it had been the desperate utterance of a goaded soul, longing instinctively, for the One only possible Redress. The sight of a pure, young, fervent faith had secretly almost assured him of that whereon it rested. The needle turned; there must then, somewhere, be a great Central Pole.

He had never forgotten the old, uncompromising Bible word, invested with such new and gracious meaning, by the sudden insight of a childlike, unseared spirit. It had whispered itself to him in many a moment since, of pain and danger, when, by the stringent call of the hour, he had been "elected" to work that only such as he could do. It had been the leaven of the kingdom lying in his soul; fermenting slowly to the softening of that hardness which was more an outer crust of habit, now, than any deeper induration. There was a place in him to be touched and occupied with a gentle interest; and this young, feeble creature, with her quiet life that showed so little joy, and yet such large, abiding peace, — with its beauty of cheerful labor, — and its sunniness of content, — had reached and held it.

He had been half afraid in his returns from sea, that there might be changes at the old corner. That the little needle-woman with her bright window, her work and her flowers, might be replaced by something common and unlovely. "My little girl," he had got to call her in his thoughts. So far as this, even, the human tenderness had repossessed him.

She would have no right to be gone; she belonged to him by a mysterious, unspoken tenure; yet it might be; it would be like all the rest. This old bitterness tinged his thought as he came homeward; saying nothing of his one secret hope and longing; cherishing it jealously, in silence; bracing himself half resentfully, in advance, against the disappointment and the end of it, that would come sometime, — might come now; wearing so, always, a certain savageness and defiance still, when he neared the home-port and came sailing in. He cheered up again and was grimly jolly, when he had once cast anchor at old Crossman's, and taken a glance around at his bearings, and found the landmarks safe.

"I might have had a child like her," Ned Blackmere said to himself. "I ought to. Was n't I made strong to take care of something like that?"

So he had sat at his window and kept his secret life, and smoked his pipe; and there was this wonderful soul-asking and answering between those two, who, until to-day, neighbors for years, had never interchanged an outward greeting.

"Land alive! Why, Grace, child, what 's happened you?" said Mrs. Hopeley, opening the door and reaching out one hand to help her in, while she hurriedly settled her cap-ribbon with the other, at sight of the "opposite gentleman," as she always called him.

Blackmere somewhat precipitately resigned his charge to the good woman; indeed Grace was aware of a certain quick movement that was not quite like his first gentleness. He was evidently in haste to be off without words.

"Now, of all things!" resumed the voluble house-lady, as he dashed across the street again with only a half-muttered, unintelligible reply to Grace's eagerly begun acknowledgment, — "to think he should go like that, as if a gale of wind had took him, and I never so much as saying 'I 'm beholden,' nor finding out his name to call him by it again! Well, it ain't all in salting tails! You may n't catch the bird no more, notwithstanding!"

"Why, you 've lost your crutch, child, so you have. And to be sure, there 's the opposite gentleman — to think I should n't be able to call him like a Christian after all, and so Christian and more as he 's behaved — a standing on the other corner with the door blowed to and the latch ketched, and no hat on, and the pieces in his hand! Maybe he 'll come back. No! there 's old Crossman, and he 's got in and took 'em, likewise. Well, here 's the amberella."

And so Grace got up stairs. That evening, by the bright light across the way through the heedlessly unshaded window, she saw, as she drew down her own blind, her new-old friend without a name, busy with the splintered bits of her old crutch, trying, evidently, if it would join. But he shook his head over it, and made up his face in the shape of a whistle; and she would not stand watching, so she pulled the cambric shade down, and settled herself behind it at her work, with many little curious thoughts glancing through her mind as to what he might do next.

Early the following morning as Mrs. Hopeley was lighting her fire and brushing up her hearth below, there came a ring. The brisk little body answered it in a twinkling. Yet, quick as she was, the opposite gentleman was ever opposite again, and on the door-stone sat a basket, and beside it a wonderful thing with a crutch-top to it, — Grace's very old crutch-top with the worn black velvet cover, — but such a stick! A slight, dark, rich, strong staff, with queer, delicate carving all up and down it, and a smell of strange spicery clinging to it, and effusing even in the frosty morning air.

"Well, if I ain't conundered, now!" she exclaimed, taking them up with a sudden hesitancy, and a glance toward old Crossman's closed door and the window above it where the curtain *was* down this time.

"Grace, here 's the elegantest thing! Stop, I 'll bring it up to you, and take away the amberella. And a big basket of great oranges as red as fire! You never see sitch! Come all in a whiff and gone again like the what 's-his-name-on-two-sticks!"

There were tears in Grace's eyes as she held the beautiful staff in her hand. Such a thing had never happened to her before in all her life. There was something in her heart as she received this gift dropped for her at her door, such as perhaps never stirred in yours, young lady, on whose table waits each morning some dainty offering of homage, and who count up your bouquets and your lovers together.

She should never lean on this, but it would seem to her like a kindly human strength. She had a friend in the world; there was a thought for her in a great, generous bosom; the world was very rich to-day for this child who had never had father or brother; who would never have a lover.

The basket was to go back. Grace and Mrs. Hopeley decided this, and the girl gathered her flowers, — her one splendid white lily with its golden spike, in the broad green leaf against which it grew, — some tender abutilons, like drops of redder gold, purple heliotropes and little English violets, a tea rosebud, just swelling into its brief perfection, and some trailing bits of yellow blossoming vine, and laid them in it, a mute, delicate thanks.

Mrs. Hopeley hoped great things from the instant in which she should deliver it. For the first time in her life she stood upon her crusty neighbor's doorstone and rung a summons.

The old man came.

"For Mr. ——," hesitating, so that anybody but old Crossman must have suggested a name. But he stood with his sharp nose protruding from a jealous crack, and waited for her to say it out by herself if she could, or give it up. He would have waited a week, morosely revelling in her discomfiture.

"For the opposite — the up-stairs — gentleman, I mean," faltered the poor woman, all of a quiver, and in utter rout.

Crossman grunted and took it in.

"It ain't all in chances, if you can't turn 'em," sighed Mrs. Hopeley to herself, recrossing. "And there 's some old sticks would chock anybody's wheels."

"I 've gin it in; but I don't know who to, howbeit, more nor ever." Mrs. Hopeley's adverbs were her colloquial accomplishment. They effected a certain point and dazzle by their recurrence, like skilful dashes upon printed calico.

After this, things went on as of old. The "other gentleman" as Mrs. Hopeley called him, in her bewildered paucity of knowledge, in contradistinction to the "opposite gentleman," who was more regularly opposite, — *the* gentleman, to Grace's distinctive perception, — came; and the corner room was bright and cheery for many weeks; then, a trunk and two chests were wheeled away, one morning, and the blinds were shut.

Mrs. Hopeley had gone out to market; the opposite gentleman knew this, doubtless; for he came very deliberately, across the street, his pipe in his mouth, and stopped upon the widow's doorstep. Before he rang, Grace, with her light spring, and the quick tapping of her deftly handled crutch, was on the stairs; and as he rang, she opened to him.

"I 'm going away," began the opposite gentleman, and paused.

"It's very good of you —." He lifted his eyes, rather, at this.

"To come and let me say good-by I mean, and thank you," said Grace hurriedly and impetuously, following up the awkward ambiguity of her first words. I have wanted to so much."

"I came to see if you 'd do something for me while I 'm gone," said the neighbor-at-intervals, ignoring the thanks. "I 'd be glad," — if you have n't any disliking to such — that you 'd take care of my parrot for me. She 's lonesome when she 's nobody to talk to."

Grace's eyes glistened with a quick pleasure. Something childlike in it, of pure delight, as well as warm readiness of womanly gratitude. A parrot had been to her childhood a thing of bright, fairy-like mystery. To have it there among her flowers, — to hear its half-human chatter, — to teach it some new phrases, — to stroke its gold-green plumage, and feed it from her fingers as she had watched her friend do, — why it would be a joy, — and she said so.

"Then I'll bring it over."

But coming back, cage in hand, he met Mrs. Hopeley herself, with basket and brown paper parcel.

"Good morning, Mr. ——?"

"Good morning, ma'am. I've brought my parrot for your daughter. She'll keep it for me, she says, if you've no objection. I'm going away."

"Look here, sir!" cried the over-aggrieved woman, bursting forth. "I guess we don't understand one another, clear. She ain't my daughter."

"For Miss —— Grace then," said the strange man, with a sort of difficulty, but never caring a whit as to Grace who. No interchange of facts to be looked for here.

Mrs Hopeley sighed a loud sigh of impatience.

"Oh dear! it was bad enough before; but this is getting to be like the House that Jack built!"

"If it's any trouble —" began the neighbor, quite abashed.

"Lor no, it ain't the parrot. Not in the least. But I'm bound to say I've been put to great inconveniences along of you; and to such roundabouts as is very tiresome. The opposite gentleman was bad enough; but the opposite gentleman's parrot, and all that, why you see it grows bigger. And the kinder you are the more so. And, moreover, after you're gone away, it can't be the opposite gentleman, withal. It's the want of the name, sir. You could n't so much as get the good of a tin dipper without one."

A half smile showed a glimpse of the man's white teeth; while a shade, at the same instant, seemed to flit over the eyes.

"My name's never been a very lucky one," he said, "The bird's name's Poll. Won't that do? And as to the rest of it, I shall be 'opposite' enough. I'm going to China."

He put the bright ring of the cage into Grace's hand, as he spoke, and turned off. Before Mrs. Hopeley could find her next words, he was striding down the street and had mixed himself and disappeared in the busy, crowded, shifting line of pedestrians that streamed up and down, to and from a great centre of labor and trade.

He could not forget that a dozen years ago, the name of Edward Blackmere had been put in capitals and cried through these very streets, as the name of a man "arrested for the brutal murder of his wife."

CHAPTER XXXIV.

OPPOSITE AGAIN; AT THE LESSER DISTANCE.

A YOUNG lady in a crape bonnet and veil, at Mrs. Hopeley's door. A pleasant voice at the stair-head welcoming her, as the door was opened by the cheery widow, and the comer put aside the folds from her face and entered. It was Sarah Gair, come for her "bit of brown bread."

One year ago there had been a little paragraph in the Selport papers, about "one of our most respected citizens." It had been headed "Sudden Death." Jane Gair was a widow.

A widow, with less of worldly fortune than she was allowed to know; for Mr. Gair's property, like that of many a man stricken suddenly down in the midst of business risks and complications, had dwindled in the "settling," and Jane, a confirmed nervous invalid, to whom quiet of mind was vitally essential, was simply to be waited on and provided for, — not burdened with any care or doubt. Reuben Gair's confidential friend and lawyer, consulting only with her young daughter, and making smooth and comfortable reports to the widow, when she was able to attend, managed everything.

There had been two or three unfavorable years; there had been failures and bad debts; losses at sea; Mr. Gair's death had happened, or resulted, at one of those critical points of a mercantile history, when life and credit are everything; when the wheels of a great enterprise are in full and complicated revolution, and, continuing so, may work out safety; but, stopping, there comes ruin. Out of all the merchants' various assets, — including twenty thousand dollars of his wife's inheritance, from the sale of real estate, which had been merged, temporarily, with his business risks, and smaller sums, invested with moneys of his own, in certain high-paying shares, — there was a bare nominal surplus, when debts were paid. The house in Hill Street remained to them; but there was a heavy mortgage upon it, with only two years to run. A present home over their heads, and the interest of some fifteen thousand dollars, remaining to Mrs. Gair, was all.

Plainly, the only thing to be done was to sell their house, pay off the mortgage, add the residue of the money to what they had, and go where they could live upon it. But this could not be done immediately. Mr. Gair had died in the spring; the summer was over before affairs were thoroughly made clear; and the only way to avoid a dangerous shock to the widow was to make her health itself the pretext for removal.

"Next summer we can do it," said Say. "For the winter we must manage somehow."

Summer and winter made a year. Two-thirds of their dividends were absorbed by mortgage interest; and their capital diminished by the cost of their year's living. And all this was a secret pain; an unshared dread and burden.

Sarah Gair came suddenly, in the midst of her bright youth, to know the grinding of that hardest kind of poverty, which is not to be confessed, and grappled with, openly; but which gnaws in secret under a comfortable outside; demanding retrenchment, as the sole salvation, when it is hard to see how an adequate retrenchment can begin. And Mrs. Gair's whims, her invalid comforts, medical attendance and nursing were expensive.

It was well known in the city that "Gair had not left so much as was expected;" but nobody supposed them poor; "*she* had money," they said; and Say was proud; she would not even let the kind aunts at Hilbury know that a piece of the patrimony had melted away; they lived on; her mother must not be worried; and she bore what there was to bear alone.

Her mother had her nurse and lived in her own room; she did not know that there was only a girl hired "for general housework," to help Say in all the rest of the house; and that the delicacies she called for, at capricious hours, according to her uncertain appetite, were mostly prepared by Say's own hands, while she, perhaps, was fretting that she did not stay and read to her, or bring her work and sit where she could see her.

"She was all pain," she said; and possessed with restlessness. The very bed was full, it seemed to her, of misery; when she lay there. It had got into the pillows and blankets, like a plague; it was associated with every line and color on the walls; with the folds of the curtains, and the pattern of the carpet. She had the furniture moved about, and changed, to break the fancy up. She was put into another room, while her own was freshly papered. This had been done twice, already, since her husband's death. There were repetitions in the first designs, that wearied her so. She had got the limit of the block, and knew just where the pattern began again; and the pain, she said, came in twinges with it.

This was Jane Gair at forty-six; who at thirty, had been the fair, unworn, happy-tempered woman, who took all things easily, and for whom the world went smoothly round.

Spring had come round again; the early spring, whose balmy days of promise alternate with chill and storm. Mrs. Gair alternated to better and worse with the weather. Say thought and planned; she could think of nothing but Hilbury; but she had only mentioned it once, and her mother had had a very bad day after it. "She never could go there; the high air of the hills would kill her; she wondered Say thought of such a thing. Could n't they go abroad? She should be better when the warm weather came; and she would get away from this miserable New England climate altogether." Say sighed, and could say no more. What ought she to do? The end must come sometime, and her mother must know; it would be worse then, for there would no longer be anything to save.

When she could get away for an hour, she went for her "bit of brown bread." She had got an hour now.

The day was lovely; a jewel of warmth and sunshine set between bleak jaggednesses of March misery. Grace's window was wide open; there were crocuses, yellow and purple, in the long narrow box upon the ledge; the parrot gyrated incessantly about her cage, clinging with clumsy beak and claw, and "picking her way," literally, with slow creep, up and down, and around; chattering, like a saucy child, all the phrases that she knew; whistling to the boys in the street; crying, like the "thousand cats;" comporting herself, altogether, with the utmost self-assertion and obstreperousness.

"My — good — friend! How dy'e do? Thank you! thank you! Gone to China! Welcome home! What's your name? What's your name" The last query had been wickedly put into the bird's mouth by the baffled Mistress Hopeley, greatly to the chagrin and trouble of Grace, who had striven in vain to make her drop and forget it.

Say sat down, in the sunshine, among the flowers. A look of rest came over her face. A very sweet face it had grown to be, though a little of the old brightness was somehow gone. She had used to seem like nothing so much as a flower springing to a breeze; there were such quick, little, graceful tossings of the well poised head, such slight, incessant motions of life and gladness, in which the fairness of feature and lovely coloring gleamed like that beauty of a wind-swayed blossom. Now, there was a quietness; an endurance; the patient look of womanhood with its burden on. Looking at the young creature, you felt that the first glow of youth, that mostly goes quickly enough, was already gone from her.

"I'm glad to get here, Grace. You don't know the comfort it is. How sunny you are, to-day!"

"Are n't we? It's sunny all down the street to where the trees are budding to make my summer 'view' again. Is n't it bright and sunny over the way? It's only at this time in the day that it ever really is. And the blinds are opened. He's coming back, Say!"

"How much you think of that strange friend of yours, Grace!"

"I have n't many friends, you know. And only to think of one that is a real friend, living anywhere on the earth, with a thought for me,—it's a great joy! I think it is a way God gives His own love to us."

"Just twice he has spoken to you. And then he went away, and has been gone a year. It's a queer friendship, Gracie."

"It is just the friendship that does me the most good. I don't think I could quite bear having a very good friend near me all the time, like people who have been used to it. A little lasts me a great while; and I want my quiet thoughts about it. It's like those weeks at Hilbury. I don't think I could have borne much more. I wanted to run back here to my little lonely nest, with the treasure I had got. I don't know what I shall ever do about heaven, Say!"

"I'm glad you've had Hilbury," said Say. "I knew Aunt Joanna would remember. I wish I could see her in her home; but I don't know when I shall ever get there, now."

"It's as lovely as anything can be," said Grace. "And we had such busy work to make it! There was nearly everything to do; for there'd only been common tidiness for years and years; nobody to really put a life into it till she came. And it kept smiling out so, with every new thing and touch; and yet, the old home expression stayed through all. 'It was the glorified body of the old home,' Mr. Hartshorne said. Such a grand man and woman as they are! They would glorify any place. And each of them thinks it is all the other. I'm only puzzled to think how they endure such happiness, when it nearly broke my heart to stay and see it. It's well there are still places for such as I, who can't bear being too glad."

"Grace! — Oh, Miss Gair! I beg your pardon. I forgot, indeed. My head's been so full of the spring cleaning, which is just the most muddling-up thing in the world, indubitably."

"Did you want me, Mrs. Hopeley?" asked Grace.

"It was only the old carpet. It's been shuck and brought in, and it's tore rather more than I looked for. I thought if you were n't too busy, peradventure, — but I see you can't."

"Oh, Mrs. Hopeley! it is n't that I'm very busy, — but let it be till to-morrow, please. It's sure to rain after this pleasant weather; and we must be in the window to-day, Polly and I, when our friend comes back. I'm sure it's all the getting home there is for him."

"You're sure of the most unprovable sort of things, Grace Lowder, forevermore," said the widow in her cheery way, coming over to the girl's side. "There's some bird in the air besides Polly that tells you stories, with neither a for nor a because to them. The carpet 's nothing, to be sure; it can wait as well as not, for a rainy day, only — well, now! as true as I'm a living sinner!"

"Gone to China! Welcome home! Thank you, thank you! What's your name? What's your name?"

Edward Blackmere stood upon the step of Crossman's door. He looked up, giving a low, familiar whistle, whereto the parrot responded with vociferation.

"Grace!" cried Say, shrinking back suddenly into her chair, "is that —— ?"

"That is my friend," said Grace, with simple, joyous warmth; her beaming face turned full toward him, with a timid inclination of the head, to which he answered with a chivalrous lifting of his cap, and a flash of soft, unused light in the dark, upraised eyes. They were gray hairs he uncovered, saluting the young girl; but the instant, happy look was new and young as hers.

Say, by a quick motion, let fall the folds of crape, to shield her side-face from the sunlight.

"And there," said Grace, still looking out, "is *his* friend, the gentleman."

Say glanced again, and saw that it was Gershom Vorse.

Nearly four years it had been since she had seen him. It gave her a quick, bewildering sensation, seeing him now and in such manner. Like that which one has at times, at sudden waking from a reverie, in which familiar things have been resolved to their ideal forms; in which one's actual surroundings have been the impalpable scenery of one's dreams; when, with a flash, one starts to find them real and at hand.

From her inner life he had never been absent. She had waited with that strange patience that only women, and, of women, perhaps a few, not all, abide in; putting by the hope that had never, indeed, been born; nerved on one side, by a human, feminine indignation, against weakness of sorrow; feeling that she had been unjustly dealt with; half cured of her love, or the sting of it, by a tender contempt of the warp and prejudice that had wounded it, and that must, sometime, be done away; of the soul that could so be narrowed by mistake; a little of her reverence, which is the essence of pure womanly passion, gone from her thought of him whom she saw not nobly reverent and believing toward heaven and fellow-men, — for a woman ever most warmly reveres, most nearly worships, the manhood that stands lowliest before God; yet looking always onward to something that, in the long history of their lives, here or in heaven, should surely come; knowing that they were not done with each other until God willed, and that the crooked should first be made straight, and that which she had prayed for, she should be given to do.

A strange, still excitement stirred her, looking down upon him,— herself unseen, unthought of, — claiming him in her heart, from these neighbors who talked of and guessed about him, not knowing even his name. This was his home then. This was his fixed, separate life, and the place of it? A pang came with that thought. A jealousy of people who had to do with him, she being shut out. Of old Crossman even, who opened the door to him, and to whom he nodded as he went in. He was set off suddenly, into a strangerhood. He was wholly gone away from her, — from them all. Gone away utterly, though making for himself an abiding place here in the same town, with the distance of only a few streets between them; a distance he had never crossed to come to her.

A chill began to come over her; over her old feeling for him, close, even, upon the first quick, warm tremble of surprise. She had not dreamed of this. She had thought of him on board his ship, — away in foreign lands, — at the farm in Hilbury; the old memories had held their places, and the old scenes were haunted. But this new place, — these altered surroundings, — this strange, isolated, secret living? It made a difference. It touched rudely upon the old charm. Place and association have curiously to do with human sentiments. Seeing him here, it was possible to see him in a new light; to discern more sharply that to which his character had grown. His very way of life, when it was a thing for him to choose, had become an embodied distrust. It was unworthy. Say felt a something widening between them that was worse than time, or distance, or mistake. Felt this with one side her nature, that recoiled from one side his, even while the old tenderness claimed him jealously, yearned over him, wrought itself into a very pain of unrest, seeing him so near again, and yet so far, far off.

Five minutes had gone by while she sat and thought these thoughts. And then Grace Lowder turned her happy face round on her. And saw nothing. Only a tired, troubled look; a flush replacing the first paleness; and a restless shine in the eyes.

"I've been selfish; tell me your worries."

She turned wholly round as she spoke; and reaching her hand along the wainscot, dropped herself off the little raised window-dais to Say's side.

"Tell me your worries, dear."

"It's no use," said Say, with a piteous, half-absent impatience. "They can't be told. Unless I could tell you all my life, and what makes them worries."

"All our lives we can't tell each other if we would. Every one of us is a secret after all. But the little bits we can tell, — they are comforts between friends."

"I can't tell you the last ten minutes, Grace, and what has come to me sitting here beside you."

Come to her in her thoughts, of course, while Grace had selfishly kept her waiting; nothing else had come to her; no other possibility entered the little needlewoman's mind. So secret, truly, are our lives.

"Tell me just what you choose, dear. Tell me nothing if you like. But let me comfort you." So she petted and soothed her, mutely, and stroked her like a tired child, holding down her head beside her, but not looking her any more in the face, till the tears came quietly into Say's restless eyes, and brought their sorrowful calm with them.

"I must go back to my mother," she said, and rose up, brushing the wet off her cheeks, and laying hold of the long crape veil to draw it down.

She felt as if she had cheated Grace of something that belonged to her. Of this knowledge that she could have given her. But then a bitter, unreasonable feeling came, — of what did Grace cheat her? What, rather, usurp from her, — sitting there in her window, among her flowers, and making friends across the way? Seeing them come out and in, — him and Gershom, — while she must go and make no sign; she, to whom they belonged by the thought and knowledge of years, — by the love of a life?

Gershom Vorse saw a figure, thick-veiled, robed in black, — come down the widow's step and turn away, quickly. An employer of the little seamstress, Blackmere's window-friend, he thought. Come to order more black bravery. "What a parade grief makes to hide itself behind! What a bother of stitches to sew up a heart-rent! If people really believed half they pretend to, — humph!" Mostly to himself, the last syllable only aloud the cynic said this; and the black-robed figure passed on, out of sight; the heart carried a thought of him in it, — a thought of pain, — as it had carried this many a year. And no little bird flew by, to tell him so.

CHAPTER XXXV.

EBEN'S DISCOURSE.

Some one had already rung, and was waiting, when Say came up the steps in Hill Street.

A tall, rough man in a snuff-brown country suit, and a snuffier brown stiff felt hat; who made room for her as she came beside him, and eyed her curiously. Say had her latch-key; it would not do to call Honey unnecessarily to the door. She made her own entrance; and then turned round inquiringly.

Either for the act, announcing herself at home, or from the putting back of her veil, giving him a better sight of her face, the stranger showed a sudden recognition. He thrust forth a hand, bare and brown as everything else about him.

"'*Tis* Say! I'll be — (buttered," in a whisper,) "if it ain't!"

"I'm not sure, — I don't know, —" hesitated Say, a little frightened, drawing back.

"Who I be? S'pose likely you don't. I did n't *recognize* you, at the first go off. You've growed, 'n I'm altered, some. Look again though, 'n I guess you'll fetch it!"

"Eben!"

"Ezer. That's it, pat as Yankee Doodle. Mother to home?"

"Come in, Eben. Mother's at home; but she never sees company. She's very feeble."

"Sho! used to be hearty enough. Guess she'll see me, though, when you tell her. Say I've come clear from Illinois, round by way 'o Hilbury. That'll fetch her."

Say's eyes opened wide at the man's manner. She ushered him in with dignity.

"I'll tell her," she said, in a tone that set aside further discussion and explanation.

She returned after some minutes, with the same quiet, unmoved air, to say to him without apparent admission of anything to be wondered at, that which did, secretly, most profoundly astonish herself.

"Mother will see you up-stairs in about half an hour."

"Whew!" Eben whistled. "Folks don't think much 'o half hours more 'n 'o half dollars, here 'n the city, 't seems!"

Say took no notice. If he had come differently, she would have had a hundred things to say to Eben, associated as he was with her childish remembrances and pleasures; to ask of Huldah; and of their western home. It was not pride, or forgetfulness; but it was the confident assertion of this man's presence, here, after such an interval of years; it was the almost insult, with which he seemed to imply that her mother would have no choice but to see him at his demand; her mother, who saw nobody; whom nobody ventured, for a moment, to disturb. It was a dark significance behind all this, which touched upon, and joined itself to those secret, terrible, vague thoughts of something that made Hilbury terrible to her mother; something which Aunt Prue suspected; a thing the clear knowledge of which she herself shrunk from, with a pain of apprehension; yet the knowledge of which she felt was sure to come; a thing that hers was, somehow, at last, to be the hand to lay hold of; to set right.

"You can look at the books, if you please;" she said, and went away.

Eben was shrewd enough to understand.

"'Taint her fault," he said, as he was left alone. "No wonder her grit 's up. It's clear sarciness to her — Well — I'm let in; and she 'll see me; I know now, I'm right; and, by Davy Crockett, I'll go ahead!"

"I'm very ill, Eben, and can bear very little; but I could n't refuse an old friend."

Jane Gair, sitting in her invalid chair, with her invalid gown and cap on, said this, as Eben Hatch came in with Say. She had sent her nurse down after being made ready, telling her she might, if she chose, go out for a turn in the fresh air while she sat up; Say would be with her.

Now, she gave Say an errand to the cook. There was to be a partridge broiled for her; and she would like some wine-jelly made. These things involved more than direction, as Jane knew. She was left alone with her odd visitor.

"How is Huldah, Eben? And where is she?"

"She 's in Hilbury, at this present speaking; but that ain't the business in hand. I don't mean to worry you about *my* affairs."

Jane Gair leaned back languidly. But her eyes were keen with questioning, as she turned them upon Eben.

"Have you any special errand to me?" she asked.

"Yes, marm. I've got sunthin' to say. A short discourse, with only two pints to it. A head an' a tail."

All but her eyes expressed the utmost quiet and lassitude. Her whole figure lay passive. Her face had the weary look of long weakness and pain. But the eyes fixed themselves, with a sharp kindling in them, on the man's face.

"It's only this, Mis' Gair, — the head of it. Them that hides can find. And they'd better be spry."

"I don't understand you in the least." Jane Gair spoke slowly, after a pause; her tone was the tone of uncomprehending, slightly surprised, indifference; but the fire in the eyes flared.

"An' I come across sunthin' to'ther day, that struck me up with a new start. 'The Lord will bring to light the hidden things of darkness.' Fust C'rinthians, fourth, fifth. *He* says so. And He mostly fetches it! That's the tail!"

The eyes blenched and the lids fell. There was a twitching of the muscles that she could not help. She sat there quivering inwardly with a detected shame. Eben never took his look from her; and she knew it.

Presently she leaned forward, with a quick anger in her movement, and raised her face again; angry, also, now.

"I think you're crazy, Ebenezer Hatch." Spoken quite quietly; the anger only in face and motion. The woman was half controlled; half self-betrayed.

"No, you don't. You did n't say that quick enough. An' I would n't talk any more, jest now. 'Taint good for you. I guess the best thing you could do would be to go to Hilbury, by'm-bye. You might get hold o' sunthin' there to your advantage — besides country air."

"Is this all you have to say?" It was an effort at dignity; but the cowering of the soul trembled in the tones.

"Yes, marm. Head, an' tail, an' application. Meetin's out." He rose and buttoned up the snuff-brown coat, and stood twirling by the rim the snuff-brown hat.

"It is nothing to me. You are either crazy or mistaken."

"Come, now! That air won't do!" said Eben, with the same drawl of imperturbability that he had all along maintained; seating himself, again, with arms across his knees, twirling the hat between them, in his hands; his head leaned forward, and his face turned confidentially toward Mrs. Gair.

"I've either told you the livin' truth, yer know; an' your conscience says the same; or else I've sarced you within an inch o' your life, an' that air bell's ben rung, an' I'm bein' turned out on the sidewalk; which don't appear. Now, yer see, I might ha' begun at t'other end; and worked it back to you; which might n't ha' ben pleasant; but I thought I'd take it reg'lar, an' begin at the beginnin.' Mebbe '*t was* a mistake, though. It's hard to ravel a stockin' the same way 't was knit. — Old Parson Fairbrother kep' a journal." He went on, meditatively, twirling the hat, and taking his eyes away from Jane, to fix them thoughtfully on the carpet between his feet. "With some view to the chance of a Me-more. An' them kind o' journals is allers full o' reflections. I don't spose he did nothin' athout moralizin' over it. Sunthin' in this fashion, likers not, 'June 27th, 18—. Advised an' strengthened Brother G. in a just act. Set my hand to it, with him. By the promptin' o' the Lord, the widder an' the fatherless are pervided for.' 'N so on. It 's an improvin' thing to look it over, seein 't the Me-more aint writ yet, nor like to be. An' Parson King, he 's got it. I don't mind lettin' out that much," raising his head, and glancing quickly at Jane's face. "'Taint stirred yet; but there 's where the light's ben throwed. An' the nex' thing's another rummage. Bindin' on you, an' me, an' Huldy. 'Cause *we* know that that air paper that 's never come to light, hed the Parson's name to it, as well as Huldy's an' mine. An' then, whatever 't was, 't was hid away in the old cubbard, for awhile, at least. You, an' I, an' Huldy, knows that. Or else, what was it waitin', unlocked and open for, that night, yer see? An' the Doctor allers kep' his keys, an' nobody meddled with his things or places; as Mis' Vorse said that day when you was up there, lookin'; Priscill' heerd it; and she named it to Huldy; she thinks it 's a chance ef 't was ever opened agin from then to the day of his death. 'Twarnt a large family, an' there warnt many comers and goers; an' it 's easy askin.' I 've got that fur; it ' a tollable strong thread; an' the toe 's started; I guess 't 'll ravel, when we once begin!"

The long speech had given Mrs. Gair time to think — to collect herself. It is not impossible that Eben's shrewdness went far enough to intend this.

He had begun to ravel. Her only alternative was to help. It was no policy for her, now, to wait; to let things take their course; to let them find what they could, or leave it undiscovered. The longer the delay, the greater the difficulty, the further she would be implicated in the investigation; the more closely circumstances would be recalled and weighed; everybody would come to know that she had been "up and round," that miserable night; how much more, depended upon Eben's counter-espial and forbearance; everybody would know that she alone had had access, since, to the place where the will had been found, and the missing paper had undoubtedly been laid away. None of these things would do.

She was quite calm, and ready with wise answer, when Eben finished speaking.

"You are altogether mistaken," she repeated. "You have

come here taking a wrong tone; an utterly unjustifiable one. If there is any written evidence of my father's wishes which has not come to light, no one can be more interested than I to find it and follow it out. I shall be in Hilbury this summer; it has been advised. I shall do what I can, acting upon your statement; provided, that is, that you refrain in future from such intimations as you have made to-day. They would only put a complete stop to any efforts on my part; I should owe it to my own self-respect to remain passive."

A very fair and clever position, this, that Jane Gair took; she actually felt it genuine, for the moment. People have two sets of attitudes that they stand in. There was quite another, grown familiar to her, that she should cower into presently, confronted only with truth and her own soul.

"I 'm agreeable," returned Eben, with the same undisturbed air of equanimity, "It's as good a way o' puttin' it as any other's fur's I'm concerned. We understand one another, — 'n that's the main thing."

Mrs. Gair passed over the under-significance of this.

"I must say, however," she returned, "that it seems very strange to me that you should rouse up on this matter again, at this late day. You have let it wait your own convenience, it seems. We had every reason to suppose that all possible search had been made at the time you first mentioned it; and that you, as well as we, were convinced that it had been a mistake."

"No, marm! I never was convinced. But I could n't help it. I was a poor man, out there in the prairies, an' no great hand at a pen, an' no way o' gittin' at circumstances, or provin' what I thought I knew. But I knew 't was bindin' — solemn — on me to fetch it some time! Or else, what 's a witness fur? Folks that makes nothin' o' signin' their names, every day o' their lives, to they dunno what, may n't feel it so; but when I put Ebenezer Hatch to that air dockyment, I made it a business o' mine afore the Lord, to see it threw, ef I could! 'T is had to lay by; I 've been hendered; but I haint lost sight of it, never. An' in consequence, here we are, Mis' Gair!"

"And your own legacy, — your five hundred dollars, Mr. Hatch? You have thought of that, perhaps, and how it might stand affected?"

"Yes, marm! The fust five hunderd I made arter I cleared my farm, an' begun to realize sunthin, I laid by in the Graysonville Bank, and there it lays; int'rest 'n all; I 'v ben ready for a reckonin' any time this ten year!"

Say came in with her mother's dinner-tray. A delicate broiled partridge, and a glass of warm, liquid wine jelly, just made, translucent as amber. To be eaten and sipped with such appetite as might be.

Eben Hatch took his departure.

"'*T was* sharp an' sudden on her; an' thunderin' sarcy, no mistake! But there warn't no other way," he said to himself, walking down Hill Street, with his hands in his pockets. "It 's laid hard on me, too! 'T warn't fer nothin' that the hendrances was took away. Well, a feller can't allers fetch everything in this world!"

Three little broken threads of life — ended in three small graves — were in the honest fellow's thought. Great drops stood in his eyes with which the March wind had nothing to do.

CHAPTER XXXVI.

MRS. GAIR MAKES UP HER MIND TO BE EQUAL TO IT.

WAS this Jane Gair's punishment, — come suddenly? — Her sin and its defeat, bearing down on her at once, force closing in around her and compelling her to restitution, — now that this Yankee honesty was on her track?

Her punishment had been upon her for long years. She had laid away a thing that she would not look at, in her soul, but it festered. She had been restless with she knew not what goadings; ashamed and afraid with a secret torment and terror; undecided with a hesitancy that unhinged her nerves, and sent a trembling of pain into every one, till it fastened itself upon her, so, and made her the helpless, diseased, unhappy thing she had become. She had had hypochrondriac fancies; she had wondered, lying by her husband's side, whether she ever talked in her sleep. She had been afraid she might sometime have a fever, and in delirium go over again and betray her knowledge and her deed. She had had her repentances; moments when God came near her in some way, and His truth admonished her; when she had almost resolved to *go and find this thing out.* She had even tried once; when Say lay ill — dying, she thought — at Hilbury, she had one day climbed again to this old cupboard; making errand of some grandmother's recipe that might be there. The letter-case was gone; it had been taken away and put elsewhere; she dared not ask for it. Say got better and her purpose was put by.

The husband of her youth had died; she had been smitten with the separate sorrow of widowhood. They had come to her with words of comfort; of faith in a continued spiritual companionship; she had shuddered; she would rather think of him who had truly had the love of her life, as gone utterly, than that he should look upon her now to know her soul. For he had been an honest man.

She shrank from her young, pure daughter. She thought of the time that might come when she should not dare to die without confessing to this child, and leaving reparation in her hands. She was afraid of the conscience-weakness that might overbear her. This was her other attitude, — before her secret soul and the truth of Heaven.

"I will repay, saith the Lord." And verily He doth repay.

It was hardly strange that now, after the first startle of Eben's unscrupulous attack, her predominant feeling should be that of absolute relief. She might openly make search again; she must; that question was decided for her; she might,— she must,— assist in the general endeavor to make clear this doubt newly arisen; the load was to be thrown from her conscience; things had worked for the best after all, and she had managed Eben shrewdly. For the money, what did she care for it now? Full of pain and discomfort, her life circumscribed by a sick-room; lonely, disappointed of all she had so striven for. She might as well be honest as not, and lie down in her grave with a clear conscience. But this was all in the fine soul-type. She only confessed to herself that she was quite satisfied with the turn things were taking, and thankful; she had never felt quite easy about the will; she would be glad to have justice done; if that paper still existed, she would do her utmost now to help the finding of it.

And so she greatly astonished Say, a few days after Eben's visit, by declaring that she had made up her mind, when the warm weather should have fairly come, to try Hilbury again.

Weeks hence she would do justice. Justice that a word, one self-humiliating word, might do to-day. Weeks hence, and she a feeble, pain-stricken woman, who could not count upon the strength of an hour.

Say wrote to Hilbury, and the days of spring wore on and softened into early summer.

Mrs. Gair seemed wonderfully better for the time; so much so that Mr Brinley, the lawyer, judged it best at last to say something to prepare her for the necessity of permanently altered plans.

He approached his subject cautiously.

"You must find this neighborhood grown very noisy, for an invalid, Mrs. Gair. Lower down, I see, they are already converting dwelling-houses into stores. The tide will creep up here at last. Has it ever occurred to you that you might sell to advantage, and find a quieter home?"

"I'm not equal to having anything occur to me, Mr. Brinley," the widow replied, with a feeble surprise and petulance. "Don't put anything in my head; for I can't bear it."

"It is difficult for me to judge how to act," said the gentleman, with a slight annoyance. "I must think for your interest. And if you could only bear a little business — it might be greatly better for you in the end."

"I don't care for business. All I want is my room, and my nurse, and the little bits I need, and not to be worried."

"You are much stronger than you were, I think."

"I'm better able to bear being alive; that's all."

"No doubt the country air will do great things for you. Mrs. Gair, don't you think you might be better to make your home in the country, altogether?"

"My gracious! Mr. Brinley, what *can* you be thinking of?"

"I'm thinking," he replied, driven desperate and feeling that his duty must be done,— "that your income would go further, so; and — this house, well — the fact is, Mrs. Gair — it is n't wholly unincumbered, you know."

Mrs. Gair sat upright, the invalid air and tone displaced by an angry surprise.

"My husband's will directed that the old mortgage should be paid off, and the property secured to me for my life!"

"Just so; but — my dear lady — it could n't be done! Not from *his* property."

Mr. Brinley put his right leg over his left knee, and gently wagged his foot from the ankle. This was the extreme of outward agitation he ever allowed himself in.

"Do you mean to tell me ——?"

"I mean to tell you only what you can safely bear to hear. But it would be best if you could hear the whole."

"I *will* hear the whole! Mr. Brinley, you have not used me well! How much have you been keeping back?"

Jane Gair spoke with strong, quick, indignant determination. For the instant, she was galvanized to a full strength.

Mr. Brinley was a bachelor. He did not know much about women, and he was quite misled. Thankful, also, to have this, at last, demanded of him.

"My dear Mrs. Gair, you have been very ill; and there was no need to trouble you before. Now, the question comes up, and it becomes my duty to advise you to part with this estate, and to make some other plan as to your own future residence. In this connection, it is my unpleasant duty also to say that you will have little beyond your own property to depend upon."

"I don't believe it! Only forty" — thousand dollars, she was going to say. A hard thing, even this, for a woman to come suddenly to know, who had believed herself possessed at least of five times that amount.

"We will leave particulars till another time, dear Madam," said Mr. Brinley, interrupting her.

He did not dare to tell the whole, even now. To announce to her how even her own inheritance had dwindled down.

Jane Gair did not dare to hear. She turned suddenly pale about the lips; there was no color elsewhere in her poor face to fade. She fell back, trembling, against her chair. Mr. Brinley brought her hastily some water and rang the bell. The nurse came in, looking forked lightnings. The lawyer took himself disconcertedly off.

After-questions upon an after-day he dodged as only a lawyer can.

"Transfer of stocks, rise in values, hopes to realize, — impossible to say just now how everything might turn out — do all that was practicable for her advantage — let her know from time to time, — &c., &c."

Somehow, he kept her quiet. Partly because of her own weak fear to face the truth.

But, the paper? The justice she was to help to do?

The secret conflicting agony began again.

She began to hope, to think, sometimes again, that the writing never would be found. They would all search. There should be "another rummage," as Eben had said, but it might end as the first had done. Could she help that?"

She meant, would it *appear* that she could have helped it?

Eben might do his worst. What then? She had gone down stairs one night, seventeen years ago, to get for Say a glass of water. She remembered it well. She had opened the old cupboard once, and hunted out a hidden volume there that she had wanted. Very well; what could anybody make of it? She had never touched the paper, that she knew of. If there were anything there in the old case that had not been discovered, it had been none of her hiding. It might come to light as soon or as late as ever it pleased.

As *what* pleased?

A vague thought of something — not blind, unconscious — ruling among earthly happenings, struck athwart her inner sense with a shudder. She dared not look that way.

She wished she had never promised to go to Hilbury at all. It was a horribly nervous business. She began to feel herself worse. She blamed Say for taking her so quickly at her word. She knew, they all knew, that the mountain air was like death to her. Well, they might finish her up, among them, and that would be the end. Say would have had her own way, and would be satisfied, perhaps.

Through such pain as this Say had to struggle, doing bravely with all her little strength what she knew was truly best for her sick, wearying, reproachful mother.

And the June days came.

CHAPTER XXXVII.

TO-MORROW.

I MUST stop here to tell you a little more exactly how the old house at Hilbury was built. I don't like, myself, to get lost among imaginary architecture, which won't stay placed, and which perpetually violates the unities. I like to have things clear before me, mentally.

The farmhouse had an extended front, divided midway by the entrance, passage, and staircase you have heard of. Below on one side was one large room, of sufficiently generous proportions to hold comfortably any possible New England Thanksgiving family party and all its merriment. On the other side, occupying the front, was the parlor, behind which the Doctor's study and certain closets intervened between it and the spacious kitchen. Something of this I told you long ago.

Up stairs there were two rooms on each side. On the left, opening from the stair landing and running from the kitchen chamber to the front, the oblong "dimity" room, where Jane and Say had slept seventeen years ago this very June, whence Jane had gone for the drink of water, and Say had listened and heard the earthquake. Still to the left beyond, in the southerly corner, separated by a long, narrow closet, and opening only into the kitchen-chamber at the head of the "end staircase," was what had been Joanna's room; occupied now, for the sake of the same telegraph of sympathy from gable to gable of the two neighboring homes, — by Rebecca. On the right the space was divided by a partitioning precisely at right angles with this last; the chambers corresponding to the situation of the rooms below. In front, with pleasant southeasterly aspect, that which had been the Doctor's, hung with chintz of buff and brown. Behind, connected by a closet entrance, and opening also to the kitchen-chamber and the entry landing, the "red-room," where Say had enjoyed and suffered. The long kitchen-chamber, with southwest end cut off, giving space for stairway, clothes-room, and Rebecca's old, cheery bedroom, where the cherry-tree came in,—ran along the rear of all, occupying the remainder of the building. Now you have it, I think, drawn out as a house should be, wherein you follow events of seventeen years.

When Jane arrived at dusk, with her daughter, and her nurse, and her trunks, and her reclining chair, and her baths, in and upon a special stagecoach from the Bridge, she was too tired to think or choose, or say a word. It was not until Mrs. Karcher was helping her into bed, and the buff-brown hangings were pushed back upon the side to give her entrance, that a sudden horrified recollection seized her, and an invisible force seemed to thrust her away.

To rest there! She saw a vision of white locks upon the pillow; of dim, imploring eyes that met her own; of lips that moved with a mute signing,—"There!"

"I can't—!" she gasped out, and fell forward as she said so, her arms thrown out across the bed. Mrs. Karcher iust went round and took her by the shoulders and turned her over, and drew her fairly on.

"The tantrums of her!" she ejaculated, finding her white, faint, and unheeding.

Rebecca came in.

Together they lifted her into a right position; and brought water and restoratives.

"Are you better, dear?" Rebecca asked, when the closed eyes reopened.

"I don't know. Where am I? What did I do?—Oh!"

"With a quick scream, she flung herself up to her elbow, out of their hands.

"I can't—I won't—it is cruel!—What did you put me here for?"

"Don't you like it? We thought it was better. Mrs. Karcher would be close by, in the red-room; and the dimity bedroom is for Say. You would be all together. It seemed to be the only thing."

"And the *cheer*, and the tubs, and the bottles, and everything, just got out and put handy! And I without a foot to stand on!" The poor nurse spoke despairingly in a low tone, to Miss Gayworthy.

"I think you must stay here to-night. You're not able to be moved."

"I am able! And I will not! Take me into the red-room."

The white lips twitched. It might be worse to persist than to let her have her way. They held her up, one at each side, and helped her slowly along, into the red-room; and got her into bed.

The faintness passed off then, and the look of life came back. But with the life came pain again. A fearful nervous agony in every limb. They stood over her and bathed, and rubbed, and gave her soothing drops.

By-and-by she quieted; and from pure exhaustion fell asleep.

"Lord save us from such another day!" sighed Mrs. Karcher wearily, dragging herself off at last, to her own uncertain rest.

Jane slept into the midnight.

Then she awoke stark, staring; alone in utter stillness.

To think.

To see the flicker of faint light through the closet door-way, from the night-lamp set upon the hearth in the room beyond.

To fancy the room in that sick glimmer; and the canopied bed; to find it impossible to picture Mrs. Karcher there its occupant; to be able to think of nothing but the white hair, the dim, asking eyes the tremulous-moving lips; to fix her imagination helplessly upon these, till they drew her with a fearful magnetism of reality.

"Daughter!"

The very tone was in her ears.

She knew it was a fancy; but if she did not go and see, it would haunt and summon her till she felt she should go wild. It was, worse here, with that door open and that sick-room gleam, and all else hid, than it would have been to stay there. She almost dreaded, in her overwrought excitement, that if she did not rise and go, her father's phantom-shape would glide from the dim room and come to her. She *should* go wild!

She was afraid she should scream out, and lose all self-control. She had been afraid of this, sometimes, before. She set her teeth, and clenched her hands. A strange shiver ran along her limbs.

She could lie there and endure no longer. At the risk of bringing back that horrible pain, she must get up, and go and see. She slid from under the bedclothes, and stood upon the floor. Noiselessly; lest Mrs. Karcher,— (she knew it was Mrs. Karcher, and no one else,— she kept saying it over,—yet she could not place her there, in the canopied bed in that next room; she could only see the old face, and the white hair, and the lips that whispered, "Daughter!") —lest Mrs. Karcher should hear, and come to her and put her back to bed again. And that threshold she *must* cross.

Was her mind going? Should she, if she once let go this clench of hands and teeth,— this clench of thought that for years had held a thing it would not unclasp to look at,—go shrieking it all out together, through the house,—a madwoman?

It was almost upon her.

How the shadows flickered as the lamp flared in the breath through the doorway! They were like things alive!

Was this room full of *guilt*, haunting and mocking her, as the room at home had been of *pain?* Had it clung there to the very walls, the breath of her old unspoken deceit, to wait for her?

"*Mrs. Karcher!*"

"The mercy!" The nurse sat bolt upright in bed.

"I must come to bed to you. I cannot stay alone. I'm —— nervous!" The word came with a low tremble of horror, through teeth clenched again.

Mrs. Karcher flung back the bedclothes, and the figure cowered and trembled in. Laid itself, cold and rigid at her side, as something might that should go wandering at midnight, and come back into a grave.

Mrs. Karcher, providentially, was not nervous. She was kindly and patient; overworked and overtired, sometimes, as humans must be.

"We'll see to this to-morrow. Lie still, now, and go to sleep," she said, coming close to give of her own abundant vital warmth, and rubbing the poor, chilled hands.

"Yes. To-morrow. We *will* see to it, to-morrow." There were separate thoughts in the two minds.

Jane Gair lay, growing calmer, outwardly; and thinking she would see to it all to-morrow. Borrowing a little peace, or stilling a little, a great torment, so.

And the gray, easterly light began to creep up against the windows. To-morrow was almost come.

"Rub my hands again. They feel so strangely."

It seemed to Nurse Karcher that she had just done rubbing, and shut her eyes, when Jane said this, an hour later.

"They're numb. I think they're gone asleep."

"You must have laid uncomfortable; and stopped the circulation."

"Rub! do rub!"

So she rubbed; and fell asleep rubbing; and Jane slept too; or some other stillness came over her.

It was broad day when the over-taxed nurse awoke. She raised herself, very gently, to look at her patient.

"Oh, my gracious God!"

There was life in the wide-open eyes; a terrible agonized life; all else — limbs and features — lay dead. There was a look of striving; a helpless, inarticulate sound came from between the lips, where the tongue lolled incapable.

Mrs. Karcher had seen it before; she knew it at first glance. Paralysis.

Here, in the very spot where her old father had lain; where she had watched, with a hard purpose of not knowing what she *would* not know, his pleading eyes, his striving lips; here, where who knows what agony of late repentance had come to her, in these hours of fear, that she could never tell nor evidence now, — the hand of God was laid upon her.

She might live, and lie here, days, in this mortal nightmare; none could know. Brain and heart beat on, alive; but she never should make utterance or motion, more.

She must live, so, and look, out of those agonized eyes, whose beseeching none might answer, on the scene of her silent sin.

She must go out of the world bearing with her, for her curse, the secret that struggled at the last within her, and anguished to reveal itself; but that God, who had had long patience, now laid His finger on her lips, forbidding her to speak.

She had "done nothing." She had "waited." She must do nothing, now. She must go away; and wait. It was her Retribution.

CHAPTER XXXVIII.

SEEKING.

"I KNOW she *wanted* something," Say said, grievingly and repeatedly.

That last, longing look, — denied speech, — from how many deathbeds has it come up, — to how many sorrowing hearts has it returned like a vision, haunting with something that was "wanted," and could never be asked for or explained.

But this, — it had not been the look of a moment, merely; of the last instant, when voice and motion fail, and the infinite yearning of all that is left unspoken, surges up with the latest flash of soul-presence, from under the fluttering lids. It had been an agony of days. It had painted itself upon Say's mental vision, displacing all other recollection of her mother's face. She could not think of her as she had been in health; she could not force her thoughts to picture her as she lay at last, stilled to the long sleep. Up, through the closed lid — the heaped-up grave even — struggled that wild imploringness of wide-open, conscious eyes. She could not think of her *at rest.* There are other hauntings, and more real, of the perturbed soul that goes unshriven, than the spectral wanderings of the old tales. The child knew that her mother had not gone to rest; that a spirit-urging was upon herself; that a something had been left undone, which she, God guiding her, must do.

Every hard, reproachful thought — if she had ever harbored such, in her pain, in time past — of the unknown thing that had lain between her mother and Aunt Prue, whereof Aunt Prue had made such seathing charge, was gone, — changed utterly. She "knew her mother wanted something." If she could have signed or spoken! There was something she would have told to Say. If for a moment, the child was left alone at her bedside, the yearning look, the terrible striving, the restless, imploring wander of the eyes grew more intense, — more fearfully earnest and agonizing.

"It is something that you want of *me?*" she had said once, bending down and speaking clear and low into her mother's ear.

And the deep, searching answer that came back from eye to eye, only! It was soul enjoining soul.

"I will think, I will try to learn; somehow, I shall be led; and, if I find it, I will do as you would have me do."

For a moment, then, there had been quiet; afterwards sudden pleading lights of inquiry came up, momentarily, from time to time, when Say leaned over her, as if the eyes said "*Will you?*" "You are *sure* you will?"

Say knew, with a sweet, filial, pious certainty, that her mother had meant justly at the last. She only pitied, now, and longed to fulfil for her. She laid away what might have been a reproach and a bitterness; it was never to be looked at again. Her poor, suffering, stricken, regretful mother! This was how she thought of her.

It was some small thing doubtless; something she had thought from time to time to set right; something she had not "considered it best"— Say knew her mother's way of judging and reasoning — to act upon it at first. She had not meant deliberate wrong; she could not think that, let Aunt Prue accuse as she might; it had only been her habit of "managing" things, which always made Say so sorry; it was such a mistake; God manages; we must only do his will, and leave it to Him. Her mother had mistaken; and it had become too late; and she had suffered. She was gone; and Say must try to find it and do it for her. Then, the look of the haunting eyes should close away into a perfect rest again.

She found Eben, one day, when he was up at the farm. She followed him down the green lane toward the sheep-pasture, and spoke to him, alone.

"I think you know, Eben," she said suddenly, looking him in the face, after she had walked a little way by his side, saying nothing.

"I know a few things," said Eben, in reply. "But — sech as what?"

"Something that my mother wanted — I must find it out, Eben!"

Eben whistled; very low. He was puzzled what to say to this child. The awful visitation that had come upon Jane Gair, had suspended all his shrewd intentions; had softened his desire of justice upon her.

"I can't work from the outside in, to the heart of the matter," he had said to himself at an early stage of his endeavors. "I hav n't got the clear track; I must work from inside out." He began at

Jane's conscience. He had got just fact enough to press upon that, and stir it to its office. Unless she would speak he knew little beyond what he had known twelve years ago; "not enough to make a rumpus, an' upset a peaceable family for."

He had kept his Yankee eyes and ears open, in Hilbury; he had talked over old times; he had been especially interested about Parson Fairbrother; he had gathered odds and ends of hearsay and conjecture; he had discussed, with the old neighbors, the changes at the Gayworthy farm; he stirred up, cautiously, the died-out "wonderings" about the will; he had felt the whole atmosphere of the place, so far as it bore, at all, upon the subject which he had at heart. At his suggestion, Huldah and Priscilla had had confidences; and Priscilla had "named" the matter of her old surprise and curiosity; and her eyes had grown round again, with a fresh and a greater wonder; and the new impression, that was to come, had come at last and mated itself to the old, that had been set away, on purpose, all these years, to cool and wait. Eben was convinced in his own mind. He "knew ther *hed* been a bob to that air kite-tail; he 'n Huldy felt convicted of it." And then, there were the "reflections" in the Parson's Diary. But, to own the whole truth of Eben, he had got at these last, in a somewhat surreptitious way, himself.

He had taken Huldah down to Winthorpe one day, when he had known that Parson King and his wife were away at an ordination.

They had found Malviny Fairbrother there; the old lady was dead; and Malviny "made it her home," now at Winthorpe Parsonage. Huldah had set her going upon old times. Eben had picked up this bright idea of some possible existing record of what he wanted to know, and worked dexterously round to it.

"He was a dreadful orderly man, yer father; allers did every thing, 't seemed ter me, 's if 't was out 'v a book, or goin inter one. 'N, by the way, they say in Hilbury, ther was to a' ben a memore, or sunthin.' Oughter ben. What 's the use 'v a man livin' a memore ef it don't get writ? Did n't Parson King hev s'm papers, 'r sunthin, 't one time?"

"He had my father's diary," replied the minister's daughter, with prim dignity. She had been the "minister's daughter," all her life, from the days of grown-up tea-parties, where she appeared on privilege, till now. The sense of it had been ever present to her; a most sustaining sense; and fortunately, since there had been little likelihood of her ever merging this in any other claim or dignity.

"And he has it to this day. Laid away in his desk, I guess; which is all that will ever come of it, most probably. My uncle

Gordon is n't exactly a *doing* man." And Malviny sniffed, as one vitally aggrieved by such incompetency.

'T must be very curious 'n improvin'," said the wily Eben. "I dursay now, 't had half the history of the town in 't, 's fur's it went. Must 'a ben a sightly vollum."

They were sitting in Gordon King's study at the moment, it being back parlor as well. Eben's eye ran over the shelves, and rested on the minister's desk.

Miss Malviny got up presently, and opened it. She took thence an old-fashioned sheepskin-covered book, of royal octavo size, with DIARY in large lettering across the back.

"This is it," she said, and turned it in her hands with pride.

"An' all full!" ejaculated Eben, with surprise. "I—! No, I don't nuther, 'twould n't be proper. I dursay, Huldy, that air 's got sunthin' 'bout you 'n me in it, 'mongst other things. October the 19th, 18—, hey? Good many things might be proved out 'v a book like that, ef there warnt no other way, mebbe."

"18—." Miss Malviny ran over the leaves in her prim, deliberate way. "Would it be a gratification to you to look at it?" and she held it out.

Eben put his hat down on the floor and took the volume on his knees open as she gave it to him.

Huldah moved toward the window, and fell to admiring the great, pink-flowered oleander that stood there in the sunshine. The two women's heads were turned away in conference over the plant, Miss Fairbrother's special boast. Somehow, by one of his clumsy motions, Eben lost the place, and had but just recovered it, when, after some minutes' talk, they turned round again.

"Here 't is, Huldy, sure enough! No gittin' away from it!" And he pointed out, with exultation, as she came to his side, the paragraph referring to the solemnization of their nuptials.

"Aint you 'horry' yet?" he whispered.

Miss Malviny turned considerately, and sensitively, away, again.

"An' 'tother 's there, too!" he got time to add, in a still lower, and more emphatic whisper, as he shut the book, and rose to give it back.

Miss Malviny took it, in bulk, with her air of pride, utterly unconscious of details. She was proud of it in bulk; she thought it ought, somehow, to be turned into a Memoir; she had never taken the trouble to examine it in its particulars.

Another most safe, though slight, concealment, this family secret of the Gayworthys' had found.

Yet, after all, if it were known? If Eben should speak out,

and direct attention to it? What did it prove? That there had been a paper. Eben could prove that, already. Something more. That the paper *had* been an act in favor of "the widow and the fatherless." But, what then? They had searched for this paper before; twelve years ago, in the first handling of the Doctor's affairs; while all such things had been scrupulously kept together; and it could not be found. The same hand which prepared, might have cancelled it. There had been, to many minds, sufficient cause. He could not say that he had not, at one time, thought it possible, himself. The only lips that could, perhaps, have told the truth, were shut, forever. He had "almost fetched it," he had said, to himself. when he had laid this hold, by sudden assault, upon Jane Gair's conscience. But she had died and made no sign. It was not an easy, or a reasonable thing, to "upset a family" upon no better grounds. And Eben could not walk into the Gayworthy presses and cupboards, with the search-warrant only of his honest persuasion and purpose. There are little every day proprieties of observance that make the firmest persuasion, the honestest purpose, unavailing against their petty bars.

"She wanted something."

"No doubt she did want sunthin'," Eben replied, to Say's eager appeal. "Dyin' folks mostly do. It's a kinder 'v an awful spell, when everything comes up together, and they aint no time nor strength to say it with. But she never said nothin' to *me*."

"What did *you* say to *her*, Eben, that day, when you came to see her in Hill Street?"

Say's eyes were turned on Eben's face, with hardly less of fearful earnestness in them, than those other eyes had held, when they turned on hers.

"Don't look at a feller so!" he cried, fairly startled. "I could n't tell a thing, ef I *did* know it!"

"What did you say to her?" Say repeated lower and more quietly, still with an earnest, demanding look in her eyes, though she tried to soften them. But it was as if another soul questioned through hers, and would be answered.

"Well, I told her I thought we'd oughter hev another rummage!"

"Rummage! Where? What for?"

"Round ginerally. Arter that air kite-bob."

"Eben! What *do* you mean?"

"Are you in airnest, Sarah?"

"In soul-earnest!" said the girl. And the words shone in her eyes.

"Well, then, I'll tell you every pesky thing I know about it. That is—hum! in proper order. Fust thing,—there was a paper. The Doctor writ it, 'n me'n Huldy signed it fur him. Parson Fairbrother signed it too, atop. I never see nothin' of it but the names. But I knew then it was a bob!"

"Oh, Eben! don't make fun. Talk plain."

"Don't make no difference what you call it. A piecin' out, or a tail end to sunthin' that was writ afore an' found arterwards, an' gone upon; an' this never was."

"Did it have to do with grandfather's will, Eben? Is that what you mean?"

"That's what I'm persuaded on, though I never witnessed nothin' but the name. I would n't do no sech a blindfold job again, though. It's a scary thing enough to be a witness, 'n ter feel that go where yer will all over the world, yer 've got to turn up again simultaneous with that air paper, or mebbe a hull posterity's in a snarl, athout hevin' it ter conjer out, besides! It's my belief, 'n I'm backed up in it strong, though that ain't needful to go inter now,—that that air hed ter dew with the property; 'n the widder 'n the fatherless. I writ t' yer mother 'n the time on 't, an' ther *was* a rummage; but nothin' come of it. 'T warn't never found."

"Why did you write to my mother?"

"Well,—cause, first place, she was the oldest; 'n yer father was egzeckitur under the will; 'n cause if the old Doctor ever talk't it over t' anybody, 't was most likely t' her; an'—well—cause I see her in 'n out o' them rooms that night arter the paper was signed, an' I thought ef anybody could make a guess where 't was put, 'n lay hands on it, she could."

"What night?"

"Seventeen year ago; the June afore Huldy 'n me was merried; the night of the strawberry frolic, when you got inter the pig's pail."

"The night I had a dreadful dream and heard the earthquake," said Say, thinking aloud, involuntarily. "And mother went down to get me a drink of water, Eben. I remember it all very well."

She said these last words very deliberately, looking him in the face as she spoke.

"Did she fetch it?" said Eben, carelessly.

"No. Her light went out and she came back. I remember it all quite well."

Her voice took almost a defiant tone, but the quick blood leaped to her check. Was it resentment at the possible shadow of an ill thought in Eben's mind? Or was it a hotter flash as she called to remembrance the old "earthquake," and the time, years after, when she heard it again; when her grandfather's will was found in the panel cupboard; and she had cried out in her surprise and her mother had clenched her hand so cruelly? Whatever it was, she crushed the horrible intuition down, and would not question it.

"It was a me*more*-able night," remarked the man, sententiously.

"Go on, Eben," said Say, in her calm, deliberate tones again. "That is n't all. Why did you think we ought to have 'another rummage?'"

"Well, ther was light throwed. On my mind. That 's the part that ain't needful ter go inter now. Ef the paper ain't never found, 't won't do no good, an' ef 't is, why then it would n't be the leastest mite o' consequence. 'T was only light throwed on my mind 'n Huldy's; that 's all."

"You must tell me, Eben. I must have all the light there is. My mother was anxious about this, I know. It was in her last thoughts. Now, it is my work, for her sake. You must tell me."

"'T might be a satisfaction, both ways, mebbe," said Eben, thoughtfully. "It 's a kinder 'v a burden to me; 'n you want it. Well, the fact is, Parson Fairbrother was a man that was livin' a Me-more, 'n keepin' a Diary accordin'. I found out that much; thought it likely; an' I 've seen the diary; Miss Malviny showed it ter me. That was all fair 'n square, warn't it?"

"Of course, Eben. Don't stop."

"I never see it but jest that once, 'n not for more 'n three minutes then; but the leaves come open, fer all the world, 's the hymnbook dooes at meetin' sometimes; t' the very number 'n line. An' there it was. I koted it t' yer mother. 'N it stirred her up. 'June the 27th, 18—. Advised an' strengthened brother G— in a just act. Set my hand to it with him. By the promptin' o' the Lord the widder 'n the fatherless is pervided fur.' Now yer've got the hull critter, horns 'n huffs 'n all."

"I thank you, Eben. I shall never rest until that paper is found."

She said it very quietly, but all the emphasis that could have been laid upon the words would have added nothing to the still force of her air of resolution.

"Only it may n't be anywers, yer know," said Eben, provisionally.

"I am glad you told me of the Diary," she went on, disregarding his words. "I know now what was in my mother's mind, and how it came. I know what it was she wanted, and why."

With these words she turned and walked away.

"Ef yer dew," said Eben, relieving his feelings as she moved out of hearing, "yer know what the old Nickerdemus hisself could n't find out afore."

It was a great comfort to know that the light "throwed" on Eben's mind, had been a light to hers, as well. That she came direct to Hilbury intent upon this duty. No wonder her poor eyes were so restless, aud eager, and distressed.

The child's heart put this pious fraud upon itself, and would discern no clearer; would glance no further back.

"I will do it *for* you, mother!" she cried out into the silence, while the quick tears sprang. And she seemed to see that quieting look again; calmed, yet pleading; as if the eyes said, always, "*Will* you? — You are *sure* you will?"

CHAPTER XXXIX.

FINDING.

"Aunt Becsie," said Say, suddenly, "I want you to tell me something. About my grandfather's will."

After a little pause, — "I stand in my mother's place, now. I shall have some business and responsibility. I want to know just *where* I stand."

"It was a very simple will, Say; made many years before his death, and never altered. All he had, except this homestead, after some legacies were paid, — your Aunt Prue's and Huldah's, and some others, — was divided equally among us. Aunt Prue had five thousand dollars. The homestead was to remain for the use of either or both of us, Joanna and me, so long as we should choose to continue here, unmarried. Eventually, if you lived, it would come to you, Say."

"To me? How?"

"To you unless — there should be a grandson. To the eldest male heir; failing males, to the eldest female. It was a little bit of his old English feeling; he wanted to keep the old estate in the family."

"Aunt Prue had five thousand dollars. Was that all?"

"Yes; we wished to make it more; for the property was far larger at the time of your grandfather's death, than when the will had been made. But she would not receive it."

"And there was nothing for Gershom?"

"He was a very little boy when the will was made; and they had not come here then, to live."

"But grandfather was so fond of him! Don't you think it strange he did not alter his will, and give him something afterwards?"

"I daresay he thought of it. But people put things off so, Say! Greater things than wills. We urged him, and his mother both; but they would let us do nothing. Aunt Prue is very proud; and very blunt and honest, Say."

"And Gershom is, too; honest and proud to hardness."

"So there it ended; we could not force them to bear an unwilling obligation."

"But, Aunt Becsie, there *was* a paper talked of, once; and searched for. There may be something yet, that is waiting to be found!"

"It was thoroughly sought for; it might have been nothing; and at all events, we had to rest content. It could never be found."

"But, auntie, think of all the places where a little paper might lie hid! And I believe it *was* something! Eben thought so, and he signed it. He wrote to mother; he was n't easy you know."

"How did you know all this? You were such a child!"

"People come to know things somehow, when it's time. And it's time now for me to know this. I am honest and proud too, auntie! I should like to search, too. It's my turn now!"

"It seemed so likely, Say, that if my father had written and *kept* such a paper, it would have been found with the will. And there was nothing there. It is very true that a small thing could be hidden away in many a common place; but there are *likely* places to look in; there are threads of probability to guide us; or we should be astray among wild possibilities always."

"It was in that old wallet. I remember when they took it out."

"Yes; quite by itself in that small pocket. The large one was full of old letters, arranged by their dates and tied. It was all looked over."

"And the wallet was in the panel cupboard. Auntie, I should *like* to look that old cupboard over. Are the same things there?"

"Mostly. But it is quite useless, Say. It has all been done before."

"*I* have n't done it; and it's my turn now," persisted Say. "Just think of the old books. It might lie between the leaves of one; or, it might have slipped down into a crack. May I look anywhere I like?"

"Yes, anywhere. I can see the uselessness; but I can understand your feeling. And I suppose we can never be too careful to be true," said Aunt Rebecca.

"And if I find a crack deep enough to hold anything, may I have Mr. Chisler here to take down the boards?"

Say spoke playfully; but her heart was in her purpose none the less. Aunt Becsie laughed; but she did not ridicule. The child should have her way and her turn.

There came a rainy day among the hills, in early August.

People who live in cities, think, perhaps, they know what a rainy day is; a day when there will be no visitors, and the bell-wire has comparative rest; when they can sit in wrappers if they like, and read books, or write letters, or do queer, stormy-weather work that they would not bring out in the sunshine; when the streets seem to them, deserted, although there is yet the rattle of incessant carriages, bearing people who must go and cannot walk; and a continual bob of shiny umbrella-tops, up before the parlor windows. They feel very safe and alone; nobody will come. But they know nothing of the utter quietude of a rainy day indoors, among the hills, and of the *still noise* out. When the drops come down with their soft sweep and whish among the leaves and grass; when nobody goes up and down the road; when the oxen are all housed, and the farmers busy in their barns; when the very chickens run under the fences and the brushpile, and only the ducks are abroad and gay. When the piles of gray clouds hang against the mountain-sides, or shift about and break away, making all sorts of new geography, of islands and mountains, where the cliffs and ridges rend them, and come through in patches; when new relays of vaporous hosts sweep up the windy horizon, and down the hither slopes like charging squadrons; when earth lies passive in the clutch of the storm, and through all the wide heaven is the thronging and hurry and rush of the great elements at work.

The separation, — the solitude, — the grandeur of a summer-day's tempest like this, is felt nowhere as in the hill-country.

The afternoon was wearing on. They had been all day sitting in Rebecca's room. The storm was wellnigh spent. The wind had lulled, and the rain came down more gently, like the tears of a half-soothed child. The mist-robe lay torn and fluttering along the hills, wreathing itself in soft folds; and here and there, behind, some crest, bared momentarily, caught the coming gleam, and lay in a green-golden light.

Say sat by the window, leaning her elbow on the sill, looking out with a restlessness in her eyes, on the shifting cloud-forms, and the fair, freshened fields, and the red gable, shiny-wet, down the hill there, between which and this old house corner, had been such secret sympathy and thought-interchange of years.

Say *was* restless; like one possessed, as people sometimes say. Possessed with a thing that would not leave her quiet, until it should be accomplished at her hand. It had been upon her all these weeks.

Aunt Rebecca was anxious about her. She had grown thin. She had little appetite. She was always preoccupied. Her eyes searched into corners; went dreamily, in wandering glances, along the very floors, as if always looking vaguely for what was lost.

There was scarcely a book in the house that she had not run through with fluttering scrutiny. The panel cupboard had been ransacked; only its thorough old workmanship, wherein no crack had been left or started, saved it, apparently, from impetuous demolition. She was determined that this thing she sought for, should be somewhere. The thought of it was upon her always. She was secretly suspicious of carpets that had been up and down a dozen times. She would have liked to get behind wall-paper, and pry away the very wainscot. It was like an insanity. Somewhere, in this old home, lay a long-buried secret; she would not be persuaded, for an instant, that it had utterly perished. Somewhere, lay, waiting, this paper that she must find. She said little; but it was in her eyes; in her whole expression and bearing.

"You are growing morbid, Say, in this fancy of yours. It is almost a monomania."

"It is laid upon me to do. It presses harder every day. The more I fail, the more something seems continually to say to me, 'You *must* not give it up.' Aunt Rebecca, I cannot help it."

They exchanged these words without preface, as Say sat there in the window, this rainy August afternoon.

Suddenly, Say started, and turned round.

"Aunt Becsie? You have never given me the old letter-case, itself!"

"No, dear; because it is quite empty."

"I have looked in a great many empty places. I must look everywhere. I climbed the other day upon the table, and felt all along the dusty top of that old chest of drawers. I pulled the drawers out, and looked underneath and behind them. I have lifted the pictures from against the walls. I am always thinking of thin, narrow spaces, where a paper might be slipped and hid."

"Say! this is dreadful! Have you thought what this implies? Such a paper could be hid in no such place by *accident*."

"I cannot help it," Say repeated, feebly, like one powerless and driven on.

Rebecca rose, and moved toward a curious, tall, triangular cabinet that stood in the corner of the room, between the fireplace and the door leading out into the kitchen-chamber. She stood up on a chair, and put her hand over the top, behind the quaint, carved moulding, and brought down a key.

With this, she opened two small, upper doors.

Say watched her eagerly. She had not asked for this, because she knew it was the one sacred place which Aunt Rebecca kept to herself. Here were her letters from her dead brother Ben, written when he was away from home, at Winthorpe school. Here were scores of little relics of the dear old past, whereof none but she knew the association. Her mother's little ornaments, that had fallen to her share, lay here. Here, also, she had put away the old, worn, yellow letters, of courtship and friendship, that had been found in the faded, shapeless letter-case. This lay with them, folded into something of its first intended form, and tied about, neatly, with its ribbon-string. But it was empty. Aunt Rebecca was very precise; and its old, bulgy, untidy look had annoyed her, among the delicate order of all else.

She opened the drawer in which these things lay, and drew forth the wallet. Say sprang to her side.

"Don't open it, auntie! Let me!"

"Poor child! When will you give this over? You pain me, Say!"

"Don't mind me, auntie. If we can only find the *Truth!*"

Then, like some dumb creature that has found a thing its instinct treasures, — she turned away and flitted to her corner with it.

Rebecca busied herself before the open cabinet again.

Suddenly a cry.

The resistless propensity to think always of "thin, narrow spaces where a paper might be slipped and hid," seized instantly the possibility that lay here. At first sight of the frayed slit in the brocaded lining, it swooped upon the truth.

"How strange! how blind!" was her inward ejaculation, as a tumult of apprehension and certainty rushed over her, and an inarticulate cry escaped her lips, as her fingers sought nervously, and touched upon — something, at last!

A tremor took her. It was coming. This that she had longed for; that she had vowed to compass. The truth should come to light.

She dared not prove it suddenly, — recklessly. It was a thing to touch with a prayer. She gathered up the loosened folds and sprang away to her own room, with that one quick cry. Round through the great kitchen chamber, to the dimity bedroom, where she shut the door and put the button over the latch, and went down by the bedside on her knees.

The old wallet lay open along the bed. Her head was down an instant between her hands. She could not think, in words. Her heart gave two great springs.

"Oh, God! — oh, my mother!"

Then she put her finger back into the opening. Her pure, honest, earnest touch fell where Jane's had fallen last.

She drew the paper forth.

A tiny thing rolled with it, on the white counterpane. A little pin-point of light.

It flashed over the whole long mystery, and made it clear. Horribly clear, to the instant apprehension of the child, bearing penance, here, for her mother's old, mute sin.

A recognition and a memory leaped, each to the other, striking fire of evidence.

This particle of precious crystal; the wonderful old ring her mother wore when Say had been a child, whose tiny gems were placed to spell a word; the empty setting at the end where a diamond had been; lost out, ever so long ago, she remembered, one summer, — when they had been at Hilbury! Cast aside ever since, and lying, now, in the little jewel-case that held her trinkets. Ruby, emerald, garnet, amethyst, ruby,— the diamond atom gone.

That which keeps the delicate links safe in the dead rock, whereby men spell the secrets of old cycles, takes care also of all minutest, marvellous, most precarious links whereby a knowledge is to come. Nothing is strange or difficult, in this old world, written all over with frail records, yet unperishing, of life, and fate, and human deed.

There is nothing hidden, but shall be made manifest — when once the hour has come.

She could not rush to proclaim that she had found it. Fifteen minutes after, she lifted the button from her latch, threw back the door, sat down in a chair, and waited.

Rebecca came. Pale and quiet, Say sat there; knowing that she would come. Her earnest eyes lifted themselves up and met Rebecca's face, with a strange calm in them.

"Here it is," she said; the paper lying open upon her lap; her hands laid, or rather dropped passively across it. "Send for Aunt Prue and Gershom, please."

She did not offer to give or show it. There was a singular still assumption in the young girl, of the right and part she had in this family event and crisis.

"It concerns us *all*, Say, you know," said Aunt Rebecca, with a shade of rebuking expectation in her tone.

"Yes, auntie," returned Say, with a look that pleaded to have its pain, its unreasonableness, even, borne with. "But them most, and me. It is between us first. It *must* be. There is no question with you. You are honest and true — you and Aunt Joanna. Wait, just a little."

For the child's sake, sitting there with this strange spell upon her, Rebecca had patience; setting aside her own rightful and grave interest. There was a something, also, that she could not have disputed if she would. Something in the girl's air, strong and authorized; something in the very gravity of this disclosure that was impending. It was not a thing to be clutched at — to be pounced upon. There is an instinct of decorous order, delaying impulse, in the momentous arrivals of life.

Miss Gayworthy went down stairs, and gave a direction.

Gershom Vorse had been for the greater part of this interval of time since that pleasant spring-day when he and Blackmere had come home together, at the hill-farm, with his mother. He had been up and down, between Hilbury and the city, and a seashore town beyond, where a great ship was building, that he was to command. But there had been long, quiet weeks, such as he might not have again for years, that he had been spending with his mother. Blackmere had been here, too, for awhile; but he was like the great amphibia; he could come up from the deep for a little, to live and breathe on absolute dry land; he could not stay long without a sniff of the salt sea. Gershom was here now by himself, with Cousin Wealthy and his mother.

Say had seen little of him; that little under restraint of her great grief, as well as of all else that lay between the two. But the feeling of his neighborhood had been a strong element in the force that had impelled and possessed her in all these weeks of one persistent thought.

If she could only do it now! He might never come back again. He might never know.

It was done. It had come. It lay within her hand.

Three quarters of an hour later a covered wagon drove into the yard.

Rebecca had gone back to Say after sending off her messenger to Wealthy's; but she had not stayed. Say hardly heeded her coming in. She was unlike herself. She sat there saying nothing, apparently feeling nothing of the pause that ordinarily seems almost to demand speech; waiting, only; holding the refolded paper fast within her hand, a pale resolve and expectation on her face. Rebecca would not watch; she asked no further question; she went away softly, presently, and waited also with an anxiety. She saw that there was something beyond the mere finding, and that the child would have her way.

"Send them into the little room, please," Say said, when Miss Gayworthy came round and looked in upon her, before descending to meet Prudence Vorse and her son.

"Send." Rebecca was to wait a little yet even. Truly,

"standing in her mother's place," the girl seemed suddenly to take the elder right upon her. The good lady was half-pained, with a little natural human hurt and jealousy; but she could not expostulate; there was too real an earnestness upon the child. Let it be so. Let her still have her way. God grant this strange high tension of nerve and will may end in nothing worse.

The two — Gershom Vorse and his mother — were led into the little room.

"It is Say who wants you. Something has happened, I hardly know what;" and very much surprised at their summons and reception, they waited there for the moment while Miss Gayworthy left them, and before Say came in. They looked up wonderingly, as the quiet figure entered, and the pale, still face confronted them. Say shut the door behind her, and the three stood there together, by themselves.

There was nothing in this of preparation for effect; no touch of dramatic climax; it was the still earnestness of a hard, imperative necessity for doing, — taxing all power and resolve, and leaving no room for thought of what appeared, that gave intensity to the little scene, and caused it to shape itself.

"I sent for you, Aunt Prue. I wanted to see you *here*. I have found something." Her voice came dry and changed, but her tones were very quiet. "Aunt Prue — Gershom — I am here in my mother's place, to-day, to give you this."

She held the paper out. Old, yellow, it almost bore its story on its face.

Prudence Vorse took it, and Say waited.

Aunt Prue was fifty-two years old. She took her spectacles out of her pocket, and put them on. Commonplaces come into everything.

She opened the folds mechanically, and her eye went over the lines almost without surprise. Nothing could have so surprised or seized such hold of her as the look and tone, restrained and simple, yet earnest to such agony, of the girl who stood before her, waiting, — Jane Gair's child.

What this thing imported to herself dropped out of sight as she discerned it, in view of what it had imported to this other.

She took her glasses off when she had read. She took off with them a look that Say had known her face by; a hard look of long years.

She reached the paper to her son, as a thing to be thought of presently; now she came straight over toward where Say stood. She would have taken her by the hand.

"Not yet," cried the girl, with a sudden sharpness. Then, with one caught breath, she toned her voice again to quietness.

"That is not all. Aunt Prue, I am here for my mother. It must be *confessed.* It *was* a hiding, and — a lie. Aunt Prue, forgive me, for my mother!"

Then Prue took her in her honest arms. Never, even as a little child, had she held her so before. She *was* a Gayworthy.

Gershom turned away a little; a red flush swept up over his face, and a great heart-throb swelled into his throat. There was no lying blood in her after all!

But Say had not come here for a scene. She had never thought of herself, or of how they would take it. It had all been for her mother. She had finished her work, and she must go.

"It is all done, now," she said, with a low, long sigh, as one might who had voluntarily and bravely borne a fearful pain.

"I am so thankful! Tell it to Aunt Rebecca."

And, almost before they were quite aware, — before Gershom had recovered himself, and come to her with his outstretched hand, she had withdrawn herself, and gone, in the same still, pale way that she had come.

Afterward, Rebecca found her lying on her bed, white, motionless, exhausted, peaceful; like one from whom a tormenting spirit had, at last, gone out.

Aunt Prue came up and kissed her, silently, before she went. At this, two tears swelled up under the half-shut lids, and rolled down, softly, over the pure, pale cheeks.

She took this, also, for her mother.

Perhaps these drops of innocent, tender, loving pain, went, somehow, in God's mercy, far to purge the sin-stain of a late repentant soul.

All Hilbury came to know it, soon; not the whole; but that this paper had been strangely found. All Hilbury wanted to know all it could; and what all Hilbury demanded and came to know, the reader has a claim for also.

This was the paper.

I hereby direct that in the division and disposal, according to any will that I may leave, or otherwise, of whatever estate I may die possessed of, Prudence Vorse, child of my late wife, Rachel, by her former marriage, or her son, Gershom Vorse, inheriting after her, be counted and considered among my heirs, to take such share and privilege as would so fall to her, or to him through her, if she, the said Prudence Vorse, were child of my own body.

This is my will, to the setting aside of anything that conflicts herewith, in any writing that I may before have made; but to the altering of nothing else, except that this is to take the place of any smaller bequest of mine, of former date, to the said Prudence, hereby provided for. And I chargo my heirs and whomsoever into whose hands this writing may fall, to see my will done in this thing.

Signed, this night, June 27th, 18 —.
BENJAMIN GAYWORTHY.

In presence of
FELIX FAIRBROTHER,
HULDAH BROWN,
EBENEZER HATCH.

They were all honest people. They asked nothing of the law. Neither party concerned questioned for an instant "whether it would stand." It was the plain will of him who had been gone from them so long, solemnly charged upon them all.

The Hartshornes, Miss Gayworthy, Sarah Gair, — they were to make this thing right.

But nobody, save Sarah Gair herself, knew what it was to be for her to do.

The sale of the house in Selport had been effected; she had had letters from Mr. Brinley, apprising her that she must come to town for the signing of necessary papers, and the final settlement of her affairs. Meanwhile, she wrote, informing him fully of this new posture of things; begging, also, that the business might be kept, for the present, carefully between her own knowledge and his.

Hilbury was greatly exercised. Eben and Huldah were under solemn promise to Say. It was thought to be pure accident or Providence, the finding of this momentous writing, so long concealed; and it was turned over and over in small mouths and minds, as great marvels and Providences are.

Eben and Huldah had their private comparison of impressions, on "the strange way things had worked."

"A feller can't allers fetch a thing, hisself," quoth the blunt farmer, "ef he *is* a witness. But, — it gits fetched!"

CHAPTER XL.

THRUMS AGAIN.

Mr. Brinley knew better. At least, man-fashion, dealing so with, and in the interest of a young, inexperienced woman, he thought he did. When Gershom Vorse, coming down to Selport, sought him out and questioned him, he let out, incontinently, all the cats Say thought she had so securely tied in his legal and executorial bag, by the hard knots of confidence and honor. He humored her in his reply; but he lifted his keen, practical eyebrows very high over her romance of self-beggary and magnificent restitution. All right, doubtless, in moral theory; but moral theory was not the only thing with him; far less, youthful quixotism of generosity. There was also common sense, which lay more in his line.

Here was a girl with fourteen thousand dollars; the sale of the house had given her three thousand above the mortgage; there had been eleven thousand beside, after paying all that had been incurred in their year's living and business expenses. All at once, she finds herself to be one of three persons who are to make up to a fourth, a withheld inheritance of thirty thousand. Everybody else concerned being amply able; she, alone, forced to render up nearly all her living. And this must be done quietly, forsooth; the friends kept ignorant of actual facts till all should be securely accomplished.

Not so fast, Miss Gair. Mr. Brinley took the reins very quietly into his own hands.

"'How will this leave her?'—With just about enough to buy her three or four gowns and a bonnet, in a year!" returned the lawyer to Captain Vorse's questions.

"And she knows this?"

"Humph! As women generally know such things. She's on the high-ropes of justice and magnanimity just now; wants it to be done at once, and kept quiet; the bonnets and gowns will come afterwards, somehow! Women can't calculate; especially girls. And of all girls, this one, more particularly."

This one! Jane Gair's child!

Gershom Vorse walked down to the railway station on the day when the Hilbury party was expected. They were all coming; his mother, the Hartshornes, Rebecca, and Say. There had been a plan for coming down, since early spring; Jane's arrival, illness, and death had put it by; now, there was all this business to do, and it might as well be all transacted together.

Captain Vorse had engaged comfortable rooms for them at a hotel; he was to meet them on this Tuesday, at the coming in of the northern train.

They were strange thoughts he had, sitting there in the waiting-room those twenty minutes before the cars were due.

Were there a thought-photograph, it might take curious instantaneous views at these momentary meeting-points of diverse and incongruous lives. For after people have got their tickets, and have asked their questions, and counted up their railway wraps and parcels, and find ten minutes or so upon their hands, they do think queer thoughts about themselves and about each other.

There was a knot of Selport-school girls, going five or six miles home to dinner, by a branch train, presently; there came in with them all the atmosphere of school-chat and young egotism, ignoring all else in the great world but its small growing self. There were girls of a different social order, going out of town to "places," with their bundles and tickets held in fast gripe; of these the greater part to come back, with turned-up noses, by return trains; there being so few "first-class" opportunities, with hot-and-cold-water-conveniences, and adequate visiting and convivial privileges, in this line of life. There was a bride of three or four hours' making, very conscious and important, in her fresh, delicate travelling dress, and lavender ribbons; there were hard, solitary men, on runs of business, with eyes and noses and chins all sharpened to the business point. There were friends to see off friends; and friends to see friends back again. There were innumerable babies. And trains were announced and departed; and peoples' thoughts were broken off short; and there was great gathering up of parcels and shawls at last minutes; and babies were taken by surprise, as the little miserables continually are, being shouldered again, just as they had settled comfortably in arms, or subsided, with no questions asked, just when the world around had begun to be vaguely intelligible and interesting from their temporary lookout. Tired mothers gave the last consolidating shake and twist, and papas came in in time to put on all the small bonnets upside down; and through all this and much more, Gershom Vorse waited and thought one thought; over and over; out and out.

Seventeen years ago, a thing had been hidden away. A thing that concerned his worldly fortune, which all this time he had done without. All this time he had gone his way, unwitting of it, and the world, so, had taken a different turn with him, for life.

Was it only this paper that had lain hidden? Was it only worldly fortune that stood affected? What other thing was this which had come to light with it, whereof he had been unknowing, unbelieving, also, all these years? What other possible gift of God that had been so withheld, or thrust away?

The truth of a human soul, that he would not see; that a falsehood quite outside of it had blinded him to. The love of a human heart that had "grown up with him in it;" that he had ignored and gone without, half-living; that he would not take when, for a moment, it lay before him; that, crushing his own love down, he had wounded sorely, and crushed out also; that shone now to his thought as something afar, that he might never reach. He — the hard man of thirty; grown into the thing that he had willed himself; distrustful, unsatisfied; "watching, carping, fault-finding;" with but one love and one friendship to keep him human, — his mother, and the man of harder life than his.

And now his very honor rose up shoulder to shoulder with his love, that sprang, as it were, from out its grave where he had buried it.

His honor — his pride — that fumed, helpless. She had him at her mercy; the foot of her nobleness was upon his neck. It was useless to resist; to say that he would have nothing of this money; it was not she alone who held it; moreover it was not his yet to reject.

They had no right, Prudence Vorse and her son, to refuse these other upright consciences a justice to themselves, — to the memory of their father, the just man gone. There was something in the clear nature of the woman who would not take a strawberry unpaid for, and who would take her due to the value of a cent, which recognized the plain right, and demanded it, wherever it lay. The right to pay, no less than to receive, a due; it was the concession, more generous often than a gift, which one honorable soul must make another.

So the strong man fought with his thoughts, waiting there, seated, regarding absently the life about him, or pacing restlessly the now vacated platform, as the time came and passed when the train should have been there.

Fifteen minutes behind; then it came thundering in.

Instantly, a crowd, and a rush, and a shouting, and a hurling of luggage, all over the space where a moment before had been almost emptiness and stillness. In the midst of the confusion he held his place, watching; and as the crowd resolved itself, they emerged from it at last,—the little party that belonged to him,—Gabriel Hartshorne, Joanna, Rebecca, Prudence, and Say.

There was a great hotel coach in waiting; there was a porter ready to take checks and transfer luggage. Gabriel took care of his wife and sister; Gershom had his mother and Say to his share. So they moved on, and went out together, after a very hurried greeting and grasp of hands. A minute that had loomed up almost like a life, to two thoughts there, had come, and was over. Over, with scarcely a word, or other outward thing to mark it; as some of our intensest moments are; she had had her hand upon his arm; he had held her close, and she had clung, in the crowd and tumult of an instant; that was all; they had been just like any other people; as Say had hoped, looking forward to this meeting with something of the old questioning and dread, they might be; as Gershom, with a strange, new apprehension, was beginning to fear they must be.

"If he would only treat her, and trust her, now, as he did the rest!"

"If he had not been a fool, she might have been to him what the whole world, perhaps, did not hold for him, now!"

The current of their two lives set together again, for awhile; neither could help that; both were strangely and secretly glad; both had felt this point of meeting from afar. Yet Gershom was writhing in his man's pride, that felt itself stabbed; under this late, stinging recognition of a thing better than legacy of land or money lost to him, hidden away, put behind him with his own hand, for years; years that had settled all his cheerless life for him. And Say was hoping, only, to be treated like the rest, at last; only thinking of this one thing that remained to her to do,—this act of restitution for her mother's sake; thinking that she should stand at last, for a moment, on the manifest level of this man that had despised her; side by side, and face to face, with him; and then go, contentedly, her own way, alone. She thought, even, that she had ceased to love him, in these long hard years.

"There is one way to help it," said Gershom Vorse to his mother, when he had ended telling her all that Mr. Brinley had made known.

"There is but one thing for you to do," said Prue, looking him straight in the eyes. "If you *can* do it, as a man should, and not make it a worse thing than the other."

Into the eyes she searched, there came a flash.

"You say it, mother?"

"I do say it," said Prudence Vorse, reading the certification of his life-story that she guessed, in that one, quick gleam.

An hour after, Prue got the rest away; Gabriel and Joanna were easily sent off together; and she took Rebecca to her own room on a pretence, and kept her there with the truth; and Gershom Vorse and Sarah Gair were left together in the parlor appropriated to the use of this family party. Alone, together, these two; who had not been so, since the moment, five years since, when Say had given him the word, — God's word, — that had come to her in her pain, and they had parted.

Straight to her side, with a purpose in his face, the sailor came. She looked up as he stood beside her, and all through her this outshining purpose of his quivered and thrilled.

"I've something to say to you," he said. It sounded short and abrupt, and he did not use her name. But there was a something, not quick and harsh, but, rather, earnest and deep, in his tone; and that she caught, and it thrilled her the more.

"Before all this is done. It is more than this will of my grandfather's that you have brought to light. You've shown me yourself. There's more than money-justice to be done. I've wronged you, in my thinking of you, all my life. I've wronged you, and myself; because — I love you."

Dead silence. A flush, that came up from her heart, and sent great tears into her eyes, lit Say's face, and went away, and left it pale again. But she could not, for the moment, speak a word.

"Is it any use, — now?" asked the plain, blunt man, humbling himself so, from his hardness, with that pause, and that "now?"

She must answer, something.

"Why have you said this — now?" She parodied, with a sudden bitterness of pain, his question. There was joy, and there was pain in her, hearing his words. But pain came uppermost. The joy had been put by, so long! She thought that she had ceased to love him, with that old, utter love, in those long hard years.

"Because — now — if you will — I must have you for my wife, Say!"

It was real, urgent, pleading passion that sent forth those words; but it sent them forth after the manner of the man.

It almost seemed as if he had come — at his own time — to claim her; who had been his, waiting his time.

"You are true and generous; be true and generous in this; forgive me; and let there be but one right between us."

He wanted this, then! To give her back her money! This was why he said it — "now!"

Her evil angel stood by, and whispered it.

"I have n't done it to *buy* your love, Gershom!" she cried, in a superb flash. Pride tingled all over her, from her head to her feet, and sparkled from her, like a thing overcharged with electricity. Whatever other force had been there, it was driven out.

"And my love is not a thing *to be* bought," the man said, as superbly. "I have told you honest truth."

She repented of her bitterness; her pain smote back, with double force, upon herself, alone.

He had called her true, and generous, at last. Had she not lived, and looked, for this?"

But, love? She would be true and generous, at least. She thought that hour of love gone by. It had been too long. Hearts miss each other, so; and lives run separate. The orbits intersect; but when the second sphere springs, radiant, to the summer-point of meeting, the other has rolled on, alone, into a winter chill.

"I have told you that I love you. As a man should love the woman he asks to be his wife. I never said the word to a woman before. Have you no love to give me? I do not believe it!"

In strange, upright, downright fashion, this wooer sued; making his virgin speech of love.

It helped her to be outright, too, as women seldom have the nerve-courage to be, answering such words of men.

"You shall have the truth of me, Gershom, as if we two stood in heaven. I cannot help what you are to me; what you have always been. God has put it into my life. Neither can you help it. It lies between us and must be. But — I will not be your wife." She said it slow and low; the words came hard, but they came clearly. "My husband must not have even the memory of a contempt for me. He must not have been persuaded or convinced into loving me. Above all, he must never have distrusted me. Gershom, you *have* distrusted me — my very nature. You have despised and disbelieved me. If you had any love for me, you fought against it and left me to fight against mine as I might. I have made something of it so that I do not understand myself; a dull, half-murdered thing that will not die; but that cannot be, I think, ever again, the old, bright, living love. What lies between us must be; we will be at peace, we will be friends with each other, but we will not marry."

"A blessed peace you give me! Say, you throw me back into my distrust of earth and heaven!"

"If that be possible, you can hardly ever have come out of it."

"You taunt me, Say!"

The pure, grieved spirit looked forth from her eyes.

"God knows I do no such thing. Did I ever taunt you? Should I be likely to do so now? Oh, Gershom! I said my husband must have faith in me; but more than all, in a higher faith he must be strong for me. He must stand nearer to God than I! It was this I meant; it was this I doubted. I *could* not taunt. I did not."

He felt that, and his look softened; his candor did her instant justice.

"You say true. You never did. It is I that have taunted. But you *punish*, Say! You show me what you are, and you tell me it is too late."

"I don't know what is too late. God will make whatever He means of it. It is between us, Gershom, as I said. We are not like other people. But — I do not think — we can be ever — husband and wife."

She said it slow and low, as before; as if thinking it out. It was worse than retaliation; it was worse than a meant punishment. It was the inevitable result of things; the attitude into which human relations, that will not stand still and wait, that can never twice in the same lifetimes be precisely the same, had come, by long bearing and pressure, and slow, imperceptible shiftings, to take between these two.

He saw; he acknowledged; but he chafed, for the moment, as men will.

"It must be all, or nothing, with us," he said, with an angry bitterness.

"I cannot make it all. It must be nothing, I suppose, if you will have it so, — for a while. Afterwards, it will be what God pleases."

It was not perversity; it was not wilful obduracy; it was sad acquiescence; it was a resigning herself to more long waiting. It was what she could not help.

Gershom Vorse turned from her, and went and took his hat. Then he stood still, a moment; and then came back, and held his hand out.

"I won't pretend not to understand — or believe you. I do, — both. I see you cannot help it. I am not ill-used; it has been my fault. — Good-by. I shan't see you again. I'm going away — on business for the ship; and next week, I sail — for a two years' voyage."

The next moment, the door closed on this rejected man, and his tardy, grand generosity.

Something, — courage, certainty, mistake, estrangement, — I know not what, — fell away, suddenly, out of Say's heart, and left a great asking, and emptiness, and misery there.

It is a story of threads and thrums; I told you so, before.

He had forgotten all about the money. He remembered it afterward.

"I will never touch a cent of hers. She may put it where she likes. It may wait. Mother, we two must make our wills."

CHAPTER XLI.

THE SUNNY CORNER.

THE business was done. Say had her way, apparently; but they had all thought, afterward, to have theirs; to prevent her ever feeling the difference. She was to go back to Hilbury; she was to live with Aunt Rebecca; she belonged there; it was her natural home.

But they found, when it came to this, that her way lay further. That it was still marked definitely out.

"I was not made to be an idle thing in the world. You have your work, Aunt Becsie, and uses for your money. Aunt Joanna has hers. I am going to have mine; *my* work, and *my* money; nobody's else earning or bequeathing. You might marry, or go away, — or die; and then — it would be neither your home nor mine. I am going to have a place of my own; I can't be a nothing; when I die, I mean to leave some sort of a little hole in the world."

Her playfulness was a cover for an evident determination; it overlaid a good deal else, also; the aching and the asking, and the misery, that were in her at sharp times.

She had already acted as well as determined. She had seen her old friend Mrs. Gorham, and set her secretly at work. There was a post ready for her as teacher in a large young ladies' school. By and by she should have a school of her own. A career of womanly independence and usefulness was before her, and her face was steadfastly set along its line.

She had been, also, to see Mrs. Hopeley and Grace. There was a third-story room, over Grace's, where she could make just such another little nest for herself.

She had gone there knowing there would be, just then, no opposite eyes to see. Captain Vorse was away upon his business for the ship; there was this two years' voyage to come; she should be safe there, as she had planned, for that time, at least; and the something that was between her and Gershom Vorse, while it made her shy of risk of actual encounter, now, yet gave a secret contradictory charm to this actual neighborhood of absence, — this nearness to the home that had been his. Two years would be a long time; they would end in a summer vacation; she should see meanwhile, how it would be. Besides, she could not give up her dream, — and Grace, — and the brown bread.

And besides, again, before all this was fully fixed, and the two years began, other strange things had happened.

Seventeen years ago, when our story opened, there had been a single night wherein we saw sown the seeds of events — mostly in quiet life-times — yet that branched forth in their results, grasping the half those lives; the intenser half, and that wherein they took direction. Now, at this point, in these few, short weeks, came a crisis and conjunction again; the culmination of much. God rounds his poems of intermingled human histories more artistically, often, than we stop to trace.

On the Sunday afternoon following the day wherein took place the interview and parting narrated in the last chapter, Say came round in the rain, when church was over, to Mrs. Hopeley's. It was quiet there; and Grace was helpful with her unconscious, tender patience; and she could not go back, for all those hours, to the hotel parlor. She did not even want Aunt Rebecca; she slipped away from her with a sudden word of excuse; she wanted Grace, and the bread of homely, friendly strengthening.

She came in the rain; and she entered by the brick alley that tunnelled the block half a dozen doors below in the side street, and led round by a wider one into which it branched, to the widow's kitchen door.

"My feet are damp; and I came round here, to dry them at your fire. Is Grace at home?"

"She's been home and upstairs; but she's gone out again. Sunday's her missionary day, you know; she's gone down to Craig's alley, to see Terny Shane. She won't be long; sit right up, and put your feet at the oven door," and widow Hopeley placed a white-scoured cricket against the faultless black of her tidy little stove.

"How nice you are here! It does look so like Sunday rest!"

"It *is* pretty comfortable," said the widow, with a distinct and rather dubious sigh, that prolonged and repeated itself, as her eyes ran complacently round the shining order of the little room.

"You sigh as if it were almost something doleful," said Say.

"Yes — well — I'm apt to be reminded sometimes of the lonesomeness; sitting here seven years of Sundays without Luke; and — furthermore — I suppose — partly — of the Sunday clutter he used to get up. It's hard to tell, after all, what our sighs *are* made of, always; or our tears, or our prayers, for that matter."

"There never was his likeness for a muss; especially of a Sunday, when there was such a good chance to begin one. He was a stiddy man, Luke was, and went to church pretty regular; and always of a morning. But, between times, and of afternoons, *sich* works of necessity as he 'd get up! Just you look there, behind the door. There 's one string of 'em."

Say glanced, somewhat puzzled as to what she was to behold; and saw a long record of something, written up in blue chalk, upon the yellow-washed wall. From as high as a common arm could reach, down to the wainscot.

1st	Sunday	after	Trinity.	Bottles.
2d	do.	do.	do.	Cats.
3d	do.	do.	do.	Clock.

And so on, twenty-seven lines of it.

"Eight years ago, last Trinity, I began, and marked it up. For him to see. First time, it was bottles. Washing 'em out to sell; lots of 'em; all we 'd gathered, of all sorts — and you 'd have thought we 'd made it a business — since we 'd lived here. Next time it was catching cats. I could n't so much blame him for that. They did yowl round the alleys, tremengious, especially Sundays. So he contrived a trap; and he was all that day, and half the night, a watching of it, and a whippin' 'em. Then it was the old wooden clock, that he took all the insides out of. I knew he'd never get 'em back again, conformable; but he said he was going to make it keep time. I told him he'd better keep Sunday, and think about eternity; but, howsoever, it was the end of time, as far as the clock was concerned; for it never moved hand or — pendleum, of its own accord again. And, so it went on. There was twenty-seven Sundays after Trinity that year; and there they all are: and I 've never washed 'em out; old sinner as I am, to keep my poor man's shortcomings, that the Lord has washed out long ago, chalked up against him! But, howbeit, it 's somehow a thing to remember him by, as nothing else would be, after all! And, as you say, the kitchen *do* look tidy!"

And Widow Hopeley ended with another indeterminate sigh, in which relief and tender recollection strove, and relief had, finally, rather the better of it.

It was not precisely what she had come looking for; but it turned, as straws do for us, the current of Say's thought. We do not always get what we reach out for; but something falls to us that works for our want as well. A whole, quiet story of homely, humble love, and petty trial, and great loss, was in Widow Hopeley's whimsical recital.

One shadow — of her own — did not quite overcast the whole

world as it had done. The world that was full of life, and endeavor, and crosses, and simple joys, — with God over all, and in all.

The smile that had come with the sense of drollness and oddity, stayed with a gleam of better things. Widow Hopeley was a shrewd woman, and perhaps she meant it, in a secondary way. Say was "brightened up" a little, by a touch that never reached the real dull spot upon her heart at all. This is the way, and these are the tools, with which life handles us.

She went up to Grace's room with a feeling of a cheer, — a pleasantness, that were somewhere. The fine inner consciousness, that, when we read it, becomes a second sight, was stirred as sensitive nerves are stirred, when over the harsh breath of the east comes the first, faint sweep of a wind from the south, — from a summer somewhere; and coming.

A gift lay waiting for her. The gift of a glad and beautiful instrumentality.

She was coming straight to where it lay, and she knew it not; but the presentiment of its delight was with her. She thought, if she thought at all, that it was all her bit of talk with Mistress Hopeley, and the atmosphere of her brightness and tidiness, and the daintier brightness she should find with Grace. The angels that led her, and knew what they had put for her to stumble on, knew better.

She had had a hard task laid on her; a thing to search for, that was pain and shame to find; she had accepted it and wrought it out, of steadfast intent and purpose; as if in a precise amends for this, a thing she looked not for, which was a joy, and a clearing off of shame, was waiting to be given her, to-day.

Up in Grace's chamber, the afternoon sun, that had dropped below the fringe of summer rain-clouds, and burnished for himself a golden gallery in the west, poured through aslant; and the plants were green in the windows; and the Sunday rest was upon all, sweeter, even, than in Mistress Hopeley's kitchen that told of toil completed. There was no breath of toil left here. The light work of the week was laid away. On the little table in the dais-window, lay a book with open leaves, as Grace had left it when the church-bells rang. Beside it, a light basket held some golden bananas. There was a plate of Indian china also, and a fruit-knife..

It was plain Grace Lowder's opposite neighbor was at home. That she looked for Say, also, for whom the little refection had been set out.

Grace herself, had not yet come. But her fan and her prayerbook lay upon her bed; and a thin shawl, that she had changed for some other garment, was thrown there also.

Say walked to the dais-window, and glanced out between the green. Nothing told her even yet, but this creeping sense of joy and pleasantness, the thing she was to have to do to-night.

Over the way a figure sat behind the out swung blinds. Another friend watching also as she did when Grace should come. Gershom's friend, too, in Gershom's sometimes home. She looked furtively, and her heart warmed to the noble sailor, of denied, sad life, who was also Gershom's friend. And nothing whispered even yet, of what was so near, — waiting her chance turn and movement.

Is anything chance? Is it not all preventing and providing,— a gift and a showing, direct?

Edward Blackmere took his pipe from his lips, and turned full round, leaning his elbow square upon the sill, with his face forth upon the street. Say drew back. She turned toward the bed. She took up, mechanically, the little worn old prayerbook, that, by some chance again, she had never handled before. Grace had another; she did not always carry this to church; she had never brought it to the Sunday School. It lay commonly with a Bible and a hymnbook, on a little bracket-shelf of Grace's own contrivance, over her bed.

The book opened, of itself, in the middle, where the Order of Holy Matrimony was set forth; where, also, at the beginning of the service, lay folded over, and fastened to the leaf, a small, written paper.

Marriage lines. She saw the names that she had never seen before. "Hugh Lowder and Grace Blackmere." A date of more than thirty years ago, and the name of a little English seaport town.

She turned the book to the fly-leaf, with a strange thrill of expectation.

There was the name repeated, — "Grace Blackmere," — and a date still older.

But up and down the cover, in a stiff, boy's, learning hand, was another name. "Edward." "Edward." Twice repeated. And then, in full, "Edward Blackmere."

Again she had brought to light a secret, hidden thing. Faithful in that which was her own, this which was another's came committed to her; to her who held in her knowledge now the two ends of this broken thread.

It was clear and sure to her. She knew there had been some strange, sad story about this man sister. That he had believed a sore, ill thing of her. That he had lost her for long years. That Grace Lowder's mother had been an Englishwoman, as was also Widow Hopeley. And now, — well, it was God's time that had come, as had come also in that other finding. And this, too, was given her to do.

After that moment's thrill and wonder, she took the book in her hand and went straight down stairs, out at the door where she saw Grace, ten steps off, coming. She did not stop to speak, or to explain. She let her act prepare her friend, and explain itself as it might. She went right over the street, and up at that opposite door, full under Blackmere's sight and Grace's.

Grace Lowder looked after her, amazed. Then a sudden fore-feeling of something coming, swept over her also, and took her whole heart in a vague storm. She went in, and up-stairs; trembling as she went; and stopped short when she reached the middle of her own room, and leaned there on her crutch, and waited.

Say rang old Crossman's bell. Blackmere was on the stairs, already, and came and opened to her. She held her hand out to him, — the hand that had come "with a gift in it," to his own feeling, years ago, — and her look, lifted to his face, shone brighter, tenderer, than she knew. His look upon her, was what she had seen in that old, first meeting. Gentle and kindly, — a rock warmed and lighted in the sunshine. She knew, now, what more she had seen in it then. What its blind reminder had been.

"I must come in. I have come to tell you something."

He was surprised, with such a surprise as the old patriarch felt when the angel came to his tent.

She could not say it here, in such a hurry. She let him lead her up into that room above. A strange place for her to be in, — a strange thing for her to do. But she never thought of the strangeness.

She stood there among Gershom's furnishings; in that chamber that was more like the cabin of a ship, with its lamp swinging from the ceiling, and its berth-like bed set in against the wall. She stood beside the table where his maps and papers lay. Blackmere drew for her the arm-chair that she knew was his; but she did not seat herself or pause.

"It is strange that it should have come to me. But I am glad and thankful that it was given to me. I have found this."

She reached him out the little book.

How *things* outlast our lives!

That little, worn old book! His childhood came back with it. The smell of the old Devonshire woods, — the farmhouse home in the river-valley; the wild breath and voice of the sea, that came up and wooed him, at last,—when bitterness and anger drove him, also,—away. The love of his dead mother; the "real mother," who had "gone to heaven as the real ones do;" the sister—!

For a moment the man's body was there, standing before Say; his soul was away off, over the ocean,—away back into long-gone years.

He knew it before he opened it. The thought and the breath of the old time came with it; he laid back the cover slowly, as one might fold back the door of a tomb.

His eye fell on the written names. He sat down on a chair that was beside him there, never thinking of Say, standing, looking on; he laid the book upon the table and his head drooped over it; tears, wrung up through the strong life of the man, along this well-shaft that had sounded down, suddenly, to the sweet springs of his boyhood, ran from his eyes upon it.

Say turned away. A strong man's tears are sacred.

Then the memory of the shame, and the anger, and the bitterness came back. *He* came back, through all the years again, to this present moment of his life.

"Where did you get it? What good does it do me now?"

"I saw this first," said Say, gently, coming back, and laying her hand on the book beside his, and turning, as his hand yielded, to that folded paper in the middle, that opened, as the leaves parted, and showed its old brown writing.

"I found it there. In Grace Lowder's room. She is my friend."

Then she moved away again, a little, while he looked at it.

"Do you know what this means that you have brought me?" He spoke, after a hushed pause.

"I think I do."

"I think you can't. It means the clearing up of a cloud, that came with a whirlwind in it, and drove me out upon the world, to be what I have been since. It means that my sister Grace—whom I *did* love, though I cursed her,—was at least an honest woman, as women's honesty is talked of in the world. It means that God has given me something of my own to care for, at last. *God?* It means that He, whom I said was nowhere in the earth, has been in all my life, and that I know it now!"

No way of writing it can show with what a burst of untrained, urgent eloquence, that had in it a great astonishment of joy,—a passion of regret,—a rush of grateful tenderness, and a grand confession of heart-faith,—Edward Blackmere spoke these words, or something like them, to Sarah Gair.

Then, suddenly, a fresh thought smote him.

"I never told her my name; because there was a shame upon it. It is *her* shame, now; and I must tell her! I believed the worst — God forgive me — of her mother. What if she should believe the worst of me?"

"You know she will not, Mr. Blackmere. The worst is never true of anybody!"

She spoke as one who knew. She who came always with a gift in her hand for him, held it out, — this grand, beautiful human faith, — and he grasped it.

The human faith came, too, — the crowning of the heavenly. He was ready, — the hard, doubting man, — at last, to believe, and to be believed in.

"Where is my little girl?"

Oh, how tenderly the rough man said it! How, with a voice of tears, he claimed and took this gift of God!

Say led him over, then, and sent him in.

There were three days before the new ship sailed. In those three days, what a carrying over of lovely things, across the way, into Grace Lowder's little room! Things that nobody, not even Gershom Vorse, had known of. Things that, for years, had been gathering in that little back upper chamber, in locked sea-chests, in old Crossman's house. Waiting for his little girl, sometime. When he should dare to give them to her, — if ever he should. All sorts of women's beautiful appointments, bought out of his hard earnings in all sorts of strange, far places where he had been, since he had first found that there was this one little woman in the world that he would like to have a right to think of and make glad! Now and then, something had gone to her; but he had kept buying, and bringing home, and hiding away, with a strange instinct, things that he never really thought to put into her hands at all. A little delusion of what might be, had embodied itself so, and so had seemed half real. The little love that had crept into his hard life had been such an intensity!

On Thursday morning the ship sailed away.

In two years he would come back again. Then they would have their little home together. Meantime, white, folded messengers would go out after him across the water, and find him in far ports. And letters, spicy from hot climes, ship-flavored from long sailing, should come back to her. He had never had anybody to write to, or get letters from, before.

All had resolved itself, in those three days. Mrs. Hopeley, — (I have not been able to pause to tell you of her ecstasy at this solution of what "*had* been, verily, her main conunderment" so long; at the opposite gentleman "coming out, after all, as handsome as could any ways be expected," with a good plain English name of his own whereby she was to have henceforth "the good of him," as if he had been a tin dipper!) — Mrs. Hopeley was to go then, to one of those likely sons of hers, that had been, long ago, so "forrard in their means," and had gone "forrard" ever since; and Edward Blackmere was to hire her house and come over to the sunny corner; to the corner of his life where the tardy sun had at last crept round.

The Captain? There was always to be a place there for the Captain when he chose to come.

It was Widow Hopeley's hour of triumph. Old Crossman's nose was decidedly out of joint.

Say caused it to be kept very quiet that, for these two years, first, it was to be her home. They would end, as she had all along said to herself, in the summer vacation. There was Mrs. Gorham, who had asked that she should come to her whenever she could and liked; there was Hilbury, where she should always go for those joy-days of the year. She should be in no one's way.

But her path tangled itself curiously with his. She felt, somehow, that they could never part, and go quite separate ways. This goes far to satisfy a woman; and Say was not so sorely sorry as she had been.

She thought, even yet, that the old, utter love was changed; that she could not be his wife; yet she looked, somehow, with a vague expectation for these two years to end.

Whatever they were to be, each to the other, in their lives, they should be; she believed in this, and waited.

Grace was content and happy; she had two years to think it over in, to get used to it, and to be ready. She could not bear it all at once, or all the time!

CHAPTER XLII.

"ELECTED!"

Do the two years dishearten you? Are they wearisome beforehand? Have you made up your mind to skip them? I may have to skip them in great part, too. Yet, let me tell you that it is the misfortune of readers that they may skip; of books that they must; that we will not accept an uneventful interval; that no life can be got, wholly, within two covers. Yet He who reads patiently the record that He lets us write, does not grow weary, nor skip; not even our times of sin. And ourselves, — out of our books, — we have to wait. We show plainly enough what we should do were the whole volume of life in our hands at once. But the dull places and the long places, the places where things won't happen, — ah, these are the very ones God means us most carefully to read!

There was much in these two years that might not be quite wearisome were we to settle down to it. Sarah Gair herself, having to settle down to it, found this. There were busy, happy days of contact with young, fresh life that she could help; there were trial days to be fought bravely through; the old word "elected," was in her heart when things were hardest; there were stanch friends, — friends of herself, not of her fortunes, — who made bright hours for her of absolute rest; there were summer days at Hilbury that gave her the elixir of her youth, and made her strong.

Aunt Prue was kind; there was no place for mean, unreasonable resentment in her honest soul, that recognized truth always, — that would have nothing else, in itself or in another. She had come to respect Say; and she showed it. There was more in her simple "I 'm glad to see you, child," than in other people's most voluble welcomes. And more than all, which proved how wholly she took her into her heart at last, she read to her bits of Gershom's letters, and told her all the news of him and of his ship. Not a hint of her knowledge of what had been, and been done with, between the two. Her native greatness turned itself, wide-armed, toward this nature that she had found to be also great.

Say grew quietly, trustfully, hopefully content. Her love for Gershom had been so much a thing born with and grown up with her, that it could not partake of the fear and the uneasiness that attach themselves to love grown out of chance meetings; where to part once is to be parted from utterly. She had "grown up with him in her heart;" Cousin Wealthy had truly said. Their lives centred themselves alike; she never dreamed of his finding for himself a new centre; she knew too profoundly that they not only could never "be quite like other people to each other," but that none other could fill the place of either.

I said she was hopeful. Hopeful of all good to come, at last, to Gershom; of a clear day that should burn away every old mist out of his soul. She was content; prevailingly content; yet there were hours of self-doubt and questioning pain, when she misgave whether or not she had done all that lay for her to do in righting the old wrong; the words of Gershom, so dear to her recollection in their vindication of her truth, — "there is more than money-justice to be done," — her heart took up in his behalf, also. The shadow of distrust and unbelief upon him, which had come so largely from that wrong which lay at her dead mother's door, — might it not, of right, have been her work to win away? Had she looked, with a strong enough faith, on her own part, through that which overlay his real nature, holding fast to that image of him, which she knew to be the true apprehension of his inward self; the self that should triumph; the glory in him that should come to be revealed?

He was very generous; he made kindly mention of her in the words that he sent home; his calm thoughts were just thoughts; she held him daily in honor, more and more.

She clung more and more, in her heart, and in little delicate ways of showing, to his mother, — the stern-judging woman, that she had been so afraid of, as a child.

When Gershom came, he would find her grown very close there, in his mother's love.

Grace Lowder's days dropped by, like the sweet, quick notes of a song. It would not be long; not anything was long, between two hearts that felt each other, and were sure; a matter of leagues and degrees is nothing to the electric wire. There was a great, strong love for her in the world; the world was one full joy; though it all lay between them, it was one great, throbbing presence; there was no such thing as separation in it.

And by-and-by, the two years were done, and came to their end. Two years, and five weeks over; they had sailed in early August, and now the September days were come. But at the last news, all was well; and they were not yet overdue.

The time had not quite come for Say's school duties; but she had returned from Hilbury, and was getting settled in her new room. The sunny corner house was ready for its coming tenant; Mrs. Hopeley's boxes were packed; her furniture sent away; Say's little nest was broken up, — built over; nevertheless, she had had her share of pleasure in the building. Grace was like a bird, hopping from perch to perch of her pretty cage. She had spent the money Blackmere left her to make this home with; spent it, turning it into wonders of pleasantness and fitness, as only a woman of delicate thought and heart can do; and from bright kitchen to bit attic, the whole place smiled.

And then there came a week of rain.

Dreary, cloudy days, at first, misting and glooming; then two days of real tempest.

And they knew that the ship was coming homeward — coastward. Grace read the prayer at night for persons at sea; it came to be in her heart all day.

Say came round in the twilight, every day, and picked up the little evening paper on the doorstep, that they left there for her to bring in; and they looked to find ships telegraphed.

How shall I tell you what they did find, one night, at last?

The weather was clear, again; people said the Line Storm was over; early, this year; and vessels had come in. For forty-eight hours, the bay had been white with them.

There was a long list of shipping intelligence.

There was a long column under the head "Disasters."

How shall I tell you what they found there? How five little lines of type quivered at them, like dusky lightning, from the page, and blinded their eyes, and smote them to the life?

How, that night, Say stayed on with Grace, and *their* storm came down upon them, and grasped them, and hurled them upon the rocks of pain, while the air was full of drowning men's voices, and too-late prayers to Heaven?

There was news of a large vessel driven ashore upon a ledge down off the eastern coast, and gone to pieces.

Dead bodies drifted ashore ten miles away; and fragments of wreck found, with a portion of a name.

"— ajestic. Selpo — "

"No doubt, the ship Majestic, Vorse, master, of Selport: from Valparaiso, June 24. All on board must have perished."

Say stayed with Grace that night.

And Grace, out of her little prayer-book, — that had brought her, in strange, long-waited answer to all her faith and rest in it, this one, short joy of her life, that was wrenched away from her again, — read the petition for persons at sea, because she could not leave it off as helpless words, even yet; though she knew her friend might be, already, where there was no more sea.

And then the two lay, sleepless, by each other's side, through the long, terrible hours; their hands clasped; sending up, heart by heart, still sobs, and speechless prayers to Heaven.

Say thought back, — how the thoughts will go back in moments like these! — and remembered the tame, habitual words that she had said for him, when his ship was going down! She had not really been afraid of the storm for him; who had come through so many storms; who was in his own, new, stout, noble ship! They had been little quiet heart-breaths, rather; such as go up from all loving souls to Him who must care for all, continually; else, though there be no cloud in the sky, we should all also perish.

"Why did she say such summer-words, and so few of them? Why did she not feel the threat of every wave, and battle, in spirit, before God, with each?

Was it too late, even now?

"Oh Thou, to Whom the Past is Present, take the prayer of agony I would have prayed, if I had known, and somehow, in Thy mysterious Power, send answer!"

He had gone without her love! Never knowing — she did not know, herself, when she gave him that hard answer that she thought true — what he was, what he had been, what he must forever be, to her! If she could but call that moment back!

The hours were not hours. They were the epitome of years. They were nameless periods of intensest life.

People expect to find friends, days after, in the first shock of sudden, terrible grief. They have gone by it, ages' length.

At first, the time went by in tears and prayers; then, at the daybreak, came a deep, strange joy.

"If it were so! Even if it were!"

The barrier was down between them, and forever.

The something, that would not let them fully understand.

That inner, real nature of his — it had gone up. The hardness, and the mistake, and the doubting — they were all beneath the sea.

Into that unseen World, where souls are — in the body, or out of the body — she felt forth, with hands of faith; she felt him near. He understood her now. He had found the Everlasting Truth. In his purified, glorified manhood, he stood nearer to God, now, than she!

Life had held them sundered: Death had brought them soul to soul.

This was the rapture of the still, sure dawn, after the darkness; the ecstasy to which grief climbed, by those steps that were Periods of Pain.

But grief must fall back into itself; and climb again; and again.

They rose up together, and shut out the daylight; the bright, riotous September sun, that came back, as if his shrouding had cost them nothing!

The life of the great city woke; wheels crashed by; merchandise was carried up and down; other ships were at the wharves, unlading; other sailors had come home; it was as if there had been no storm, and no brave vessel and no loving hearts had been borne under, and gone down.

In the broadening, busy day, they could hardly feel it true.

Night came again, and night thoughts, and certainties of suffering. They cried, and prayed; and slept, at length, from utter weariness.

In the second morning, Say gave her friend long kisses, and went home.

Aunt Prue came down from the country in the afternoon. Say knew that it would be so. She had the paper always, only twelve hours late, up there in her hillside home; and these tidings would bring her; down, at least nearer to this terrible sea, and the news of it.

The two women met there again, in the crowded station. They grasped each other's hands and never said a word.

Until Say led Aunt Prue into her own quiet room, and turned with arms held out.

"Aunt Prue! you do believe me now, and I must comfort you."

And Gershom's mother called her "child," and held her close.

○ ○ ○ ○ ○ ○ ○

The last gasps of a southeasterly storm down on the Atlantic.

A great vessel out of her course, dismasted, leaking, drifting, broadside on, to a lee shore.

Twelve men, clinging to the wreck; eight washed away into the hungry sea, with sails, and ropes, and spars, and boats, that had gone, sweep after sweep, crash after crash.

In the deck cabin lay the master, sorely hurt; the bones of his foot and ancle broken by a falling timber, as he helped to cut away the mainmast with his own hands.

Beside him, Blackmere, his first officer and friend; nothing to do now but to stand by loyally, to the last plank.

They heard the sound of the great seas as they shattered into breakers over the nearing rocks.

A heaving, as if the soul were going out of her, which, indeed, it was, — a grinding, — a shock, that flung them helpless across her deck and floors, — and the vessel that had had such glorious life in her, lay, a dead thing, cast up, at half tide, on a cruel, outlying ledge.

Fast, by her stern, between two griping crags; but she parted, forward, and the cargo came out of her. Three more men upon the forecastle went down then.

Nine souls were left upon the fragment of her; and the tide was going out.

Night, and darkness, and shivering timbers, that might go with any shock. But the morning was coming, and the storm that had done its worst, was dying down; the wind was changing, and the tide was going out.

Broad day at last, and the tide upon the turn.

Before them, the tumultuous ocean, seething after its long scourging, and turning its face this way, with death in it. Behind the ledge, a calmer water; and more than half a mile away, showing between wave-tops, as they lifted and lowered, a line of sandy, island beach.

Men might live to get there. The ship could never last that tide out. The sea would sweep clean over the whole reef.

Two men, strong, hardy swimmers, lashed themselves to planks, and flung themselves off, to be borne back by the fearful under-tow, and dashed lifeless among hidden crags.

High on the topmost point the five men left got up a staff and a white signal. A boat might, by some wonderful chance, come out to them. All up and down among those islands into whose broad fringe that eastern coast was torn, were homes of small sheep-farmers and hardy fishermen.

Long before noon the golden sun shone clear in the blue heaven. And out there, over the dark points of rock, against the blue, two brave 'long-shore men saw the fluttering gleam of white. A vessel gone aground in the night; and souls waiting there to perish. For the tide was three hours in.

Help coming. A boat with men and ropes, and poles, daring the waters, out of which the wrath had but half subsided. Climbing, and pitching, — toiling against the great incoming tide. But the wind had come out fair from off the shore, and they had set up a pole, and spread a bit of sail.

Pollock's Ledge is a great sea-mountain, sloping up its gradual mass from the ocean-front, and running abruptly down into the water on the shore-side; at one point, showing a bare perpendicular face at ebb. Near up here, alongside the rock, buried two-thirds, now, under the rising tide, knowing their one safe approach, the fishermen came; holding themselves off, at cautious distance, against the strong force of recoiling waves, with their stout boat-poles planted against the ledge.

Three men stood by their frail signal-staff. Down from the wreck, along the slippery crest, dashed, even now, with the advance of the coming flood, — where, through clefts, the water rolled already, clutching with its wavering, deadly embrace, the huge, worn body of rock that twice daily, it drew down into its sea-grave, — where the curling breakers bursting, nearer, every one, along the crags, might grasp and carry them away in the very face of hope, — struggled two more, bringing a berth mattress with them. For the Captain, insensible with the long pain of his broken bones, and the harder pain of his proud, brave sailor heart. The boatmen flung their ropes, and the quick sailors caught them, and the bed was so swung over.

Blackmere, giant of love and muscle, came, toilsomely and perilously, last of all; stooping, clinging; hands and feet in the creeping water; salt spray in his face; bracing himself with every forward movement, against a possible, threatening wave-shock; bearing his friend, unconscious, swathed in blankets, on his true, chivalrous shoulders.

They fastened sling ropes about the Captain's body; they watched their time when the boat, lifted on the surge, swayed nearest; they passed him safely. Blackmere's work was done, — almost.

Then three seamen swung themselves after. Only three.

"We can't take more! You'll swamp her! We'll come back!"

And the boatmen flung off the ropes, drew in their poles, set their oars in the rowlocks, and turned their faces toward the shore.

But the sailors knew that there would be no time. The sea was upon them. The tide was more than four hours in.

They would have plunged down into the water, after the boat; those two left standing there with Blackmere.

"Hold back!" cried the mate, grasping them each by an arm. "Will you lose eight lives instead of two? God's here as well as there!"

There was an angry, desperate blow; the brave man held on; another, and he fell back against the rock. There was a plunge into the sea, but the boat, lifted and swung upon the tide, had passed over in that moment, from their reach ; English Ned had saved his friend ; the boy who had once saved him.

He was hurt by that ruffianly blow, and fall ; there was a shoulder crippled. He could not swim for it now, were it not even a hopeless thing to try.

If he must go, he would go with the ship ; with what was left of her. He crept down and up again, through the clefts of crag and the dashing water, as he had come. He went back — the last man, alone — to face his death. He climbed upon the trembling timbers, lying even with the topmost rocks, over which the sea, returned to find its prey, began to break with every burst that came more eager than the rest.

He held fast while he could hold.

He had one thought, with a long pang in it.

" My little girl ! "

And then came Peace.

Till in the seeming pitiless black wall of water that rose up at last with gathered, towering bulk above and toward him, he saw, as in the last extreme souls only see, a Love and Pity bending in the Might that smote. A still, small voice within the roar, spoke a triumphant word to him — " Elected ! "

And on the seaward sweep of that backward-thundering wave, a great, brave, *believing* soul went forth to God.

A strong thread, holding fast to many hearts, was — broken ?

Loosed from earth, and drifted out to the Unseen.

Upon such lines hearts follow, and find Heaven.

CHAPTER XLIII.

LAST, BUT NOT FINAL.

Aunt Prue had not come down to sit and grieve, and wait for certainty of ill to come to her.

"Pollock's Reef." "And the news came by telegraph from Landhaven. I'm going to Landhaven to-morrow morning, and from there, as near to Pollock's Reef, wherever it is, as I can get."

A longing hesitancy came into Say's face.

"Of course," said Aunt Prue, reading it. "You, too, child. Your heart 's there. Why should you act a lie?"

And Say was glad, and not ashamed, to be read through, and to be made welcome so.

At Landhaven, they got more news. The blessed news of life, at least. For a little, only, perhaps. There was terrible injury and danger.

They thought that he would die. Say looked for nothing else. But if she could only take back that word of hers, so false as she felt it now! If she could only give him her love at last, to go from life with! If she could but cancel that sharpest agony, before the tide of her grief surged back upon her!

If there were a chance given her! What had the two years done with that love of his, and his stern, strong nature?

Two days after their first meeting, Prudence Vorse and the "child" were together in the little fishing village of Wyacumsett, ten miles below the place of shipwreck; where the bodies and the drifting timbers had come ashore, and where Gershom Vorse lay with his shattered limb, and the sore anguish at his heart.

* * * * * * *

Back, out of strange confusion and wild dreams. Back, through a dreamless void and horrible pause. Groping back into the world of life again; feeling one by one, after the old fibres of mysterious association and relation, whereby, in delicate poise, identity swung — somewhere! Back out of emptiness; the atoms of consciousness regathered; the soul, in short, come again into its body.

"Say!" It was his first word. How did he know that she was there?

"I've been — a naked soul. I've been out — into Nowhere. Thank God — for Here, again!"

He had been under the effect of ether. They had amputated his left foot.

"How did I know that you were here?" He asked the question himself, now.

"I felt you as I came back, through the darkness. It was the first I knew that I was coming. It seemed to bring me back again. Back, to my *place*, — among created things."

He spoke dreamily; words perhaps, that would have waited, had the restrictions of a full consciousness been upon him. But it was the truth that came.

"Gershom!"

She could only speak his name, after all. She could only put her hand in his and hold fast by him; as if so she would hold him to the world and to her love. The tone and the touch said all. A grasp and a look lifted up at her, in which the soul flashed full to its presence-chamber, answered her. It was right between them; though it should be only at the end.

Clear recollection, as it came back, sent his thought a moment after, to the live point of pain. A great groan surged up from the depths of his being.

"Oh, mother! Oh, Say! — Blackmere! — The noblest soul I ever knew has gone out of the world!"

And for days after he scarcely spoke again.

They kept him quiet. If they had known the sort of quiet that it was!

He lay there doing double battle; his life fighting for itself against bodily outrage; his love against its loss.

Secretly waging a deeper, more interior strife than either, that none else knew; the truth that had come close to him in an awful, new experience, — a something different from all experience of conscious, self-governed life, — measuring itself with old doubts; resolving slowly, old problems of obscurity; working out a way for him, — a strange and special way — toward the light.

He had trembled almost out of life — the strong man, who had never felt physical helplessness, or any brain-bewilderment before.

In that mysterious anæsthesia, he had left sense and certainty behind him, and fluttered, a naked soul, into the void. He had barely, it seemed to him, fluttered back.— What was it? He lay here, and tried to sift, from among fearful impressions, what it had been.

Days after, at a moment when Say sat alone, by his bedside, he spoke something of it out. In words different from any she had heard from him before; words great and full, with a great pondering.

"Back again. Back to my *place.* Say, I know something about it now. I know what death may be. I know what madness may be. I've let go the little anchorage we call our life, and drifted out into the great emptiness that lies round it. Going out of one's self is an awful thing! The danger and the pain — everything else was nothing to that! I have laid here and thought of it, till it seems, sometimes, as if a very little would make me let go again, and drift away. What is that we hold by? A few little outside appearances, that hedge us in. Things round us, that we see, and hear, and touch. When we lose these, and go off — is there nothing, any more? Say! I seemed to leave all these; they jumbled up together, and fell away; and I went out — out — where there was nothing!

"There was nothing, and there was everything. It was not sea, nor wind, nor fire; but it was the possibility of them all. The world snapped like a bubble, and went out. There was an emptiness — a seething; as if awful forces might break loose, and take no law, perhaps. As if all things were resolved; and what *had* made life, and safety, *might* make anything; any wild confusion, terror, pain. I cannot tell you, Say; my words seem wild; but no words could be strong enough, or wild enough, to speak it.

"Does n't the Bible say something about the 'secret chambers of the Most High?' I feel as if I had been taken in there, Say!

"I lie here, and think — of Blackmere; my friend — oh, my friend! The noble, noble fellow, who gave his life for me! —— And I wonder if souls go out into this, when they go wholly out of life!"

"'Even in the valley and the shadow of death, I will fear no evil, for Thou art with me; Thy rod and Thy staff, they comfort me.' 'When thou passest through the waters I will be with thee; and the rivers, they shall not overflow thee.'"

Say could answer nothing but this.

"I cannot find it, Say! There was *nothing* there!" This was all, for long, that Gershom answered back.

And other days, again, went by.

And they had other talk. Gershom, and his mother, and Say. Of the storm, and the wreck, and the saving of those four men, only, out of all the great ship's company. Of what they could easily fill out, from the facts known, and their own larger knowledge of the man, of Blackmere's heroism and fate. Of his "little girl," to whom Say wrote, every day; from whom came such sweet, sad, submissive answers; who should be their care, now; Gershom wanted his mother to take her home to Hilbury; there was money for her, — all Blackmere's savings; Gershom almost wished there had been nothing, that he might provide for her; that he might have this, at least, to do for his friend. But they would never lose her out from among themselves; they would give her love, and home, and cherishing, for his sake.

And through and under it all, — all tender, almost remorseful sorrow, and reverent memory, — through all bodily pain, and slow convalescence, and thoughts of himself and his future, — and even the love of his life, borne back upon him so, and whispering an unsyllabled promise in the midst of all, — through everything, wrought still, incessantly, the deep spirit-lesson God, in His own way, was teaching Gershom Vorse.

He had to sound the very depths. He had to feel what death and the grave *might* be; what the viewless forces were, that worked about his puny life; he was given an awful, wordless revelation of wreck and horror that were possible. For some mysterious instants, he had been taken from out the harmonious working and relation of life, and thrust, — a faint trembling point of consciousness, — into the elemental waste. He had felt the pregnant void, from which life might, or might not, according to some Unknown Will, be born; he had touched unfirmamented space, where seethed the unshaped principles of things, that, leaping to an equilibrium, might coruscate in worlds; that worlds, with one electric flash, might crumble to, again.

It lay in his memory; it came back to him in the nights; the physical loss, — the mutilation, — he had suffered, was forgotten in this experience of soul that had come with it. He thought of his old talk with Say, — of the "strength of the hills;" of the still, solid, earth, and the silent gripe that holds its atoms; of all that he, that day, had talked of; the fury and riot of elemental and brute force, and of human passions; of all the horrible clash of Life with unheeding Law; and he knew that nothing less than GOD was in and over it all.

That, he had never really doubted. But, man? And what this God would do with him?

He came round, so, at last, to the Light.

As if he had never seen it, in all his life, before. It was given, now, a new and special gift, to him.

One still, flushing, creeping dawn, he lay, alone with his deep thoughts; and it was given to him.

Christ!

It was what He came for, — out of the bosom of the Almighty. It was what He laid His finger on the tempest for. What He touched disease and discord for, and set them right. What He went down into the grave for, where men must go; and out of its blank and nothingness came back; in His own, glorious, unharmed individuality.

It was so He saved the world!

It was that His words meant, that came thronging so.

"I am the Resurrection and the Life. Whoso believeth in Me shall never die."

"In my Father's House, are many Mansions."

"I go to prepare a *Place* for you. That where I am, ye may be also."

"Of all that my Father hath given me, I have lost none; and I will raise them up at the last day."

"Say! tell me the words of the Creed, that you used to say on Sundays, when you were a little girl."

And Say repeated to him the grand, Apostolic confession of faith.

"*I believe*," he said solemnly repeating, when she had ended. In that full manly tone, that had never been afraid to utter a belief. "I *believe* in God, the Father Almighty; and in His Son, Jesus Christ, our Lord.— Who was crucified, dead, and buried. And who rose from the dead. I *believe* in the Holy Ghost; the Communion of Saints; the Forgiveness of sins; the Resurrection from the dead; and the Life Everlasting!"

There was a deep silence between the two.

"Thank God! — Maimed, I have entered into life!"

It was only a whisper; with a hand over the face, and the face turned toward the pillow; but Say heard it.

Maimed, heart and body; yet, by divine paradox, a *man* made whole.

What more is there to tell?

He had come nearer, at last, to God, as she had said,— through his fiercer pain, and loss, and wrestling, than even she!

They could not help what they were to each other; it came to be as it was meant.

"Will you take me after all, Say, as I am?"

And she took him as he was; not in his first, young achievement, when she had craved to be nearest to him; when she had longed to say, "I had the dream of it with you, Gershie; I knew that you would do it: it is done!" Not in the full pride of his successful manhood, nor when she had just proved herself to him, and he had owned her truth; not in any way, according to any hope or longing that was past; in no moment of triumph or of surprise, for him or her; in no climax of a common love story; but in quiet acknowledgment of the truth that lay between them; after all, and as he was; under misfortune; his life crippled in its activity; but his soul whole. Years gone by that might have been years of a young joy; a fresh, unthinking love. Years come, with grief that was dearer than delight; with memories as holy and as heart-grasping as their hopes.

There came to be a Home, again, at the Old Farm; and the wide house was full.

And Grace? She was there, with them; Aunt Rebecca and she with their sweet, denied lives, were the embodied peace and serenity of it.

"The whole, great earth was warm and close to me," Grace Lowder said; "because there was this love in it for me; and now, all heaven is warm and close, because the love is there."

My story does not end as you would have it? It does not end, at all. We make an end of our tellings; but the stories of life go on. You may stop at a pain, or at a pleasure; it is all the same. The threads run on, and out of sight.

I know there has been more of waiting, here, than of fulfilment. That not one life, of all that are interwoven in these pages, achieves a perfect earthly destiny. That in all, first or last, there is something missed, or failed of; that each may seem, in part, defrauded; that the web is not woven without flaw or break, and finished with a hard, sharp selvage. Is any, in this mortal weaving?

At the best, there is always more warp than woof. The tissue falls from out the loom, at last, fringed with the thrums of unfulfilled, procrastinated hopes. The threads float forth into the infinite.

Not yet, — but surely, — shall an hour come, when the pattern shall be made complete; when every filament unweft shall be gathered from its aimlessness or its entanglement, joined to its own appointed fibre of immortal Life, and woven into the one, great, golden web of Joy!